THE FALL-OUT

SOPHIE RANALD

Storm

PUBLISHING

Ebook ISBN: 978-1-80508-671-0
Paperback ISBN: 978-1-80508-673-4

Cover design: Rose Cooper
Cover images: Shutterstock

Published by Storm Publishing.
For further information, visit:
www.stormpublishing.co

ALSO BY SOPHIE RANALD

The Love Hack

The Girlfriends' Club series

P.S. I Hate You

Santa, Please Bring Me a Boyfriend

Not in a Million Years

The Ginger Cat series

Just Saying

Thank You, Next

He's Cancelled

The Daily Grind series

Out With the Ex, In With the New

Sorry Not Sorry

It's Not You, It's Him

No, We Can't Be Friends

Standalone romcoms

It Would be Wrong to Steal My Sister's Boyfriend (Wouldn't It?)

A Groom With a View

Who Wants to Marry a Millionaire?

You Can't Fall in Love With Your Ex (Can You?)

For STBC (again) – the best friends in the world (still).

ONE

The first time I saw Patrick naked, I couldn't believe my eyes. A few minutes later, I couldn't believe my luck.

I can remember telling my friends about it, once I was sure it was okay to tell them anything at all. 'I mean, my God. Seriously. I thought it was only, like, marble statues made by ancient Greeks with massive hard-ons over some twenty-three-year-old discus thrower that looked like that. But no, he genuinely does. It's ridiculous.'

'Has he got – what are they called again? – semen gutters?' Rowan asked.

'Stop!' Kate put her hands over her eyes. 'We're friends with the man. We don't want to think about his semen. Never mind it trickling down his— Ugh. Just no.'

'It must be like dating a fitness guru,' Abbie suggested.

'Yes, only without the wanky posing in front of the mirror,' I said.

'And the grunting,' said Kate. 'Although of course, that might happen later. Go on, Naomi, share it with the group.'

'Share wha—' I began, then I was overcome with reticence.

'I'm not going to. Suffice to say, if there is any grunting, it happens at the appropriate time and place.'

'I bet it does.' Rowan giggled. 'Zara always said—'

And then it was her turn to shut up, and the conversation moved on, thankfully, to other things.

Now, though, too many years to think about had passed, and whole days – weeks even – went by without me giving Patch's ripped physique a second glance.

His snoring, not so much.

It was a Friday in January, a day I'd been dreading for as long as I'd known it was going to happen. Appropriately, the weather was foul – the app on my phone had warned me what to expect, and the glimpses of dark sky showing through the gap in the curtains, the swish of rain on the street outside and the occasional blustery whistle of wind confirmed that it had known what it was on about.

It was five in the morning and I wanted nothing more than to go back to sleep for another hour and put off the inevitable awfulness of what lay ahead. But, with what sounded like a pneumatic drill going at full volume on the pillow next to mine, the chances of that were growing more remote with every minute that passed.

'Patch.' I dug an elbow into the ridge of muscle that ran down his side, none too gently. 'You're snoring. Turn over.'

'What?' he muttered, rolling over away from me. 'Sleeping. Leave me alone.'

'Jesus. I know you're sleeping. At least one of us is.'

I was fully awake now, the jangling, unrested wakefulness of a disturbed night. I should be used to it by now – I literally couldn't remember the last time I'd slept uninterrupted for eight hours. There must have many nights like that, back when Patch and I first got together, when we'd go out, have a few drinks, come home and shag ourselves senseless before sleeping and sleeping, waking up to have sex again and sleeping some more, on and on into the morning, until eventually we got up because we were so hungry from all the sex we couldn't stay in bed any longer.

But those days were all kinds of gone.

I closed my eyes, turning over and fitting my body into the curve of his. At least if I stayed there, it would make it harder for him to flip over on to his back, and hopefully keep the snoring at bay for a bit. I rested my hand on his arm, feeling the definition of the muscles there, just as clear as they'd been the first time I'd touched him. Once, feeling them would have ignited a flame of desire deep inside me, but now the only thing I desired was sleep.

How long has it been? I thought fretfully. *Three months? Four?* The last time would have been on Christmas Eve. Which was pretty grim, now I thought about it. *Tree given a top-up of water, check. Sprouts prepped for the morning, check. Presents wrapped, check. Now a bit of sex for him indoors and Santa's little helper's work is done.*

Ee-eww.

And the time before that? On Patch's birthday, obviously. In June.

Shit. It's not good enough, is it?

I turned over again, resisting the urge to open my eyes, and listened to the rain. Today was going to be bad enough if I was rested and refreshed, but the chances of that were diminishing by the second. The thought of our dwindling sex life had added a spark to the pile of worries that seemed to permanently inhabit my brain, and – like a fire starting in a hoarder's home – there was plenty of fuel for it to feed on.

Was I going to be able to fit into my purple dress? Did I have a pair of tights that weren't laddered or bobbled? Was I going to be able to get everyone up, breakfasted and out of the house on time?

Why was life so fragile, cruel and short, yet each day simultaneously so damn long?

Was my husband going to stop loving me?

Had he already stopped loving me?

Damn it. It was no good. I raised my wrist to my eyes and the clock on my fitness tracker told me it was five to six. When I connected to its app, it would tell me what I already knew: that I'd had about three and a half hours of restless sleep.

There was no point trying for more – I knew from experience that now, if I managed to fall asleep again, I'd only be jerked awake from a dream that I'd struggle to shake, and spend the day feeling groggy, anxious and even more tearful than I was bound to feel anyway.

I turned back to Patch's warm body and wrapped my arm round him, pulling him close. He grunted sleepily and I kissed the back of his neck, inhaling the smell of him, trying to recapture the way that smell used to make me feel.

But I didn't feel anything – just a deep weight of sadness that I feared would never go away. Having sex with my husband on his birthday and at Christmas was one thing, but I wasn't going to be able to get myself in the mood on the morning of a funeral, pecs or no pecs.

At any rate, the closeness of my body had roused him into a lighter sleep, and the snoring had stopped for now. Looking at his back in the blueish early-morning light, his shoulders relaxed in sleep, his hair mussed where it had pressed against the pillow, I felt overwhelmed with tenderness. It was like when we'd been on a date, years ago, to see an afternoon showing of *E.T.* at the cinema, and at the moment when the boys soared into the sky on their BMX bikes, I'd glanced sideways at him and seen that he was crying.

I was already in love with him then, but that moment – seeing him so moved, so vulnerable, like a little boy himself – had made me think, *I'm going to spend my life loving this man.*

And here we were. Still together, married, the parents of two children. Still in love – mostly. I hoped.

I turned over on to my back, reaching for my phone and releasing it from the charging cable one-handed. As soon as the book-end of my body left Patch's back, he turned over too and the snoring began again, even louder than before.

Soft thoughts of love forgotten, I dug my elbow into his ribs – more than a shove but not quite a blow.

'Whatcha doing?' he mumbled.

'You're snoring. Stop it.'

'You hit me.'

'No, I didn't. Turn over.'

'I'm sleeping.'

'No, you're not.'

But as if to prove me wrong, he let out another thunderous snore.

I rolled my eyes – pointless, given his were closed – and shuffled my pillows higher to sit up, flicking my phone to life. My notifications screen told me nothing I didn't already know – I had no new emails, one event that day, and the weather was awful. Oh, apart from the FTSE 100 being up and the Nasdaq down, which I hadn't known but didn't need to.

I tapped the WhatsApp icon, as I did almost first thing every morning. There had been no new messages on the Girl-friends' Club chat since we'd all wished each other good night, like we were girls whispering in the dark in a boarding school dormitory.

Now, it was time for the process to happen in reverse.

NAOMI:

Good morning

Then my thumbs paused over the keypad. There was so much to say, yet also nothing at all. *How are we all feeling?*

Scared, sad, still disbelieving. *How did everyone sleep?* Not much. *Is it really happening?* Yes.

Then, as I watched, three new messages flashed up on my screen, just the same.

KATE:

Good morning

ROWAN:

Good morning

ABBIE:

Good morning

I imagined them all thinking, just as I had, that there was nothing else to say – not yet, anyway.

Then I heard the thud of footsteps outside the bedroom, the rattle of the latch and the thump as the opening door rebounded off the wall.

'Daddy, Toby says he needs a poo.' My daughter's voice pierced through the half-light.

'Why's Daddy making that noise?' her brother demanded. Next to me, Patch muttered in his sleep and pulled a pillow over his head.

'Come on then,' I said. 'Let's go to the bathroom.'

TWO

Half an hour later, I was in the thick of what felt like a normal morning. Patch was in the shower. I was spreading toast with peanut butter (Meredith) and strawberry jam (Toby), making sure not to use the same knife for both even if I'd wiped it (okay, licked it before showing it back in the jar) in between, because I knew a hunger strike would ensue.

I'd already put my coffee in the microwave twice to warm it up, and still not drunk it. I still hadn't checked whether my purple dress fitted (or even still existed – there was a very real chance it had been sent to the charity shop months before) or I had any intact tights. The window of opportunity for my own shower was narrowing at speed, and I'd said goodbye to any prospect of giving my hair a decent blow dry.

'Okay, breakfast.' I plonked one plate in front of each twin and took a sip of my coffee – lukewarm already.

'Can't I have Coco Pops?' Meredith asked, looking mournfully at her toast.

'No, you can't.'

'Why?'

'Because they're full of sugar.'

'Why?'

'Because otherwise they'd taste like cardboard.'

'I want cardboard,' announced Toby.

'Well, you can't have it. I've made you toast and jam and anyway cardboard isn't food.'

'Why?'

Teeth gritted, I put my coffee back in the microwave. Upstairs, I could hear the water still running – clearly Patch was having one of his mega-showers, involving exfoliating his face, shaving with a cut-throat razor and putting a treatment on his hair before nicking my hairdryer to style it.

'Can we have *Peppa Pig* on the tablet?' Meredith asked, sensing weakness.

'No.'

'Why?'

'Because it's upstairs.' *And once I go upstairs, I don't intend to come down again until I'm showered and dressed in whatever I can find that fits.*

'Why have we got to go to Granny's?' asked Toby, for the millionth time.

'Because Mummy and Daddy have to go to a funeral.'

'What's a funeral?'

I sipped my coffee, wincing as it burned my lips. I felt like we'd done the careful, age-appropriate explanation a million times before, but with four-year-old twins, stuck-record territory was familiar to me.

'It's when someone dies and all the people who love them get together to say goodbye to them.'

'Like when Daddy goes to Aberdeen?' asked Meredith.

'No! Nothing like that at all, because when Daddy goes to Aberdeen he always comes back, doesn't he?'

Two pairs of wide, dark eyes, identical to their father's, gazed at me, then Toby said, 'When's Uncle Andy coming back?'

I closed my eyes. I felt like I'd spent the past ten days either crying or about to cry, and here I was again, about to cry.

'Uncle Andy's not coming back.'

'Why?'

'Because he died.'

And if you ask me why, I'll legit scream, because I've already tried to tell you about six million times, even though I don't really understand it myself, because it's the most fucking unfair thing that's ever happened.

'Why did he—'

Hearing the hairdryer shut off, I fled upstairs.

'Patch, please can you get the kids to your mum's, like, now?'

'There's no rush, is there?' He hitched the towel higher up on his hips. 'We don't need to leave for another hour and I'm not dressed.'

I could see his suit hanging on the wardrobe door, encased in a dry-cleaner's bag. There'd be a lengthy faff while he dressed, I knew, with me expected to play personal stylist and advise on his choice of everything from shirt to socks.

'Just put on jeans and go, please? I've been getting the third degree down there and I can't stand it any more.'

For a second, he looked mutinous, the way his daughter had earlier when I'd vetoed the Coco Pops. Then his face softened and he hugged me, fragrant from the shower. 'On it. Are you sure they'll be all right with Mum all day?'

'More like whether she'll be all right with them. But what can we do? We couldn't exactly take them, could we?'

'Well, we—'

'Couldn't. Come on. It's out of the question. It's not going to be one of those funerals where the person's led a long and happy life and died in their sleep at ninety, and everyone goes on about how they had a good innings. It's going to be fucking traumatic.'

Patch pulled a jumper over his head and forced his feet into trainers without undoing the laces. 'Right. I'll be back in fifteen.'

'I'll be in the shower, so don't forget your keys.'

I heard his feet thumping down the stairs and his voice calling for the children to get their coats on because he was taking them to Granny's in the car, and flopped down on the unmade bed, immediately remembering that I'd left my phone downstairs. The effort of getting up to fetch it, straightening the duvet and hanging up Patch's wet towel on my way, felt almost too much to bear. Then I remembered my half-drunk coffee and the children's breakfast plates, the dishwasher still unemptied from the previous night, the load of wet stuff in the washing machine.

The ache that had settled on my heart days before had gradually spread, infecting every muscle and bone in my body so I could only move very slowly; like an old woman, I got up.

But I did nothing about the dishes or the laundry. Instead, I sat down at the kitchen table, surrounded by toast crumbs and butter smears, winced at the taste of my cold, stale coffee and opened WhatsApp.

There'd been no new messages since our greetings half an hour earlier – like me, everyone would have been getting ready for the day. Kate would have spent the night in the converted South East London warehouse where her boyfriend, Daniel, lived, maybe getting up to feed Jigsaw, their kitten – or maybe still in bed having the kind of life-affirming shag that would temporarily banish the shadow of death. Rowan and Alex would be having breakfast with Rowan's daughter, Clara, assuring her that crying at funerals was fine, everyone did it and there was no shame in it. Abbie and Matt would be getting dressed together in silence, knowing each other's thoughts so well neither of them needed to say anything, only occasionally locking eyes or touching hands to reassure the other that they were there and they felt the same.

All of us, getting ready for an event we'd dreaded on one level for a long time, but also blindly, bloody-mindedly believed would never happen.

And how do you? I thought despairingly. *How do you even prepare for this? You can't. And it's not just one day that'll be over soon, like going to the dentist. It's one day that's just a kind of punctuation mark in a story we've all been living for years and will have to carry on living forever.*

Someone had to get the day's conversation under way, I thought, and it might as well be me. I knew that when we saw one another later, there'd be tears, reminiscences and laughter – now, though, some instinct told me that what my friends needed was what I needed – a brief interlude of normality.

> How's everyone doing?

I posted.

> Patch has taken the kids to his mum's. God knows whether we'll get them back – she'll probably take them to McDonald's and lose them en route.

There was a pause after my message popped up on the screen. I pictured my friends glancing at their phones, seeing it was me and thinking, *I don't need to leave for an hour and a half. There's time for a chat.* Just the same as I'd thought.

> ROWAN:
>
> Clara just puked up her breakfast. I'm hoping it's nerves not bulimia (jokes). I'm kind of tempted to puke mine up too, I feel horrible.

NAOMI:

Maybe if I'd spent more time puking I'd have a chance of fitting into that purple dress. Someone bring safety pins.

ABBIE:

Matt's gone for a walk. He didn't sleep at all last night, just lay there next to me pretending. Of course I was pretending too, so…

KATE:

I'm shitting myself about that reading. What if I cry when I get to the 'Let me go' bit?

ABBIE:

What Andy would've wanted, innit? Max drama. Everyone weeping and rending their garments.

NAOMI:

You flinging yourself on top of the coffin demanding to be buried – OK I'll stop. Too soon, right?

KATE:

Damn it, I'm laughing now. That's way too dark but you just know Andy would love it.

ROWAN:

Has anyone spoken to his mother?

ABBIE:

Yep, Matt did yesterday. She's in bits. He thinks she mostly feels like crap because she and Andy weren't in touch for so long before it happened. She's okay with us having organised just about everything – says she's far too emotionally fragile but actually he reckons she knows she doesn't have a clue what he'd have wanted.

I raised my eyes from the screen and stared out into the gloomy, barren garden for a moment. The branches of the silver birch tree, naked of leaves, were whipping in the wind. The kids' plastic toys, which we should have put away in autumn but hadn't, were up-ended and splattered with mud.

I'd never met Andy's mother – as far as I knew their relationship had been somewhere between frosty and non-existent for years – but the guilt I imagined she must be feeling now was almost unbearable. I wished I'd kissed my own children goodbye instead of hustling them out of the door with Patch.

NAOMI:

And we do know. Right, gang? So come on, let's get out there and smash it.

ABBIE:

We've got this. Purple frocks on, chins up, tits out. Those of us that have any tits to speak of, that is.

KATE:

First I need to decide which purple frock to wear. I ordered six off The Outnet and I haven't tried them on yet.

ROWAN:

Give Daniel a fashion show and let him decide.

NAOMI:

Hope you bought purple underwear to match.

KATE:

Actually, I hate to admit this but I did. Mad OTT but...

And then Abbie, Rowan and I all typed the same thing at the same time, almost as if we'd been practising.

It's what Andy would have wanted.

To my amazement, when I put down my phone and went

up to get ready, I was actually smiling.

THREE

NOVEMBER 2007

As friendships go, ours didn't get off to the most auspicious start. After all, the sidelines of a five-a-side football match in the autumn rain, with your boyfriends' team already four-nil down before half-time, is no one's idea of fun. I remember watching Stuart, the guy I'd been dating for about four months after getting stuck in a lift with him on my way up to the office where I worked as a junior legal secretary, miss the ball over and over, sliding around in the mud like Bambi on ice and losing his cool with the referee. *This evening is not fun*, I thought, *and I don't think this relationship is much fun either*.

To distract myself from the carnage on the pitch, I glanced sideways at the other spectators. There was a woman in a parka, a few years older than me, sipping something from a hip flask and occasionally yelling encouragement at her husband, who'd scored three of the four goals for the opposing team. There were a couple of teenage boys, occasionally hoofing around a football of their own, clearly convinced that they could do a better job than their father. There were the reserve players, bored and resentful in tracksuits, occasionally half-heartedly stretching their hamstrings.

And, I saw through the thickening twilight, there were four other women about the same age as me. One was bundled up in a faux (at least, I assumed it was faux – later, I changed my mind) fur coat, her gleaming dark bob beaded with drizzle, the heels of her suede boots sinking into the mud.

Another was wearing faded jeans and wellies, her hair scraped into a messy bun, a too-big leather jacket clutched round her shoulders with one hand while the other held her phone.

Standing a few feet away from her was a woman with swishy mahogany-coloured hair in a long cream trench coat, who managed to look like she'd stepped out of the fashion pages of a glossy magazine; she was even wearing lipstick, which I found quite awe-inspiring in the circumstances.

And there was a curvy woman in leather trousers and trainers, an oversized red scarf wound high under her chin, emphasising her perfect porcelain skin, which – unlike mine – hadn't turned blotchy from the cold.

As the match dragged on, the five of us began to kind of sidle closer together, exchanging pained glances and eye-rolls as the other team scored yet again – in fact, it was one of the guys on Stu's side who'd committed the ultimate screw-up of landing an own goal.

'God, this isn't much fun, is it?' remarked the woman in the wellies.

'"Come and watch me and the lads play footie," he said.' The trench-coated woman's teeth were chattering so hard she could hardly get the words out. '"It'll be a great match," he said. Not.'

'And I worked until midnight last night so I could knock off early for this,' said the one with the scarf. 'I'm seriously tempted to call it right now and go back to the office.'

'It's freezing, isn't it?' I ventured, and immediately wished I could have come up with something even slightly witty to say.

'Look, you know what' – an immaculately manicured hand pulled the fur coat closer around the sharp line of its wearer's jaw – 'we don't have to do this. We can just sack it off and go to the pub. They'll find us there when they're done.'

'What pub?' I asked, rendered stupid by cold.

'Any pub,' said the one in the trench coat. 'Literally any one. I don't care if there are fag-ends on the floor and piss in the fruit machine coin trays so long as it's warm.'

'They normally head to the Prince Rupert after,' said the woman in wellies, who was the warmest and driest of us and therefore the most capable of rational thought. 'It's about five minutes away.'

'Take us there,' urged the one with the scarf. 'Please. First round's on me.'

And so we squelched away across the muddy field, towards the line of lights that marked the road, civilisation and warmth, five strangers with a shared goal of getting dry and getting a drink. One the way, we introduced ourselves: the one in the wellies was Abbie, whose long-term boyfriend, Matt, was captain of the team. His brother, Ryan, was dating red scarf-wearing Kate, although I could tell from her extreme narkiness that Ryan was already halfway to Dumpedville, population him. The beautiful one with the lipstick was Rowan, and although I didn't catch her boyfriend's name at the time, I got the impression she must be deadly serious about him to put herself through this. And the fur-clad one with the jawline introduced herself as Zara.

'It was my fellow that scored the own goal,' she said. 'Which hopefully means he'll be dropped from the team and I'll never have to do this again. Not that I would anyway, because frankly it's hell on earth, isn't it?'

'I mean, I don't mind so much in summer,' said Abbie. 'When you can wear shorts and sit on the grass with a bottle of wine. But this…!'

'Wine in summer sounds all right,' I admitted.

Already, I was imagining the five of us being friends – at least, to be more accurate, I was sure I wanted to be their friend. Whether they'd want to be mine was another matter. Glancing surreptitiously at each of them in turn as I sheltered with Zara under her giant umbrella, I confirmed my first impressions of Rowan's beauty, Zara's glamour, Kate's confidence, Abbie's air of serene self-assurance.

In contrast to these women, what did I have? An ordinary job I was averagely good at; a just-getting-off-the-ground relationship with a man who'd never made my heart soar; a disparate circle of friends left over from school, university and part-time jobs who were gradually dispersing in different directions.

According to my nan, I made the best cup of tea in the whole world, but I couldn't imagine putting that one forward as a reason why these women should embrace me as a friend.

So I kept quiet and listened while Zara and Rowan chatted.

'My God, that coat is so lush,' Zara said. 'It's Burberry, isn't it? Must've cost a bomb.'

'Actually' – Rowan smiled sideways from her position on the other side of the umbrella – 'it was a freebie. I do a bit of modelling and I was wearing it for a shoot and butterfingers here spilled nail polish on the cuff. Oops. So they let me keep it.'

'Strong work,' Zara said. 'I'm a fashion editor and you won't believe the stuff that gets minor damage during shoots. People are ever so careless.'

They both laughed, complicit in their experience of a world I'd never be part of.

Then we arrived at the pub and the warmth and dry, the smell of beer and stale cigarette smoke and the familiar babble of voices made me feel better, more at home.

'There's a table over there,' Abbie said. 'Why don't you

three nab it, and a few extra chairs, while Kate and I get a round in?'

'Merlot do everyone?' Kate asked. 'It feels like a red wine kind of evening, doesn't it?'

'You read my mind,' said Rowan. 'And how about some crisps as well? Or better still, pork scratchings.'

My stomach rumbled at the prospect of food – maybe we could order burgers and chips later, or soup with crusty bread.

Then Zara said, 'Anything that comes in a packet's safe enough, I guess. Anything from the kitchen in a place like this...' And she drew a finger across her throat and rolled her eyes theatrically.

Rowan hurried ahead of us, swooping down on a table for twelve with practised ease, turning a megawatt smile on the group of guys who were vacating it. As they moved towards the exit, I saw at least two of them looking longingly back at her, like dogs being taken for a walk just as you're getting the roast beef out of the oven.

'So what do you do for work, Naomi?' Zara asked, slipping into the chair next to mine. As she shrugged off her coat, I got a waft of her perfume, heady with vanilla and neroli.

Here we go, I thought. *Now comes the bit where I bore you to death.* 'I'm a legal secretary, but I'm hoping to do a law conversion course in a year or two and qualify as a solicitor.'

'Blimey.' Zara fixed me with eyes as wide and green as a cat's. 'So you're bright and motivated. That's a new one on me. The clever people I know are all lazy fuckers and the ones who work hard are thick as mince. And you must tell me about your hair. Is the colour natural?'

Automatically, I tugged a strand over my shoulder and looked at it, like I'd forgotten what colour it was – as if twelve years of being called ginger minger and copper crotch at school could be forgotten. 'Yeah, unfortunately for me.'

'What are you talking about? It's glorious. And so on trend

right now, like Julianne Moore. Don't ever change it. I'm a closet blonde and the upkeep is hideous – I even have to wax off all my pubes. It's totally not worth it.'

Then why do it? I wondered, but I could feel myself thawing, not just from the warmth of the pub, but from the glow of Zara's friendly attention – oh, and the massive glass of red wine I'd almost finished.

'Look,' Rowan said. 'Here come the boys. They don't look too happy – I can hardly see Paul for mud.'

In they trooped, and the next few minutes were taken up with post-match recriminations, a pretence that they'd been sure we'd dumped them en masse because they'd been so hopeless, and another round of drinks orders.

Off the football pitch, I found it even harder to sort out which of the mud-splattered, heavy-footed men was which. Stu, of course, I knew, although I found myself thinking how much I'd prefer spending the rest of the evening with my new female friends than with him. The two tall men must be brothers, and therefore belong to Abbie and Kate. The earnest-looking one with the beard had kissed Rowan and sat down next to her, apparently all set to monopolise her for the evening.

So Zara's boyfriend must be... Oh. The one who'd just come back from the bar, a tray of drinks balanced on one hand, a rueful grin revealing teeth that were just shy of perfectly straight, a lock of dark hair flopping down over eyes the colour of strong coffee, and a body that would make a Greek god cancel his gym membership because it was too depressing using the same changing room.

The tray still held aloft, bicep flexing impressively, he unloaded drinks on to the table.

'Pint of Guinness for you, sir. Stella for you, mate. Two Peronis, one IPA and a bottle of merlot. Oh, and all the crisps. Phew.' He dropped a kiss on the top of Zara's glossy head and sat down, resting a hand casually on her thigh. 'How's it going, Zee?'

'I could ask you the same thing, David Beckham,' she said, giving him a sideways stare under her eyelashes. 'Made a right arse of yourself back there, didn't you?'

'Oh God.' He pressed a hand dramatically to his face. 'I'm shit, right, but not normally that shit. Must've been stage fright because we had an audience.'

'Don't worry' – Zara grinned – 'we won't come again. We've already discussed it and we're in agreement. This is Naomi.'

The man smiled at me, and for a second I felt like I was the only person in the world – and, disloyally, as if poor Stu had never even existed. His gaze was level, direct and warm. He extended a hand across the table and I took it, expecting three hundred volts to shoot through me, but it just felt like a hand – albeit an exceptionally warm, strong, callused one.

'Patrick,' he said. 'But everyone calls me Patch. Good to meet you.'

'And you,' I said.

I wasn't lying. I was elated to meet him, filled with a thrilling sense of new possibilities opening up with this group of new potential friends.

'Anyway,' Zara was saying to him, 'now that I've endured this, you've got no excuse whatsoever not to come and visit me in Paris next weekend. None.'

'Not exactly a hardship, is it?' Patch asked, and Zara brushed a finger over his cheek in a way that made me turn away from them, feeling suddenly superfluous.

'This wine is practically taking the enamel off my teeth,' Abbie was saying. 'It's like I'm experiencing tomorrow's hangover today.'

'It'll be totally worth it though,' Rowan replied. 'You know there are some hangovers where you wake up and think, *Why did I even do that?* and some where you're like, *Fair do's, I'll take how I'm feeling right now?*'

I laughed. 'When you're trying not to spew on the Tube, but at the same time you're looking round at everyone else and thinking, *I bet you wish you had as good a time as me last night.*'

Abbie glugged some more wine. 'And your boss gives you a bollocking for being late and you just grin inanely at her.'

'And then you go and buy a bacon roll and a KitKat and you're instantly cured,' Rowan chipped in.

We all laughed, and I was sure we already knew we'd still be friends tomorrow. I barely registered when another man joined the party – a blond, movie-star-handsome guy who seemed to immediately hit it off with Kate.

'What's your favourite colour?' I overheard her ask.

'Purple, obviously. The colour of royalty, mystery and of course Cadbury's Dairy Milk. Yours?'

'Purple too,' Kate replied, and the two of them burst into laughter so infectious the rest of us couldn't help joining in, even though we hadn't heard the lead-up to the question and had no idea what was so funny.

But my pleasure in the evening was tinged with something else – a sense that something had changed that night. That because of this random meeting on the side of a rainy football pitch, my life was going to travel in an entirely different direction from the one it had been on before.

And as it turned out, I was right.

FOUR

And so, here we were. Sixteen years later, sixteen years older, in another nondescript pub in a different part of London. It was late morning now, not evening. It was January, not November. Rowan's then-boyfriend Paul wasn't with us and nor was Matt's brother Ryan; they'd been replaced in Rowan and Kate's lives by Alex and Daniel.

Zara wasn't there and of course nor was Andy.

It was by no means the first time all of us had been together; it was only the latest in a series of countless meet-ups – the second Wednesday of every month had become the regular date for what we'd come to call the Girlfriends' Club; there'd been birthdays and pre-Christmas drinks and weekends away and, of course, weddings.

But this was the first funeral. A shiver passed over me as it occurred to me that it wouldn't be the last – but even that could barely darken my gloom.

I was gloomy enough in the present without thinking what the future might hold.

'We should've got them to put some booze in this coffee,' Kate said, wrapping her hands around her mug.

'It's shit, isn't it?' said Abbie.

'The coffee?' Rowan sipped hers gingerly. 'It tastes like it's been brewed from burnt sawdust.'

'The coffee, and also – you know – everything.' Kate bit her lip. Her lipstick was a deep plum colour to match her dress.

'Funny that we're talking about booze, in the circumstances.' Abbie tried to smile but it came out more like a grimace.

'Hey,' I argued. 'Remember, it's what—'

'Andy would've wanted,' finished Rowan.

We all tried to laugh, but Abbie's turned into a sob and Kate wiped away a tear, carefully angling her finger so as not to smudge her mascara.

'Andy wouldn't have just been talking about it,' she said. 'He'd have been getting a round of tequila shots.'

'And then another,' I agreed.

'And we'd all have been so shitfaced we'd have missed the funeral,' said Rowan.

'If there's anyone capable of missing their own funeral because they were getting bladdered in the pub, it would've been Andy.' Abbie tipped sugar into her coffee, stirred it, sipped and winced. 'If you know what I mean.'

'Back in the day, sure,' I said. 'Damn it, though, why did this have to happen? Like, why? It's so unfair.'

'Life's not fair,' Rowan said. 'Like I tell Clara all the time.'

'He was clean for so damn long.' Kate's sadness was mixed with fury. 'So long. We tried so fucking hard. He tried so fucking hard. And then that car accident in Turkey, and the drugs they gave him there, and it all kind of spiralled.'

'Even after that.' Abbie pushed her cup away. 'He relapsed and then he was okay again. We all thought it would be all right.'

'Until it wasn't.' Kate finished her coffee, drinking it down like she wasn't tasting it. 'Daniel and I went to visit him in

Manchester, like we'd been doing every couple of weeks, and we just knew, as soon as we walked in the door.'

We all knew the story. We'd heard it many times before – she'd told us as soon as it happened, desperate for some idea, some miracle suggestion that would make everything okay again. She looked over at Daniel now, standing in the cluster of men, all of them solemn and upright in their suits and purple ties. It was like she hoped he'd overhear and move over to her, laughing, and tell her off for going on about that mad, upsetting dream she'd had a couple of months back.

'That first time – it wasn't like before, when he quit the drugs the first time. Back then when he was using his flat was like a shell; he'd sold everything. This time he was still living almost normally, going to work and stuff.'

We all nodded, letting her talk it out.

'But me and Daniel knew. Andy was expecting us – we'd got into a kind of routine with visiting him. He'd found this gelato place down the road and he was obsessed with trying all the flavours, which would've taken forever because they kept introducing specials. We'd even been discussing on WhatsApp how we were going to try the pistachio and lemon that weekend. But then when we got there he said he wasn't hungry. And we just knew.'

'It's not your fault,' Abbie said gently. 'You tried to get him to go to a Narcotics Anonymous meeting, remember? You even took him there and waited outside for him.'

Kate nodded sadly. 'He didn't go to the meeting. He fessed up afterwards – he locked himself in the toilet and watched old episodes of *The Simpsons* on his phone until it was time to come out again. It was like he thought we'd think it was funny.'

'I remember,' I said. 'It wasn't one bit funny.'

I could feel the weight of Kate's guilt and the load of our shared grief spreading over us, darker even than the lowering clouds outside.

'Remember when Andy bought that teddy bear?' I said to break the silence.

Abbie looked up, a reluctant smile on her face.

'He thought he'd be like Sebastian from *Brideshead Revisited*,' she said. 'All charming and whimsical, carrying it everywhere with him.'

'Except he didn't,' Kate chipped in. 'He kept losing it. He left it in a pub one time, and I put a call out on Facebook for it, and some sweet couple brought it round to my flat. They were so proud they'd found my little boy's comfort object, and I was like, "Actually, he's thirty-two."'

I looked at my watch and saw it was ten to twelve. Time to go. Somehow, we seemed to have mustered enough courage between us to get this done. Around the table, my friends shuffled their feet. Rowan and Abbie got up, wordlessly, and went to the toilet. Kate took out a compact mirror from her bag and topped up her lipstick. I pulled a comb through my hair, more for something to do than because I thought anyone would or should care what I looked like.

Then Patch came over to our table and laid a strong, warm hand on my shoulder.

'We should probably head over,' he said. 'Daniel and Matt are already there, doing the meet and greet thing outside the church.'

Church. I felt myself flinch at the idea, but it had been the one thing Andy's mother had been insistent on, Abbie had told us on WhatsApp.

ABBIE:

Matt tried to suggest that something secular might be a bit more – you know…

KATE:

What Andy would have wanted.

ABBIE:

Exactly – apparently she reacted like we'd
suggested we chop his body into bits and feed
it to our cats. So church it is.

And church it was – the one across the road from the pub, a hulking neo-Gothic building which I supposed would have appealed to Andy's sense of the dramatic even if he deplored the spirituality it represented.

Together, we all left the pub and crossed the road. The rain had stopped and a thin winter sun was beginning to brighten the cloudy sky. The road was wet and the wind cut through my coat and the gap where the zip of my purple dress was held together by a safety pin.

People were trickling through the arched wooden doors: some I recognised from various parties Andy had thrown over the years, but most were strangers – family, I guessed, or friends of his mother's, or perhaps even people he'd met at the twelve-step programmes he'd attended before he stopped attending any of them.

As we approached the doors, a long, shiny black vehicle pulled up outside the church.

'Oh my God,' Kate muttered. 'I can't watch this bit. Let's go in and leave the boys to do their thing.'

'Let's,' I agreed, reaching over to squeeze her hand. It was icy cold.

'Are you worried about your reading?' I asked.

She shook her head. 'That'll be fine. I'm scared of lots of things, but not that. It's just... you know.'

'Everything,' said Abbie.

'Yeah.' Kate sighed. 'That. It's fucking grim, isn't it?'

'All of it,' agreed Rowan.

'Mostly not seeing him again, ever,' said Abbie. 'I mean, that's been a done deal for a while, obviously. But this kind of makes it official.'

'Come on,' I said. 'Let's get this over with.'

'Then we can go and get drunk.' Kate managed a smile.

And so, at least, we were all half-smiling when we entered the church and found seats near the front, a pew to ourselves, guarded by Ryan.

I hugged him briefly. 'Don't drop the coffin.'

'We should've let Patch carry it on his own,' he whispered, then turned and walked back down the aisle, towards the waiting hearse.

I could barely watch as the wooden box containing what was left of our friend was carried on the shoulders of my husband and the other men to its place by the altar. Each breath I took felt painful, as if my body was resisting being alive. When Patch, his duty performed, slid in next to me and took my hand, the relief was overwhelming.

I focussed my eyes on the brim of Andy's mother's black hat in front of me, but I could still see the coffin, topped with a wreath of violet orchids. And beyond that, the pale, grave face of the vicar – his funeral face, I supposed, perfected by years of practice.

He intoned a few words of welcome, something about brothers and sisters and the memory of a life well lived, then the organist began to play *Dear Lord and Father of Mankind*, and everyone stood up and sang as best they could.

Then Matt, looking taller and more stooped than ever, slipped out from the end of the pew and walked to the lectern, white-faced. Abbie had told us he'd wrestled for hours over his eulogy, and in the end it was briefer than it was meant to be, because he started to cry and couldn't stop.

And then it was Kate's turn. Looking almost regal, her chin held high and her eyes dry, she walked gracefully to the place where Matt had stood, cleared her throat and began to recite.

When I come to the end of the road
And the sun has set for me

Her voice was perfect – low and slow and carrying, each word seeming to come out exactly as the poet had intended it to sound. She carried on through the first stanza and second, unfaltering.

And then something weird happened. At first I thought it was to do with the acoustics in the church, but seconds before everything had been fine. Then I wondered if Kate had rigged up a recording of the poem and was reading along to it through an earpiece, which had malfunctioned somehow.

But the echo wasn't coming from the front of the church. There was another voice, almost but not quite in time with Kate's, saying the words.

For this is a journey we all must take
And each must go alone.
It's all part of the...

I couldn't help it – I craned my neck and looked behind me. And there she was, silhouetted in the doorway against the winter sky. Although I hadn't heard her voice for several years, it was instantly recognisable, carrying through the space as clearly as the clock that had chimed midday a few minutes before. Although the veil on her hat half-obscured her face, it couldn't hide the way the light from the stained-glass windows reflected off her hair, creating green and purple highlights on the jet black. Even the sound of her heels, like twin drums on the stone floor, was familiar.

It was Zara.

FIVE

JUNE 2008

It was half a year before I saw Patch again, at least in the flesh, although he appeared regularly in pictures on Zara's Facebook feed. Along with Abbie, Rowan and Kate, the five of us had added each other as friends and had arranged to meet up the following month while our boyfriends played football. *Although nowhere near a fucking football pitch, obviously*, Kate wrote.

And so the second meeting led to a third, and soon it was clear that the Girlfriends' Club was a thing. I can't remember who came up with the name first, but whoever did, it stuck, even though Andy complained that it was a classic example of reverse sexism, surely in contravention of the Equality Act, and what were we going to do next, have jam-making competitions like the Women's frigging Institute?

Outside of the monthly meetings, I saw my new friends sporadically but increasingly frequently. Kate and I met for lunch in the City and she gave me excellent advice on dealing with a difficult colleague at work. Abbie, Rowan and I went to a French art-house film together, although none of us could understand it so we sacked it off halfway through and had a boozy brunch instead.

I went on a few more dates with Stu before mutually calling it a day after an awkward chat during which we both edged towards admitting that although we liked each other, we didn't like each other that way – translation: didn't like each other enough. I got promoted at work and became Executive Assistant to one of the partners. I went on holiday to Tenerife with friends and had sex with a handsome, drunk Spanish man on the beach.

Summer turned to autumn. At work, everyone was back from holiday with renewed energy and the release of the quarterly financial results led to a frenzy of additional work as everyone geared up for year-end. I was working long hours, trying to do my best for Nerine, my new boss, and was relieved that she seemed pleased with me. But it left little time for socialising – I was getting back to my flat after nine most nights (the second Wednesday of the month excepted) and often having to take work home on weekends too.

So when I received a surprise text from Zara asking if I was free the following Saturday, I read it with excitement and then doubt.

Then I made up my mind. Work could wait until Sunday. Sleep was for the weak. And Zara was in some ways the most fascinating of my new friends, with her glamorous job in fashion and her impossibly handsome boyfriend. So, without knowing what she was going to suggest, I agreed.

NAOMI:

> Great!

She messaged back.

ZARA:

> Meet me at Notting Hill Tube station, 10a.m.?

I was intrigued and puzzled, but no further details were forthcoming, so I turned up as arranged and waited for her in the street outside the station. It was a gorgeous late September day, still properly warm although the leaves on the plane trees were just beginning to turn. I was wearing a cotton skirt, denim jacket and boots – an outfit I'd dithered over for ages before realising that whatever I wore, I'd never look as effortlessly stylish as she did and so there was no point worrying about it.

Sure enough, she emerged from the Tube wearing a high-necked, sleeveless brocade mini dress, a squashy leather jacket slung over her shoulders and dark glasses obscuring most of her face. My breath misted them up when she leaned in to kiss me.

'Hello!' she cooed. 'Isn't this the best fun?'

I smiled. 'I don't know – you have to tell me what we're doing first.'

'We're going shopping,' she announced. 'It's Patch's birthday next month and I've decided to have a few people round. It's going to be a surprise – he gets back from Aberdeen that evening and he was going to stay at mine for the weekend. I'm thinking balloons, a banner with his name on – all the tacky stuff. But I've got nothing to wear, and I needed help.'

'That sounds amazing. But you've asked the wrong person. Rowan would have been a much better personal stylist than me.'

'I doubt even Rowan would have been up for a shopping trip with a four-week-old baby,' Zara said. 'Besides, I wanted you.'

Feeling a little glow of pride at having been chosen, even if I was only the second choice, I followed Zara into a vintage shop, an Aladdin's cave of sparkling lurex, embroidered silk, velvet in jewel colours and even a few forlorn-looking furs draped over a dressmaker's dummy at the back.

'This place is the business.' Zara moved over to a garment rail and began rifling through the contents. 'When you're buying second-hand, the trick is to always come to areas where you could never afford to live. Rich people have amazing clothes – especially the dead ones.'

I laughed. 'How do you know whether things will fit? I mean, sizing's changed so much. Wasn't Marilyn Monroe a size sixteen?'

Zara snorted. 'Of course she bloody wasn't. She was tiny. I reckon that's a lie fat women have made up to feel better about themselves. Anyway, you can always get things altered. Seam allowances used to be so much more generous. How about this?'

She pulled something off the rack. It was a long-sleeved, short-skirted dress with a zigzag pattern in psychedelic shades of purple, yellow and green.

'It's... it's quite full-on,' I said. 'But if anyone can carry it off, you can.'

'Not for me, for you.' Zara pushed it into my hands. 'It's original Biba, I'd lay money on it. Try it on.'

Bewildered, I followed her pointing finger to a curtained-off corner of the shop, tugged off my clothes and pulled the dress over my head. Even in the dim light, I could see that it worked. The colours made my hair look brilliant red instead of dusty copper. The bodice made my waist look tiny and the hem finished at just the right point, making my legs look endless. My freckled arms – my least favourite body part – were concealed by the sleeves.

I pushed the curtain aside and emerged to find Zara hovering outside.

'It's all right, isn't it?' I asked, beaming.

'Off the scale,' she said. 'You'll stun everyone at Patch's party in that. My single male friends will challenge each other to a duel over you.'

'What about you?' I asked. 'Aren't you trying anything on?'

'Oh, I picked up a few things.' She showed me a bulging carrier bag. 'Now we can go and have lunch.'

We went to a Polish café Zara knew and had pierogi, giant

blinis piled with smoked salmon, fat slabs of poppyseed cheese-cake and several shots of vodka each, because Zara said she wanted to try all the flavours. After about the second round, I found myself confiding in her about the dire state of my love life.

'I mean, I'd love to settle down and have kids some time,' I said. 'But it feels so kind of final. I knew Stu wasn't right for me, but how do you know who is?'

'Isn't that the million-dollar question?' Zara knocked back a shot of bison grass vodka. 'Shall we try the sour cherry next? The thing is, you're supposed to know – like bam, fireworks etcetera, but I don't think people really do. I certainly don't.'

'Do you mean Patch...' I began. I thought of the photos I'd seen on Zara's Facebook feed of the two of them together – gorgeous, smiling, apparently in love.

'Patch is a lovable hunk of meat.' She smiled wickedly. 'And he's so delicious to look at it's easy to forget his other short-comings.'

I couldn't resist asking what those were, but she answered only obliquely.

'Ah, I suppose no one's perfect. But fortunately I travel so much and he's always working away, so we have lots of time apart. Absence makes the heart grow fonder – and the fond heart wander.'

I laughed, even though I wasn't sure what she'd said was even funny.

'You know,' she went on, leaning confidingly across the table to me, 'no matter what happens with him and me, I'll be grateful to him always, because without him I wouldn't have met you. And Abs and Ro and Kate, of course.'

'I feel the same about Stu. Funny how things work out, isn't it?'

'I guess it's fate. I've never really had friends before – not close ones, anyway. I don't think I've ever mentioned it, because

I hardly tell anyone, but I grew up in care. I'm an orphan – or I was, I'm not sure how old you have to be before you stop being one. But my parents died when I was six, in a plane crash. There was no one else to take me in, so the children's home it was.'

'That's awful, I'm so sorry.' I looked at her, shocked and disbelieving. I'd always assumed that Zara, with her poise and confidence, had come from the most privileged of backgrounds.

'It was grim at the time.' She frowned, then broke into her usual bright smile. 'But it made me who I am. It taught me resilience – but it also taught me to put up walls. And you're teaching me to break them down again.'

I reached across the table and squeezed her cool, slim hand. 'I'm glad. I'm glad we could do that for you.'

Then our conversation moved on and it was late afternoon when we eventually left, saying we'd see each other at Zara's for Patch's surprise party. I found myself looking forward to it, eager to understand more about the workings of this relationship that seemed so perfect on the surface but appeared to be anything but.

Then, at five o'clock in the morning on the day of the party, I pinged awake the way you do when you've forgotten something you ought to have remembered.

I hadn't bought a present for Patch. It was his birthday and I'd be arriving empty-handed, apart from a bottle of fizz I'd planned to buy at an off-licence on the way, which would pretty much empty my bank account until pay day the following week.

In the end, in desperation, I decided to make a mix CD from the year from he was born. It felt personal – too personal, maybe, more than something like a bottle of aftershave would have been – but I was skint and I couldn't think of anything better. His Facebook profile told me it was 1985, and when I started googling I was pleased to find loads of familiar tunes

from that year, songs my mother had played to me in the car
while she drove me to swimming and ballet when I was a child,
which I still had on my iPod because – in spite of their gloomy
content – they made me happy. Soon, I had a properly gothic
compilation going: The Smiths, The Cure, Siouxsie and the
Banshees, The Jesus and Mary Chain and loads more.

When I'd finished that, I spent two hours getting ready and
got the Tube to Zara's flat. The door to the balcony was open to
the late summer evening, fairy lights were strung everywhere
and with Zara's fashionable friends standing around sipping
champagne, I felt like I'd stepped into the pages of *Tatler* magazine. When Zara saw me, she rushed over and folded me into a
CK One-scented embrace, taking my bottle of supermarket fizz
like it was vintage Veuve Clicquot and handing me a glass of
something that I thought might actually be the real thing.

'You look so stunning, Naomi. Love you in that dress – we
did good work.'

'You look incredible too.' It was true – but then Zara always
looked incredible.

'You're the first of the Girlfriends' Club to get here,' she
said. 'Let me introduce you to some fun people.'

She did – whisking me round the room inserting me into
groups of her old uni friends, Patch's old uni friends, women
who worked with her in fashion. Soon after, Rowan, Paul,
Abbie, Matt, Kate and Andy arrived, and to my relief I found
myself enclosed in a chattering, laughing, champagne-drinking
group of my own.

'So where is the birthday boy, anyway?' Abbie asked.

'Probably decided to dodge the whole thing and go to the
pub,' Andy replied. 'Surprise parties are the ultimate double-
edged sword.'

'Why do you think that?' I asked.

'They're all about the surpriser, not the surprisee.' Over
time, I'd learned to expect these off-the-cuff, yet seemingly

deeply considered observations from Andy. 'Has anyone asked Patrick if he likes surprises? Clearly not, because that would have spoiled the surprise.'

'So this way, Zara gets to look like a genius surpriser, and if Patch doesn't like it he just has to suck it up,' concluded Kate. 'I never thought of it that way.'

'Oh come on,' argued Rowan. 'You two are so cynical. Maybe Zara just wants to do something nice for her boyfriend.'

'Trust me,' Andy said, 'when you've been round the block as many times as I have, petal, you'll have learned that the Zaras of this world never "just" want to do anything for anyone.'

But before I could ask Andy what he meant, the longed-for ring of the doorbell sounded.

'Quiet, everyone!' Zara hissed over the chorus of voices and clink of glasses. 'He's here! Everyone hide.'

Somehow, with much giggling and jostling, everyone did.

'Wait until you hear me say happy birthday,' Zara commanded in a whisper, then I heard the click of her heels on the parquet floor as she hurried to open the door.

'Hey,' she said, almost purring, 'how was the journey?'

'Shit,' Patch said. 'Hot as hell and took forever.'

'Well, you made it,' Zara soothed. 'Welcome back. And happy birthday.'

There was a moment of silence, then the rustling of many bodies and the shuffle of many feet all awkwardly moving together, then the first voice called out, 'Happy birthday!' and another added, 'Surprise!' and soon everyone was shouting at once, crowding round Patch and Zara to share in his amazement and her achievement. Patch looked tired – as he would after two weeks of long, physical days doing whatever engineers did on North Sea oil rigs – and a bit scruffy, as he would after a seven-hour train journey.

His jaw was shadowed with stubble and there were shadows under his eyes, too. His faded grey T-shirt was creased and I could see a darker triangle of sweat on the back of it. His hair looked like he'd showered that morning and just left it, without putting on styling products or whatever he normally did – it was sticking out at the sides and the fringe wasn't lying smoothly over his forehead.

Not so delicious to look at now, I thought, wondering if Zara thought the same and if she was reminded of his other short-comings, whatever those were.

But Patch was certainly putting on a brave face. After the initial, *What the fuck just happened?* moment, he was laughing and shaking his head, rueful at how thoroughly he'd been surprised. He'd accepted a beer from someone. He had his arm round Zara's waist and was giving the right answers to all her questions – no, he'd had no idea she was planning this. Yes, it was totally amazing. Around me, the party seemed to be gathering pace. Zara was handing around plates of food – 'Oh God, I didn't cook it myself! I called in a favour from the caterer we use for work events' – some people had drifted out on to the balcony to smoke and others were kneeling around the coffee table while someone tipped white powder out of a Ziploc bag.

I saw Andy glance in their direction, then break away from us to join the group. Kate took a step after him, then changed her mind, sighed and turned back to us, her smile a frozen facsimile of what it had been before.

There was no sign of Patch.

Without really thinking about it, I went towards the door that had to lead to the bathroom, turned the handle and pushed it open.

And there he was.

Not having a wee, thank God – if I'd walked in on him doing that I'd have been mortified. He was standing at the basin, splashing water on to his face, his long dark fringe dripping, his shirt on the floor at his feet.

'Oh my God, I'm so sorry,' I gasped.

'No worries, at least I'm decent. Give me a second, I'll just – would you mind passing me that towel?'

'Sure.' I handed it over. 'Don't mind me, I can come back. I was just—'

I broke off. Patch was towelling his face, his arms flexed, and the beauty and power of his body took my breath away. His back and chest were sculpted like he was made of marble. A kite shape of dark hair began at his throat, spanned his nipples and trailed down to the waistline of his jeans. His abs were so defined they cast shadows on his skin.

Okay, Zara, I thought, *I'd look past shortcomings too, for that.*

'I'm Patrick, by the way,' he said, 'in case you hadn't guessed. But everyone calls me—'

Embarrassed for him as well as for myself, I said, 'I know. We met a few months back – pub after football? I'm Naomi.'

'Of course. I'm so sorry – I should have remembered. I thought you looked familiar – your hair...'

'That's okay. And happy birthday. I brought you a thing.' The home-made CD felt foolish now, almost inappropriate given he hadn't even remembered meeting me. But I'd mentioned it now, so it was too late to change my mind. I fumbled in my bag and took out the gift, wrapped in paper with birthday cakes printed on it. 'It's a mix CD. I'm not fourteen, I promise.'

He laughed. 'I can see that. Hey, I really am sorry I forgot your name. It's just – this is a lot, you know. All these people.'

'I'm not great with crowds either. Forget my own name, never mind some random who I met months ago.'

'You're not a random.' He smiled the smile I remembered from before, which made me feel like I was being bathed in sunlight. 'And I should open your present.'

'It's a bit daft,' I apologised. 'I didn't know what else to get you.'

'The man who has everything, right?' He unpeeled the sticky tape and took out the case, on which I'd carefully hand-written the names of all the tracks. 'Oh my God. This is seriously cool.'

'You like alternative music?' I asked, surprised.

'Love it. You know when you're a teenager and you feel like no one understands you—'

'Especially not your mum and dad?' I smiled, imagining a surly boy with oversized hands and feet.

'Exactly. And then you discover Morrissey and Marr and you're like—'

'I've found my people?'

'Just like that. I even went vegetarian after I listened to Meat Is Murder for the first time. Think it lasted all of four weeks.'

I laughed. 'Are you serious? Me too. Then my mum took to cooking sausages for breakfast on Saturdays and—'

'Game over?' He smiled, holding the box closer to decipher my handwriting. 'Ah, you've got *Just Like Honey* on here. And *When Love Breaks Down*. Awesome.'

'I would never have guessed. I'd have thought you were more into... I don't know.'

'What?'

'Bruce Springsteen, I guess. Or Bon Jovi. Something more... blokey, maybe.'

He laughed. 'Not me. I like the dark stuff.'

He grinned and sang a couple of lines from *She Sells Sanctuary*. His voice was another surprise – a perfectly pitched tenor.

Or maybe the acoustics in Zara's bathroom were just off the scale.

'Well, I'm glad you like it,' I said, smiling. 'You can pretend you're a kid again when you listen to it, only without the angst.'

My words were light, but I was surprised how pleased I was – almost moved.

'I really do. Thank you. Now, I guess I should let you...'

'Sure.'

We stood together for a moment, the bathroom suddenly feeling even smaller than it had before. Then he edged past me and left, the CD cradled in both his hands like it was something precious.

SIX

All around me, I could see other faces turning towards the back of the church, bewildered, aghast or – in the case of Andy's mother – furious. Kate's voice fell silent; Zara's continued for two more words: 'To home.'

Then she said, 'Sorry, sorry. Don't mind me,' and slipped into a pew at the back of the church.

I could feel my heart hammering in my chest. Today of all days – a day that was ostensibly about celebrating Andy's life but couldn't possibly be, because the shock and grief of his death were still so raw. A day when my friends and their support mattered even more to me than they did every other day. A day when the past felt even more present in my marriage than it usually did. And she was here. From the jumble of my thoughts, one clear one emerged: *She didn't get the memo. Literally didn't get it – about the purple.*

Then I thought, *What the fuck, Naomi, now is not the time to obsess about fashion choices, is it?* I forced myself to look at Patch next to me, and saw that he'd gone white as a ghost – as if he'd seen a ghost. I slipped my hand into his and squeezed it, but he didn't squeeze back – his normally strong grip was ice-cold and clammy.

Then, into the silence, Kate's voice resumed again, with a faint tremor at first, then settling into calm clarity.

When you are lonely and sick at heart
Go to the friends we know.
Laugh at all the things we used to do
Miss me, but let me go.

As she recited the final stanza, I wondered how many of the congregation were actually listening. Probably some thought it was nothing – just a random, slightly eccentric woman who'd turned up late and disrupted the proceedings before settling down and behaving herself.

But we knew it was more than that. I could see it in the slight wobble in Kate's legs as she walked carefully back to her place in her high heels; in Abbie's wide-eyed look of shock – almost fear; in the way the tears were no longer falling from Rowan's eyes.

I could feel it in Patch's hand, still and rigid in my own.

She's back, I thought. *Today of all days, she had to pick to come back. And it's not going to be pretty.*

Absurdly, I thought how much Andy would have relished the moment of drama – how he'd have retold the story again and again, adding new embellishments every time.

But Andy wasn't here any more.

Finally, the organist played *Amazing Grace* and we all joined in as best we could, before filing back outside into gently falling rain.

Zara didn't come over to speak to us, not then. I determinedly avoided looking at her, but I couldn't help catching glimpses of her in my peripheral vision, malignant as a crow in her black dress, flitting around talking to Andy's NA sponsor, the vicar, Andy's mother – anyone but us.

I stayed close to the little group made up of Patch and our friends, as if there'd be safety in numbers.

'What are we going to do?' Kate whispered.

'We can't uninvite her to the wake. She's here now,' said Abbie.

'And she wasn't invited in the first place.' Rowan was clinging to Alex's arm like she was having difficulty staying on her feet, Clara watching wide-eyed.

'You don't get invited to funerals, anyway,' Daniel pointed out grimly. 'You just turn up. And she has.'

'We could go somewhere else,' I suggested desperately. 'A different pub. There'll be others nearby.'

'We can't do that,' Patch said. 'Not when we've organised it all, and Andy's mum and all these other people are going to the Watley Arms.'

His face was frozen and his voice sounded stilted, as if it was an effort for him to speak at all never mind sound almost normal. It was the first time he'd spoken since asking me if I wanted espresso or cappuccino, over an hour before. I wanted to hold him tight, let him tell me if he was feeling as shocked as I was, hear him reassure me that he loved me. But it was almost like he'd forgotten I was there.

'We could go.' I looked up at my husband pleadingly, then around at my friends like I was asking for permission. 'Just us.'

'We can't,' Abbie said gently. 'You know we can't.'

Of course, I knew we couldn't.

'This isn't about us,' Rowan said. 'Come on, Nome. It'll be okay.'

I waited for Patch to echo her reassurance, but he didn't. The cold weight I'd felt in my stomach since learning of Andy's death, which had been heavier since I woke that morning, had been joined now by a swarm of icy butterflies.

The rain had intensified. Zara had produced a giant black umbrella, and Andy's mother was sheltering under it with her, like the two of them were official NBFFs. People were starting to look at their phones and drift off in the direction of the pub we'd so carefully chosen for its proximity to the church and its upscale buffet menu – Andy would rather have died than have wilting egg sandwiches and mystery meat sausage rolls at his wake.

Except obviously he wouldn't have had a wake if he hadn't already died.

'We're just going to have to front it out,' I said. 'That's what she's doing, after all.'

'You sure, Nome?' Rowan asked. 'You and I can slip off early if you'd rather. Or go home. It's fine, you do you.'

I shook my head. 'I'll come if Patch still wants to.'

Patch kind of shook himself, like a dog that's just been for a swim. 'We're coming. Let's do this.'

He took my hand, squeezing it quite hard. My fingers were cold now, and damp from the rain, whereas his felt as warm and reassuring as usual, the chill I'd felt in the church gone. But I wasn't quite ready to be reassured.

Ahead of us, I could see Zara's patent black stilettos with their scarlet soles striding along the wet pavement. There were seams running up the back of her tights, and the coat she'd put on was swishy cashmere, exactly the same length as her dress. I wondered if she had an outfit specifically for funerals tucked away in her wardrobe, or whether she'd bought this one for the occasion. I wondered how long she'd known she was going to be coming, and where she'd been.

I looked at Patch, but his face gave no sign of what he was thinking.

Soon – too soon – we reached the Watley Arms. From the outside, it looked like an old-school London boozer, complete with a swinging board bearing a coat of arms, leaded windows and a heavy, studded door. But I knew from the website that inside it was all sleek and modern, with beige suede banquettes, engineered wood floors and abstract art on the walls.

We all paused outside for a moment.

'Come on, team,' said Kate. 'We've got this.'

'We knew it was going to be bad,' Abbie said. 'And the worst bit's over.'

'The worst bit's just starting,' Kate muttered, and I knew she wasn't talking about the wake, or Zara's surprise appearance, but about the days, months and years that lay ahead, without Andy.

'This is about him, not us,' I said. 'Zara doesn't matter. It's fine. She can't hurt us.'

'So let's all get in there and get shitfaced,' Rowan said.

Our eyes met and we all recited our funeral mantra: 'It's what Andy would've wanted.'

Inside the pub, it was blissfully warm. I took my coat off and draped it on a pile of others, feeling the polyester of my dress damp under my arms.

'Bottle of fizz?' Daniel asked.

'Better make it two,' said Matt. 'Abbie and I will stay here by the door to meet and greet.'

'I'll stay too,' Kate said.

'I'd better go and speak to Andy's mum.' Reluctantly, I left the safety of my husband and friends and edged through the small crowd of people in the direction of Mrs Sinclair.

She was standing alone as I approached her, a glass of what looked like brandy clutched in both hands. She was a tiny woman, fair-haired like Andy, with echoes of his face in her razor-sharp jawline and high forehead.

'Hello,' I said. 'I'm Naomi, one of Andy's friends.'

She took my hand in her tiny, bird-like one. 'Ah yes, the famous Girlfriends' Club. Lavinia.'

'I'm so very sorry for your loss.'

She looked up at me, her eyes twin splinters of blue glass. 'It's your loss as much as it is mine. Andrew and I weren't close, as I'm sure you know. But no mother should have to attend their child's funeral.'

She said it with something almost like disgust, as if Andy had insisted she come and watch him cavort at a sex party, I thought. Then I instantly felt terrible for my harshness – how could I know how I'd react in her situation? For a moment, I allowed myself to imagine organising Toby or Meredith's funeral, and I felt the tears that hadn't been far from the surface since learning of Andy's death threaten to start leaking from my eyes.

'Of course not,' I said gently. 'It's a terrible thing. We all loved Andy very much.'

And Andy must have loved her, at some point. But ever since I'd known him, he'd referred to his mother as 'the gorgon' and barely seen her – and, to be honest, I was starting to under-stand why.

'We mustn't speak ill of the dead,' she said, in the tone of someone who was about to do just that, 'but I sometimes think my son only loved himself.'

'He was very troubled. We all have our demons, I guess, but he brought us all so much joy. He had so many friends.'

Zara's face appeared in my mind, so clearly it almost seemed as if she'd materialised from across the room and was standing right there, smiling at me. But she wasn't.

'So I see.' She looked coldly around the room. 'And I suppose I should circulate among them. If you'll excuse me.'

She turned away without another word and disappeared into the crowd, leaving me clutching my glass, trembling.

I felt tears welling up again, and saw the sign for the ladies' toilet in front of me. I'd take a moment, I decided – have a quiet cry, sort out my make-up and then brave the rest of the afternoon. We needn't stay long, I promised myself. We had to pick up the children. Soon I would be home.

I pushed open the door, already rummaging in my bag for tissues. But as I did so, I felt a sudden twang between my shoulder blades, and something sharp piercing my skin.

'Ouch,' I muttered. 'Shit.'

I'd completely forgotten about the safety pin holding the top of my dress together where the edges of the zip wouldn't meet. The air in the pub was so warm I hadn't felt the coldness where the gap was, and hadn't kept my coat on as I'd intended. As I approached the line of washbasins, I heard a tiny clatter as the pin fell to the floor, and as I bent to retrieve it, I felt the zip unfasten all the way down.

'Damn it.'

Twisting in front of the mirror, I could see a bead of blood where the point had pierced my skin. There was no way I'd be able to secure it again without help – earlier, it had taken Patch five minutes of fumbling to get it right. I'd have to text Abbie or Rowan and get them to come and rescue me.

But as I was rummaging in my bag for my phone, I heard the sound of approaching heels on the floor outside and the swish of the opening door. Some instinct told me I should duck into a cubicle and hide, but my feet refused to move. In the mirror, I saw my eyes widen in alarm and I gripped the safety pin so tightly its point drew blood from my finger. Then the door swung open and Zara stepped in.

I hadn't been in the same room as her for more than half a decade. I knew perfectly well what parenting twins had done to me – the changes pregnancy had made to my body and sleepless nights had wrought on my face. And the changes weren't just physical. I was different in other ways too, deeper ones that were even more uncomfortable to think about. But it was like time had stood still for Zara – like she'd spent the intervening years in an alternate universe, or in a coma or something, and stepped back into the world utterly unchanged.

She was still blade-slim. Her pale skin was still unlined. Her dark hair was in the same asymmetric bob with the same brutally short fringe that said, *With my bone structure I can do what the fuck I like to my hair and look great.* Her cat-like green eyes were the same, with the same wings of black liquid eyeliner.

All of this I noticed in a few seconds, the safety pin clutched in my fingers, feeling a trickle of blood oozing down my back.

'Naomi.' She moved in and air-kissed both my cheeks. 'Are you okay? God, this is tragic. When I heard I had to come.'

Unable to speak, I stared at her. I could feel the blood from the safety pin turning tacky on my hand and felt a flare of resentment – *Look what you made me do!* – mingling with a suffocating sense of dread.

'Poor Andy. He was always so full of life – you know what I mean? The most alive person ever. I can't believe it.'

'No one can,' I said, twisting the pin in my hand.

'I'm back in London,' she went on. 'For the moment, anyway. I don't know how long I'll stay, but I couldn't not come today.'

'It's what Andy would have wanted,' I parroted mindlessly, although I was fairly sure it wasn't true.

'Are you having a wardrobe malfunction? Can I help?'

Don't touch me, I thought. I could still feel the places on my cheeks where her kisses had almost landed, as if they were stained with her red lipstick, except Zara's lipstick never smudged. But I found myself standing, frozen, while she took the pin from me and moved behind me.

'I see the problem.' I could feel her breath on the back of my neck – it made the hairs there stand on end – and smell her perfume.

I breathed in while she pulled the zip as high as it would go, then stood very still, feeling her knuckles pressing against my skin as she pulled the gaping the sides of the dress together.

I felt as if I, too, was being precariously held together, at risk of unravelling.

'There,' she said. 'Job's a good 'un. But you don't want to go out there like that, do you?'

'I left my coat by the—' I gestured.

'Want me to fetch it for you? What's it look like? No, wait, I've got a better idea.'

She plonked her bag on the vanity unit and undid the clasp. The bag was large, pewter leather that I knew would feel buttery-soft. And I knew, because seemingly nothing else about Zara had changed, that it would contain everything from make-up to tampons to a shiny little notepad and pen – although perhaps Zara used her phone for note-taking now, like everyone else.

'Pashmina.' Proudly, she produced a rolled-up cylinder of black silk and shook it out. 'I never go anywhere without a pash. Places get so cold.'

She handed it to me and I draped it round my shoulders.

'I'll give it back as soon as I've got my coat.'

'No rush.' She smiled. 'We'll be in touch soon, won't we?'

'Thank you.' The words came out automatically. *Damn it, Naomi*, I castigated myself. *Why do you have to be so damn British? Why can't you tell her you're not friends, everyone's horrified by her turning up here, and what's more, 2003 called and would like its fashion accessory back?*

But I couldn't. I couldn't betray any anger, any sign of weakness.

Zara turned to the mirror, laser-focused on her face, dusting some sort of powder from her make-up bag over her cheeks, making her skin look even more luminous than it already did. I backed into a cubicle and locked the door, pressing toilet paper against my hand, which was damp now with sweat as well as blood. I could hear myself breathing effortfully, a tightness around my chest that wasn't only to do with the newly secured zip of my dress. Although I could no longer see Zara, her scent clung to the pashmina, surrounding me like a miasma – or a memory.

I waited until I heard the door open and close again, the click of her heels receding then abruptly vanishing. Then I exited the cubicle, washed my hands and inspected my own face before deciding there was no point bothering to try and make myself look any different – besides, when I looked in the mirror, I couldn't shake the sense that she was there, watching me over my own shoulder.

Bracing myself, I pushed the door open again, immediately hearing the low buzz of voices and clink of glasses again. I'd find Patch, say goodbye to our friends, deposit Zara's scarf on the pile of coats, and leave. And hopefully that would be the end of it – she'd be out of my life once more, this time never to return.

I saw Patch straight away. He was standing by a window, looking out into the rain-soaked beer garden where a few hardy people were smoking under umbrellas. And he wasn't alone. Zara was standing next to him, her arm round his waist, her hand held aloft as she snapped a selfie of them together.

SEVEN

Patch and I were at home, sitting at the kitchen table surrounded by the detritus of the children's tea: scooped-out eggshells, toast crusts and banana peels. I could feel an early hangover beginning to descend, and was making my way through a pot of lemon and ginger tea. Patch was drinking beer. We'd been half-arguing, half-discussing whether to order curry or Chinese for our own dinner, and no compromise looked like being reached any time soon.

So I changed the subject. 'What do you think about what Meredith said when they were in the bath?'

'What, about Uncle Andy being in the sky with the angels? Pretty harmless, isn't it?' He stacked the plates and started scraping scraps into the food waste caddy.

'I mean, actually, I don't think it is. I've asked your mother before about not filling the kids' head with that nonsense.'

'As opposed to the nonsense we fill them with about Santa, the Easter Bunny and the Tooth Fairy?' He took another beer out of the fridge and gestured to me with it, but I shook my head.

'That's different.'

'How's it different? Look, I really fancy chicken madras. We should order if we're going to.'

'It's different because whole nations aren't oppressed on the basis of belief in the Tooth Fairy.' I half-stood, sat down again, then abandoned the pretence that I wasn't going to drink any more and poured a glass of wine from the fridge. 'If we order from Deliveroo you can have that and I can have sweet and sour pork.'

'But the Bengal Palace does ten per cent off if you order through them directly.' His face looked just like Toby's when he opened negotiations for a third bedtime story.

'So order directly and I'll get mine from Deliveroo.'

'They have a minimum spend. Twenty-five quid, and chicken madras is only eleven. Go on, Nome, we can have Chinese next time.'

I was reminded of our son again – *Just a short one, Mummy. Please? Just tonight?* – and relented. 'Oh, for God's sake. Fine. Get me a lamb biriyani and we can share some samosas and that should make up the total.'

'On it.' He slid his phone across the table and started tapping at the screen. I waited in silence – when it came to ordering food online, my husband had the concentration span of a washing-up sponge. 'I got some bhajis as well, and a garlic naan.'

'Good job. Anyway, I didn't mean about heaven and stuff. I meant about her calling Toby Patrick.'

'She's always done that. Even when we were kids, she'd call me Niamh and my sister Patrick.' He stretched out his legs, interlacing his fingers behind his head like he was on a deck chair at the beach.

'Yeah, maybe. But it sounded like this was different. Like she was insistent that Toby was you and Meredith was your sister.' Propping my elbows on the table, I leaned closer to him.

'They're four. They're probably remembering wrong. Or she was teasing them.'

'Patch, those kids have got memories like elephants. Look how they spouted chapter and verse about the whole afterlife stuff, right down to the harps and Saint Peter. I'm worried about her.'

He shrugged. 'She clearly remembers all she got taught in Sunday School about Saint Peter.'

'Yeah, sure. But the short-term stuff – when I took the kids to see her last week she'd completely forgotten we were coming. And normally she looks forward to it for ages and bakes and everything.'

'She's seventy-five. Doesn't everyone's memory get a bit shit?'

Frustrated, I set my wine glass back on the table so hard the liquid sloshed inside it. One of Patch's most appealing traits was his positive outlook on the world, but it was also one of his most annoying. *She's teething. Don't all kids scream a lot then?* he'd asked, when nine-month-old Meredith had kept me up all night with a temperature of 39 degrees.

'Not to the point where they think their grandchildren are their children. I'm not sure we should be leaving the kids there on their own. I wasn't crazy about doing it today but there was no alternative. And I think she should see a doctor.'

'Good luck with persuading her to do that.' He glanced at his phone, then towards the door, clearly listening for the sound of an approaching moped. 'She barely leaves the house these days.'

'Patch, I know. That's why I showed her how to do her shopping online. I thought it was a great plan at first, and it was, but now she forgets how to do it and I end up spending ages on the phone taking her order down and doing it myself, because last time she ended up with three kilos of baking potatoes instead of three potatoes.'

'Easy mistake to make – I've done it myself.'

He turned back to his phone and, after a couple of seconds, I did too, avoiding my social media and instead flicking through random news articles. The emotion of the day had left me utterly drained, and I realised I didn't even feel particularly hungry any more – I wanted to get in the bath with a scented candle and a book and wallow for an hour, then go to bed.

But I also needed to talk to Patch – and not just about his mother. About Zara, and her reappearance in our life. I thought of her black scarf, rolled up in my handbag – a physical reminder of her, still smelling of her, as if she was right here with us in our kitchen.

If I closed my eyes, I could see them together again – Zara and Patch. Not only how they'd been a few hours ago, their faces tilted upwards to get the best angle on Zara's phone camera, but how they'd been back in the beginning, the unassailable, beautiful couple.

Patch was mine now, I told myself. We had our home, our children. We were a unit. We were the unassailable ones now.

But what if that changed?

The chime of the doorbell made me jump and I realised I'd been staring at my phone, not really seeing the images on the screen, for ages.

'Food's here,' Patch said, springing out of his chair to answer the door.

'I'll grab some plates.'

I sorted the table while Patch levered the lids off plastic boxes, releasing their fragrance into the warm air. Even though I knew I'd regret it when the twins woke me at five a.m., I poured myself another glass of wine.

I waited until Patch had started tearing into his chicken madras, then said, 'Zara looks well.'

'Probably got a picture in an attic somewhere going all wrinkly,' he replied.

I forced a laugh. 'It'll be Botox, more likely. And fillers, and face cream that costs eighty pounds a pop. Was it weird, seeing her?'

'Not really. Funerals are like that – you see people you haven't seen for years and then you don't see them again until the next person carks it.'

Casually, he spooned more curry on to his plate, tore off a chunk of naan bread, dunked and ate. But I noticed that he wasn't quite meeting my eyes either – instead, he was looking sideways at his phone, face down on the table next to him. As I watched, I saw a faint glow appear round its edges as the screen lit up. Patch saw it too – the involuntary movement of his hand towards the device told me that.

'Someone texting you?' I asked.

'Dunno.' He licked his fingers, then flipped the phone right way up. I could see an alert from WhatsApp on the screen. 'Yup.'

I paused, a samosa halfway to my mouth. *Ask him. Don't ask him. It's okay to ask. It's mad and controlling to ask.*

I asked. Actually, I didn't need to ask, because I already knew. 'It's her, isn't it?'

He nodded, chewing. I put the samosa back on my plate.

'Why did you give her your number?'

'I didn't. She already had it – it hasn't changed since before.'

'What does she want?' I tried not to sound needy, jealous and controlling, but failed on all three.

'Don't know, do I? I haven't read it,' Patch responded casually.

'Okay. Look, I'm done here. Will you put the dishwasher on before you come up?'

He nodded, still chewing. I picked up my wine glass and climbed the stairs, my legs leaden with exhaustion and my heart just as heavy.

EIGHT

DECEMBER 2009

I don't know whose idea it was to have a party on New Year's Eve. Quite honestly, it could have been any one of us – we were all young enough not to know that it's categorically the worst night of the year: a night that over-promises and under-delivers, inevitably ending in drunkenness and despair.

It was probably Zara. Lately, when Patch was in town, she'd been very keen to bring him along to gatherings – to Kate's housewarming, of course, but also to Rowan's baby shower, which seemed a bit random. And when the Girlfriends' Club met up on Wednesday evenings, Patch would often turn up towards the end of the night, have a drink with us and then go off somewhere else with Zara, Andy occasionally joining them.

'It's like she wants to show him off,' remarked Abbie.

'Well, I mean, you would, wouldn't you?' asked Kate, who was currently single. 'He is hot as fuck.'

'But we all know he's hot as fuck,' Rowan pointed out. 'It's not like there's some big reveal. It's more, "Oh hi, Patch. How are the biceps doing?"'

We'd all laughed, slightly awkward because we'd been – not

bitching, exactly, but talking about Zara when she wasn't there, which was bitching's more subtle little sister.

I wasn't so sure, though. Of course, given the long-distance nature of their relationship, Patch and Zara would want to see as much of each other as they could. But it felt like more than that – it felt as if when they weren't kept apart by distance, Patch literally didn't want to let Zara out of his sight.

I remembered Zara's quip: *Absence makes the fond heart wander*. And I wondered whether Patch was aware of the possibility of Zara's heart wandering, and was doing whatever he could to stop it happening.

So I approached the New Year's Eve party planning with a degree of misgiving. But none of the others seemed to notice that I was less than enthusiastic; every time we met up or someone posted on the Facebook event page that had been created for the occasion, the plans seemed to be getting more elaborate.

No one had a flat big enough for us to use, so Abbie hired the function room of a pub near where she and Matt lived. Andy's friend Daniel offered to be DJ for the night. Kate spent ages negotiating the food menu with the landlord over email. Zara announced that she'd bought an outfit in a sample sale, but wouldn't show anyone photos of it because it was going to be a surprise. I felt I couldn't give the vintage Biba dress I'd purchased with Zara another outing so soon, and ended up panic-buying a black lace number in the Boxing Day sales. When New Year's Eve eventually came, I arrived at the Barley Mow almost half an hour late to find the party already in full swing. Handsome Daniel, who I'd only met once before, was presiding over the decks, Oasis blaring out at full volume. Andy, Matt and Paul were playing a good-naturedly tipsy game of pool. Kate, Abbie and Rowan were drinking champagne.

Zara and Patch were on the dance floor, Zara in a silver sequinned dress that left the whole of her slender, toned back bare. I noticed how Patch's hand rested possessively on her skin and he leaned over occasionally to whisper in her ear. She, on the other hand, was holding a glass of champagne, her eyes flitting constantly around the room over his shoulder.

'Bloody hell, missus,' Kate said when she saw me. 'That dress is off the scale.'

'You look gorgeous,' Abbie confirmed, pressing a glass into my hand.

'Honestly, your legs,' said Rowan. 'I don't know why you ever cover them up.'

Wrapped in the comfort blanket of my friends' admiration, I set about enjoying myself. I drank the champagne and then had another glass. I asked Rowan how Clara was doing, left for the first time with a babysitter for the evening. I ate three miniature burgers. I danced with my friends, although Zara didn't come over and join our group.

Perhaps things were okay between Zara and Patch after all, I thought.

But when I glanced over my shoulder fifteen minutes and two more glasses of fizz later, Zara was nowhere to be seen and Patch was standing unsmiling by the bar alone, one elbow propped on the wooden counter top, a beer in his hand.

I nudged Rowan. 'Do you think he's okay?'

'He looks kind of down. Why don't you go and ask?'

Empty glass in hand, I strolled over to him.

'Hey,' I said. 'You look like you could do with some company.'

'And you look like you could do with another drink.'

'Well, now you mention it...' I smiled and he smiled back. The warm, easy smile that revealed his slightly crooked front teeth changed his face completely – he was still dazzlingly handsome, but it made him look more normal somehow, less like a brooding hero on the cover of a trashy romance novel. 'Are you having a good time?'

'Hey' – he shrugged – 'you know me and parties. We don't get along so great.'

He clearly remembered the brief conversation we'd had in the bathroom of Zara's flat.

'Maybe that should be your New Year's resolution. Find your inner party animal. I bet it's lurking just under the surface.'

'Like your inner goth,' he teased.

'What do you...?' I felt myself blushing. 'Oh, the dress.'

'You could use a bit more eyeliner and maybe some black lipstick,' he suggested, grinning.

'Wasn't it more leather and corsets?'

He pressed a hand to his face. 'Stop. I don't want to imagine you in a leather corset.'

What was I doing? Was I flirting with Zara's boyfriend? Was he flirting with me?

'Don't worry,' I said hastily, 'it's never going to happen.'

'A guy can dream, though. I still have that CD you made for me, you know. I listen to it all the time, while I'm driving up to Aberdeen. It helps with the...' He trailed off with a vague gesture of his hand, like he was trying to grasp a word that wasn't there.

'The what?'

'Loneliness, I guess. I'm used to it now, but I always feel it anyway, when I leave. Like going back to school. Like I'm leaving something important behind.'

His openness – vulnerability, almost – was another surprise. 'You mean Zara?'

He nodded slowly. 'Does she ever talk to you about... you know. About me?'

I wasn't sure what to say. The truth was, Zara didn't. She only mentioned him with a kind of glib casualness, as if her handsome boyfriend was another accessory to her life, like her Fendi handbag.

Patch took my silence as an answer. 'I thought not.'

'She really likes you,' I said hastily. 'Anyone can see that. I mean – anyone would like you. Obviously.'

He laughed, but it didn't sound genuine. 'That's sweet. Thank you. But sometimes I'm not so sure.'

'You could try asking her.'

'I could. But then I might not like what I heard.'

'But you should. You should go and talk to her right now.'

'Only she's outside having a fag with the DJ.'

Automatically, I glanced up. The decks where Daniel had been standing were abandoned, the music pausing then moving on to the next track.

'I'm sure they won't be long.' And they weren't. Just a couple of seconds later, I felt a cold blast of air from outside and saw Zara and Daniel re-enter the room. Her face was turned up to his and she was laughing, one hand raised to brush raindrops off her gleaming dark hair. I saw her look around the room, her chin tilted upwards, her green eyes bright as lasers. When she saw me and Patch, her smile faltered, then reappeared even more dazzling than before.

She didn't come over to us. Instead, she said something to Daniel, her smile dialling up another notch. He shook his head, laughing. She spoke again, inaudible over the music, and took his arm, leading him on to the dance floor, Daniel laughing and protesting as Lady Gaga's *Just Dance* began playing.

Zara, though, was doing more than just dancing. Her body was moving as sinuously as water in her sparkling silver dress. Her slim arms reached up to Daniel's shoulders and she pulled him towards her, Daniel still laughing and shaking his head. Her hands found his hips and she moved him closer still, until their groins were touching, their bodies moving together in time to the music, Zara's smile unfaltering.

She didn't look in our direction, but I was sure she knew we were watching. The smile had vanished from Patch's face and I felt a pang of sympathy for him.

'They're just dancing,' I said, although I knew that from his perspective, it would look like far more than that.

'Do you have your phone on you?' he asked.

'My— yes, of course.' Automatically, I reached into my bag and took it out.

'Give it to me.'

I was too bewildered to refuse. I watched as he swiped the screen to life and tapped it a few times, then entered eleven digits and returned it to me.

'Is that...?' I asked.

'My number. "Just" my number. Use it, don't use it. But I've given it to you now. You can tell her if you want.'

But I knew I'd never tell Zara. I took back the phone gingerly, as if it was an unexploded bomb. And then, my fingers fumbling because I was a bit drunk and a bit shaky, I typed in his name. It took me three goes to get it right.

Patrick Hamilton.

NINE

'I don't want to go to nursery,' Toby wailed, almost as loudly as he'd wailed that he didn't want to go home when I'd picked them up the previous day.

'Well, you have to.' With an effort, I kept my voice calm and reasonable, resisting the urge to physically chuck both children out of the door just so we could get on our way. 'It's good for you. You like it there. It teaches you valuable social skills.'

'But I don't want—'

'Valuable social skills? I can tell.'

'I want to ride on my scooter.' Meredith looked at me, eyes narrowed, lower lip jutting out menacingly.

'Merri, you can't. There's nowhere to leave it there, and I need to go and see Granny after and drop off her shopping, and I don't want to be lugging a scooter around with me. Okay?'

'But I want to!' My daughter's wailing joined her brother's.

I stood up from tying Toby's shoelaces, pushing my hair out of my face. The kids going to nursery three days a week was meant to be a break for me – give me a chance to get on top of the million other things I needed to do, which seemed impossible with two small children constantly underfoot, bickering with each other because one of them wanted to go to the park and the other wanted to watch CBeebies.

Ultimately, it was supposed to pave the way for me going back to work, but the chances of that looked about as remote as they had when I'd had one of them clamped on to each of my breasts, chomping away at my nipples like a pair of flesh-eating bacteria.

At least Patch will be home tonight, I consoled myself. I still found myself flying solo with bathtime and bedtime most nights – and, now, dealing with the carnage of getting the pair of them ready in the mornings alone.

In a few months, hopefully I'd be getting myself ready for a day in the office too. Just as soon as I got around to writing my CV, creating a LinkedIn profile and actually finding a job.

It gets easier when you're back at work, everyone said. *You rediscover your sense of self.*

Well, wouldn't that be nice? Right now, it felt as if my sense of self had got lost somewhere along the way, possibly in a plastic box under a pile of Duplo, at the bottom of the over-flowing laundry basket, or in the same place as my phone – wherever the hell that was.

Finding it (my phone, not my sense of self – although that would be a bonus) was on my to-do list for the morning, along with tackling the backlog of washing, cleaning up after the kids' breakfast, having some breakfast myself, scrubbing off the sticky footprints that always seemed to appear on the kitchen floor (sticky feet? How?) and identifying the source of the mysterious beeping sound that had been driving me intermittently crazy all morning.

And that was just the beginning – there were numerous other items to be checked off, but I wasn't sure what they were, because the list was on my phone.

'Come on, now, darlings. Coats on. Let's go.'

I wrestled up the zip of Meredith's jacket and shoved a hat

on Toby's head. Looping both their rucksacks over my arm along with my own handbag and fumbling my keys into my jeans pocket, I grabbed their hands and began frog marching them down the street.

'You're hurting me,' Toby protested.

'Mummy, stop.' Meredith turned up the volume of her shrieks, the sound penetrating my head like a dentist's drill.

Jesus, I thought. If one of my neighbours called social services because they thought I was torturing my children, I had no idea what I'd say. 'You've got me bang to rights,' would make a good start, possibly followed by, 'Yes, please take me away and lock me up in a lovely quiet police cell and bring me a cup of tea.'

The twins' joint tantrum continued throughout the ten-minute walk to nursery. First Meredith threw herself down on the pavement and refused to move, forcing me to carry her. Then Toby cottoned on to this and tried the same trick, so by the time I arrived at Busy Bees, I was a sweating, frazzled mess, laden with three bags and two wailing children.

It was all I could do not to face-plant on the ground and howl myself.

And, of course, Princess Lulu arrived at the gate at the same time as we did.

Her name wasn't Princess Lulu, obviously. It probably wasn't even Lulu at all. But every morning, she strolled up in her Lululemon athleisure wear, poised and serene as if she'd just done half an hour of yoga nidra, her blonde hair sleek, her make-up perfect. Her little girl was immaculate in a corduroy pinafore dress and white (how?) tights. Her baby was asleep in his pram.

As always, I felt like we were two illustrations in a parenting how-to book, me with a massive red cross in the corner of mine, hers with a tidy, smug green tick.

'Morning, morning,' Bronwen, who looked after the four-year-old group, greeted us at the gate. When they saw her, the twins' tears instantly stopped. Resisting the urge to drop them both, I squatted down, released them from my arms and kissed their cold, salty cheeks.

'Off you go now. Be good, love you,' I said to their rapidly departing backs.

Princess Lulu, meanwhile, was handing over her smiling daughter, saying something to Bronwen about picking her up early to take her to a violin lesson.

I imagined her day: her yoga class, her manicure, her lunch with a friend, the healthy yet elegant dinner she'd share with her banker husband. Whereas I hadn't had a manicure in years, could barely touch my toes, and if Patch got pasta with sauce from a jar for dinner I reckoned I was making a decent fist of this being-a-wife/mother/housekeeper thing.

And far from a leisurely lunch with a friend, the social highlight of my day was going to see my mother-in-law.

Fighting down the sense of resentment that these visits always seemed to awaken in me, and the accompanying sense of guilt (more guilt. Item one on the 'things they don't tell you about motherhood' list, surely – you'll feel guilty every day for the rest of your life), I boarded the bus that would take me the few miles across North London to the house where Bridget had lived all her adult life, where Patch and his sister had grown up and where my father-in-law had died, three years before.

She's lonely, I told myself. *She's elderly and she's confused, and your visits mean a lot to her.* Except it never seemed as if they did, not really – and I couldn't quite understand how it had come to pass that it was me and not her son who dutifully paid them, once or twice a week.

He's busy. He's at work. Which was true, but I knew with the same certainty I knew Patch wouldn't have unloaded the dishwasher before he left for work (*You have one job! One!*) that even once I too was gainfully employed, the visits to Bridget would remain something I did, not him, and that his own visits on high days and holidays would be greeted by her with far more enthusiasm than mine.

I got off the bus a stop early and joined the small throng of mid-morning shoppers at the local supermarket. What did she need? I'd made a list, lying next to Patch in bed the night before, but of course it was on my phone, and therefore might as well have been on the surface of the moon.

Teabags – she usually needed teabags. And washing-up liquid, and some fancy biscuits. And a few of the frozen ready-meals she always complained about, but seemed to eat and enjoy. And bread, milk and some blister-packs of cooked ham so she could have a sandwich for her lunch.

I paid for the groceries and for a heavy plastic carrier bag, because predictably I'd forgotten to bring one of the many reusable fabric ones that hung on the overloaded hooks in our hallway, and made my way down the familiar street, the wind biting through my coat.

Hurrying down the pavement, I barely glanced at the passersby: more chic young mums, heading for the gym or the hairdresser or out for coffee; elegant women my mother-in-law's age carrying expensive handbags and browsing the windows of the local boutiques and bookshops; young men in cheap suits who could only be estate agents, their eyes on the prize of a multi-million-pound property deal.

And then, in the darkened window of a brasserie that hadn't yet opened for lunch, I caught sight of my own reflection and stopped.

God. I looked a mess. My hair was scraped back in a pony-tail, the ends showing under my woolly hat, parched and split. My face, bare of make-up, was doughy and pale. My jeans were baggy around the knees, my boots had collapsed at the heels and my navy down coat looked like the Primark purchase it was.

I barely bothered any more, that was the problem. I hadn't

the time or more importantly the inclination. There seemed no point in buying nice clothes, having my hair done or putting on make-up when no one ever saw me apart from the nursery staff, my children and my mother-in-law. Oh, and my husband. But sometimes I wondered if he did actually see me any more – or rather, look at me as anyone other than the mother of his children, keeper of his house and warmer of his bed.

Yet another thing I'd need to sort before I presented myself, faded and out of practice, to the waiting job market, I thought. Yet another thing to add to the to-do list on the phone I didn't have on me.

I made a face at my reflection in the window and turned away from it – out of sight, but unfortunately not out of mind – and continued down the road towards Bridget's house.

A few minutes later, I was knocking as I usually did at her front door, which had been painted dark red many years before but was now faded and peeling. The knocker itself had seen better days – rust made it sticky to lift, and I knew from experience that the only two sounds it would produce were a tentative tap and a resounding crash.

I settled for a tap, but there was no reply. I tapped again, waited a minute, then resorted to a crash: there was no way she wasn't there; she was always in on Tuesday mornings, and besides, I'd let her know I was coming with her groceries.

I strained to hear the familiar sound of her footsteps, and just as I was about to knock again, I heard them, followed by the click of the latch. But instead of swinging open like normal, the door parted just a crack.

'Oh, hello, Naomi, it's you.'

I was used to Bridget not sounding exactly elated to see me, but today she seemed downright hostile. Through the narrow gap, I could see her face looked almost furtive. As usual, she was dressed as if she'd raided the costume department of a long-closed theatre, in a long paisley skirt and tapestry slippers, a shabby jade-green waterfall cardigan draped over her tie-dye T-shirt.

Not so usually, she was wearing lipstick – a bold slash of scarlet.

'Morning,' I said cheerily. 'Delivery for you. I got those florentine things, but I couldn't remember if you preferred dark or milk chocolate.'

'Lovely' – but she didn't sound particularly enthusiastic – 'thank you, Naomi. I'll take the bag, shall I?'

I paused, startled. She always asked me in. Always, no matter how much of a rush I was in, I stayed for a cup of tea and to update her on how the children were doing. Did she have a man with her? But the idea seemed vanishingly unlikely.

'Oh, don't worry, I'll bring it in.'

'Well, I'm not sure—' she began, then she appeared to capitulate. 'Come on in, then. There's tea on the go, or would you prefer coffee?'

'Tea's great.'

The door inched open and I stepped inside on to the shabby Turkish carpet that covered the wooden floorboards. Around me was the familiar clutter of my husband's childhood home – the dusty seashells lined up on the windowsill, the dreamcatcher that was now mostly cobwebs suspended from the light fitting, the console table littered with handmade clay pots and metal trinket boxes containing loose change, keys, acorns and a crochet hook that had been there for as long as I could remember without ever having been used.

But there was something new – an unfamiliar smell hanging in the air, expensive and musky, not like the herbal perfume Bridget wore.

'I'll unpack this lot in the kitchen, shall I?' I suggested, moving automatically through the house, feeling the carpet give way to a quarry-tiled floor beneath my feet.

'There's no need to bother, I can manage.' Again, there was that evasiveness in Bridget's voice.

Then I heard the sound of heels tapping on the floor. The unfamiliar scent intensified. And Zara appeared in the living room doorway, silhouetted against the cold winter light, her dark hair gleaming.

'Hello!' she said, like seeing me was the best surprise. 'We were just playing cribbage. Shame you can't join in, it's a game for two really.'

TEN

NAOMI:

She fucking ambushed me

I typed into the Girlfriends' Club WhatsApp later, aware that I
was maybe being just a tiny bit of a drama llama but not caring.

At the time I'd been first blindsided, then genuinely furious.
My mother-in-law, as guiltily as a woman surprised with her
lover when her husband arrives home, had immediately insisted
on offering me tea and switching the game from cribbage to gin
rummy, and I found myself unable to refuse. So I endured a
tortuous hour playing cards – which I sucked at; I'd started
losing to the children at snap about a year before – drinking the
kind of herbal tea that tasted of grass clippings, and listening to
Bridget and Zara chatting about Paris.

'Such a beautiful city,' Bridget rhapsodised. 'And always so
clean! When I compare the London Underground to the Metro
– ugh.'

'My apartment's right in the centre of the *dixième*,' Zara
said, 'so I mostly walk everywhere. But yes, arriving here has
been quite a shock to the system, haha! I'm only out for a few

weeks and then I'll be heading back home. It truly does feel like home now.'

I gritted my teeth and checked my cards – a useless collection of unconnected, off-suit low numbers, apart from the jack of hearts. *Why are you staying, Naomi?* I asked myself. *You're a grown-up – just make your excuses and go!*

But somehow, I couldn't. It felt almost like leaving them to it would have been somehow perilous – as if allowing Zara unfettered access to my mother-in-law, her tea, the biscuits I'd brought and a pack of playing cards would be the beginning of a dangerously slippery slope that could lead anywhere.

'You should come and visit, Nome,' Zara said, casually laying down the king, queen and ace of spades. 'It's been years.'

'Patch has always loved travelling,' Bridget said, as if I kept him chained to the kitchen table or something.

At last, I was rescued by the British Gas man turning up to read Bridget's meter, and I was able to say goodbye. Zara did, too, kissing Bridget as if she was her long-lost aunt and promising to visit soon.

Then, as soon as the front door had closed behind us and I was preparing to say the briefest possible goodbye to her, Zara said, ever so casually, 'Oh, Nome, about my pashmina.'

Startled, I replied, 'Yes – what about it?'

'You do still have it, don't you?'

'Of course.' What did she think I'd done, flogged it on Vinted in the four days since Andy's funeral?

'Do you mind awfully if I pop back to yours and pick it up? It's just, I'm so used to having a black pash in my bag. In case of emergencies, you know, like the one on Friday. And I'm getting all twitchy without it. It's like my Linus blanket.' She gave a tinkly, self-deprecating little laugh.

Put on the spot, I couldn't think of a decent excuse. It was too early for needing to collect the children from nursery to be plausible. I clearly wasn't going out to lunch or to the gym.

So I said, 'Okay. I mean, of course you can. Shall we get the bus?'

'Haha, no need for that. Come on, let's Uber it.'

'You – okay, let me get my phone and I'll order one.'

Except I didn't have my phone. So I heard my voice giving her my home address, and watched helplessly as she entered it into hers.

I half-expected the cab journey to pass in awkward silence, but I'd reckoned without Zara's Teflon self-confidence – or was it just the hide of a rhino?

As soon as the car door thumped shut and we settled into the pine-scented interior, she began giving me what I later described to the Girlfriends' Club as an interrogation the Stasi would have been proud of.

'So – E17. Where's that postcode exactly?' she asked, frowning earnestly down at her phone. 'My London geography's gone to shit since I've lived abroad. Is it Hackney?'

'Haha, no. We couldn't have afforded Hackney if we wanted to. It's further north than that and a lot less fashionable.'

'And you've lived there how long?'

'Four and a bit years.' I hesitated, torn between wanting to give away as little information about my life as I could and needing to emphasise its stability, its permanence. 'We moved in just before the twins were born.'

'Twins! Oh my God, I did not know that. How adorable. Identical? You know I have an identical twin sister, Zoe? What are yours called?'

'They're a boy and a girl. Toby and Meredith.' It felt odd telling her our children's names – frightening, almost. Like I was handing her some sort of power over them. And as for her twin sister, who she'd never mentioned before – I wasn't sure I wanted to ask her about that.

But what else could I say? *I'm not telling you what they're called and you can't make me* – way to make myself look like I was the weird one here, not her.

'That must be quite the handful, with Patch being away so much.' She smiled sympathetically.

'He isn't so much any more,' I replied defensively. 'He got promoted so he doesn't do the six weeks offshore thing any more – he's mostly based in London and only travels sometimes.'

And now I'd given her a clue to my husband's whereabouts.

'And you?' she probed. 'Still doing the old nine to five?'

I shook my head, watching her wide, guileless eyes follow the movement. 'I'm a stay-at-home mum, for now. I went back after maternity leave but it was too much, so we decided I'd best pack it in for a bit. But I'm thinking of going back once they start school.'

'And how about the old gang? Abbie, Kate, Rowan – you guys still see each other?'

'Yes, same as always. Second Wednesday of every month. But we talk online every day.'

'Ah.' She sighed, her fingers pressed against her lips like she wanted to be blowing out cigarette smoke, not just air. 'You know, I miss that. I've never had a group of friends like you guys, and I don't expect I ever will again. It gets harder when you're older, doesn't it?'

Then why did you fuck it up so badly? So deliberately and unnecessarily? I wanted to know the answer, but at the same time I couldn't bring myself to ask – because how would I know if what she told me was even true?

So I just said, 'Yeah. We're all really lucky.'

And then I asked her a bit about her time living and working in New York, and it turned out she'd spent a couple of years in LA as well, and a year in Hong Kong before returning to Paris. If, of course, any of that was true.

To my relief, the cab drew up outside my house, and Zara jumped swiftly out, thanking the driver and strolling up to the front door before I had the chance to offer to go in and fetch her scarf while she waited in the car.

'Do you mind if I use your loo?' she asked. 'I'm absolutely bursting after all that tea.'

'Uh... sure. It's just up the stairs on the left.'

I watched the high heels of her boots disappear on to the landing. *Don't go into our bedroom. Or into the children's bedroom. And if you could possibly close your eyes when you're in the bathroom so you don't notice the state of the floor, that would be good too.*

But Zara gave no sign of having noticed anything untoward when she came strolling down the stairs a few minutes later. I'd done a hasty rummage through the blue Ikea bag of dirty washing that was spewing its contents out on to the kitchen floor and located her scarf (thank God I hadn't put the delicate cashmere and silk garment through a hot wash), as well as my phone (likewise).

'Love your tiles,' she said. 'Honestly, this place is so lovely. It really feels like a home. You should see the hovel I'm renting – it might be central but there's no room to swing a cat. Not that I'd try swinging Bisou, obviously, she'd never put up with it.'

So then of course I had to ask her about her cat, and listen to a run-down of how she'd adopted a Bengal kitten when she was in Paris and it had been all over the world with her, and was getting on now but she loved her so much she sometimes felt like she might die.

And then, politely refusing my offer to have her scarf dry-cleaned and post it back to her, she left.

NAOMI:

So that's what happened

I typed in the Girlfriends' Club WhatsApp.

I was perched on the edge of the bathtub, where Toby and Meredith were currently contentedly splashing each other (and me). I reckoned I had about five minutes to finish updating my friends on the day's events before the twins got bored and started demanding more bubbles or wanting to get out.

KATE:

OMG I can't believe the brass neck of her! Just turning up like that.

NAOMI:

I mean, to be fair, it's just paying a social visit on an elderly woman and playing cards. It's not like she was stealing the silver.

ROWAN:

Still. That must have been awkward.

NAOMI:

Like you won't believe.

'Mummy, I'm cold.' Meredith's inevitable announcement came a good three minutes later than I'd been expecting it – a welcome reprieve.

'Come on then, darlings. Bedtime and a story?'

For the next half an hour, I was distracted from any thoughts of Zara by *The Cat in the Hat*, *Aliens Love Underpants* and the intoxicating smell of my children, all soapy and sleepy – although I didn't particularly rate the chances of them staying that way, given Toby's recent habit of pinging into shouting wakefulness the moment I left the room.

I waited while they fell asleep, perched on the end of Meredith's bed, not looking at my phone or even thinking about anything much except the way the shadow Toby's eyelashes cast on his cheek was more visible than the pale ginger lashes themselves, and how Meredith's lips drooped downwards towards the pillow as she fell asleep, her favourite teddy clamped under her chin.

At last, I felt it was safe to leave the room. I stood,

infinitely slowly so as not to cause any vibration in the mattress, tiptoed to the door and stepped out on to the landing.

Only then did I allow myself to breathe.

Retrieving my wine glass from the bathroom, I walked downstairs. The kitchen was a mess – the children's coats dumped over the backs of chairs, their lunchboxes unwashed next to the sink, my handbag spewing its contents over the kitchen table, which was still littered with the remains of spaghetti bolognese.

It was far from the scene of domestic serenity I'd imagined welcoming my husband home to, back when we'd decided it made sense for me to give up work. And, even though the child-related chaos was somewhat worse now than it had been earlier, it wasn't the image of mine and Patch's home I'd have chosen to display to Zara, either.

I glanced at my phone again and saw that the chat had been updated.

ROWAN:

That's so weird. It sounds like she was almost... Nice?

ABBIE:

She was always nice. That was one of the things about her. Dangerously nice.

NAOMI:

I know, right? I could feel my guard coming down all the time, and I really didn't want to let it.

KATE:

Want to know something else?

NAOMI:

What? Tell us quick, because I need to get cracking.

KATE:

> She messaged me on LinkedIn. She's asked
> me to meet her for a cocktail next week.

I put down my phone, leaving the others to react to Kate's announcement. I took the defrosted chicken breasts out of the fridge, along with a couple of bendy carrots, a head of broccoli that was going brown round the edges and some wilting spring onions. My hands moving without my mind being fully engaged, I started vigorously peeling and chopping.

Zara was back. It seemed like she intended to infiltrate our lives as if nothing had happened – as if she could turn the clock back to when we were all friends and none of us would notice, or remember what had happened in the intervening years.

And I had absolutely no idea what to do about it.

ELEVEN

MAY 2010

'Ooooh!' Rowan clutched the handrail, her ankle almost turning over as she stumbled down the stairs in her high heels, just making it safely on to the pavement outside the bar. 'I think that last round of strawberry mojitos was a mistake.'

'Strawberry mojitos are never a mistake,' Kate scolded. 'Strawberry mojitos are the bomb.'

'Bet you won't be saying that at seven a.m. tomorrow,' pointed out Abbie, who'd been held up at work and was therefore the most sober of the five of us – not that that was saying much.

We all paused, blinking in the glare of an oncoming bus.

'I need a fag.' Zara fumbled in her handbag for her cigarettes, but the strap slipped off her shoulder and the bag crashed to the ground, sending its contents spilling out. 'Oh, bollocks.'

I dropped to my knees to help her, but she dropped at the exact same time and our heads bumped together with an audible thud that made my eyes water. On all fours, I looked up at her and we both started giggling helplessly.

'Come on, you two.' Abbie scrabbled on the ground for Zara's scattered belongings. 'Is that the new Tom Ford lipstick?

Cool. Get up now, or you'll be on the front page of the *Daily Mail* illustrating an article about ladette culture.'

I scrambled to my feet. Rowan held out a hand to help Zara up, but she was like a baby giraffe taking its first steps, her legs in her patent slingback stilettos going in every direction except the one she wanted them to. Eventually, with Rowan holding one arm and Abbie the other, she made it up.

'God, I love you guys so much,' she slurred. 'You'll always have my back, won't you? Won't you?'

And then she started to cry.

'Oh, babe.' Kate found a tissue in her own bag and Zara's cigarettes in hers, and lit one for her with the practised eagerness of an ex-smoker. 'Come on, no need to get all emosh. We've got you.'

'No one's ever said that before,' Zara sobbed. 'I've always been alone until I found you guys. I don't want to ever be alone again.'

I put my arm around her and she buried her face in my shoulder, the smell of perfume and smoke surrounding me. 'Sssh, you're not alone. We're here. And what about Patch?'

'Patch doesn't love me.' Zara's voice was muffled the fabric of my coat. 'He can't possibly. I don't deserve to be loved.'

'Oh, darling. He does love you.' I said it even though I had no way of knowing whether it was true. The number Patch had given me at New Year's Eve was still saved on my phone, uncalled and unmessaged by me. I was glad of that now, because even a 'hello' would have made me feel horribly disloyal to Zara.

'And so do we.' Abbie moved in closer, enfolding both Zara and me in her arms.

'We need to get her home.' Rowan's voice was full of concern.

'She can't get the Tube on her own,' Kate agreed.

'Where are you staying, Zee?' I'd never used Patch's nickname for Zara before, but it came quite naturally now.

'Bloomsbury.' She lifted her head from my shoulder and took the cigarette from Kate, inhaling deeply, then coughing.

'I'm going north too,' I said. 'Why don't we share a cab? I can drop you at your hotel and then go on home.'

The cost of a taxi all the way home would be prohibitive, but Zara didn't need to know that. I'd see her safely back to her hotel and then get a bus, I decided.

'No dodgy minicabs for you, mind,' Rowan said.

'Here we go.' Kate flagged down a black taxi. 'In you get. Message when you're both safely home, okay?'

'I haven't finished my fag,' Zara complained.

'Come on.' I took her arm and opened the car door. 'One more drag and off we go.'

'Can't I finish in it in there? We'll open the window for ven-ven-titilation.'

'Not in my cab you won't, love,' barked the driver. 'And if you throw up on my upholstery...'

'She won't,' I promised, although I was far from certain. 'What's the hotel called, Zee?'

'The Regency.' Reluctantly, Zara dropped her cigarette and allowed herself to be bundled into the back seat.

I followed her, sliding across and pulling Zara's rucked-up skirt down over her thighs as best I could. Her legs were as limp and floppy as a rag doll's.

'Regency? Never heard of it, love.'

'It's just behind the Brish Mushum,' Zara slurred.

'Just behind the British Museum,' I translated.

I was surprised. I knew that when Zara visited from Paris, where she was now living, to see Patch, they tended to stay at his parents' place, or went away to some romantic hideaway together. But when she came to London alone to join us for the Girlfriends' Club on Wednesday evenings, which she didn't manage every month but did at least several times a year, I'd assumed her work put her up somewhere properly posh, which any cab driver would have known how to find instantly. I didn't have time to analyse that, though – my priority was keeping Zara awake until we reached our destination.

'When are you heading back?' I asked her. 'Hope you're not getting the Eurostar early tomorrow. You'll have the hangover from hell.'

'Never get hangovers,' Zara insisted, her head flopping against the seat back. 'Too much practice. Patch says I've got a liver of steel.'

I laughed. 'Your liver and his abs. You're quite the pair.'

Zara laughed, hiccupped, then started to cry again.

'Oh God, I'm so sorry.' I knew from experience that anything could have set her off at that point, but I still felt awful. 'What did I say?'

'I don't deserve him,' she said. 'I shouldn't have... I should never...'

'Sssh.' I stroked her shoulder. 'Don't worry. Everything's okay.'

She lifted her face and looked at me, her eyes bright with tears but her mascara still, impossibly, in place. 'You don't know what it's like. If you haven't been through what I've been through, you can't understand how it feels not to be able to trust anyone.'

I'd seen this side of Zara before, when she'd had too much to drink – a dark, paranoid, melodramatic side. I remembered her telling me about her childhood in the care system, and there'd been something else, too, once – about a boyfriend who'd sexually assaulted her. I'd been drunk too, when she'd whispered the story to me in the pub toilet with a broken lock, and we'd had to stand guard while the other one had a wee, so my memory of it the next morning had been so hazy I'd wondered if she'd actually said it or it had only been a dream.

'You can trust me,' I soothed. 'Don't worry.'

'Can I, Naomi? Can I really?' The question didn't sound hopeful or needy – it sounded deeply cynical – almost angry.

'The Regency,' the cab driver announced, swinging over to the kerb and then muttering under his breath, 'And not a moment too soon.'

Hastily, I thrust a ten-pound note and two one-pound coins through the slot, thanked him and opened the door. There was no question of leaving Zara to make her way in alone. Possibly if it had been the sort of hotel I'd imagined, with a smiling, uniformed porter waiting outside a brightly lit lobby where tourists were nursing post-theatre drinks, I would have – but not here.

The place was on a side street. From the outside it looked like just another of the terraced Georgian houses that surrounded it, mostly converted to offices, their stucco fronts pristine and their windows dark and shuttered. But I could see lights on in several upstairs rooms here, dim as if cast by single filament bulbs or flickering televisions, and the lights revealed ragged, grubby lace curtains half shrouding the windows. On a faded board in a downstairs window, I could see the words 'Bed and breakfast' with two red stars below them.

I wonder how long that's been there, my logical brain registered cynically. *When was the last time the AA inspected this place – 1998?*

I hurried round the back of the cab and opened Zara's door. She was slumped down in the seat, her chin on her chest.

I gave her shoulder a gentle shake. 'Up you get, we're here. Do you have your keys?'

'Home sweet home,' she said, swinging her legs out of the cab and clutching my arm for support as she stood up. 'The good old Regency.'

Old, maybe, I thought.

As if she'd recovered the homing instinct of the drunk

person, Zara found her keys quite easily, and I followed her up the three steps to the front door. The mosaic tiles in front of it were chipped and dirty. Zara fitted a key into the lock and turned it, and as the door swung open a dim light clicked automatically on.

Inside, the air was cold and sour smelling – a hint of industrial cleaning products not quite masking whatever grime was lurking. The hall light switched off and another above us came on, revealing a carpet that had once been dark green but had worn away to reveal its brownish-grey underlay in the centre of every step.

It wasn't just the shabbiness of the place that unsettled me; I'd lived in more than my share of sketchy student houses and my current flatshare certainly wouldn't be appearing as the 'after' picture in a bleach commercial any time soon. There was something else – an air of seediness, almost of despair, that seemed to seep from the walls as clearly as the unpleasant smell.

Zara didn't seem to notice. Purposeful now, she climbed the stairs swiftly, past the first floor and on to the second. On cue, the stairwell light went out and a fluorescent strip illuminated the corridor.

Dimly, I could hear a woman's voice moaning wordlessly.

Zara stopped three doors along, raised her key and fitted it into the lock at her second attempt.

Then she turned to me, smiling. 'I'm all good now. Thanks, Naomi.'

I looked at her, appalled. Before, all my energy had been focused on getting her back to base – but now I'd seen what base was, the idea of leaving her here was unthinkable. As she turned the key and edged the door ajar, I could see it was barely thicker than plywood.

'You can't stay here on your own.' I took a step towards her. Through the crack in the doorway, I could smell damp, overlaid with a blast of her perfume. 'It doesn't feel safe.'

She laughed. 'Of course it's safe! I've been staying here for years. All the models use this place as a base for fashion week – it's dirt cheap and obviously dirt everything else as well, and the breakfast's inedible so they all stay lovely and thin.'

'Seriously?'

'Seriously.' She seemed to have sobered up a bit, recovering some of her usual poise.

I still wasn't sure. I was far from sober myself, and the shock of finding myself here made me feel kind of distant from reality, as if I'd fallen into a weird drunken dream and I'd wake up any minute to find myself standing in a warm, fragrant corridor at the Dorchester.

Zara moved swiftly, as if to take advantage of my confusion. 'Nighty night, Nome. Thanks for looking after me. You can tell the girls Cinderella's safely back from the ball.'

She leaned in and pecked me on both cheeks, then opened the door and darted through it. I glimpsed the interior of the room for only a second, but afterwards I was almost certain of what I saw: a person in the bed, silhouetted in the light from the street lamp shining through the curtains. And I was equally sure that, over the hum of traffic from outside, I heard a man's snore.

Then the door clicked shut behind Zara and I heard the key grind in the lock.

There was nothing more I could do there. I wanted nothing more than the comfort of a crowded night bus and the familiarity of my own bed. My mind made up, I turned and hurried away, the lights snapping on and off and on and off as I made my way out into the street. All the way home, the details replayed in my mind: the shape under the bedclothes, the rasps of a sleeping breath. Thinking about it, I was almost sure I had smelled something, too – a masculine fragrance like juniper, entirely different from Zara's perfume.

I tried to convince myself that I was wrong. Zara didn't keep secrets – if anything, she over-shared, freely spilling out details about her life and feelings. If she'd been there with someone – a man – surely she would have told us. But then, perhaps she wouldn't – because of Patch, who was our friend too.

However much I tried to convince myself that my mind – helped along a bit by the strawberry mojitos – had been playing tricks on me, I couldn't quite do it. I thought, when I messaged Rowan to tell her that Zara had got back safely, about mentioning what I'd seen to her, but I couldn't bring myself to. It would have felt like a betrayal of Zara, who I'd promised to take care of.

Unlocking my own front door half an hour later, I realised something that had never occurred to me before. I thought of Zara as one of my best friends – but, really, I knew almost nothing about her.

TWELVE

'Well, cheers. I guess.' Rowan raised her glass of chardonnay, and Abbie and I followed, our glasses clinking in the centre of the table with a sound more cheerful and celebratory than any of us were feeling.

It was the first meeting of the Girlfriends' Club since Andy's funeral, and we were in a bar we'd visited before. It was not a particularly nice one – the tables were small and cramped, the music was too loud to hold a conversation over, the wine was indifferent and expensive and the food was limited to packets of crisps with fancy and off-putting flavours like Brie and prosecco or fried egg.

'What happened to our reservation at that new place in Shoreditch?' I asked.

I didn't want to seem as if I was complaining – this was more of a second, mini-wake for Andy than our usual monthly catch-up, and crisps that made you burp sulphurically for hours after eating them were an insignificance compared to the loss we'd all suffered.

'Kate cancelled it.' Abbie took a sip of wine and winced. 'She's not coming, and the reservation was on her credit card.

Apparently they've got some weird policy about the person who made the booking needing to be there.'

'Is she okay?' I asked, concern flashing in my mind like the red police car light emoji.

Of all of us, Kate had always been closest to Andy – just how close, we'd only discovered recently. Andy's bisexuality and his physical relationship with Kate had been a secret they'd kept for years, placing enormous strain on both of them.

'She's devastated, obviously,' Abbie said. 'You know, she never got over the idea that she'd be able to save Andy somehow – that if she loved him enough and gave him enough and tried hard enough, he'd eventually be okay.'

'But that's not true.' I looked at my friends' faces, mirroring my sadness and worry. 'There was nothing she could have done. Nothing any of us could have done.'

'I think,' Abbie went on slowly, 'she thinks that if she'd somehow made her and Andy's relationship work, she'd have been able to stop him taking the drugs.'

'But she tried that,' Rowan said. 'She tried for years and years.'

'And if she'd carried on, she'd still be being made miserable by Andy, instead of being happy with Daniel,' I added.

'But then Andy might still be alive.' Abbie put her feet up on her chair, her knees tucked under her chin like it was cold in the bar, although it wasn't. 'Maybe she thinks her happiness would be a price worth paying for that. But I'm not sure, because she won't talk to me about it.'

'She's grieving,' I said. 'It makes people behave strangely. Maybe she just needs some space.'

'I hope so.' Abbie gazed miserably down into her glass. 'I just wish she'd open up about it. It makes me feel kind of helpless.'

'Maybe you could ask her for a coffee or something,' Rowan suggested. 'Just the two of you.'

'I tried. She says she's busy.'

Rowan and I both glanced involuntarily down at our phones. I knew she wanted – just the same as I did – to look at the Girlfriends' Club WhatsApp chat, to see when Kate had last posted, analyse the tone of her messages for something different, something wrong.

'If you'd offended Kate, she'd tell you, right?' Rowan asked.

'I hope so. I thought so.' Abbie sighed. 'But now I'm not sure.'

A sudden thought occurred to me, and I took a large gulp of wine, barely noticing how bad it tasted. 'She said she was going for a drink with Zara. Does anyone know if she did?'

An image sprang into my mind: another bar, a chic, glamorous one like the place Kate had originally booked, not like this slightly seedy pub. Two women sitting opposite each other, wearing designer clothes and drinking complicated cocktails. Their faces alight with laughter, leaning in to talk, exchanging memories and secrets.

Zara dripping poison into Kate's ears with the same precision and delicacy as the barman would have added bitters to their drinks.

'I don't know.' Rowan frowned. 'Did she tell you, Abs?'

Abbie shook her head. 'I mean, she mentioned it like it was a totally normal thing for them to do. But it's not, is it?'

'If Zara asked you out for a drink, would you go?' Rowan asked.

Abbie didn't answer. I remembered how she'd found it in her heart to forgive Andy, even after his betrayal of her and Matt years before, when he'd stolen money from them to buy drugs. To accept overtures of friendship from Zara – even after such a drastic fall-out, even after so long – might seem quite minor by comparison. What I knew of Abbie's kindness, the value she placed on friendship, her willingness to see the best in everyone, gave me the answer she hadn't.

And what about me? I had met up with Zara, even if it had been involuntary. I'd invited her into my home, even if it was only because it had felt impossible to refuse.

There was silence round the table. Then Rowan said, 'Look, shall we have another bottle of this pencil-shavings chardonnay, or shall we call it a night? I think we're all a bit knackered.'

'There's no point staying here,' Rowan agreed. 'Vibes are officially not good.'

'I think we should go round to Kate's place,' Abbie suggested. 'See if she's home. If she's okay.'

'It's only a few minutes' walk away.' Suddenly, I felt like the disappointing evening could be redeemed. 'Let's do it.'

'We can swing by Tesco and get supplies.' Rowan was already on her feet, slipping her arms into her coat.

Ten minutes later, we were walking over the bridge across the river, laden with carrier bags containing bottles of sparkling wine, crisps and frozen pizza. Buoyed by excitement, I barely felt the bitter, sleety wind.

'This is just like when you moved into your flat after you and Paul split up, remember, Ro?' Abbie's smile flashed out in the darkness.

'Ah, I remember that! It was just the best thing. I was so sad and skint and Clara wouldn't stop crying, and I was thinking, *What the hell have I done?*' Rowan recalled. 'And then you guys turned up and we had gin and tonics and a kitchen disco.'

'I got so pissed I had to sleep on your sofa.' I laughed. 'And do the walk of shame to work the next day in yesterday's clothes, and everyone thought I'd had a one-night stand.'

I felt a pang of something that felt like longing for the young woman I'd been then – laughing with my colleagues in the office, insisting that I hadn't got lucky but had been up late with my friends, inhaling a bacon sandwich and fixing my make-up in the ladies' toilet before going into a meeting with a client.

How simple life had been then – how spontaneous, how free of any responsibilities.

'Here we are,' Abbie said, looking up at the glass-and-steel front of Kate's riverside apartment building.

'Her light's not on.' I felt doubt creeping in, my excitement cooling as the wind cut through my scarf. 'Maybe she's asleep.'

'Kate never sleeps.' Confidently, Rowan extended a gloved hand and pressed the buzzer.

I felt myself beginning to shiver as we waited for a response that I was already suspecting wouldn't come. Rowan pressed the bell again, but we were met with silence.

'Maybe she's still at work,' Abbie said.

'Or at Daniel's,' I suggested, but I was thinking, *Or out with Zara*.

'We should've rung first, I guess.' Abbie smiled bravely.

'We'll tell her we tried,' said Rowan. 'It's the thought that counts, right?'

There didn't seem to be much point in extending the evening after that, standing out in the cold in the hope that Kate might return or trying to find somewhere else to go. So we divided up the shopping, exchanged hasty hugs and went our separate ways.

My hands deep in my coat pockets, I walked slowly towards the Tube station, alone. Tonight had felt strange – like we were a table with one of its four legs missing. It reminded me of when we'd been a group of five. The heady optimism we'd briefly felt raiding Tesco and going to surprise Kate made the disappointment of her absence even more acute.

I remembered how I'd felt all those years ago – that the friendship between the five of us was in peril, and it was my fault. I felt the same way now, although there were only four of us. Or were there? And if so, which four?

THIRTEEN

'Daddy,' said Meredith, clambering on to the sofa next to her father.

'Daddy!' Toby followed, taking the other side.

'Daddy, Daddy.' Meredith turned the volume up a notch.

'Daddy, Daddy, Daddy,' echoed her brother, his voice taking on the high-pitched sing-song quality that cut through my ears the way the whine of a mosquito cuts through sleep.

'Patch,' I said, adding my own voice to the chorus.

'What?' He looked up from his phone. 'Come on then, you two. Who wants to see Jackson score against Arsenal?'

The twins couldn't have cared less about Chelsea scoring a winning goal, but they instantly squealed, 'Me, me, me!' and scooted up closer to their father. Patch slipped an arm round each of their shoulders and angled his phone so they could see.

'Look how he cuts through the defence. Beautiful pass from Fernandez, and...'

Tuning out his commentary, I remembered the first time he'd left me alone with the children to go up to Aberdeen for work, just after his paternity leave ended. I'd tried to put a brave face on it, telling him I'd cope just fine on my own, that his mother would drop in and help and stay overnight if necessary, that he wasn't to worry.

Then, at the last minute, just as he was zipping up his bag ready to leave, I'd broken down.

'They're so little,' I sobbed. 'And I haven't got a clue what I'm doing. What if one of them gets sick? What if I drop them down the stairs?'

When I looked up, I saw his eyes were full of tears too. 'Fuck it. I'll stay. I'll tell work I can't do being away from home any more. If they sack me, they sack me – we'll manage.'

I felt a brief leap of relief and joy, but stifled it straight away. 'You can't.'

'I can. You just gave birth – having a tricky talk with work is nothing compared to that.'

'It's not just the tricky talk.' I wiped my nose on my sleeve, glancing automatically over my shoulder to check that the twins were still asleep on our bed, where they'd finally conked out after a lengthy screaming session and a feed. 'If you lose your job we'll be fucked.'

'We'll find a way. It's only money. You need me, and besides...'

'Besides, what?'

He reached out and stroked my cheek, rubbing away a tear with his thumb. Then he sat down on the bed, gently so as not to wake the babies.

'I hate leaving them, Nome.'

Looking down at him, this strong man next to his tiny son and daughter, I felt like I needed to protect all three of them. I sat down too, and took his hand.

'Even when I go to the supermarket, I miss them,' he went on. 'Everyone says you'll fall in love with your babies, but I didn't expect it to be like this.'

'I know.' I managed a watery smile. 'Me neither. It's worse for you because you have to be away for so long.'

'Six bloody weeks. What if they smile for the first time while I'm away and I miss it?'

'I won't let them. I'll be the most boring mum ever. If they look like they're about to try I'll tell them something really sad.'

He laughed. His vulnerability gave me a confidence that hadn't been there before – an awareness of the resilience that was there somewhere inside me – at least, I hoped it was.

'We'll be okay,' I went on. 'Promise. We'll FaceTime every single night – just let me know what time your shifts are. I'll take videos of them in the bath and if they crack so much as a hint of a smile—'

'You'll delete it off the recording so I think it's me that made them do it first?'

'Exactly.'

'Nome?'

'Patch?'

'I have to go.'

'I know.'

'I love you.'

'I love you too.'

As it happened, Meredith did smile for the first time while her father was away – although Bridget said it was probably just wind. But Toby held off until the day Patch got home, and when his dad lifted him up, smothering his face with kisses and saying, 'Where's my big boy?' he cracked a proper, unmistakeable grin.

Patch had cried then too.

He'd loved them so much – he still did love them. But somehow, somewhere along the way, he'd stepped back from the day-to-day grind of parenting and I'd taken over. When his job had changed to be office-based, he'd announced with delight that he'd be able to do more with the children now, but it hadn't happened. Of course he cuddled them and played with them and kissed them good night if he was home early enough. But

when Toby resisted sleep at night, Patch didn't know it was
because someone had to check the wardrobe for monsters.
When Meredith needed to be taken to try on new shoes for her
ballet class, he didn't know whether they needed to be pink or
black.

And the loneliness I'd dreaded that first time he went away
had become so much of a fixture in my life that I barely noticed
it any more.

I finished stacking the children's plates in the dishwasher
and gave the left-over pasta sauce that was destined for our
dinner a stir. Then I opened the fridge, looked at the half-
finished bottle of wine on the shelf, and closed it again.

'Come on, Meredith and Toby,' I said. 'It's time for your
bath and then bed.'

'But Daddy!' Meredith's voice was entering full whine
mode, and I knew tears would shortly follow if someone didn't
apply some distraction – and fast.

'Daddy's busy,' muttered Patch. 'Go and have your baths
and I'll come and kiss you good night.'

'Daddy, play with us.' Toby's lower lip was thrust out
mutinously.

'Mate, I'm busy.' Patch's eyes had returned to his phone.

'But I want—' began Meredith.

I put the wooden spoon down on the counter with unneces-
sary force, red sauce splattering around it. Clearly, Patch wasn't
going to take over the bedtime routine. I could bawl him out for
ignoring them when I was busy, but we'd often had conversations about how to withstand their divide-and-conquer strategy,
and had agreed that arguing in front of them about who did
what was an instant route to defeat. Besides, bathtime was my
job. Quite when it had become my job, even on the nights when
Patch was home, I couldn't recall – but my job it was, as firmly
entrenched now as the bins being Patch's job – except, of
course, when he wasn't here, when it became mine by default.

'Toby and Meredith,' I said in my I-mean-business voice, 'if you're upstairs in thirty seconds, you can have some of Mummy's special bubble bath.'

That worked. The promise of a squirt of L'Occitane's finest was a sure-fire way to make the kids cooperate – not because they appreciated its moisturising, almond-scented, fifty-quid-a-bottle glory, but because they'd seen how badly I'd freaked out the one time they'd tipped half a bottle into their bath before I could stop them, and it was now kept securely out of reach in the same cabinet as the Calpol.

Come to think of it, the twins were the only members of the household who ever got to use the stuff; I couldn't remember the last time I'd had an uninterrupted wallow in the bath. I could barely remember the last time I'd shaved my legs.

The children dashed upstairs and I followed more slowly, with a last longing glance back at the fridge. If I got through bedtime without losing my shit, I promised myself, then I'd have the massive glass of chardonnay I so badly wanted.

Forty-five minutes later, splashed with expensively scented water and with a numb arm from where Toby had lain on it while I read *The Very Hungry Caterpillar* through three times back to back, I returned downstairs.

Patch was still on the sofa, still on his phone, the football still playing on the television with the sound still off.

I stirred the pasta sauce again. It was starting to catch on the bottom, so I added a splash of wine before sloshing a load more into a glass.

'Any chance there's a cold beer in the fridge, Nome?' Patch asked.

Any chance you could get your arse off the sofa and actually help? I thought. But there was a time and a place for a row, and that time wasn't now – not yet, anyway. I took our drinks over to the living room and sat down next to him.

'You know, the kids really love it when you're here,' I said.

'I really love it when I'm here.' He stretched out his legs, taking a long swallow of craft IPA. 'Work's fucking brutal at the moment. I'm knackered.'

'I get it, I really do. You haven't been home much before eight for the past couple of weeks. So it's exciting for them when you're here. They love having their dad around. And – you know – I get tired, too, doing all the parenting and house stuff on my own.'

'What's this, the tiredness Olympics?'

'Of course not. I know how hard you work. It's just, sometimes I wonder if you know how hard I work.'

'Sure I do. That's why we put them in nursery three days a week, even though it costs a fucking fortune.'

'But on the days they're there – come on, Patch. You've seen what carnage it is getting them out of the house in the mornings. And then there's all the shit I have to do – cleaning, shopping, seeing your mother, all that. And then it's time to pick them up again and I've got them all afternoon and evening until you get back.'

I could hear the tone of my voice changing – no longer calm and soothing, but querulous, almost carping. *Dial it down, Naomi*, I told myself, *or that row you didn't want to have is going to happen.*

'So what do you want me to do about it?' His tone had changed too – no longer genial, becoming combative. 'Jack in my job, and then we can both stay home and do the shopping?'

'Patch, don't be daft. Like I say, when you're here, it would be nice if you spent a bit of quality time with your children. That's all.'

'I take them to swimming every Saturday.'

Sure you do, Dad of the Year. Giving me a precious one-hour window which I spent – if I was honest – messing about on my phone, jumping guiltily to my feet and dragging the Hoover out when it was nearly time for them to get home.

'And they love it,' I said. 'Just like they'd have loved it if you'd given them their bath and put them to bed just now.'

'Toby won't settle for me,' he pointed out, as if our son's behaviour was some force of nature beyond his control. 'When I try, he just yells for you.'

'Of course he does.' I could hear my voice rising again. 'Because I do it every bloody night and it's what he's used to.'

'Because you're here every bloody night and I'm not.'

And here we were again, right in the middle of the same circular argument we'd had dozens of times before.

'I'd just like some time to myself,' I pleaded. 'Like you do, when you leave the house at six three times a week to go to the gym.'

'Do you seriously think I like having to drag myself out of bed at five thirty?'

Well, obviously. Because otherwise you wouldn't do it.

But I didn't get a chance to say that.

'If you want to go to the gym, knock yourself out,' he went on. 'I'm not stopping you. You can get up and go right now if you want.'

He was right, of course. I could, if I wanted to.

'I would.' I felt like I was caught in a trap – the trap of an argument I wasn't going to win. 'But come on, I'm tired. Like I told you. It's eight o'clock and I just want to eat and go to bed.'

'And? That's what we're going to do, isn't it? Eat and go to bed. Living the dream.'

'Fine.' My glass was empty and I was fresh out of ideas, too. 'Set the table. I'll cook the pasta.'

'Want me to make a salad?'

Aware that the point I'd been trying to make had been – again – lost in the familiar pattern of our bickering, Patch became conciliatory. He filled up my wine glass without being asked, made a dressing for the salad, complimented my puttanesca sauce, asked how the children had got on at their street dance session that afternoon.

And I should probably have left it there. Taken the easy way out, gone to bed, accepted that this was a situation of my own making and wasn't about to change.

But I didn't.

When we'd eaten and I was ferrying the dishes from table to counter while Patch – still in co-operative mode – stacked the dishwasher, I asked, 'What were you doing on your phone earlier, anyway?'

'What do you mean?'

'The kids were clambering all over you. They wanted their dad, and you just blanked them. What was so important?'

'You seriously expect me to remember what I was looking at on my phone two hours ago?'

'You seemed pretty engrossed in it. Typing away.'

'Jesus, Naomi. Maybe I was answering work emails. I don't know.'

'It wasn't your work phone.'

'So maybe I was messaging the guys on the gym WhatsApp. Or checking the football scores. I can't remember.'

Maybe he couldn't. But I wasn't sure I believed him. There'd been something about the way he'd gazed at his screen, ignoring the children as if they weren't even there, that had seemed... different. Off.

'Patch?' I asked. 'Has Zara been in touch with you at all?'

He gave me a long, cold stare. Then he said, 'Actually, yes. She wants to see me.'

'Why? What the hell for?'

'She has something of mine, and she wants to give it back.'

I have something of hers, my mind echoed, *and she wants to take it back.*

I forced air into my lungs. 'Patch, I'm not sure I'm comfortable you seeing her.'

He laughed shortly. 'Don't be ridiculous. What do you think's going to happen?'

'I don't know. It's not that I don't trust you. It just feels – wrong, somehow.'

To my surprise, he said, 'Okay. In that case I won't. It's only an old DSLR camera – I'll never use it and it'd fetch pennies on eBay. I'll tell her to take it to a charity shop.'

Relief and gratitude washed over me. He cared – he'd heard my concern and fear and taken it on board. Everything would be okay.

'Look,' I offered, 'why don't I pick it up? I can go when the kids are at nursery. And then you can decide if you want to keep it or not. I'll message her now.'

In my eagerness to make amends, to be as selfless as he'd been, I grabbed my phone and started typing. When I looked up to ask Patch for Zara's number, I thought I saw a look of something like panic on his face, but it vanished before I could be sure it was ever there.

FOURTEEN
OCTOBER 2010

'Oh my God.' Seeing Abbie and Matt approach me across the crowded concourse of St Pancras station, I abandoned my wheelie case and dashed to meet them, skidding to a stop and almost spilling my coffee. 'How exciting is this?'

'We're going to Paris.' She hugged me tightly, making my coffee slosh dangerously again. 'We're going *en vacances*.'

'We're going *chez* Zara,' I agreed.

'*Sur le Eurostar*,' offered Matt.

'*Et voilà* – or is it *voici*? – Rowan,' I said. 'At least one of us can speak French properly.'

In her swishy taupe trench coat and high-heeled boots, Rowan looked the epitome of Parisian chic. She joined our huddle, grinning excitedly but apprehensively.

'God, I hope I still have a daughter when I get back,' she fretted, checking her phone. 'Paul's never looked after Clara on his own for this long before. What if he breaks her, or leaves her in Sainsbury's or something?'

'He won't,' Matt assured her. 'Apart from anything else, he'll be too shit-scared of what you'd do to him if he so much as dressed her in odd socks. Here's Kate – but no Andy?'

Kate was approaching almost at a run, her case trundling behind her.

'Sorry I'm late. Fucking nightmare of a morning. Andy's not coming. He woke up this morning with a severe case of man flu.'

We all met each other's eyes, but said nothing. We knew that Andy's ailment was far more likely to be a bad hangover or come-down than any sort of viral infection, but we didn't want to bring down the mood by discussing it. This weekend had been weeks in the planning, a surprise visit to see Zara in Paris, and a much-needed break for all of us.

'Shame,' Rowan said, 'but I guess that means we've got an extra room, so you and I won't need to share if we don't want to, Naomi.'

'I mean, I'm totally happy to. But to be honest, I snore terribly when I've had a few drinks and since you've not got Clara with you, you'll probably be glad to get some sleep.'

'So we're just waiting on Patch.' Matt glanced at his watch. 'Hopefully he's not been struck down with a lurgy too?'

'He said he'll meet us in Paris.' I tried not to blush, feeling as if everyone could guess how long I'd had Patch's number saved on my phone before I'd finally dialled it. 'His flight from Aberdeen was delayed so he's getting a later train.'

Rowan gave me a searching look and said nothing. But, as we moved to board the train, she hung back with me, letting the others go ahead, and we found seats together a couple of rows away from them.

'It's going to be kind of weird seeing Zara on her new turf,' she began, handing me a can of pre-mixed gin and tonic from her bag.

'Yeah, although Patch has been out to see her a couple of times already, so it's not so new to him.' As soon as I'd spoken, I wished I hadn't.

'You two have been chatting, then?' Rowan asked faux-casually, her eyes narrowing.

'Me and Zara? Yes, of course. We—'

'Nome. You know that's not who I meant.'

I ducked my head, then took a gulp of my drink. I hated lying to my friends – hated even the idea of it, which was why, up until now, I'd been careful not to. Or at least, to lie only by omission. When the first of Patch's texts had arrived on my phone a month before, I'd felt a thrill of excitement so intense it had shocked me – almost as much as my own urge to keep the to-and-fro messaging that had followed a secret.

Even though our exchanges had been entirely innocent: him sending me a photo of some dolphins in the North Sea, me replying with a picture of autumn leaves in a London park; him asking me how work was going, me telling him about a disastrous first-and-last date I'd been on with a friend of a colleague; and, more recently, us sharing plans for this Paris getaway, they still filled me with guilt. Guilt that was almost as potent as the pleasure our sporadic exchanges brought me. Guilt that was only intensified when I remembered what I was almost sure I'd seen in Zara's hotel room six months earlier – because now I was not only hiding something from Zara, but hiding something from Patch, too.

'Oh, me and Patch?' I replied casually. 'Yeah, we text sometimes. It's no big deal. We're just mates.'

Rowan pushed her sunglasses up into her glossy hair. 'Naomi, babe, I want you to hear me out. Just this once, then I promise I'll never mention it again, okay?'

I felt the kind of hollow apprehension I used to get when I was summoned to the headmistress's office for bunking off a hockey match. 'Okay. But seriously, Ro, there's nothing—'

'Going on between you and Patch? I didn't think there was. At least, not yet.'

'What do you mean?' That twist of guilt again, with a thrilling side of, *Does she truly think something might actually happen between him and me?*

'Nome, I'm sorry to mention this. I really am. I don't want you to think I'm lecturing, because I'm not. But I've noticed – it's been pretty obvious to be honest, for ages – that you like him.'

'Of course I like him. We all do.'

She gave an impatient little shake of her head. 'Duh. But you *like* like him.'

'I... Ro, if I did, what would it matter? He's with Zara. I'd never, ever do anything to hurt her or spoil what we've all got as a group. You know I wouldn't.'

'I know you wouldn't,' she echoed. 'But here's the thing. You might not mean to, but sometimes things happen when two people like each other. And with Zara and Patch having this long-distance thing, it makes their relationship that little bit more fragile.'

She thinks he likes me! But I concealed my pleasure. 'Ro, there's nothing to worry about. Truly, there isn't. I promise.'

'Okay.' She reached over and squeezed my hand, her cashmere wrist-warmer soft against my palm. 'Because I really don't want anyone to get hurt. And you really, really don't want to make an enemy out of Zara.'

'What are you talking about, Ro? I'd never make... Zara's my—'

'You two are looking very serious.' Matt's grinning face loomed above us. 'I'm off to the bar for a bottle of fizz. Want any crisps with it?'

The rest of the journey passed uneventfully. Rowan fell asleep; I closed my eyes, but couldn't stop thinking about what she'd said. I remembered the last time I'd seen Patch: the pain on his face when he'd watched Zara and Daniel dancing, then the recklessness with which he'd given me his number, like it was some sort of final throw of a dice. I didn't know what was going on between him and Zara or how deep the cracks I'd witnessed in their relationship ran, but I did know that distance was only a part of what was wrong.

And what about me? Did I fancy Patch? There was no point denying it to myself any longer, even if I continued doing the equivalent of putting my fingers in my ears and going la-la-la when Rowan brought it up. Would I ever do anything about it? Of course not. Absolutely, categorically not.

Except that, by not deleting his number from my phone straight away and now exchanging messages with him, I already had.

It was going to have to stop, I told myself. This weekend would be safe – Zara and our other friends would be there. Nothing could happen between us, even if Patch wanted it to. Did I want it to? Not at the expense of hurting Zara and destroying our friendship, that was for sure. And as for what Patch wanted – it was impossible to imagine him wanting to put his relationship with Zara in jeopardy for me of all people.

What I felt for him was just a crush. A stupid teenage thing based on nothing but a few minutes in a bathroom and another few at a bar, and magnified through the twin lenses of secrecy and distance. Now I had the opportunity not only to see Zara, but also to put the whole thing into perspective and knock it on the head once and for all.

So why did that prospect make me feel bereft?

My gloomy musings were banished from my mind the second Patch arrived at the apartment we'd rented in Montmartre. It was tiny – the room that had been destined for Andy had only a single bed, pressed tightly against one wall – but the ceilings were high and the walls painted a sunny yellow. On the walk there, I'd already found myself falling in love with the city: the graceful tree-lined boulevards, the wrought-iron pavement tables where people chatted over glasses of red wine, the first glimpse of the Eiffel Tower on the horizon.

It was enchanting – but even Paris paled in comparison with Patch. As soon as I heard the rattle of the door and his footsteps on the wooden floor, it felt like the whole atmosphere of the place changed, as if the heating had been turned up a notch or music had started playing or some exotic scent had filled the air.

But it was only him. Calling out a greeting, apologising for being late, hugging and kissing us all (including Matt – I loved how unrestrained Patch was in his displays of affection), depositing a supermarket carrier bag bulging with wine and cheese on the kitchen table.

I hung back, longing for his embrace but also wary, conscious of Rowan's watchful eyes and my own emotions, kept so precariously in check.

'Naomi.' He hugged me and I allowed my cheek to rest for a second against the sleeve of his woollen coat, feeling the fabric scratch my skin and the hardness of his bicep beneath it. 'How are you, sweetheart? First time in Paris?'

'I think I came here on a school trip ages ago, but I can barely remember it. It's beautiful.'

'We should sightsee properly tomorrow,' Abbie said. 'Go to the Louvre, see Jim Morrison's grave—'

'Take lots of photos to send to Andy,' Kate went on.

'Get Zara to show us the good shops,' added Rowan. 'I'm sure it's all changed since I lived here.'

'What's the plan tonight, anyway?' Matt asked. 'Does she know you're here?'

Patch nodded, smiling easily. 'She's booked a table at a bistro near her flat. I had to ring them and tell them there'd be seven of us, not two, and it was a surprise. Which was kind of tricky, given my non-existent French. Anyway, we're meeting there at eight; I'll go back to her place afterwards.'

Abbie glanced at her watch. 'That gives us two hours. I'm dying for a shower – why don't we get ready, then head out and explore a bit and have a drink somewhere?'

So I hurried to the bathroom I shared with Rowan, determined to make myself look as beautiful as I possibly could, but painfully conscious that it would be nowhere near as beautiful as Zara looked without even breaking a sweat.

By ten that evening, we were all seated at a long, paper-covered table in the restaurant, surrounded by the remains of steak-frites, mussel shells, baskets of bread and almost-empty bottles of red wine. Zara had reacted with amazed delight to our surprise. The food had been delicious. Crème brûlée and brandies had been ordered. Patch was safely on the opposite side of the table to me, down the other end next to Zara, and I was allowing myself to enjoy his company at a distance, the intensity of my feelings mellowed by wine and the company of my friends.

We were all pleasantly tipsy – except for Zara. As soon as we sat down, she'd ordered a kir royale and then another, then drunk wine at what seemed like twice the pace of the rest of us, barely touching her food. Paris seemed to have changed her – or maybe not so much changed her as intensified her, distilled the essence that made her Zara. She'd lost weight; her legs in her black leather trousers were model-thin and the bones of her wrists clearly visible where the draped sleeves of her silk blouse ended. Her hair was cut more sharply than ever, her eyeliner more heavily applied, her lips stained now with red wine as well as her dark lipstick.

There was something about her – there always had been – that made you just want to gaze and gaze at her. She wasn't conventionally pretty like Rowan, but she had something – glamour, magnetism, charisma; I didn't know the word for it and I didn't want to know, because whatever it was, it was part of what must make her irresistible to Patch. And that night, I could hardly bear to look at her, partly because of how her beauty made me feel – small, nondescript, shabby – and partly because looking at her meant looking at Patch, and every time I did that he would look back at me, as if he somehow knew, and I'd feel a twist of pain deep inside me that even the wine and laughter couldn't muffle.

'I'm going out for a fag.' Now I had to look, because Zara was standing up, swaying slightly in her high-heeled boots and steadying herself on the table before making her way to the door.

She passed me on her way and I felt her hand brush my shoulder.

'Come out with me, Naomi.'

I didn't smoke – I never had. But it was a summons I couldn't ignore. Abandoning my untouched dessert, I got up, shrugging my arms into my coat, and followed her outside. Apparently impervious to the cold, she was leaning against the stone wall of the restaurant, one ankle crossed over the other, her cigarette lighter illuminating the sharp planes and angles of her face.

'It's so amazing to see you,' I said. 'Are you having a good time?'

'The best.' Smiling, she blew out a long plume of smoke. 'I can't believe you all came here just to visit me. And see Paris, of course.'

'Yeah, it's all about Paris really,' I joked. 'You just happened to be here.'

She laughed. 'The truth comes out. Tell me, are you seeing much of Patch in London?'

Her normally clear voice was a bit slurry and I realised she was even drunker than I'd thought.

'Not really. I mean, he's up in Scotland most of the time, and when he comes down he gets together with the guys, but I haven't seen him since New Year's.'

Apart from those text messages. My phone was in my bag, back in the restaurant, but I felt as if it might be sending out a hidden signal, telling Zara the truth about what was stored in its memory.

'It's shit, the long-distance thing,' she went on. 'I mean, we see each other maybe once every six weeks. We message all the time, obviously, and sometimes it gets quite – you know – spicy.'

I flinched, not wanting to imagine her and Patch sexting each other, sharing over their phones the things they wanted to do in real life – had done, would be doing later that night.

'Are you embarrassed?' She laughed. 'Bless you, Naomi. If you knew the stuff we get up to, you'd just die. I'm very highly sexed, you see, and so's Patch.'

I remembered that dingy hotel room, the shape beneath the bedcovers, the sound of a snore that I could have sworn was a man's. Was that an example of Zara being highly sexed? If so, surely it was something Patch couldn't be expected to put up with, no matter how enthusiastic about bedroom shenanigans he was himself.

What went on between them was none of my business. But I felt compelled to know – did they have some sort of consensual open relationship thing going on?

While I was trying to frame the words to ask, Zara took another long drag on her cigarette and then went on, 'Here's the thing – I trust him, obviously. I know he's smitten with me, and I am with him. But I meet loads of hot men at work. Most of them gay, obviously, but not all of them. And I have to admit I sometimes feel – you know, tempted. And I can't help wondering if it's the same for him.'

'Honestly, Zara – how many hot women do you think work on oil rigs? Gay or not? But if you're' – I could hardly bear to use the words – 'seeing other people, don't you think he deserves to know?'

She laughed again, that throaty cackle. 'I'm not "seeing other people". Bless you, Naomi. Not in the way you mean, anyway. I'm not unfaithful in any sense that matters. But Patch is different. For him, when he's back on shore, letting off steam, or in London seeing his mates when we haven't been together for weeks – if something happened, it would matter. To him and to me.'

'But you trust him, surely? He must trust you, knowing all the hot men you meet here in Paris.' Did he, though? I remembered the shadow of sadness I'd seen on Patch's face at the New Year's Eve party, right before he'd given me his number. He hadn't looked particularly trusting then.

'Trust.' She grimaced, her crimson lips curling downwards like a sad clown's. 'I mean, it's all well and good, isn't it? But I'd rather have certainty than trust.'

'You can't be certain though, can you?' I leaned in closer to her, feeling the warmth of her shoulder, smelling her perfume and her cigarette smoke. For a second, I felt like I'd felt back in the very earliest days of the Girlfriends' Club, when we'd all got drunk together and shared secrets, revelling in the joy of our new-found friendship. Before I'd known how I was going to feel about Zara's boyfriend. And feeling as I did, who was I to judge what Zara was doing?

'Sure, there are no guarantees. I can't keep the man under lock and key – although if I could, he'd probably quite like it.'

'So then all you have left is trust.'

'Trust – and maybe a little insurance policy as well. Belt and braces.'

'What do you mean?'

'I mean you, Naomi. Will you help me? As my friend?'

'Help you do what? Seriously, Zara, I don't under—'

'It won't take much. It'll be the ultimate cushy number, actually.' Again, I heard the slurred mushiness in her words. 'Just touch base with him. When he's in London, meet up with him. Go for drinks. Have coffee. Go see those action comedy films he likes so much. Hang out. That's all.'

'You want me to spy on him?' Her request took me

completely by surprise – as did the spark of excitement it gave me. She wasn't just giving me permission to see Patch when she wasn't around – she was practically ordering me to.

'Haha. Not spy. That would be mad. Just be his friend. And if he suddenly isn't free to see you, or he mentions another woman, or you think something's off, you let me know. Simple.'

'Zara, this is mad. You can't be serious. It's no way to have a relationship – you doing… whatever you're doing, and then asking me to keep tabs on him. It's not healthy. You need to tell him what's going on.'

She looked at me through a haze of smoke, her eyes narrowed. 'Why? You don't want to split us up, do you, Naomi? Because if you did, I'd have to wonder about the reason for that.'

'No!' I felt like I'd walked into a trap. 'Of course that's not what I want.'

'That's settled, then.' She dropped her cigarette butt and ground it under her heel. Then she reached out and gripped my hand with her cold fingers, so hard it hurt. 'Naomi?'

'What?' I wanted to pull back from her, but I couldn't.

'You won't tell anyone about this, will you? Because it could literally destroy me.'

Her intensity frightened me. I wanted this conversation to end; I wanted to get back inside the warm restaurant and drink wine and laugh with our friends. So I said the only thing there was to say.

'Of course I won't.'

'Thank you, Naomi. I knew I could count on you.'

FIFTEEN

'It's just an Airbnb.' Zara touched a fob to a panel next to the door and I heard a muted beep before she pushed it open. It was two days later, and I'd arrived at the address she had given me a few minutes early, and almost given up and gone away again when there'd been no answer to my ring.

It felt almost like a reprieve – like having an appointment for a smear test cancelled at the last minute. I could just go home, tell Patch Zara wasn't there, was being flaky as she often was and offer to arrange a courier to pick up the camera. I could avoid having to see her on her own turf, alone and undefended.

But just before I turned to leave, I'd seen her hurrying up to the building, gushing apologies.

A steep flight of stairs led upwards beyond a rank of letterboxes. 'I don't know how long I'll be here – I'm contracted to do a series of stories on the London fashion scene but if things get busy back in Paris or New York they might whisk me out again. It's kind of like a working holiday, I guess.'

'That sounds fun.' She'd already reached the first bend in the stairs, climbing easily, her wide-leg trousers swishing above her high-heeled boots.

No one in London wears heels any more, I thought unkindly. *Maybe you should put that in the first of your dispatches from the Big Smoke.*

'I've got used to embracing uncertainty over the years. Paris has been home mostly, of course, but I've been all over. Luckily Bisou loves travelling. Are you all right back there, Naomi?'

'I'm fine,' I panted. We were two floors up now and she showed no sign of slowing, but I slogged grimly on after her.

'I could have found somewhere with a lift, but that would have cost more, and I reckon this is doing wonders for my cardiovascular fitness. You know I've always detested the gym.'

This was true – I remembered from back in the day how Zara seemed to never do any exercise, yet drank and often ate enormously when we were out, while remaining as thin as a shop-window mannequin. Rowan and I had once speculated that she probably lived on lettuce leaves and cigarettes the rest of the time.

'And here we are.' Zara finally stopped on the fifth floor – or it might have been the sixth – in front of a shiny black-painted door. She fitted a key into the lock and turned it. 'Home sweet home – for now.'

Stepping into the apartment, I felt a pang of envy. My own house was – well, it was home. But it was nothing much to look at. Patch and I had bought it before I stopped working, when I'd still been earning enough for us to get the mortgage. We'd chosen it because it was big enough for a family and close enough to his mother, and figured on fixing it up later on.

But later on hadn't happened yet, and our kitchen was still shabby and inconvenient, our stair carpet a threadbare trip hazard, our windows rattly and draughty. The twins had added their interior design touches too – piles of plastic toys in the living room, high chairs we'd found second hand on Facebook, and liberal felt-tip pen artworks on the fridge and of course the walls.

This was like something out of a magazine. The floor was shiny parquet, a lush green palm grew in a brass pot, a marble sculpture of a woman's torso stood on a mid-century modern sideboard, and one wall was painted deep magenta. Even the cat looked like it had come from some swanky designer cat department store – a slinky dark brown-spotted Bengal with wide amber eyes and an implausibly long tail.

Zara scooped it up and kissed its pointy nose. 'Have you missed me, darling? Say hello to Auntie Naomi.'

I felt a jolt like I was waking from a dream. From the moment I saw her a few minutes before, I'd let myself be swept into my old patterns of thinking and being around Zara: envy, guilt and an over-riding sense of inadequacy. That wasn't good enough. What had happened in the past was just that – the past. Patch and I had been together for more than ten years. We were married, we were parents.

If Zara hadn't moved on from that, it was long past time she did. And I needed her to know that I'd moved on – that she no longer had the power to manipulate me.

So I made clicking noises at the cat, cooed, 'Hello, you,' like meeting it was the best thing that had happened to me all day, and reached out a hand to stroke it.

The cat regarded me with disdain, then wriggled out of Zara's arms, stalked over to a gold leather-covered chaise longue and began sharpening its claws energetically.

'I really shouldn't let her.' Zara shrugged. 'But what can you do? If they allow cats in the apartment they have to expect some damage. I guess I'll kiss goodbye to my deposit. Coffee?'

'Coffee would be great.' I'd drink it with her like the old acquaintance I was, I resolved, then pick up Patch's camera and get the hell out. And that would be that – no need to see her or speak to her ever again.

'Give me a second.' She gestured to a chrome-framed yellow sofa and disappeared into what I presumed was the kitchen.

I perched uncomfortably on the edge of the seat, turning towards the window, which overlooked a garden square surrounded by black-painted railings. The trees were leafless now, their branches skeletal against the leaden sky, and where there would be flowerbeds in summer were now only rectangles of bare, wet soil.

The cat approached me, sniffed my trainers, then backed away as abruptly as if I'd kicked it – which I hadn't, of course – and, in a sudden burst of athletic indoor parkour, jumped from the floor to the coffee table to a low bookshelf and up on to the mantelpiece. Then it sat down, washing its face in between regarding me distrustfully.

Don't worry, I thought. *I feel just the same about this.*

Zara returned with a cafetière and two white china mugs on a tray. 'I hope you don't take milk, because I'm afraid I never have any in. It only goes sour and I have to throw it away.'

'Black will be fine.'

Somehow, it was impossible to picture Zara doing something as ordinary as going into a supermarket and buying a pint of milk. I bet if I'd asked for a piece of toast, she wouldn't have had any bread in, either – I could imagine her fridge, empty apart from a bottle of champagne and a bottle of vodka, the way Kate had told us Andy's was when he was in the throes of drug addiction, only classier.

She poured the coffee, handed me a cup and sat next to me on the sofa, perched as I was on its edge, because it was one of those pieces of furniture that if you ever managed to get comfortable on it, you'd never get up again. Except Zara probably would, having abs of steel from all the exercise she didn't do.

'We were in touch quite regularly before he died, you know,' Zara said.

'What, you and Andy?' I couldn't have been more surprised if she'd chucked her coffee in my face. Andy had been a notoriously fickle correspondent, occasionally sending long stream-of-consciousness voice notes then not replying for weeks if you texted to wish him happy birthday. And yet he'd stayed in touch with Zara? It was far more likely that Zara, aware of Andy's vulnerability, had stayed in touch with him as a way of keeping tabs on the group she'd chosen to leave. Realising that, I felt a flare of anger at her for using him for that purpose.

She nodded. 'He used to come to Paris quite often, when he was in funds. He had a boyfriend there for a while, and when that ended and he was sober again he'd come and spend weekends with me. He loved the city.'

This I could imagine – Andy, always stylish to the max, heading out on shopping trips with Zara, eating with her in fancy restaurants, going to art galleries.

'I'm sure you had loads of fun,' I said, sarcasm creeping into my voice. 'Must have been a good chance to catch up on all the news from London.'

'Oh, it was.' Her smile was half-obscured by her coffee cup, which she was holding with both hands, as if to warm them. 'You know how Andy loved to gossip. He told me all about your babies, and Rowan's new chap, and Kate kicking him out of her flat. He was quite cut up about that, bless him.'

'So you didn't need me to tell you Patch and I had twins, and what they were called' – I smiled sweetly, pleased to have caught her out in what hadn't exactly been a lie, but had certainly been an omission of the truth – 'because Andy already had.'

'Oh, it must have slipped my mind.' Zara had reverted to her usual airiness; I remembered now how, Teflon-like, she was always able to deflect any suggestion that she was wrong. 'I've never been that interested in children and nor was Andy. He might not even have told me their names – I can't remember. There was always so much else to talk about.'

'I'm sure there was.' Even as I spoke, I hated the bitchy

defensiveness in my voice. I didn't sound like myself, but like a stranger – one I wouldn't particularly like. 'You must have loved reminiscing about the old days – that place in Bloomsbury where you used to stay, the last time you came to the Girl-friends' Club, Abbie's wedding – good times.'

The cat had left its spot above the fireplace and sprung up on to Zara's lap, its claws rhythmically piercing the wool of her trousers. She put down her coffee cup and buried her fingers in its fur, as if now she was trying to keep them warm that way.

'Actually,' she said, with one of the sudden switches from merriment to mournfulness I remembered, 'we didn't talk about those things. I preferred not to remember how it all went wrong. Having Andy with me reminded me a bit of how it was before all that, only without the feeling of being...'

I waited for her to continue, but she didn't. I heard my voice asking, 'Being what?'

'Being the odd one out. You know, among the five of us. If someone made a sitcom, like *Friends* or something, Kate would be the successful one, Abbie would be the nice one, Rowan would be the beautiful one and you'd be the clever one.'

I knew what she wanted me to ask, and in spite of myself I asked it anyway. 'What would you be?'

'I'd be the one who wasn't important enough to be in every episode,' she said sadly. 'On the fringes. My name last in the credits.'

And here it was again – Zara's familiar pattern of making herself appear marginalised and hard-done-by, all the while also making herself the centre of attention. But this time, her words resonated with me. I remembered that first meeting, looking at my new friends (at least, I already hoped with all my heart that they'd become friends), and categorising them: Kate, the chic City professional; Rowan, strikingly beautiful even with the rain frizzing her hair and mud on her shoes; Abbie, so at ease in her own skin people would gravitate towards her wherever she was. And to that list, of course, I'd added Zara, who wore an air of mysterious glamour with the same assurance she wore that coat that might or might not have been real fur.

It was I, back then, who'd felt out of place, not good enough. Compared to the others, I was just ordinary – not particularly good looking, not particularly successful, just muddling through my life while I waited to discover where it would lead and what kind of person I'd become.

That feeling had persisted for a long time, I realised. I couldn't quite remember when I'd stopped worrying and realised that my friends loved me for who I was. It was probably round about when Patch and I got together, or when Zara stopped being part of the group.

I didn't really want to think about why those things might have coincided, or speculate about whether Zara might have realised all along how I felt and how that knowledge could have influenced her behaviour towards me.

'That's why it was so important to me that you and I were friends,' she went on. 'I felt that you and I... we had something in common.'

No. I'm not letting you do that. I'm not having us painted as fellow outsiders.

I forced a laugh, hearing myself adopt the same tone I used when one of the children launched into a complaint about the unfairness of life. 'Don't be silly. You were always at the heart of the group, even though you were living in Paris. We tried our best to include you in things. It was you who was always wreaking havoc, you who decided—'

'I had no option! They chose you, same as Patch chose you.'

I was silenced. I didn't want to go into the details of how Zara's version of the truth might differ from mine, but I couldn't deny that fundamental reality.

But even if I'd known what to say, Zara didn't give me a

chance. 'And speaking of Patch, let me go and fetch that camera for you. It's in the bedroom somewhere.'

She lifted the cat off her lap, draped it over her shoulder and drifted out. I gulped the rest of the bitter, cooling coffee and stood up. The apartment didn't feel spacious and elegant now – it felt stifling.

I waited impatiently for Zara to return, hearing her moving about in the next room, making scraping sounds as she dragged what might have been a suitcase across the floor, chattering away to her cat.

'Here you go,' she said at last, returning with a black nylon camera bag in her hand, the cat following her. 'I've got no idea if it even still works, but I expect Patch will be glad to have it back. Would you like another coffee?'

I shook my head. 'Thanks, though. I need to pick the children up from nursery.'

'Of course you do.' Her smile was wistful. 'It's been lovely talking to you, Naomi. Maybe we should do this again? I feel like there's so much you and I need to talk about.'

'I'm not sure that's a good idea,' I said. 'There's no point raking over ancient history. We've all moved on now. And besides, I'm really busy with Patch and the children and everything.'

I hadn't meant to, but I realised I sounded spiteful, like I was rubbing her face in all the things I had and she didn't.

'I understand. Take care, Naomi.'

I said goodbye and left, the camera slung over my shoulder with my battered leather handbag. Before I reached the bottom of the stairs, I became conscious of the familiar, creeping feeling of guilt. I wished I hadn't come – I felt as if I'd opened a door that should have remained closed.

SIXTEEN

For the next couple of weeks, my life was just the same as it had been before Andy's death. It just felt different.

Although I hadn't heard from Zara or seen her again, my visit to her was preying on my mind. I was furious with myself for the way I allowed her to wind me up – to manipulate me, to make me behave in a petty, spiteful way that wasn't like me. I was angry with her for what she'd told me about Andy, and the way she'd turned my anger around to make me feel like she was the victim. And – entirely unreasonably – I was annoyed with Patch. I'd made the effort to pick up his camera, which had involved an unpleasant encounter with Zara, and he'd merely glanced at it when I handed it over, mumbling a 'Thanks,' before chucking it in a drawer.

I felt on edge all the time, as if whenever my phone rang or there was a knock on the door, it might be her. When I passed a woman with a dark bob while walking the children to nursery, I'd had to stop and look back over my shoulder, only to realise that it was a complete stranger. I'd asked Bridget if Zara had visited her again and felt my whole body tense when she said she had, but in the next sentence her visitor had become

Niamh, Patch's sister, so I couldn't be sure whether it had actually happened. After her non-appearance at the last Girlfriends' Club meet-up, Kate had begun posting on the WhatsApp again, although her messages were briefer, less frequent and somehow more distant. When I'd apprehensively asked whether her cocktail date with Zara had taken place, she'd vaguely replied that they were both really busy, which when I thought about it was no answer at all.

And now, the next meet-up had come round, a month later. It was in Patch's and my diaries, a three-line whip: the second Wednesday of every month. As soon as the children had been old enough for me to leave them, we'd reached an agreement that childcare on that night was his problem and his problem only. If he needed to work late or otherwise couldn't be home, he organised a babysitter, not me.

Because on the second Wednesday of the month, I. Was. Going. Out.

Sure, there'd been times when our meet-ups hadn't taken place. During lockdown, when we'd tried the first time to drink champagne and talk on Zoom, but found it too depressing and reminiscent of the grim work socials that everyone was enduring at the time, so abandoned the idea until we could meet in person again. When everyone had been away on holiday one summer. When – totally coincidentally – Abbie, Rowan and I had all come down with flu at the same time, and Kate had said she was damned if she was going to drink cocktails and eat crisps on her own like some kind of tragic loser.

Almost always, though, it went ahead. Sometimes, when life was getting me down to an even greater extent than usual, I found myself looking at my diary a week or even ten days ahead, counting the sleeps until the second Wednesday like a small child looking forward to Christmas. Once, I'd even caught myself leaving the house to go and meet my friends and feeling a shadow of sadness because after just a few hours it would be a whole month before next time.

But as it turned out, fate derailed my plans. I was woken just after midnight by a plaintive call of, 'Mummy,' closely followed by the unmistakeable sound of Toby being sick. As night follows day, Meredith woke up and puked about half an hour afterwards – just as I'd got her brother settled and his sheets changed.

And so the rest of the night passed in a kind of vomit relay – one of them threw up, I sorted them out, then the other did. Rinse – literally – and repeat until six in the morning when Patch woke up, looking so healthy and rested I almost vommed myself.

Except I didn't – not until he'd left for work. By that stage I'd rung nursery and told them the kids were ill, started a boil wash with all the soiled bedding, given the children glasses of flat Coke (their dentist would have had a coronary if she'd known, but it was what my mum had always done and therefore so did I), and made myself a coffee.

It tasted funny. What should have felt like a healing wave of caffeine entering my exhausted bloodstream was more like ingesting poison. I paused, the mug halfway to my lips.

No fucking way. I'm fine. I'm going out tonight.

But my body had other ideas. Within seconds, my stomach had given a horrible lurch, my mouth filled with saliva, and I sprinted upstairs to the bathroom, just making it in time.

The rest of that day passed in the seventh circle of parenting hell: trying to look after sick children when you're as sick as a dog yourself and all you want – literally all, ever – is to lie down and concentrate hard on not dying. But as soon as I did, a plaintive voice would call out, 'Mummy,' and the whole cycle would begin again – one would be sick, then the other, then me. My entire world shrank to a relentless treadmill of buckets and bleach and the inside of the toilet bowl.

I'd have happily died, only it wasn't an option.

At some point, I managed to focus on my phone for long enough to send a WhatsApp saying:

NAOMI:

Struck down by stomach bug from hell. Not going to make it tonight. Pray for me

My friends' loving messages gave me some degree of comfort, until the next wave of nausea hit me.

To his credit, when Patch arrived home he sprang into action like some kind of United Nations rescue force arriving in a disaster zone. The children had been able to keep water down for a couple of hours, so he made them dry toast and that stayed down too. He got the tumble dryer going on overdrive. He offered me toast too, and when I replied, 'Are you trying to fucking poison me? Go away,' he just stroked my hand, turned out the light and departed, leaving me with my sick bucket for company.

I pinged awake at four the next morning. For a moment I wasn't sure what was happening – I could hear no sounds from the children's room or elsewhere in the house. Somehow, my internal calendar informed me that it was the second Thursday of the month – the day after the Girlfriends' Club meet-up. But I didn't have a hangover, which I'd normally have expected. I felt fine. In fact, I felt absolutely brilliant.

Then I remembered – I'd been ill and so had the kids. Maybe I was still ill. Maybe the children were too, and needed me. I lay motionless on my back for a minute, then cautiously sat up. But I still felt well – the kind of well you only feel when you've been really sick and now you're better. I had a vile taste in my mouth and I was thirsty and hungry, but it was nothing compared to the horrors of the day before.

I was alone in bed. Patch must have decided to spend the night downstairs, either because he didn't want to disturb me or for fear of catching whatever it was the twins and I had had. I strained my ears, but I couldn't hear a sound. Everything was peaceful.

I turned over, pulling the fresh-smelling duvet up to my chin and closing my eyes. But just as I felt myself drifting into sleep, a thought woke me as suddenly as a cry from one of the children would have.

I'd kept hoping Patch would take out the camera I'd collected from Zara, but it remained in his bedside table. And now he wasn't in the room.

I remembered handing it to him and him barely looking at it, then putting it away in the drawer where he kept his passport, cufflinks and an unopened box of handkerchiefs his mother had given him for Christmas a few years back.

I rolled over on the mattress, using my phone as a torch and sliding the drawer open as silently as I could. The black nylon case was still there. I lifted it out, surprised at its lightness, and sat up, resting it on my crossed legs. The zip slid open easily, as if it had been oiled. The camera inside was just that – a camera. Quite a high-end one, I guessed – black and silver and slim – although like all technology presumably almost worthless over a decade after its purchase.

I didn't know how to use it – even how to switch it on. If there were photographs stored in its memory, I didn't know how to get them off. Presumably it needed a cable to connect to a computer, but there was no cable in the bag. Probably, it would need a separate cable to charge.

What was on there? Why had Zara kept it all those years, while she moved from apartment to apartment in Paris and from city to city around the world? Why had she chosen to return it to Patch now, rather than posting it back years ago, donating it to a charity shop or just throwing it away?

There must be pictures on there. Pictures of her and Patch, from when they were together. Pictures she wanted me to see –

or wanted me to want to see. But I didn't want to see them. I didn't need to torture myself with images from long ago, of her and Patch young and beautiful and in love.

I wasn't going to play that game. It wasn't my camera. Whatever images were stored on it weren't my memories. Guiltily, I replaced the camera in its case and put the case back in the drawer.

Silently, I sprang out of bed and dressed, glancing into the children's room on my way to the bathroom and seeing them both sleeping peacefully. I cleaned my teeth, not wanting to rouse the household by showering, and tiptoed downstairs. Patch was asleep on the sofa, covered by a blanket. I shut myself in the kitchen and drank two glasses of water followed by a cup of tea, then devoured three slices of toast and Marmite.

Then, fortified, I picked up my phone. There were a handful of messages from Kate, Abbie and Rowan saying they missed me and hoped I felt better, but no clue as to what I might have missed the previous night.

I flicked through to Instagram. Kate and Abbie didn't post frequently – just the occasional picture of their cats. But Rowan, possibly inspired by her teenage daughter, had become quite prolific on there recently, posting pictures of the properties her estate agency had on the market, clothes she'd bought and selfies of her with Clara and with her boyfriend Alex (who admittedly was so hot anyone would want to show him off).

Sure enough, there was a picture from the previous night. A familiar scene – a table in a bar, several cocktails, a bottle of wine, a carafe of water and bowls of rice crackers. A bit of Rowan's arm, where she was holding the phone high to get everyone in the picture at their best angle. Her face, luminous and beaming; Abbie, caught as usual in a not-quite-smile, her eyes half closed; Kate, her face enigmatic as ever, lips only just parted because she was self-conscious about her slightly crooked front teeth.

And there, on the edge of the picture, in shadow and half cropped out, was another face, in profile. A slice of defined jawline, a ski-jump nose, long feathery eyelashes, dark lipstick and the line of a cropped, angular bob with a brutally short fringe.

Zara.

SEVENTEEN

For a second, I wondered whether I was going to throw up again. I could feel the toast churning uneasily inside me, but I quickly realised that I'd seen off whatever bug I'd had – this was something different. Surprise, of course – but more than that. Shock. Betrayal, even. And along with all that, a kind of sick sense of foreboding.

But that was ridiculous. I'd done nothing wrong. It was Zara whose behaviour had alienated her from the Girlfriends' Club inner circle – Zara who'd been in the wrong. I'd done nothing to be ashamed of, nothing that would earn me retribution or ostracisation. Of course, the way things had turned out for Zara hadn't been ideal – but whose life was, really, ever? Certainly not mine.

My friends knew what Zara was like – they'd been on the sharp end of her behaviour for years. They had no reason to trust her and no reason to mistrust me. And I had no reason to be feeling the way I was now – nervous, furtive and discombobulated, as if I'd done something terrible and been caught out and now everyone was talking about me, and once they'd finished talking they'd have all made their minds up to hate me.

I shook my head, gulping the dregs of my tea, then grimacing because it had gone cold. I was being ridiculous.

Perhaps she hadn't even arranged it – perhaps she'd just coincidentally been in the same bar they'd been in the previous night and joined them for a quick drink and a selfie.

But my rationalisation of the situation totally failed to reassure me.

I switched on my phone and looked at the image again. Zara's face was still there. I didn't press like on it.

Instead, I tapped through to WhatsApp. Normally, we'd check in once we got home from a night out, all of us tipsily saying what fun we'd had or carrying on the threads of conversations we'd begun earlier. Almost always, whoever woke first the next morning would kick off the day's chat when she was still in bed, and we'd all compare notes on our hangovers before getting on with our days.

But this morning there was nothing – silence, a blank screen apart from a final message Abbie had posted the previous evening saying she was stuck at her desk and would be half an hour late. I hesitated for a moment, then grasped the nettle and posted.

NAOMI:

> Morning gang! How was last night? Did I miss anything interesting?

There was no response.

Come on, Naomi, give them a break. It's still early.

Trying to stop the niggling voice in my head that told me something was up, I forced myself into a whirlwind of activity, making beds, tidying the kitchen and ironing a shirt for Patch to wear to work.

Then, like a moth drawn to a life-threatening naked flame, I picked my phone up again.

ABBIE:

Hey, Naomi, glad you're back in the land of the
living! Are you feeling better?

KATE:

These twenty-four hour bugs are the worst but
when they fuck off you feel SO good, like a new
person.

ROWAN:

We missed you xxx

Which was all very well, but told me precisely nothing
about what had transpired the previous night.

I wanted to ask – I needed to ask. But I found I couldn't.
These women were my closest friends in the world. They must
know how I'd feel about Zara having been there – so either they
didn't know I knew, which seemed unlikely given the photo-
graphic evidence, or they didn't want to talk to me about it.

It felt confusing and frightening and unfair. Part of me believed
– or wanted to believe – that I was being silly and irrational, that I
was acting as if we were all teenagers instead of grown women who
knew how to navigate relationships and use our words. But the
problem was, I didn't feel like a grown woman – I felt just like a
teenager who was being left out by a clique of her friends.

'Babe?' Patch's voice interrupted my thoughts. 'Are you
going to stare at your screen all morning, or are you going to kiss
me goodbye?'

'Sorry.' Without me noticing, he'd showered and dressed. I
reached up and gave him a peck on the lips, barely noticing the
fresh oak moss smell of his aftershave and the breadth of his
shoulders in the crisply pressed shirt. 'Have a good day. Will
you be home for dinner?'

'Doubt it. Got a late meeting. I'll grab something in town.'

'Okay.' Suddenly needy, I added, 'Love you.'

'See you later.' He shouldered his laptop bag and hurried through to the hallway. I heard the brief pause and rustle as he pulled on his coat, then the rattle of his keys, then the crash of the front door closing behind him.

'Mummy!' Toby's voice immediately pierced the silence. 'I'm bored.'

'How would you like to go to Granny's?' I asked.

Both children leaped up from the sofa like it was an ejector seat, sending the blanket they'd been snuggled under flying, along with their empty toast plates.

'Yay!' Meredith squealed.

'Can we go now?' demanded Toby.

'Can we stay all day?'

'Yes, you can. Come on, let's get our coats and I'll take you there on the bus.'

I felt a twinge of guilt, but it melted away almost immediately. Patch's mother loved having the children – the longer the visit, the better as far as she was concerned. The games that left me seething with frustration after playing them for twenty minutes would keep her happily engrossed for hours. And as for my worries about whether she was capable of looking after them alone – well, nothing had happened so far, and there was no reason to think that it would today.

So I wasn't surprised that she replied to my text delightedly agreeing to my last-minute plan, assuring me that she had a cast-iron stomach and hadn't come down with anything worse than a cold in years, and telling me to leave them there as long as I liked.

'And what are you going to get up to today, then, Naomi?' she asked when I dropped them off. 'Anything nice?'

'I'm going to meet a friend for lunch in town.'

'How lovely – good to see you getting out like a proper lady who lunches. You deserve a break.'

If only you knew, I thought, kissing her and the children

goodbye. I wasn't so much a lady who lunched as some kind of guerrilla, planning a surprise hit on an unsuspecting victim – one who I wasn't even sure would be where I was expecting at the time I made my attack.

But she was. When I arrived in Mayfair an hour later, the streets were already packed with people braving the grey, drizzly afternoon: office workers hurrying to meetings with their laptop bags and take-out coffees; tourists shrouded in rainproof plastic capes; glamorous women sheltering under umbrellas as they made the short journey from taxi to boutique.

This used to be my turf, back when I was working. Or near enough – the law firm where I worked was headquartered on the other side of Central London to Rowan's West End office. But still, I found myself rediscovering the familiar rhythm of the crowded lunchtime streets as I dodged slow-moving tourists, threading my way expertly through the crowd while simultane-ously glancing in tempting shop windows and looking at my phone.

I hadn't properly appreciated it at the time, I thought with a pang. I'd been too busy being stressed by work, hurrying out for a sandwich before the next meeting or averting a crisis caused by something my boss had neglected to tell me to do. But I'd loved it. I'd loved the cut and thrust of office politics, the chal-lenges that came my way almost hourly, which I'd need to solve without appearing ruffled or unprofessional. I'd loved being a tiny cog in the huge machine of corporate London.

I'd loved it when my boss smiled at me over her coffee and said, 'So when are you starting that law conversion course, Naomi? You're wasted as a secretary.'

I'd lost that opportunity – or given it away – when I'd decided to stay at home with the children. At first, I'd told myself it would only be temporary, but now I wasn't too sure. Had I left it too long? Was I too old, too out of touch? Would I ever stop missing it?

I approached the plate-glass window of Walkerson's Elite, the estate agency where Rowan worked, as warily as if I was a burglar planning a midnight hit on the place. But I realised almost immediately that there was no point attempting stealth. Rowan's desk was right there at the front of the office, facing the window, and she was there, her phone pressed to her ear, a pen in her hand as she jotted on a spiral-bound notebook.

At first, she didn't notice me. I hesitated outside the door, waiting to catch her eye, then pushed it open and stepped inside, the warmth of the interior welcome after the gusty cold of the street. Hearing the door – or feeling the chilly blast of air I brought with me – she glanced up, her expression changing immediately from polite enquiry to surprise and then something like bewilderment.

'Yes, of course,' she said into the phone. 'I'll relay that to the vendor this afternoon. I agree it's a bold offer, but they're keen for a quick sale and you're in a good position to proceed, so I think we can be optimistic. Leave it with me. Okay. You too. Bye now.'

Then she replaced the handset on its cradle with a clatter and said, 'Naomi! Hi!'

Her tone was bright and welcoming – almost too bright and welcoming. Her face didn't look particularly welcoming at all.

'Hey,' I said, leaning in for a hug, but it proved impossible thanks to the desk between us, and I almost knocked over her computer screen. 'I came to see if you fancied lunch.'

'Lunch?' She sounded like I'd suggested we spend the hour between one and two climbing Ben Nevis. 'Why?'

'Because...' All at once, the impetus that had brought me here – *Rowan's my best friend. She'll tell me what's going on* – had deserted me. 'It's lunchtime. I thought you might be hungry, after last night.'

Normally after a night out, we'd spend the morning eagerly discussing the bacon sandwiches and filthy Maccy D's we couldn't wait to eat. There hadn't been any of that chat on the WhatsApp today, I realised.

'Hungry? Sure. I mean, I guess I am. I'm just a bit snowed under. I was going to grab a sandwich and eat here – I've got a viewing in forty-five minutes.'

'Oh.' I stepped back, feeling a bit like I might be about to cry. 'I'm sorry, Ro. I ought to have checked. It's just, I thought—'

'Don't be ridiculous.' She stood up, pushing back her hair and reaching for her coat. 'Of course we can have lunch. It'll have to be quick, that's all. There's a Pret just round the corner.'

Not quite what I had in mind, I thought. I'd imagined us going somewhere quiet, where I could treat Rowan to a pizza or maybe even Welsh rarebit, which she adored, and a pudding afterwards, and find out properly what was going on. But I had to work with what was on offer.

So, five minutes later, I found myself perched on a high stool at a counter, picking at a cold, rather damp salad while Rowan spooned up chicken and mushroom soup next to me.

'So how are the twins?' she asked. 'Over their bug?'

'Yeah, they're all good. How's Clara?' I was itching to get past the formalities, but if she was standing on ceremony, I'd have to do the same.

'She's all good too. Looks like her and Jonny are an item again. To be honest I think I'd be more upset than she would if they broke up.'

'I can imagine.' Then I leaned closer to her and asked, 'How did last night go, anyway?'

'Ah, it was lovely to catch up. You know, it always is. I was home by eleven, though – I think we're all getting old.'

'No strawberry mojitos, then?' I felt as if the time we had together in this narrow window in Rowan's day was slipping away, and wanted to bring the conversation round to Zara – but, at the same time, I didn't.

'No strawberry mojitos.' Rowan's smile was wary. 'So you know Zara joined us.'

At least she wasn't trying to deny it, or hide it from me. Although even if she was telling me the truth, it wouldn't necessarily be the whole truth.

'Did she say...' I began, then changed tack. 'How is she?'

Rowan shrugged. 'You know. She's Zara.'

I tried to laugh, but it came out all shaky.

Rowan went on, 'I think she regrets what happened. She didn't say so, of course. But I got that sense. Because, Nome, you know...'

'What?'

Rowan looked down, twisting her paper napkin. 'I regret it. At least, I regret how it all turned out.'

What did she mean? Did she mean that if things had been different, Zara would still be part of the group – or that I wouldn't?

'Do you mean if she and Patch—' I began.

'No!' Rowan dug the wooden spoon into her cup, fishing out a final bit of mushroom, then looking at it and putting it back again. 'Don't be mad. If you and Patch weren't together, what would have happened about my godchildren?'

I laughed, slightly reassured. 'I'd have married someone else and you'd be fairy godmother to my kids with him.'

'I suppose I would. Maybe. But still, I think that we—' A shrill trilling sound came from Rowan's bag. 'Sorry, Nome, I just need to... Hello, Rowan speaking. Of course. Two fifteen works great. Give me five minutes and I'll see you there.' Rowan tucked her phone away in her bag. 'Shit. They're early. I'm so sorry, babe, I'm going to have to dash. I'd have told them no but it's a five million quid listing and it's just not shifting and the commission...'

'That's okay. I get it.'

Abandoning my salad with no great regret, I hurried after

Rowan to the door, fighting my way into my coat as I walked. She was already striding away, her long legs scissoring effort-lessly along, but she stopped to wait for me.

'We must do this again properly. Promise?' She pulled me into a hug.

'That would be great. Listen, do you mind if I text you? I really want to—'

'Here's the thing, Nome,' she said, smiling in a way that looked almost forced. 'I've been wondering if we were wrong about Zara. But we'll talk later, okay?'

EIGHTEEN
MARCH 2011

It was a perfect Saturday morning in late March, the sun shining warmly in a cloudless sky. Only the faintest breeze stirred the buds on the magnolia tree that grew outside my bedroom window. I lay on my back in bed, relishing the fact that I didn't need to get up for several hours – and that when I did, it was to do something I'd been looking forward to.

Smiling, I reread the text that had just pinged on my phone. It was from Patch:

PATRICK HAMILTON:

Still on for this afternoon? Fancy a movie?

We were indeed still on, but it had been a close call. The previous afternoon, while I was at work, Rowan had rung me in a panic to ask whether I was free to look after Clara for her.

'That fucker Paul's let me down. Again,' she said. 'I'm booked to do the make-up for a massive wedding, which means loads of cash, which means I'll be able to pay my rent this month. So—'

My eyes fixed on my computer screen, not really seeing the note that had been in my calendar for a couple of weeks, but knowing that it was there. But I could cancel – of course I could.

I just didn't want to.

'Naomi? Are you still there?'

'Yes, I'm here. Sorry – I think the reception cut out there for a second.'

'You do have plans, don't you? You're just wondering if you can cancel them.'

Damn it, Rowan, why do you have to see straight through me every single time? 'I'll cancel them. It's fine.'

'You're seeing Patch, aren't you?'

Shit. Busted. But why did I feel like that when I wasn't even doing anything wrong? I'd told my friends, on the train back from Paris, about Zara's request. What I hadn't told them was what I suspected Zara might be up to behind Patch's back, and what that might mean for them as a couple.

And the few times I had met up with him – to go for coffee, grab a sandwich while he waited for his train, help him choose a birthday gift for his sister – I'd told my friends about it. Every single time. Even though there'd been nothing important to tell.

'Yeah, we said something about meeting up. He can't see Zara because she's in Stockholm for work. But it's nothing definite. I can take Clara, no problem.'

I heard Rowan take a deep breath on the other end of the line. 'I'm going to ask Abbie. If she and Matt can help, I'll take them up on it. If they can't, I'll ring you back, okay?'

'Seriously, Ro, I'll do it. It's not a problem at all. It's—'

'Love you, hopefully I won't need you.'

She ended the call. I spent the rest of the afternoon jumping like I'd been poked with something sharp every time my phone rang, and felt almost shocked at my relief when, at five o'clock, the text from Rowan arrived:

ROWAN:

You're off the hook. Have a lovely day xxx

And now here I was, with plans to go and see a movie with him. Just a movie. The kind of thing teenagers did on a first date. Only we weren't teenagers, and this wasn't a date. But it was also the kind of thing friends did together on a Saturday afternoon when they had time on their hands, I reassured myself. I'd be able to text Zara afterwards – *Saw Patch today, we went to the cinema. He's missing you like crazy xxx* – with a clear conscience, because there was no way it could be interpreted as anything other than innocent.

And it was innocent, I told myself. Since that New Year's Eve, there'd been no repeat of the moment of connection I'd felt with Patch – the pang of heartache for him that had made me want to hold him close and protect him from hurt.

And now I felt as if he needed protection more than ever. The promise I'd made to Zara when we were in Paris – that I'd see Patch, hang out with him, report back to her if his behaviour seemed suspicious in any way – had troubled me at the time. And now I had the sense that there'd been something else behind her request: a need for me to keep Patch busy on his free weekends while Zara herself was otherwise occupied.

Earlier in the week, we'd exchanged text messages that had left me feeling profoundly uneasy.

ZARA:

Hey Nome, what's up?

NAOMI:

Not much. Work's hectic. How about you?

ZARA:

Same, same. Listen, did you know Patch is in London this weekend?

NAOMI:

He mentioned he was on a break from work but I thought he'd be going to Paris to see you. Why?

ZARA:

Yeah, no, he's not.

Then my phone had rung and I'd spent half an hour franti-
cally juggling my boss's diary to fit in an important client who
wanted to meet with her urgently, but only had three half-hour
slots available over the next fortnight.

When I next checked my mobile, there'd been another,
longer text from Zara.

ZARA:

I just spoke to him. I said he should go to
London and hang out with you if you're free.
But Nome, if he asks, I'm in Stockholm for
fashion week, right? Actually if anyone asks.
Okay?

I felt as if I'd entered into some kind of unholy pact with her
– and with myself. Lying on her behalf, because that was the
only way to protect Patch from being hurt. Having to deny any
feelings I might have for Patch – because it would be disloyal to
her. And now, lying to Rowan about both those things.

It made the innocent plan Patch was suggesting feel grubby
and illicit. It made me feel bad about something I should be
feeling good about. It made me feel like a bad friend for not
helping Rowan out when I could have cancelled Patch's and my
arrangement before anything was even properly arranged.
Except then he might have altered his own plans and gone to
Paris to see Zara and found – what?

I was caught in the middle of an ever more complex tangle
of lies and half-truths, and I didn't feel good about any of it.

Still lying in bed, I checked my phone and saw another
message from Patch.

PATRICK HAMILTON:

> Hold on, just looked outside. It's gorgeous!
> Maybe we should go for a picnic or something
> instead?

A picnic? I imagined telling Zara that. *We went for a picnic on Hampstead Heath. We had smoked salmon and champagne.* No. Just no. My discomfort about coving for Zara would only be compounded if she got the sense that her boyfriend had been up to something on-the-face-of-it romantic with me.

NAOMI:

> Movie sounds good

> Redheads like me can't take any chances in
> this weather. If I go out in the sun I'll get
> freckles.

PATRICK HAMILTON:

> No worries

> My mum's got red hair too so I get it. Although
> Dad always tells her a woman without freckles
> is like a night without stars.

And he added a semicolon and a closed bracket – a wink.

Shit. But it meant nothing, I told myself. It was just a sweet remark about his parents – the kind of thing a friend would say. So I responded with a 'lol' and I swiftly arranged to meet him in town to see *The Girl With the Dragon Tattoo*, even though I had no interest in it at all.

In the event, though, I found myself transfixed by the film. From the opening credits, I almost forgot that Patch was there next to me, until my shoulder accidentally brushed his arm or our hands met when we reached for popcorn.

Afterwards, we walked out into the bright afternoon and stood blinking in the sunlight like people who'd just arrived from another planet.

'Wow,' Patch said. 'I could use a drink after that. How about you?'

'For sure. And some food – I hardly got a look-in on that popcorn.'

'Really?' His face fell. 'Sorry about that.'

'Just kidding. I had loads. Still hungry though.'

'Me too – even though I scoffed all the popcorn. Where shall we go?'

'There's a place – someone at work was talking about it. Like a diner, that does burgers and cocktails and stuff. All very trashy. I'm sure it's around here somewhere.'

'Sounds great.'

Vaguely, I started walking, and Patch fell into step next to me.

'Nome?' he asked after a few seconds, and I felt a little glow of pleasure at him using the same pet name my closest friends used for me. 'Have you spoken to Zara recently?'

Oh no. I felt suddenly aware of those texts on my phone, right there like an unexploded bomb. If I got run over by a bus right now, I thought absurdly, and the emergency services had to look for a contact number for my next of kin and Patch was there, he might see them.

That was ridiculous – it wouldn't happen. But what was going to happen was I was going to have to lie to him: do the thing I'd promised Zara I would do, fulfil my side of the bargain that meant I got to see him.

'Not spoken. She texted me a few days ago – she's somewhere with work, I can't remember where exactly.'

'Okay,' he said. 'I was just wondering whether she was okay. Last time we spoke she seemed a bit... I don't know.'

'I'm sure she's just distracted with work,' I answered, hating myself and praying he wouldn't ask anything more, force me to elaborate on what I was pretending to know.

To my relief, it turned out my memory of my conversation

with my colleague was clearer than I'd thought. Patty Palace was just round the corner from the cinema – a noisy, warehouse-style place with paper tablecloths and chefs with bandanas round their heads sweating over a sizzling grill.

'Does this look okay?' I asked.

'Brilliant. I feel like I just spotted a mirage in the desert.'

'I think you mean an oasis. They're the things with water and date palms and shit. Mirages are—'

'The things that aren't real?'

'Correct.'

Laughing, we pushed open the heavy glass door and found a table in a corner, surrounded by pop-art posters and noisy groups talking and laughing over their meals. I was reassured – this was as far from a romantic destination as it was possible to get. I could tell Zara about it in detail and she wouldn't need to worry. I just needed to distract him from asking me any more about her.

We sat down and studied the menus, which didn't take long, because they consisted of just a few items printed on yellow A4 paper.

'Negroni?' I suggested.

'For sure. And a beer, so we stay hydrated.'

'Good thinking. There's going to be a lot of salt involved here, I reckon.'

'There'd better be. Double cheeseburger with extra bacon?'

'Fries, obviously. Plain or dirty?'

'Dirty for sure. And onion rings?'

'Be rude not to.'

Grinning at each other, like we were complicit in some kind of secret ritual, we ordered our food and drinks. Damn, he had a great smile, I thought. I couldn't help noticing a girl at the table next to us nudge her friend and whisper something, and them both surreptitiously have a good old stare at Patch.

This must be what it was like for Zara every time she went

out with him, I thought. Except Patch probably got the exact same with men checking out Zara.

Then Patch asked, 'So what did you think of the film?'

I took a gulp of my negroni, the giant ice cube pressing cold against my nose. 'It was – complex.'

'Why do you say that? It was a great thriller for sure.'

'Yeah, I could have done with a bit less violence if I'm honest.'

'You were watching through your fingers at one point, I noticed.'

'Was I?' So he'd been looking at me in the darkness.

'I wondered if I needed to hold your hand.'

I laughed awkwardly. 'I could've done with a hand-hold.'

'Damn.' He took a swallow of beer. 'A missed opportunity.'

Stop flirting with me, I thought. But his words gave me a small glow of pleasure I couldn't quite suppress.

I was saved from having to respond by our food turning up, and we dived into it as if we hadn't eaten in days. I was too hungry to care if I got ketchup on my chin and had to blow on my onion rings because they were too hot to eat.

See, I told myself. *You don't fancy him. If you did, you'd be licking your fingers seductively instead of scattering paper napkins everywhere.*

'Anyway,' he said, adding salt to the already salty chips, 'What did you mean by complex?'

'The film? Like you said, it was a thriller – and a good one. But there was a message there, too, I thought.'

I paused, thinking, and took another bite of my burger.

'About how women could be driven to violence, because society is so full of violence towards them?'

Surprised, I swallowed. 'Yeah. That. All that suppressed trauma needing some kind of an outlet.'

He nodded. 'That was hard to watch. I couldn't help thinking – if it had been my sister, or Zee, or you...'

His words touched me. I was reminded of Zara's dismissal of her boyfriend – *a loveable hunk of meat*. But it felt unfair – just because he wanted to protect the women he cared about didn't make him some knuckle-dragging chauvinist. And to have been included in the list of women worthy of his protection made me feel absurdly pleased.

'What are you thinking?' he asked. 'You've gone all serious all of a sudden.'

'I'm just thinking – I like seeing you. I'm glad we're friends.'

'I'm glad we're friends too.' He smiled, took another swallow of his cocktail, then added, 'Except when I'm not.'

I felt a tingle of anticipation – part excitement, part apprehension. 'What do you mean?'

'That us being friends means we're not more than friends.'

The mouthful of burger I was eating suddenly felt too big to swallow.

'I'm sorry,' he said. 'I shouldn't have said that.'

'No,' I agreed sombrely. 'Probably not.'

His face was serious, all the lightness of a few moments before wiped away. 'Have I offended you?'

I shook my head. 'I just think – we shouldn't talk like that.'

'I know.' He sighed, his eyes holding mine. 'And nothing's going to happen. But I just wanted you to know something, Naomi.'

'What's that?'

'Things aren't great between me and Zee. I'd never cheat on her, but I – it helps to see someone else, sometimes, and forget about it all.'

'Why are you...' Voicing the thought felt terrible, like a betrayal of Zara. 'I mean, if things aren't great, why don't you...?'

'End it?' he finished for me. 'I can't. What you said about trauma – there's a lot of that in her past. She – it's not my place to tell you, really.'

'She what?' I asked, dry-mouthed.

'She tried... a few years back, when a relationship ended, to – you know. Harm herself.'

'Oh no, Patch. That's awful.' I felt like another link had been added to the tangled chain that bound me to Zara. She was fragile, I knew, but it had never occurred to me that she might be suicidal, or had been in the past. I could never do anything that might trigger that again.

'So you see,' he went on, his eyes cast down, 'I could never hurt her like that.'

'I couldn't, either,' I agreed, feeling the knot in my stomach grow tighter.

He reached over and put his hand over mine. I felt the warm pressure, the rough skin at the base of his fingers. Then, after a second or two, he moved it away.

We finished our burgers, had more beer and more cocktails and didn't talk about Zara again. By the end, we were giggly and silly, but we didn't mention anything serious like feelings, and when we parted at the Tube station it was with a hug that felt almost brotherly.

That night in bed, I replayed every moment of the day, preserving the memory of everything he'd said, holding on to the knowledge that we'd done nothing wrong, nothing to betray Zara's trust.

But the knowledge brought me no comfort – it was as bitter-sweet as the fading taste of vermouth on my tongue.

NINETEEN

It had been three weeks, and I couldn't stop thinking about my meeting with Rowan. Of course, there'd been the bad stuff – the coolness and awkwardness there'd been between us, which had never been there before. And that coolness – that sense of distance – seemed to have extended to the rest of the group as well. The WhatsApp group, normally filled with a steady flow of chat from when the first of us woke up in the morning until the last of us turned out the light at night, was more silent now, less intimate somehow. Some days had always been busier than others, of course; some were quieter, with just quick 'Hello's and 'Crazy busy, love you all's. Now, however, my posts were often ignored for several hours at a time, then responded to with just a love heart or a thumbs-up.

I couldn't suppress a fear that if my friends weren't chatting on there, they might be chatting somewhere else. What if Rowan had been asking the others the same question she'd asked me – had we been wrong about Zara? I was certain that I hadn't been wrong: that Zara's reappearance in our lives would lead to more drama, more manipulation, more fall-outs. But then I had skin in the game. It was my actions that had triggered

Zara the most, and now I was the one with the most to lose if my friends were to decide that, back in the past, they'd made the wrong decision – backed the wrong horse.

I felt stuck, wanting to know if something was going on behind my back, but also not wanting to know, hoping that whatever it was, it would all blow over and things would return to how they'd been before.

But I was also thinking about how I'd felt walking through town to meet Rowan. I mean, it wasn't like I'd become some country mouse with hayseeds in my hair (okay, maybe a bit); I went into Central London a couple of times a month. But for some reason, that last time had awoken something in me that had been dormant before.

My vague intention to brush up my CV and start looking for a job had become a burning desire. Everything about that day – the Tube journey, the crowded streets, even the too-cold, under-seasoned salad, had made me long to have a job again, a purpose outside motherhood, a commute, a desk, colleagues to bitch to when things were going badly – the lot.

It won't be like it was before, I reminded myself. *You won't be able to go to the pub after work for a few drinks on a Friday. Hell, people don't even go to offices on Fridays any more. You'll still have other responsibilities. You can't turn back the clock.*

But I didn't care. After I'd dropped the children at nursery, I dug out my laptop, made myself a coffee and sat down at the kitchen table. The last time I'd looked at my CV had been six years ago, when I'd applied for the last job I'd got before the children were born. I logged on to LinkedIn for the first time in ages. To my surprise, I had a bunch of new notifications – people I'd worked with in the past wanting to connect with me, people endorsing me for skills, a handful mistaking me for another Naomi Hamilton who was apparently a shit-hot data analyst.

Lucky you, Other Naomi, I thought, deleting the messages.

But I accepted the connection requests and updated my own profile, making sure to tag all my previous employers. I sent connection requests to a few old colleagues. Almost immediately, I found that the algorithm had sprung into action and begun recommending pages to me – law firms, recruitment agents, people I'd worked with whose names I could only just remember.

By the time I needed to pick up the twins, I'd been on there for hours. I felt I'd made progress, but I hadn't achieved anything tangible yet. I didn't even know whether I was going about things the right way. *I should ask Kate*, I thought. *Kate spends half her life on LinkedIn.* But something that would have felt totally normal a few weeks ago now seemed like an imposition, like asking a stranger for help rather than one of my best friends.

'It's a start,' I told myself, closing my laptop and putting it back in the drawer where it had languished for so long. As I closed the drawer, I gave its aluminium casing a pat and whispered, 'Don't worry, I'll be back.'

Then I put on my coat and hurried out to walk to nursery, my mind already on what I was going to feed the twins and, later, Patch and myself.

A few hours later, the dishwasher gurgling softly in the background, we were on the sofa, Patch flicking idly through the channels on the TV. I'd had a couple of glasses of wine, Patch's arm was around my shoulders, and I found myself overwhelmed with an urge to confide in him about my worries.

'Patch, there's something weird going on.'

'What, with the kids? Why didn't you—?'

'Not with the kids. Well, no weirder than usual. With the Girlfriends' Club.'

'Really?' He found a football match, a replay of some European game that neither of us had any particular interest in watching – certainly not me – and turned the sound down a bit.

'You know how we chat every day on WhatsApp? Just about how our days are going, stuff like that?'

'Look at that. Blatant foul. That referee needs to go to Spec-savers. Yeah, you chat every day and stuff.'

'Recently, it's been kind of quiet. It's like...' *It's like all the usual chat is going on somewhere else instead. Somewhere I don't know about.* But I could barely articulate that thought, even to myself – it made me feel all strange inside, cold and sick and frightened.

'People are busy. Hell, we're busy.'

Except I wasn't busy. No busier than usual, anyway. And as far as I was aware, my friends weren't either.

'It's like, since Andy's funeral, something's different.'

'Of course it's different. It's a lot to process, right? Losing a mate, at our age. That stuff's not meant to happen yet. Not for years and years.'

'Sure. But normally, after something big like that, we'd talk more, not less.'

'But there's no "like that", is there? It's not like this has ever happened bef— What a goal! Get in!'

My voice small, I said, 'I don't think it's about Andy. You know, next week's the second Wednesday of the month and no one's made plans for the Girlfriends' Club. That never happens. I think it's something to do with Zara.'

Like always, I said her name cautiously, as if she was Lord Voldemort. It was a habit I'd developed early, and sustained so long it was automatic now.

'What about her?' Patch asked, equally warily.

'I'm worried that now she's back, they'll want to be friends with her and not want to be friends with me any more.' As soon as I'd said it, I realised how pathetic it sounded.

'What, and you're also worried Mrs Jones will put you in detention because you got caught smoking behind the bike sheds?'

'Stop it. I know it seems so childish and dumb but it feels real. You know what Zara's like – you know her better than anyone. She's used to getting what she wants and I know her – she might still be mad at me because of what happened way back when, and if she decides she wants to take things that are mine then she will.'

I sniffed and pulled a tissue out of the sleeve of my jumper to wipe my nose. I'd wiped Meredith's with it earlier, but that didn't seem to matter much right now.

'Nome, you're being ridiculous. Come on. Zara's just a girl – a woman, even – she's not some wicked fairy going to turn up at the feast and curse everyone. Or however it goes in those stories that give the kids nightmares.'

'She did though. She turned up at Andy's funeral.'

'And have we been cursed?'

'I don't know yet.'

'Come on,' he said again. 'Come here.'

I edged closer to him on the sofa and he put his arm round my shoulder and pulled me against him. The warmth of his body felt comforting, but also not – the fact I felt like I needed to be comforted and protected was unsettling in itself.

I turned my head and buried my face in his shoulder, so when I spoke my voice came out all muffled. 'I'm worried she wants you back.'

I felt Patch's chest shake with laughter. 'So what if she does? I'm not her Oasis CD you borrowed and haven't given back. She's got no claim on me.'

And I do? I thought. If Patch was an autonomous adult, which obviously he was, I didn't have any more of a claim on him than Zara did – apart from the slender gold band on my finger and the two not-so-autonomous non-adults tucked up in their beds upstairs. And I couldn't imagine those things holding much sway with Zara if she decided to trample over my life in pursuit of what she wanted.

You didn't have too much of a problem trampling over hers, though, said a niggling voice in my head, but I silenced it as quickly as I could. *It was over; I did nothing wrong.* But the refrain I'd repeated so often over the years seemed to have lost some of its power to reassure me.

'Patch?'

He brushed a kiss on the top of my head. 'What?'

'If she did anything – said anything to you – that I wouldn't be okay with, you'd tell me, wouldn't you?'

I felt his chest rise and fall again, this time in a deep breath that ended in a sigh. 'I can't promise you that.'

'Why not?' I jerked my head up, craning my neck so I could see his face. But it was expressionless.

'Because I wouldn't want to hurt you.'

'It would hurt me far worse if you were keeping secrets from me.'

'People always say that, don't they? But I don't reckon it's always true.'

'Of course it's true! If there was anything I needed to worry about, I'd want to know.'

'So you could what? Worry about it more?'

'So I could do something about it.'

'Babe. If – massive if, obviously, because this is categorically not happening, okay? – Zee suddenly said she wanted us to be an item again and I wanted it too, what exactly do you think you could do about it?'

The thought felt like one of the players on the TV had kicked a football through the screen and it had hit me in the stomach. 'I'd tell you not to.'

'And what difference would that make, if I wanted to?'

'I don't know.' My voice was a hoarse whisper.

'Exactly. So you have to trust me, right? I don't want to – I wouldn't want to even if she did, which as far as I know she doesn't. It's you I married. It's you I love. It's you who's the mother of my kids. Okay?'

'Okay.' His words soothed the hurt a little bit, like when one of the kids fell over in the park and grazed their knee and I gave them a chocolate button so they'd stop crying.

'And speaking of the kids...' Patch began, then stopped.

'What about them?'

'I've been thinking, Nome... Now's probably not the best time to talk about it.' He kissed the top of my head, like I was one of the children and he was about to turn out the light.

'Damn it, Patch, what? You can't just say something like that and then say you're not going to say whatever it was.'

'I've been thinking... I've been wondering whether we should have another baby.'

'What?' I jerked away from him. 'Patch, what the fuck? Because I've been wondering whether you should have a vasectomy.'

We pulled apart and looked at each other. His face was as shocked and wounded as if I'd suggested carrying out the procedure right then and there with a butter knife from the kitchen drawer.

'You're joking,' he said.

'I'm not.' I swivelled round to face him, hugging my knees to my chest. 'I know now's not the best time to bring it up and obviously it's your body and totally your choice but I've been on the Pill for ages and I'm sick of it. It kind of feels like it's your turn. Because I definitely don't want another baby.'

'Why not? You're a fantastic mum.'

'I'm not. I'm mostly average and often a bit shit.' I took a gulp of my wine; the glass had been standing there for so long its sides were weeping with condensation. 'The twins are... you know. I love them so much it hurts, sometimes. But I can't do it again. I'm knackered. I want to go back to work and have something for me again.'

'You'd be more knackered if you went back to work.'

'Not as knackered as I'd be if I had another baby.' Only now that we were actually discussing it did I realise how much the prospect terrified me. 'Seriously, Patch. My body's fucked. My feet are a size bigger than they were before. I've still got a stone I want to lose. I haven't had a decent night's sleep in four years.'

Patch looked as surprised by the intensity of my reaction as I was – surprised and hurt. 'They'll start school in September. It'll be easier then.'

'And that's why I want to go back to work.'

'But what about when I'm working late, or away?' His tone was almost pleading.

'I don't know. I haven't thought about it,' I lied. 'We'd make a plan. Other people manage. Your colleagues must manage.'

'They mostly have wives who stay home and look after the kids.'

'Yeah, well.' I shrugged. 'I've done that. I've done my time. I need to move on from just being a mum now. You don't get it – you don't know what it's like being with them twenty-four-seven with no time to yourself.'

'I bloody wish I could.' His hurt was turning to defensive-ness now. 'You don't know what it's like working ten-hour days and being away from home and never seeing them.'

'So let's swap.' I called his bluff. 'You stay home, I'll go to work.'

'And who pays the mortgage? Father Christmas?'

I felt my cheeks sting with anger. Back when we first got together, we'd earned about the same. Then Patch had got a promotion and another one, and then I'd got pregnant and that had been that. If I did find a job, whatever school-hours-friendly role I secured would command a salary maybe a quarter of what he brought home now.

'Okay, so you can't stop work,' I admitted. 'But that doesn't mean I can't start. There are ways – like I said, people manage.

It's months away, anyway – maybe next year. Let's think about it, please?'

'Haven't you given me enough to think about for one night?'

'Probably.' I forced a smile. 'I'm sorry, Patch. It's a lot. The Zara stuff and now this. We can talk about it another time. Let's go to bed.'

He picked up the remote control and turned the sound back up. The roar of the football stadium crowd filled the room. 'You go. I might come up later – or sleep down here.'

I opened my mouth to argue, but thought better of it. Too much had been said and nothing resolved – and nothing would be, not tonight. So I said good night, kissing his cheek because he wouldn't turn his head, went upstairs and got into bed.

Normally, I'd have gone on to WhatsApp to pour my heart out to my friends. Normally, even though they couldn't solve my problems, their advice, virtual hugs and outrage on my behalf would have made me feel better. But now I couldn't do that. I felt as if the hands I'd been able to reach out for in the dark were no longer there – or if they were, they wouldn't reach out to me in return, and my fingers would be left scrabbling at empty air.

TWENTY

'Mummy?'

'Mummy, where's Daddy?'

The sound of my children's voices and their footsteps on the wooden floor jerked me out of sleep. The patter of little feet – if only whoever had come up with that cliché knew that first thing in the morning, it was more like a herd of wildebeest invading my bedroom.

I reached automatically over to Patch's side of the bed, but encountered only chilly, empty sheets, same as I had the previous six nights.

My head pounding and my eyes scratchy with tiredness, I sat up. 'Daddy slept downstairs.'

'Why, Mummy?' Meredith asked.

Why indeed? Work was hectic and he needed his sleep. He was training for some hardcore fitness thing and getting up early to go to the gym. That was what he said, anyway.

'Meredith, could you stop asking why when I don't know? Just maybe for one day. Even a couple of hours.'

'Why don't you know, Mummy?' chimed her brother.

Oh, for God's sake, just shut up. Fortunately, I managed to say the words in my head rather than out loud. But I'd been more snappy with the children than usual, more absent. *Not as absent as their bloody father*, I thought, in an unsuccessful attempt to mitigate how guilty this made me feel.

'Come on then, you two.' I forced a cheerful note into my voice and pushed the duvet aside, my ears straining to hear sounds of life from downstairs. But there was nothing – Patch had already left for the day.

When I'd dropped the children at nursery, been to see Bridget and returned home, the house felt emptier than ever. The central heating was off and I shivered when I removed my coat, but I couldn't be bothered to go upstairs and find a warmer jumper. I could see drifts of dust on the skirting boards and crumbs on the floor under the kitchen table, but I couldn't summon the energy to run the Hoover round, even though a bit of housework would warm me up.

I made a coffee and sat down, looking out into the garden hoping for signs of spring. It was already April, but it had been raining relentlessly and the drifts of blossom that had appeared on the trees had been stripped away by wind. The blackbirds I'd seen flying to and fro from the overgrown ivy on our neighbour's wall weren't there – I imagined them deciding to raise their family somewhere that felt more like a happy, welcoming home.

'Come on, Naomi,' I told myself. 'Get a grip. It's not that bad.'

But it felt that bad. It felt worse than when Patch had returned to work after his paternity leave and I'd been left with alone with two tiny babies, exhausted and terrified. Worse than when I'd woken up the morning after Abbie's engagement party with the hangover from hell and a sense of impending doom. Worse than when Toby got croup and I'd rushed him to Accident and Emergency in the middle of the night, the sound of his rasping breaths making me feel sick with fear.

Because at those times, I'd known that the Girlfriends'

Club had my back. I'd had Rowan to come and change nappies, feed me cake and bundle me into a hot shower. I'd had Kate to commiserate with over a bacon sandwich and a Bloody Mary, agreeing that was the only thing that would take the edge off. I'd had Abbie to do a late-night mercy dash to sit with Meredith overnight and cuddle me the next morning when I cried with relief that Toby wasn't going to die after all.

Automatically, I reached for my phone. The impulse to talk to my friends when I was sad, or happy, or even just plain bored was so deep-rooted than even unease about the response I might get couldn't overcome it.

NAOMI:

Morning gang! What's going on? Feels like it's been quiet on here the past few days.

ROWAN:

I'm all good – work's just crazy. What's up with you?

ABBIE:

Bloody April, innit. Feels like Narnia, where it's always winter and never Christmas. This too shall pass.

KATE:

I'm just eating my body weight in pasta, trying to get through it. At least Daniel and I are off to Sicily in a few days so we'll see some sun.

My best friends in the world, and all they seemed to want to talk to me about was work, the weather and their holiday plans. *I might as well try confiding my worries to a bloody hairdresser,* I thought miserably.

I set my phone aside and poured the dregs of my coffee down the sink, resigned to the fact that I was going to have to tackle the cleaning before it was time to pick the children up again, bring them home and watch everything descend into chaos again.

Then I heard its cheerful ringtone trilling from behind me and abandoned the bottle of anti-bacterial kitchen spray. An incoming call wasn't exciting in itself – I often got phoned by the twins' nursery, by my mother-in-law and by scam numbers trying to sell me non-existent phone upgrades. But this was a withheld number, and that almost never happened.

I considered ignoring the call – if whoever it was wanted to speak to me, they could leave a message – but at that moment I was bored enough and lonely enough to want to talk to anyone, even if it was about a car accident that hadn't been my fault (and had never happened).

'Hello? Naomi speaking.'

'Naomi? Hi. It's Zara.'

I was so surprised my legs almost gave way under me, and I sat down hard on the thing nearest to me, which happened to be a plastic basket half-full of dirty laundry, in which I found myself trapped, my legs and arms sticking out of the top, the phone pressed to my ear.

Maybe we should do this again, she'd said, the last time I saw her. It felt like far longer than six weeks ago when I'd picked up the camera from her – the camera, still in the drawer, its secrets locked within. I'd been clear I didn't want to see her again, or have anything more to do with her.

But that had been before she'd turned up at the Girlfriends' Club, taking the place that should have been mine.

'Naomi? Are you there? Please don't hang up.'

'I haven't hung up,' I gasped, fighting to extricate myself.

'I guess this call's a bit of a surprise. I'm sorry. But I wondered if you're free tonight?'

'Tonight? Why?'

'I thought maybe we could meet up for a drink.'

Seriously? A drink? Which part of *I'm not sure that would be a good idea* hadn't she understood?

'Hold on,' she went on, her voice husky and strained. 'Hear me out. I know you're busy and everything. But I could do with some company. I've been staring at the same four walls every night for the past week and I think I might be going a bit mad.'

You and me both, I thought. *Except the difference here is, you were always a bit mad. We just didn't see it.*

Although the idea of Zara not having a glittering social life that involved going somewhere different every evening was so alien as to be almost laughable. It couldn't be true – she must have loads of friends. And she hadn't exactly held back when it came to turning up on an evening out with my friends – in fact, she'd seen them together more recently than I had. Perhaps she'd be able to tell me what had happened at that meeting – what had led to Rowan's comment about them having been wrong about Zara – because it didn't look as if anyone else was going to.

'Okay,' I agreed reluctantly. 'But I'll need to check if Patch is going to be home. Can I text you?'

'Sure. Do you still have my number from... you know, before? I'm sorry, I withheld it because I thought you might not answer if you knew it was me.'

Damn right I wouldn't have. But in spite of myself, her admission of vulnerability touched me.

We ended the call and I fought my way out of the laundry basket. Then I texted Patch, telling him that he really, really needed to be home by seven, because I was going out. I didn't tell him where and he didn't ask; perhaps he assumed that I was meeting up with Rowan and the others to make up for the night I'd missed. To my surprise, he agreed, saying that his right hamstring had been playing up and his trainer had said to rest it for a few days, so a quiet night would do him good.

By now, the adrenaline from Zara's call had worn off and

my sense of urgency was replaced with scepticism – surely this was some sort of joke? But when I texted the number she'd given me, she replied straight away saying she was so excited to see me, and giving me the address of a bar in Covent Garden.

And so I found myself there at the appointed time. At least, I found myself pacing up and down an unfamiliar street, my umbrella protecting my blow-dried hair from the drizzle, damp soaking through the soles of my ancient suede boots, increasingly convinced that this was a joke – a trick to get me out of the house, or make a fool of me, or just waste my time.

Because Bar Chloe didn't appear to exist. The door numbers either side of the one Zara had given me were there – a dance studio and the offices of a design agency – but in between them was what looked like a residential townhouse: a tall, white-fronted building with a few early petunias struggling in planters underneath the windows. The shiny black front door was closed, the three buttons on the entry panel were blank and I didn't have the courage to buzz them and see what happened.

It was seven twenty-eight. I'd wait another ten minutes, I promised myself, then I'd go home and block and delete Zara's number, as if she was a Tinder date who'd ghosted me.

Then I heard the click of heels on the pavement behind me and whirled around. Zara was hurrying towards me, her black trench coat shiny with rain, her glossy hair reflecting the street lamps.

'There you are, Naomi. I'm so sorry, I should have warned you – this place is an absolute fucker to find. You're in the right place, they just deliberately make it all mysterious.'

And she'd chosen it knowing that – knowing I'd feel out of place and foolish, my defences down before I'd even seen her.

Well, I wasn't going to let my defences down, not if I could help it.

I forced a casual laugh. 'If you know, you know, right?'

'Exactly! And thanks to me, you didn't know. What an idiot I am. Come on.'

She pressed the middle bell, said her name, and within seconds a buzz sounded and she pushed open the door. We stepped into a warm, brightly lit hallway, an Oriental rug on the wooden floor, gilt-framed paintings lining the walls. A handsome young man in a white dinner jacket stepped out of a doorway to meet us and Zara gave her name again.

'Ladies. Good evening, and welcome to Bar Chloe. May I take your coats and show you to your table?'

Zara shrugged off her coat, scattering raindrops on the carpet, and handed it over. Humbly, I removed my shabby parka and relinquished it too. I glanced at her wine-red cashmere mini dress and over-the-knee suede boots and felt dowdy and out of place in my scarlet Primark tunic and leggings, which were similar on the surface to her outfit and yet as different as night and day.

I imagined her getting ready to meet me, turning and smiling in front of the mirror in that elegant apartment, knowing full well that she looked chic and put-together and I wouldn't.

But I didn't have time for in-depth style analysis.

The waiter said, 'Come this way, please,' and Zara and I followed him into a spacious, dimly lit room with a high ceiling and sage-green walls, hung with more pictures. Low, copper-topped tables were dotted around, velvet chairs in jewel colours surrounding them. There was a grand piano in one corner and lush potted plants in the corners. Soft music was playing and I could hear the muted hum of conversation and the occasional burst of laughter. It was the sort of place I might have come to with Patch before the children were born, if we had something special to celebrate like an anniversary or a birthday – the sort of place I hadn't been to for years and had never felt truly comfortable in.

And Zara must have known that too.

'Your table, madam,' the guy said to Zara, and we sat down.

'Isn't this fab?' she said, smiling happily and crossing her legs. 'My favourite place in London. Nothing bad ever happens here.'

There's a first time for everything, I thought, picking up the printed menu card and studying it. The cocktails, which were called things like 'Limerence' and had descriptions like 'Monkey 47, Amontillado, Clarified Yuzu', were priced at north of twenty quid a go.

I realised she was looking at me expectantly, as if seeking approval.

'It's very glamorous,' I said, in the same tone I used when I told one of the children that their nursery scribbles had all the promise of an early Picasso.

'There are just so few places where you can have a good drink and a conversation, and sit in a comfy chair.' Zara smiled confidingly at me – *Look at us two old birds on our night out.* 'I can't be doing with standing around slopping a shit cocktail down my front and being hit on by men who work in insurance any more.'

I couldn't think how to respond to this other than with overt snarkiness – *Better a man who works in insurance than no man at all, surely?* – but I was saved by a waitress bringing water in short-sided glasses so thin and clean they looked like they weren't there at all, and a bowl of olives.

'I'll have the Bellmont Number Five, please,' Zara requested, smiling.

'Um... a Limerence for me.'

'Good choice.' Zara smiled again, as if she was enjoying some private joke and leaning over the table towards me, although we could hear each other perfectly well if we sat back in our chairs. 'Anyway. How've you been?'

I took a sip of water, carefully weighing up my response to

this seemingly innocent enquiry. I didn't want to reveal how much the landscape of my life seemed to have shifted since Andy's funeral, but at the same time I didn't want to reveal just how mundane it had been before – and still was, outwardly.

'You know. Same as usual. Pretty busy,' I said guardedly.

'Been seeing a lot of the girls?'

'Not as much as usual,' I admitted. 'You know, we meet up regularly, but I missed last time because I wasn't well, and I guess everyone else is pretty busy too.'

Tell me, I urged silently. *Tell me you were there, and why, and what happened.*

The waitress brought our drinks. Zara's was purple, with crystals that might have been salt, sugar or something entirely different crusting the rim of the glass. Mine was pale orange, like overdiluted squash, with a brighter orange sphere of something resting atop the huge cube of ice in it.

She took a sip and sighed with pleasure. 'Here, try this. It's glorious.'

I hesitated before accepting her glass and tasting the drink – *What could she have done, bribed them to poison it? If they had, she'd drop dead too* – then passed mine over for her to taste as well. The exchange felt uncomfortably intimate as if we were the very best of friends who swapped sips of our drinks all the time.

Then Zara said, 'I hope you don't mind that I gatecrashed the last Girlfriends' Club. I asked if I could go along, you know, for old times' sake. And Kate agreed to have me. I didn't realise you weren't going to be there, or I'd have said something to you first. They all told me you wouldn't mind, but I know how it must have looked. Anyway, I'm sorry.'

Her apology was clearly intended to disarm me, and I didn't want to let it. Still, what could I say? *If I'd known you were going to be there, I'd have turned up and puked all over you?* Not really. And I certainly wasn't going let her know how her unexpected presence that night had brought all my old insecurities to the surface. *Naomi won't mind* – as if, once again, she was part of the inner circle and I was outside it, an irrelevance being talked about dismissively by the others.

'It's okay,' I said.

Smiling, she went on, 'I'd forgotten how much fun those evenings were. I'd forgotten, I suppose, what it feels like to have friends.'

'You must have loads of friends,' I protested involuntarily.

'Not really. I've been moving around a lot, you see, and it makes it almost impossible to form proper connections with people. You meet someone you like, you go for a coffee or whatever, or you work together for a bit, and then you move on and you promise to stay in touch but you never do. There's Gabrielle, who I used to share a flat with, but she's married with kids now, same as you. And that makes you grow apart from people. You of all people must know that.'

I laughed. If she thought I was going to empathise with that, she was wrong. 'Actually, me having the kids hasn't made any difference. I see the girls just as much as I did before. They were amazing when the twins were little – they really rallied round. And now they're older, I can leave them with Bridget sometimes, or get a babysitter. We have our monthly meetings, same as always.'

At least, they were the same as always until you showed up.

Zara sighed. 'They were such good times. I think about those Wednesdays often. Remember when Rowan brought Clara along? She was only tiny and breastfeeding and the bar tried to kick us out because they had a no-under-18s policy.'

The memory made me smile in spite of myself. 'And Kate demanded to see the manager so she could explain the Equality Act to him and give him a lecture about reputational risk.'

'Except then the waiter realised he was going to get to look at Ro's tits all night, and changed his mind,' Zara finished, with a throaty laugh.

I took a swallow of water. My cocktail was almost finished and I could feel my defences slipping. *I must not allow that to happen.*

I didn't join in Zara's laughter and after a couple of seconds her face became serious again.

'You know, I do regret how things turned out.' She licked a few grains of purple salt off the rim of her glass, her tongue precise as a cat's. 'It was partly my own fault, I know. I have trust issues. And of course when you and Patch got together... well, that was hard for me. I never saw it coming.'

Even though you were shagging around for months, I thought.

But I hadn't come here to have a confrontation with Zara or to score points in a competition that, by any reckoning, I'd already won. I'd come here to hear her out, try and establish what her intentions were, let her know I wasn't going to be manipulated or walked over.

I said deliberately, 'Zara, I'm genuinely sorry you were hurt. That was never my intention, and I would never have chosen to damage our friendship like that. But I'd have hoped we would all have moved on from it by now.'

Zara waved a hand as if to dismiss my apology, but our waiter misread her signal and hurried over. Against my will, I found myself ordering a second complicated, expensive cocktail.

'You're right, I suppose,' she carried on once he'd gone, 'it's all water under the bridge now. Life carries on and changes. Apart from the Girlfriends' Club. I've always thought of the Girlfriends' Club as a kind of constant in the world, one of those things that'll never change. Like Quality Street selection boxes at Christmas.'

'They change those all the time,' I pointed out. 'And whenever they do, there's practically a riot about it.'

Zara laughed. 'You're so funny, Naomi. You always were. I do hope you're right. And I hope we can – maybe not be friends again, but at least let bygones be bygones. Can we?'

Our next round of drinks arrived, and she extended her glass to me. I raised mine too, but withdrew it before it could touch hers.

'Zara,' I said. 'There are a few things you need to know. One I've already told you – I'm truly sorry you were hurt and I regret my part in that. Two, the promise I made to you – I've never broken it and I never will. And three, my friendship with the Girlfriends' Club is the most important thing in the world to me, apart from Patch and our children. And I won't put it at risk for anything or anyone.'

She looked at me appraisingly and then nodded. 'I understand.'

Slightly mollified, I went on, 'But of course I can let bygones be bygones. I don't want to hold grudges.'

She smiled. 'That's good to know. To friendship, then.'

Reluctantly, I extended my drink again. This time, I heard the faint, musical clink as the glasses connected.

'Cheers,' I said. I felt there was nothing else I could say.

'Excuse me' – Zara got to her feet – 'I have to use the loo.'

Taking advantage of her absence, I signalled the waiter for our bill and when she still hadn't returned by the time he brought it, I paid.

It was only after we'd said a brief, coolly civil goodbye in the rainy street that I realised two things – or more like two parts of the same thing.

Zara had led me into revealing my weak points: my family and my friends. And she'd engineered the situation so I'd paid a hundred-pound bar bill I could ill afford.

She'd manipulated me, just the way she used to, despite my determination not to let her. Come what may, I wasn't going to let her do it again.

TWENTY-ONE

MAY 2011

'Wow, Naomi!' Amina, my flatmate, squealed when she saw me. 'What the actual fuck are you wearing? And your hair...!'

She put down her cup of tea next to her laptop and doubled over laughing.

'I know, right?' I paused in my bedroom doorway, caught between shyness and amusement. 'Is it too much?'

'Depends what you're doing. First date with Mr Might-be-Right? Get right back in there now and change. Fancy dress party? You're all good.'

I turned back into my room and looked at myself in the mirror for the millionth time. My hair was gelled, back-combed and sprayed into wild spikes. My eyes were heavily ringed with black, my face even paler than usual thanks to thick ivory foundation. My lips were blood red. My tights were ripped below a tiny pleather skirt and my feet were squeezed into pointy, silver-buckled boots.

'I think I'm all good,' I said. 'I'm off to Camden to see a Cure tribute band.'

'That's a relief.' She picked up her tea again. 'You'll fit right in.'

'So long as I can get there on the Tube without seeing anyone from work.' I grimaced at my reflection, suddenly doubtful. 'I'd never live it down.'

'Frankly, they wouldn't recognise you. Who are you going with, anyway?' She eyed me beadily. 'Do you have a whole circle of punk mates no one knows about?'

'Negative. Just Patch, and he's not a punk. We just like some of the same music.'

'Patch? The one with the girlfriend?'

'No – I mean, yes.'

'Got to be one or the other.'

I minced over to her and sat down. 'Jeez, these boots are killing me already. I'll be in agony by the end of the night. Yeah, he's got a girlfriend. My friend Zara. But the thing is '

'The thing is you fancy the pants off him and you don't want to do the dirty on your mate?'

'No! Sisters before misters, like always. But she's not really acting like she's got a boyfriend right now, and I don't know how to tell him. Or even whether to tell him.'

Amina pushed the teapot over to me, reaching behind her for another mug. 'Go on.'

I hesitated, inhaling the steam from my tea. I'd made a promise to Zara two months before, when she'd asked me to tell Patch she was in Stockholm. As it happened, he hadn't asked, but I hadn't told anyway – not him, and not Rowan, Kate or Abbie. I felt even worse about keeping secrets from them than I did about keeping them from him.

And now I felt worse still. Because Zara had asked me to lie again, and the lie was bigger. A few days before, I'd woken up to a text from her that had made me feel kind of cold and dirty, like I'd fallen face first into a muddy puddle.

ZARA:

Shit, Naomi. I have the hangover from hell and I'm the worst person ever

The message had been sent two hours before, at what would have been about five in the morning in Paris. I lay on my back in bed, my phone propped on my chest, and replied:

NAOMI:

> What happened? Are you okay?

Her answer came straight away.

ZARA:

> Apart from poisoned by absinthe. Yeah, I guess I'll live. Not that I deserve to.

Concerned, I pushed myself higher up on my pillows.

NAOMI:

> It can't be that bad! You've got beer fear, that's all. Or absinthe anxiety, which must be worse.

ZARA:

> Haha, v funny. You always make me feel better. Please, Nome, tell me to stop getting pissed and doing things I shouldn't do.

NAOMI:

> Stop getting pissed and doing – whatever you did.

I didn't want to know. I really didn't. But I could sense that she was going to tell me anyway, and there was nothing I could do to stop her.

Sure enough, she texted back:

ZARA:

> As Oscar Wilde didn't say, to shag one random stranger looks like misfortune, to shag two looks like carelessness. I've been careless, Nome.

Before I could compose a reply, she messaged again.

ZARA:

Please don't tell Patch. Pleasepleaseplease, I
beg you.

'Shit.' I frowned at my phone's screen, torn between anger
at Zara – why was she doing this to me, putting me in this
impossible position? And even more to the point, why was she
doing this to Patch? – and my instinct to support my friend
when she needed me.

NAOMI:

That's not cool, Zee. You know it's not. You
should tell him. Or just end it. If you're shagging
other people, it can't be working with him.

Even as I pressed Send, I felt a stab of guilt – *Yeah, you
want her to end it, don't you, Naomi? And why might
that be?*

ZARA:

It is working though. I need him. He's the only
good thing in my life right now – apart from you,
obviously. I'm such a terrible person and I don't
deserve anyone to love me but he does, and I
need that.

NAOMI:

If he loves you, he'll forgive you.

Even as I typed, I doubted it – and a selfish part of me
hoped it wasn't true.

ZARA:

Why should he? Come on, Nome. But if I never
do it again, it might be like it never happened.

Again, before I could find words to answer her, another
message flashed on to my screen.

ZARA:

> When you see him again – he's in London this
> weekend, right? – can you talk to him? Like,
> sound him out. Maybe he's been seeing
> someone else too and that would kind of
> cancel it out. Will you? I promise I'll never ask
> you another favour again as long as I live. And
> whatever you do, don't tell anyone.

So, reluctantly, I'd said I would try my best.

'What a mess,' Amina said, when I'd finished pouring out the story to her.

She didn't count, I told myself. She didn't know Patch or Zara and she'd never tell anyone anyway. She was a solicitor and probably bound by some code of confidentiality or something.

'It's grim,' I agreed. 'So I'm seeing him tonight and I don't know what to do. It feels all kinds of wrong.'

'You know what my advice is?'

'What?'

'Stay out of it. Don't tell him anything. And don't ask about his love life either. Tell her you didn't get a chance, or whatever. It's not your fuck-up to fix, it's hers.'

Feeling like a burden had been lifted, I said, 'You really think so?'

'I honestly do. Now take yourself and your ridiculous hair off and have a fun night.'

'I'll try. Thanks. And, Amina...?'

'Mmm?'

'Can I borrow your leather jacket?'

As it happened, I couldn't have asked Patch anything even if I'd wanted to. By the time I arrived at the pub, a cavernous space by the canal near Camden Market, the gig was already in full swing and I could barely hear him when he asked if I wanted a beer. For the next three hours, we communicated mostly in hand signals, when we weren't dancing, singing along to our favourite tunes, or admiring the outfits around us, most of which were even more outlandish than my own.

Patch himself was wearing black jeans, a faded black T-shirt with a Bauhaus logo on it (kudos to him, I thought – he'd either had it for years or hit the jackpot in an Aberdeen charity shop), and eyeliner. I had thought his eyes looked larger and more luminous than usual. I imagined him walking out of his mother's house wearing it, getting on the Tube, not caring what people thought of him. It was a side of him I'd never seen before, and a side I realised I liked very much – probably too much.

But I didn't want to think about liking him, because that would immediately lead to thoughts about Zara. I wanted to drink beer after beer, sing along as loud as I could to *Just Like Heaven*, join the moshing crowd by the stage, and forget my troubles.

And it worked. By the time the band finished at almost two in the morning, my throat was raw from singing, I was light-headed from drinking and my hair was sticky with sweat as well as gel. Patch put his arm round my shoulder to guide me through the press of people towards the exit, and the cold, damp night air filled my lungs as we stepped outside.

'That was pretty awesome, right?' he asked.

'Totally awesome. The best time. God, I'm actually quite pissed.'

'Quite right too.' He grinned. 'Like a proper rocker.'

'Goths aren't rockers, though,' I argued. 'Aren't they meant to get high on amphetamines and... I don't know. Misery?'

He laughed. 'I don't feel miserable tonight. Not a bit. Makes a nice change.'

What did he mean? Was he talking about the loneliness of working offshore for weeks at a time, or something else? Did he know about Zara's infidelity? Had she taken my advice and told him, or had he guessed? Or was it about something else entirely?

I didn't know. But I was distracted from my bewilderment by a sudden awareness of the pain in my feet. While we were dancing, I'd been able to ignore it, but now it came back with renewed force.

'Ouch.' I winced, stumbling slightly so I cannoned into him. 'My feet really, really hurt. These shoes are a size too small.'

'Problem. We've missed the last Tube, so we'll have to get a bus. Or a taxi, I guess.'

We'd paused now, leaning on a railing overlooking the canal, waiting for the crowd around us to thin. It was almost but not quite raining, a light drizzle shivering the dark water below us, the reflections of the lights blurry and indistinct.

'I'm going to have to take them off.'

'Or I can carry you. But first...'

He reached into his pocket and pulled out a hip flask, handing it to me. It was warm from his body. I unscrewed the cap and took a sip, fiery bourbon searing my throat.

'You came prepared,' I said.

'Think of me as a Saint Bernard dog, rescuing stranded goths from the streets of London.'

I laughed. 'Isn't it water they carry? This is better, though.'

I returned the flask to him and he said, 'Cheers. To an amazing night.'

'And friendship.'

As soon as I said it, I regretted it. I didn't feel friendly towards him right in that moment – I felt something else entirely, and what it was made me no friend at all to Zara.

I took the hip flask and had another gulp. The spirit went down more easily that time, pleasantly warming rather than blazingly harsh. Then I passed it back to him.

He hesitated, took another drink and cleared his throat. 'If I say something, promise you won't be offended?'

'Yeah, like I'm going to get the hump and hobble off into the rain.'

'Fair point. Not a bad strategy, actually – when you want to tell a woman something and you're not sure how it's going to land, make sure she's wearing shoes she can't walk in.'

'Exactly – talk about a captive audience. So go ahead.'

I had no idea what he was going to say – I genuinely didn't. But something in me must have sensed it would be important, because I felt my breath coming faster and my heart beating hard in my chest.

'I've never seen anyone look as beautiful as you do now, with eyeliner all over your face,' he said.

And all at once, something inside me changed – only it wasn't really a change but a thing that had been there for ages, which I'd become so used to burying and denying I'd become able to pretend it wasn't there. My desire for him sprang out like the shoots of a long-dormant seed, or a chemical reaction that had needed just the right conditions in the test tube to make it happen.

I didn't think about it – I wasn't capable of thought. I just swivelled my body around and took a step closer to him, so I could feel the warmth of him.

'If I kissed you, would that be a really terrible idea?' I whispered.

'Probably,' he said, his face gently leaning towards mine.

And then he kissed me.

TWENTY-TWO

'Meredith and Toby, we need to be out of the house in five minutes.' I heard my voice rising as I hurried downstairs, a tiny backpack in each hand. 'Have you cleaned your teeth?'

There was silence from the children, both of whom were in front of the television, half empty bowls of porridge on their laps, glazed expressions on their faces.

'I'm going to count to three,' I said. 'One, two...'

With glacial slowness, Meredith stood up, putting her bowl down on the sofa, where it tipped precariously over.

'Don't put that there!' I snapped, snatching it just in time.

Calm down, Naomi. They're four. Thinking about upholstery cleaning is exactly what they don't do.

I forced myself to take a steadying breath, then remembered that they still – clearly – hadn't cleaned their teeth and that the received wisdom was that children should only be permitted to do so unsupervised round about the time of their sixteenth birthday.

'Come on. Upstairs – teeth. Now.'

I remembered – not for the first time – how, when I was pregnant, I'd imagined what kind of a mother I'd be. The idea that these two minute proto-people were growing inside me had felt so daunting it was almost terrifying – that, somehow, I'd be responsible for not only getting them to full gestation and out of my body in one piece (or, ideally, two), but that I'd then need to rear them to adulthood.

And, even though I'd only seen them in grainy grey images on ultrasound scans and didn't even know their names, the love I felt for them had been overwhelming. I'd nurture, cherish and protect them always, I'd promised myself. I'd lavish all the love and attention I possibly could on them. I'd never, ever shout at them.

Ha. As if.

It had only been a few weeks before I'd lost my shit the first time, during one late-night feed when Toby had been fussing at my breast. My already shredded nipples were screaming with pain, my teeth were clenched and every cell in my body was crying out for sleep – even though I knew that when sleep came, I'd be snatched from it almost straight away and wake feeling even worse than I had before.

'For fuck's sake,' I'd half sobbed, 'please just latch on!'

Next to me, Patch sat up in horror. 'You can't speak to him like that.'

'He doesn't understand.'

But still, shame had flooded me. I'd sworn at my baby. I'd failed as a mother. I'd probably scarred my precious son irreparably, before he was even two months old.

When I confessed this to Rowan, she'd laughed. 'Welcome on board the guilt train, Nome. Next stop, death.'

Since then, I'd learned to set aside some of my images of perfect parenthood and accept that I was doing my best – I could only do my best. But the mother I'd imagined myself being – the one who'd happily play with her kids for hours, never lose patience, always serve healthy, nourishing meals, dispense stickers and praise for good behaviour rather than chocolate buttons for bribes – her best would be better than this.

As I quick-marched the children to nursery, I found my feet beating out a rhythm on the pavement: *this isn't enough, this isn't enough*. Being my children's mother and Patch's wife wasn't enough for me, even though it was the thing I'd thought I wanted most in all the world. Or maybe I wasn't enough for them, or didn't have enough: enough patience, enough love, enough self-sacrifice.

That's selfish, Naomi, said the guilt-loving voice deep inside me. *You wanted someone else's man and you took him, and now you want something else. Maybe now you've made your bed, you should try lying in it a bit longer?*

I was so distracted by my thoughts that, turning into the nursery gates, I almost collided with Princess Lulu. Actually, I did collide with her, but she did a strategic last-minute side-step that meant my shoulder only just caught the shoulder of her cashmere coat, and she narrowly avoided tripping over Meredith.

Hold on – cashmere coat? I stepped back and looked at her. Instead of her usual designer athleisure, she was wearing what looked like a navy trouser suit underneath the expensive outerwear. Her hair was up in a bun instead of in its usual beachy waves, and she didn't have her daughter's scooter in one hand as she usually did, but instead a rose gold leather laptop bag.

'Oh my God,' I said. 'Sorry about that.'

She smiled. 'One of those mornings? Me too.'

'Aren't they all those mornings?' I pushed my hair back under my woollen beanie and squatted to kiss the twins. 'Off you go now. Be good. Love you.'

'I mean, yeah...' Princess Lulu looked down at her pointy black boots as if she was surprised to find herself wearing them – or perhaps checking they were a matching pair. 'But today's worse for me. I'm starting back at work and I'm properly shitting it.'

I did a double take. It sounded almost as if this perfect woman was actually human. 'Wow. Yes, that must feel like a lot.'

'It's terrifying. I'm worried I'll get lost on the way to the office, I've forgotten how to send emails, and when my PA gets up to go to the toilet I'll tell her not to forget to wipe her bottom.'

I burst out laughing. 'I'm sure you'll get the hang of it. I'm thinking of doing the same, later in the year, but...'

'It's a lot,' she echoed. 'I'm only doing three days a week at first. We should have a coffee sometime and compare notes.'

'That would be great. My name's Naomi, by the way.'

'Imogen.' She extended a cool, pale hand and I shook it. 'I must dash, I don't want to be late. But coffee, for sure – maybe next week?'

'Sounds good.'

She hurried away, the tails of her coat flying out behind her. I watched her go, torn between pleasure at having had a normal, adult encounter with a woman I'd assumed would never deign to talk to me, and my usual envy. Of course Princess— Imogen had a job to return to. Some sort of highly paid City gig, I was willing to bet, in which her experience and knowledge were so highly valued she'd been able to dictate her three-days-a-week terms and her employer had willingly sucked it up.

But she'd seemed nice. She'd seemed as nervous as I knew I'd be in her position. She'd suggested we meet for a chat, so she must think I was a potential friend – unless she was just lining me up to invite her daughter home for playdates and fish fingers when she was kept late in some high-powered meeting.

But the encounter had reminded me how nice it was to talk to another adult who wasn't Patch, Bridget or the woman who checked my age when I bought gin in Sainsbury's.

It had reminded me how much I needed friends. It had brought home to me that I needed Rowan, Kate and Abbie in my life – I couldn't allow Zara or ghosts from the past to damage our friendship.

I turned away from the gates of Busy Bees and walked back the way I'd come, more slowly this time, taking my phone out of the pocket of my coat. The last time I'd tried to speak to Rowan, it hadn't ended well. That had been my fault, I realised – I'd basically ambushed her at work. I should have known that she'd be busy. It hadn't been fair.

I needed to try again – to be more considerate, more strategic. I needed to get to the bottom of what Zara had meant when she'd said they'd been talking about me – whether it was something important or just a fabrication to make me feel uneasy.

I tapped the WhatsApp icon and began typing, not in the Girlfriends' Club group but in the private chat I had with Rowan.

NAOMI:

Hey. Hope everything's okay with you. I wanted to talk – are you free in the next few days?

Leave it open-ended – don't give her a chance to say she's busy on a particular day.

There was a pause, and I felt an anxious knot in my stomach, the way you always do when you're waiting for a reply to a message you're not sure will have been welcomed.

But it took her just a few minutes to respond.

ROWAN:

You're right, we need to have a chat. I'm sorry about what happened last time I saw you. Shall I come round to yours tonight?

NAOMI:

That would be amazing. P working late then at gym. Shall I cook?

ROWAN:

> Don't go to any trouble. We can get a takeaway
> or something. Be there about 7.30 x

Just one kiss? And her message sounded oddly formal. 'Don't go to any trouble' – well, it wasn't like I was going to prepare a four-course menu for my closest friend. But I stopped off at the supermarket and stocked up on hummus, pita bread, olives, random pastry things and (of course) wine, and then spent the morning blitzing the house and baking a batch of my chocolate brownies, which had achieved something akin to legendary status within the Girlfriends' Club over the years.

By half past seven, the children were bathed, in bed and under strict instructions to stay there. And I – I realised – had worked myself up into a right tizz, as if it was a hot date coming round rather than my best mate.

When I heard the doorbell buzz, I literally jumped, even though it was seven thirty-five and I'd been expecting to hear it for the past ten minutes. I dashed to the door and flung it open.

'Hey.' Rowan smiled, but without her usual warmth. She looked tense, and for the first time I wondered what conversations had been going on behind the scenes – whether she'd been briefed by the others on what to say to me, how to act, the importance of reporting back after our meeting.

'Hey. Come in, it's so nice to see you.'

I took her coat – which normally she would have dumped over the bannister – and she offered to remove her shoes, which she surely knew wasn't necessary.

While I poured merlot into glasses and ferried bowls of snacks over to the coffee table, we made stilted conversation about how our days had been. Then we sat down, the foot or so of distance between us on the sofa feeling like an unbridgeable chasm.

'Look—' I began.

At the same moment, Rowan said, 'Listen, Nome—'

'It's okay, you go first.'

'No, you go.'

We laughed, and I felt the tension ease a bit.

I tried again. 'I wanted to talk to you. Because it feels like things have been weird, and I don't understand why. I spoke to Patch about it and he said it all sounds like a load of playground drama, and maybe it is, but...'

'Playground drama's kind of a big deal when you're in the playground.' Rowan's lips moved into something that wasn't quite a grimace but definitely wasn't a smile.

'Exactly.' I took a gulp of wine and bit an olive in half. The salty morsel felt almost too big to swallow.

'The thing is, Naomi...' She shifted uncomfortably. 'Ugh, this is horrible, isn't it?'

I nodded miserably. 'Whatever it is, you might as well just come out and say it.'

'Okay.' Rowan also gulped at her wine, taking such a big sip that it left stains on the corners of her lips as if she was smiling, although she wasn't. She dabbed her mouth with a napkin. 'Look, we always knew you liked Patch, even when he was still with Zara.'

'Guess I didn't do as good a job of hiding that as I thought,' I quipped.

But Rowan didn't laugh. 'No, you didn't. And when you two got together – well, it felt kind of inevitable. We were all really happy for you. But we didn't know...'

'Didn't know what?'

Her words came out in a rush. 'That he'd actually cheated on her with you. And I know he was the one in a relationship and it was on him and it's all ancient history. But if we'd known at the time, we'd have told you to wait. We'd have said it wasn't worth hurting a friend for a man. Because Zara was terribly hurt. And if we had – if we'd known, and you'd waited – we could maybe have avoided it all going so horribly wrong.'

'But I did wait,' I insisted. 'Patch and I – okay, there was one kiss. Just the one. I know it wasn't right, but nothing more than that happened until after he'd split up with her. I would never have let it happen.'

Rowan sighed. 'Nome, that's not what Zara says. And – I'm really, really sorry to say this – I believe her. We all believe her.'

'But she—' I began.

'Look, she got into a bad place. She did some bad stuff. It's just...' Rowan looked miserably down at her hands, twisting the napkin between them. 'We never thought you were that kind of person, Nome. I never thought that.'

'I'm not that kind of person,' I insisted, my voice sounding high and thin. 'I don't know what Zara's told you, but it isn't true. Patch broke up with her before we got together. I'd never have done what you think I did. Honest.'

'That isn't what Zara says,' she repeated wearily.

'But Zara—' I began, but then I stopped. Even all these years later, it felt wrong to tell Rowan that Zara hadn't been faithful to Patch, either. Even now, the weight of the promise I'd made to her (*promisepromisepromise?*) was too heavy a burden to set down.

'Ro, are you saying you believe Zara and not me?' The sense of injustice hit me with the force of a wave at the seaside, tumbling me, making it hard to know which way was up and almost impossible to breathe.

'It's not really about who I believe.' Rowan sighed. 'The thing is, I think we treated Zara unfairly back then. Not just you – all of us. We knew at the time she had a lot going on in her life and not everything she told us was true, but that was all... you know. All part of the same picture. All the trauma from her past.'

What trauma? I thought. *The trauma she told you about or the trauma she told me about or the trauma she told Kate...*

As if she could read my mind, Rowan said, 'And I know she made stuff up. But that's kind of to be expected, when someone's damaged like that. But she didn't make it up about her and Patch still... you know. When you...'

I sat there in silence, the accused in the dock, my defence suddenly gone AWOL. The only way I could justify my actions would be to tell Rowan what Zara had been up to, but the promise I'd made to her was one I still wasn't able to break.

'I know it was a long time ago.' Rowan reached over and squeezed my shoulder. 'It's just all been a lot to take in. And Zara really needs friends right now. She really needs us. And we – I – we didn't think you'd be willing to offer her friendship, even now. Even though...'

'Even though what?' I took another gulp of wine. The tannin in it made my mouth dry – or maybe it wasn't only the wine.

'This isn't really for me to share,' Rowan said wearily. 'But I don't see how I can not tell you. You'll find out sooner or later. Zara's... she's not well, Nome.'

I almost joked, *Well, we all knew that!* But I realised Rowan didn't mean what I would have meant – she meant something else. Something serious.

My voice sounding thin and strained, I began, 'Are you saying she's—'

'She's got cancer, Nome. She got a call from her doctor in Paris with some test results. She's had to go back there and start treatment.'

'Ro, I hate to ask this. It's awful to ask. But are you sure?'

'Jesus, Nome. Can't you ever let up? Look.'

She took her phone from her bag, tapped the screen a few times and handed it to me. On it was a post from Zara's Facebook feed – the feed I'd blocked years before. It showed Zara in what was clearly a hospital ward. She was wearing a white cotton gown with a geometric print, her shoulders resting against a blue pillow. She was wearing make-up: smoky eyes and red lipstick.

Got my slap on for the occasion, she'd written.

Wouldn't want to frighten the nurses – or M le Docteur, who I've developed quite the crush on. No nail polish allowed, though – how random is that? I'm going in in fifteen minutes. They don't know yet how much they're going to have to take out. See you on the other side.

'What... Do you know what kind of cancer it is?'

'Cervix, apparently.' Rowan took back her phone and tucked it in her bag. 'So, you see – it feels like it might just be time to let go of the past, right? Have a bit of compassion.'

I nodded mutely. I felt almost as if I was being crushed by guilt. Even though the rational part of my mind knew full well that you didn't develop a potentially fatal disease because your boyfriend kissed someone else more than ten years ago, I still felt responsible. And Rowan was right – I hadn't been compassionate. My first instinct had been to doubt what Zara had said, not offer friendship and support.

Another part of me was thinking, *First Andy, and now this. It's too much, too soon. It's not fair.*

And then I realised how incredibly selfish that thought was too.

'That's awful,' I managed to say. 'Just – terrible. What can we do?'

'Nothing,' Rowan said. 'She says she'll tell us how it goes. I guess you could send her a message or something, if you want.'

Us – you. I got the sense that the 'us' didn't include me.

'Nome, I should go.' Rowan reached over and zipped up her

bag, not meeting my eyes. 'I don't want to get home to Clara too late.'

'Have another glass of wine, at least.' She'd barely touched the first one.

'I can't. I'm driving.'

She stood up and we looked at each other for a moment, then stepped closer and touched each other's shoulders in something that should have been a hug, but wasn't. I fetched her coat and we said goodbye at the front door, watching as she climbed into her battered turquoise car and drove away.

Then I went back inside, looked at the undrunk wine and the untouched brownies and threw myself down on the sofa, and burst into tears.

TWENTY-THREE

SUMMER 2011

I don't think I've ever felt as horrible as I did that Sunday morning. I had a hangover, obviously – not the worst one ever, but a strong contender. I woke up with my mouth tasting disgusting, smears of make-up all over my pillow, my hair matted and sticky and a banging headache.

But all that was nothing compared to the guilt. All the elation of last night had faded – the rush of joy and excitement that had carried me through that first kiss, and the one after, and the one after that. I remembered the feeling of Patch's hand in mine as he'd walked with me to the bus stop, slowly because of my shoes and because we kept stopping to kiss each other again – it had felt so right at the time, like our hands had been waiting for each other, all these years, and now they were linked together at last. I remembered thinking that no one had ever kissed as well as he did, and I'd never kissed anyone as well as I kissed him. I remembered us singing *The Walk* and how the lyrics – midnight, the rain, the kisses – felt like they'd been written just for us.

I remembered seeing my bus approaching, leaning into

Patch for one final kiss, gazing into his eyes, made almost luminous by make-up, and saying, 'I have to go home.'

He pressed me close against him and I pressed back, wishing I never had to leave the warmth of his body, the strength of his arms.

'Don't worry.' His voice was gentle. 'It's going to be okay.'

'Really?' My face was pressed into his chest, my words muffled. 'How will it be okay?'

'It will. Trust me.'

And I had trusted him. I'd allowed myself to relive those kisses over and over, all the way home as the bus crept through the rainy streets. I'd imagined us having a future together, our friends saying they'd always known it was meant to be, Zara magnanimous as she embarked on a relationship with someone new, admitting that she'd never cared that deeply for Patch.

What a fool I was. What a duplicitous, horrible person. What a bad friend.

I spent the rest of that day wallowing in misery. Part of me longed for Patch – to speak to him, find out how he was, get reassurance from him that what we'd done wasn't that bad, it would never happen again and no one would ever find out. Part of me wanted to confess to Zara, to Rowan or to everyone en masse, and receive some kind of absolution – but I was too ashamed to do that. And anyway, I knew it would do no good – what had happened had happened; telling anyone would only help assuage my conscience while hurting Zara terribly. So I kept quiet, clinging to the knowledge that eventually the pain would ease and perhaps, with time, I'd be able to see Patch as just a friend again.

For a couple of days, I heard nothing from him. I knew it was for the best, but the pain was awful. I couldn't concentrate at work; every time my phone buzzed I grabbed it with wild hope that it might be him, immediately turning to horror when I realised it could just as easily be Zara. I couldn't sleep at night. I could barely eat.

Tortured with guilt, I thought again about confessing – to Rowan, to Zara, to someone. Then, on Tuesday, I received a text from him. When I saw his name on my screen, my heart leaped and then plummeted again. *She's found out. He blames me. Everyone will hate me.*

But the message said only:

> **PATRICK HAMILTON:**
>
> I broke up with Zee. You don't need to worry. Xxx

> **NAOMI:**
>
> What?

I texted back, my fingers fumbling on the keypad.

> **NAOMI:**
>
> When?

> **PATRICK HAMILTON:**
>
> It doesn't matter. It's been over for a long time. I haven't seen her in about six weeks and it wasn't working long before that.

It's been over for a long time – what did that even mean? That kissing him had been okay? That the way I felt about him was okay? I didn't know. I didn't want to know.

> **NAOMI:**
>
> I'm sorry
>
> Is she all right? Are you?

> **PATRICK HAMILTON:**
>
> Honestly? I've never been better. I'd love to see you. I'm back in London in a couple of weeks.

My heart went, *Yesyesyesyes!* But my head said, *No way,*

Naomi. Too soon.

NAOMI:

We could meet for a coffee, maybe?

So we met for a coffee. I told him how bad I felt, and he told me I'd done nothing wrong; it was him who'd been in a relationship and that relationship was over. He said he wanted to be with me. I said I wanted to be with him, too, but I didn't want to rush into anything. He said he respected my feelings, and we'd take things at whatever pace I wanted.

Six weeks later – waiting for him to return from Aberdeen, it felt like an eternity – we met up again.

This time, I suggested he come round to my flat. Amina was away for the weekend, and I knew what the invitation meant – I couldn't have been more obvious if I'd said, 'Netflix and chill,' instead of, 'I'll cook.'

I spent the day making a lasagne – the kind of proper, home comfort food I reckoned he'd have missed while working away. I cleaned the flat to within an inch of its life and shaved every bit of superfluous hair off my body. I lit scented candles and put fresh sheets on my bed.

When Patch turned up with a bunch of roses and a bottle of champagne, I knew he'd understood the message just as clearly as I had. As soon as he walked in the door, we hugged each other as if we were nothing more than friends, but the tension was as palpable as the relentlessly fluttering butterflies in my stomach.

'This is nice,' he said, looking around the tidy living room and inhaling the smell of cooking. 'It feels... homely. I never thought of you as a domestic goddess.'

'I'm not any kind of goddess,' I said. 'But I cook a mean lasagne.'

'Music to my ears.'

'Shall I open this?' I took the champagne from him.

'I think we could both do with a drink.'

I poured two glasses and we sat on the sofa, a polite few inches of fabric between us. We clinked our glasses and drank. He asked me about work and I did the same. We talked about the weather – how boiling it was in London but Aberdeen was still cool during the day and chilly at night.

I began to panic. I was shy and awkward around him in a way I'd never been, with none of the easy companionability I'd felt before. It felt like there wasn't just one elephant in the room but a whole herd of them, waving their trunks and stomping all over my carefully curated romantic evening.

'Have you heard from Zara?' I asked carefully.

Patch shook his head. Then he said, 'Look, is that lasagne almost ready?'

I thought, *Shit. Now he can't wait to eat and get the hell out of here, and I don't blame him.* 'Just a couple of minutes.'

'My mum reckons it's best if you leave it to rest for a bit. Like, half an hour or so.'

'Really?' Now we were exchanging cooking tips. *There's no coming back from this*, I thought.

But when I looked at him, he met my eyes with a smile that suggested food was the last thing on his mind. The butterflies sprang back to life inside me.

'I'll take it out of the oven,' I said.

My legs suddenly seemed to have been replaced by strands of wet spaghetti. I got up and opened the oven door, leaning my face into the blast of hot air to hide the fact that I was blushing. I lifted the dish out and put it on the worktop, then turned off the gas.

Patch poured more champagne into our glasses.

'This is all kinds of weird,' he said gently. 'It is for me, anyway, and I reckon for you too.'

I nodded, taking a gulp of my drink, the bubbles tingling my nose.

'I care about you, Naomi,' he went on. 'I don't want to do anything that doesn't feel right for you.'

'Same,' I muttered.

'Come here,' he said.

I put the oven gloves down and stepped towards him, into the warm circle of his arms. He held me tenderly, stroking my hair. And then I felt what I'd felt before, by the canal in Camden – a steady flame of desire like the pilot light on a boiler that burns unnoticed in the background until you turn up the heating.

I turned my face up to his and kissed him on the lips, hesitantly at first and then more passionately, remembering what it had been like that night, the feel of his back and shoulders under my hands both familiar and exciting.

His hands moved from my hair to my face, down to my arms, round my waist, touching me like I was made of glass. But I didn't feel fragile – I felt suddenly powerful, ready, sexy.

'Come on.' I broke off our kiss and smiled up at him. 'Bedroom. Let's do this.'

He laughed. 'Wow. No messing about, then.'

'Lots of messing about,' I promised, reaching up to undo the buttons of his shirt. 'All the messing about you could possibly want.'

By the time we reached my bed we were both naked, a trail of garments following us from the kitchen, up the stairs and to my door. There was no need to close it because no one would see us.

The light from the landing illuminated his perfect body – the kind of physique I'd thought didn't exist other than on Greek marble statues and the cover of *Men's Health* magazine. But now I could see that – although breathtakingly desirable – he wasn't flawless after all. There was a mole on his right shoulder, a tiny egg shape of darker skin. He'd missed a bit on his jaw when he was shaving, and I could feel the roughness of it when he kissed me. On his left thigh, right up near his hip, there was a scar – an irregular bit of white skin where no hair grew.

I ran my thumb over it. 'What happened there?'

'Gunshot wound,' he murmured, his voice muffled by my hair. 'You should see the other guy.'

'Really?' I was almost sure he was joking, but not quite.

'Nah.' He raised his head and grinned at me. 'Wiped out off my BMX when I was eight.'

I laughed, my nerves vanishing as I remembered that we were friends – we'd been friends before all this, and we'd still be friends after. I didn't care that I was far from perfect myself and hadn't been near a gym in months – I knew he wanted me just as much as I wanted him.

I pushed him gently down on the bed and straddled him, smiling down at him, my hair brushing his chest. Then I lowered myself on to him and kissed him again, feeling us begin to move together, fitting together perfectly.

TWENTY-FOUR

'They're asleep,' I told Bridget. 'Fingers crossed they'll stay that way – at least until four in the morning, when they wake me up.'

'Oh, bless you.' She reached over and touched my cheek. 'I remember those years like they were yesterday. Funny, because it was all a blur at the time. You think it'll last forever, but it's over in the blink of an eye.'

You think it'll last forever. Her words seemed to have a different meaning – one I really didn't want to consider right then, or ever, if that was an option.

'There's a lasagne in the oven. It'll be ready in half an hour, but I've set the timer just in case.'

Bridget looked doubtfully at the cooker like it was some piece of space-age technology that couldn't quite be trusted, then at her watch.

'Delicious,' she said. 'Wherever you're off to, I doubt they'll feed you so well.'

'It's just a Thai place round the corner. Patch is meeting me there when he's finished at the gym.'

Which hopefully wouldn't mean me sitting there on my own for ages drinking wine like a Tinder date gone wrong.

'And you look beautiful. You should wear green more often, with your colouring.'

'Thank you.' I'd only had time to throw on a clean jumper over my jeans and put on some mascara while the kids were in the bath, but her compliment made me smile. 'We should be back by ten, and then Patch will get an Uber home with you.'

'All set then. Have a lovely evening, Zar— Naomi.'

I hesitated, doubt creeping into my mind. Bridget's absent-mindedness seemed to come and go – when I'd asked her to babysit so Patch and I could go out for a date night, she'd seemed alert and eager to help. But her vagueness troubled me – what if there was an emergency and she didn't know what to do?

We're only down the road. The children are asleep. This is important. What could possibly go wrong?

So I kissed her on the cheek, picked up my bag and left.

The clocks had gone forward the previous week and it was still light, the new leaves on the chestnut trees acid green against the sapphire sky. Soon, the children would be playing in the park in shorts and T-shirts instead of coats and wellies; soon, we'd be planning outings to the seaside, sandcastles and fish and chips.

Maybe. If my conversation with my husband tonight went as I hoped it would, rather than as I feared it might.

As I'd expected, Patch was late. I sat on a wooden bench, my back to the distressed brick wall, sipping pinot grigio and trying not to scoff all the prawn crackers in my anxiousness. The restaurant was busy – couples out for early dinners, families with older children, groups of students drinking lager and making the most of the Tuesday night all-you-can-eat special. Alone on the end of the long communal table, I felt shy and out of place.

It wouldn't have been my first choice of venue for the conversation we needed to have, but the words 'all-you-can-eat' had always been music to Patch's ears. So I wasn't surprised when he came striding in, just ten minutes after I'd arrived, his face wreathed in the easy-going grin that had always melted my heart.

'Hello, beautiful.' He leaned over and kissed me, and I smelled the shower gel I'd given him for his birthday, which was perfect for the gym because it came in a tiny bottle but cost about a tenner per squirt.

'Hey. Good day?'

'So much better now I'm here with you.' He swung a long thigh over the bench and settled down. 'God, I'm Hank Marvin. That workout they made us do was extra.'

He launched into what would have been a long explanation about sets of burpees, snatches and cleans (whatever they were – certainly not something he did a good deal of around the house), but fortunately was interrupted by a waitress bringing over our menus.

'How shall we do this?' I asked, knowing that there was no point expecting him to focus on anything until the pressing issue of food was dealt with. 'One each of the starters then share a couple of the mains?'

'Maybe double up on the chicken wings?'

'Really? You know I don't really like them.'

'But I really, really do.' He smiled at the waitress, who smiled back. I wondered whether she was thinking: *Look at this hunk of a man with his healthy appetite*, or *God, we always get the greedy bastards on Tuesday nights*.

I wasn't exactly sure what I was thinking myself.

'Whatever you think,' I said. 'Go wild. And I'll have another glass of wine, please.'

'And a beer for me,' Patch said, when he'd finishing placing a lengthy food order.

Soon, platters and bowls began arriving at our table, occupying more than our share of space and forcing the students next to us to budge up. I lifted a couple of sweetcorn fritters and a pork dumpling on to my plate and ate slowly, waiting for Patch to placate the ravening beast that was his post-workout hunger.

'So,' he said at last, when the starters had stopped coming and dishes of noodles, red curry and rice had arrived. 'This is nice. We haven't had a date night in ages.'

'Yeah, and your mum said it was a while since she'd had an evening with the kids. So I thought, why not?' I raised my wine glass and tapped it against the rim of his beer bottle. 'And besides, there's something I wanted to ask you.'

'Is it about you going back to work? Look, we can make it work if we have to, I guess. But are you sure it's what you really want? You'll end up spending virtually everything you earn on childcare and—'

I dug my chopsticks into the bowl in front of me and lifted out a prawn, but my hands weren't quite steady and I fumbled, letting it fall back before it reached my mouth.

'It's not about that,' I said. 'Don't worry – we can talk about that another time. This is something else.'

'Jeez,' he grumbled. 'Here I am thinking I'll have a nice evening out with my wife and it turns into a summit conference. Okay, hit me with it.'

I waited until he'd piled his plate with rice, pork and salad. 'Okay. It's more of a question, really. When did you actually break up with Zara?'

'Oh, God, Nome. Not this ancient history.' He put his chopsticks down and raked a hand through his hair. 'I can't remember. What are you looking for – day, month, hour?'

I felt a flare of annoyance at his flippancy. 'Patch, come on. It's important.'

'No, it's not. You and I are together now – that's the important thing.'

'It's important to me,' I insisted. 'I mean – not the day or the hour, obviously. But whether it was before or after... you know.'

'Before or after we shagged?' he asked, too loudly.

The girl sitting next to him paused, a forkful of food hovering mid-air. Then she put it down and whispered something to the bloke next to her. *Give me a second, I need to hear what this couple are saying,* maybe.

'Yes. I mean, no. More like before or after we started going out, like, properly.'

'Oh, come on.' He rolled his eyes. 'What's properly? We'd known each other for years. We didn't need to do the whole "exclusive" thing and have a coming-off-the-apps ceremony.'

'No, we didn't. Because after we'd got together, I would never, ever have had anything going on with anyone else.'

And for ages before, because as far as I was concerned no one else could ever have measured up to Patch.

'Naomi.' He put his chopsticks down and took a long swallow of lager. 'Here's the thing. As soon as I met you – okay, maybe not the very first time, but pretty much straight away – I fell for you. I knew it was you I wanted to be with. I tried to do the right thing by Zee. I really, really didn't want to hurt her. So I put aside my feelings for you for a long time, but it was hard.'

As soon as I met you, I fell for you. He'd never told me that before. Even now, with all the years that had passed, all the times we'd said we loved each other, it gave me a thrill of happiness. If I'd known back then that he'd felt the same as me, right from the beginning, would I have done things differently?

The knowledge was bittersweet. *If only you'd told me, everything would have been so much easier.*

'But you were with someone else.'

'But you were hanging around looking so bloody pretty I could barely keep my hands off you.'

'That's sweet. But you did keep your hands off me, because you were with Zara. Until you didn't. And I need to know whether you were still with her then or not.'

'For God's sake. It doesn't—'

'Yes, it does.'

We looked at each other across the table. His face was so familiar – as handsome as it had always been, his eyes the same rich, deep brown, just a few wrinkles at their corners. His hair the same glossy black, just a few silver threads running through it.

I remembered how it felt to love him so much it was like a pain.

He sighed. 'Okay. Let's not beat around the bush. There was an overlap.'

'When we went to that gig in Camden?'

'Then, and... after. For a bit.'

'How long of a bit?'

'I can't remember!' He raised his hand, making a fist as if he was about to thump the table, then brought it down again, gently, and placed it over mine.

'Was it, like, days? Or weeks or what? Longer?'

'It was... weeks. Maybe a month. Or two.'

My mouth felt dry. I drank the last of the wine in my glass and then a gulp of water. 'Why did you tell me you'd ended it with her?'

'Because I didn't want to fuck things up. I knew, really early on, that you were right for me and Zee wasn't. You were – you are – everything I'd always needed. Smart, gentle, loving. I wanted you to be the mother of my kids, even back then. I knew how amazing you'd be at that. But Zee – come on, you know her as well as I do.'

'What about her?'

'She's volatile. Unstable. I didn't want to hurt her. And...' A shadow passed over his face – an echo of the conflict I'd seen back when I was first falling in love with him.

'And what?' I asked gently.

'I was worried about what she'd do – how she'd react.' He twisted his paper napkin like he was wringing water out of it. 'I had to time it right, let her down gently.'

'Your timing doesn't look like it was so great from where I'm sitting.'

'Yeah, well.' He shrugged. 'Maybe I should have done it sooner. My bad. Hindsight's twenty-twenty, right? But at the time, I thought I was doing the right thing.'

'I tried to do the right thing, too,' I said. 'But I still don't know if it was right.'

'If what was right? You and me, or – something else?'

I remembered how I'd felt back then, about the secret Zara had asked me to keep. How dishonest it had felt – how disloyal to Patch and mostly to myself. But loyalty to Zara had won out – until it hadn't.

I still hadn't broken that promise, not for all these years. Should I break it now? Could I?

'Patch,' I began hesitantly, 'did you know – when Zara couldn't see you on your weekends off – did you ever suspect there might be something else going on?'

'What are you talking about? I knew what was going on.'

My mind whirled. Patch was a kind, tolerant man – always had been. But surely he wouldn't have blithely carried on a relationship with a woman he knew was cheating on him, however deeply he'd been in love with her?

Before I could formulate a question, he carried on. 'She told me about her brother. She was ashamed – she didn't want anyone else to know, so I promised I'd never tell.'

I leaned in towards him, confused. The restaurant was noisy – the students next to us had given up eavesdropping on our conversation and were laughing and cheers-ing one another; perhaps I'd misheard him. 'Brother? What brother?'

He shrugged. 'See? She never told anyone but me. But I don't suppose it matters any more; he'll have been released by now.'

'Released? From – prison?'

Patch nodded. 'He was serving a sentence in Greece, for smuggling cocaine. She said he'd always been troubled. She went to visit him there when she could, and sometimes that coincided with my weekends off so we couldn't see each other. It was one of the reasons why I – why I wanted to protect her. I didn't want anything else bad to happen to her.'

My chopsticks were frozen halfway between my bowl and my mouth. I had no idea what to say. Maybe the story about Zara's brother was true and what she'd told me about seeing other men wasn't. Maybe it was the other way round. Maybe both things were true – or neither.

But I knew one thing for sure – I'd wanted to protect Patch from hurt then and I still did now. Telling him she'd lied to him and betrayed him might have helped me get what I wanted then, but it would achieve nothing now that I had it.

His lie about having broken up with Zara made a bit more sense now. He'd wanted to protect her, even though he'd gone about it in the clumsiest possible way. But his actions had had another consequence – one I doubted he'd even considered at the time. He'd made me into the other woman; he'd made me betray my friend. And now all my protestations to Rowan about how things had happened had turned out to be lies, and Zara's version of events the truth.

'Still though,' I said. 'It doesn't feel right. It feels like you've been lying to me, all this time.'

'Oh, for God's sake. Naomi, stop raking over the bloody past. It's done now. What matters is— Is that your phone ringing?'

'My – shit.' I bent over to retrieve my bag from the floor, banging my head on the table on the way back up. My eyes watering, I fumbled through it until I found my phone.

'It's your mother. God, I hope the kids are—' I swiped to answer the call. 'Bridget? Hi. Is everything all right?'

For a moment, I thought the call had failed – all I could hear was a high-pitched electronic wailing.

Then I heard my mother-in-law's voice, sounding panicked and shaky and suddenly very old. 'Naomi? The smoke alarm's going off and I can't make it stop.'

TWENTY-FIVE

Patch leaped to his feet, signalling to the waitress and pulling a few twenty-pound notes from his wallet. 'Do you know if they include service? I don't want to stiff our poor waitress.'

'Let's just leave extra and get back,' I urged.

I was already standing up, my coat on and my bag over my shoulder. My phone was still pressed to my ear. 'Don't worry, Bridget. We'll be there in five minutes, tops, okay? Are the kids all right?'

But I couldn't hear her answer over the wailing of the alarm in the background and the buzz of voices around me in the restaurant.

'Right, sorted.' Patch headed for the door and I followed him, weaving my way between the crowded benches, feeling as if I was in one of those nightmares where, no matter how quickly you move, you can't seem to reach your destination.

As soon as we turned the corner into our road, we heard the alarm, its shriek cutting through the still darkness. Patch increased his pace and I jogged to keep up, my mind filling with horrors. The top floor of the house on fire and the children trapped in their bedroom. The fire service turning up, flames silhouetting Toby and Meredith perched on the windowsill and me standing helplessly below exhorting them to *Jump, jump!* Fire engulfing the loft where all the kids' baby clothes, our Christmas decorations and my wedding dress were stored.

Ahead of me, I could see our open front door, smoke hovering in the amber light of the street lamp above. Its colour reminded me of flames. As we drew nearer, I could see Bridget standing in the doorway, her arms wrapped around her. Above the din of the alarm, I could hear Toby crying and Meredith screaming, 'Mummy! Mummy!'

The neighbours' upstairs windows were open and pale, anxious faces peered out.

Patch reached the house ahead of me. He put a hand on his mother's shoulder for the briefest second before nudging her out of the way and entering the house. I imagined him dashing up the stairs, taking them two at a time, reaching the first floor and finding – what?

'What happened?' I gasped, squatting down in the doorway and pulling the twins close against my body, hearing Meredith's screams turn to sobs, feeling Toby's tears hot and wet against my face. 'It's okay, darlings. Mummy and Daddy are here. It's going to be all right.'

'The lasagne.' Bridget dropped to her knees next to me, clutching the door frame for support. 'I left it in the oven like you said, but I was watching television and I didn't hear the timer thing. Then when I remembered and opened the oven there was smoke everywhere and the alarm went off and I couldn't make it stop.'

Thank God. There had been no fire – just a minor domestic crisis and the alarm doing its job.

'It's okay, Bridget. Deep breaths.'

I could see she was trembling and beginning to cry. 'I'm so sorry, Naomi. What was I thinking?'

Abruptly, the alarm stopped. From the kitchen, I heard the roar of the extractor fan start up.

Patch emerged, a wooden spoon in his hand. 'Those sensors are too high for Mum to have reached,' he said, 'even if we'd shown her the old kitchen utensil hack. I've opened the back door and the windows upstairs – the smoke should clear in a few minutes. Let's all get inside, shall we?'

'See?' I told the children. 'Everything's okay. Look at that horrid burnt dinner, though. Poor Granny must be starving. Would you like some toast, Bridget? And a cup of sweet tea?'

'There was smoke everywhere,' Toby said, his eyes wide.

'And then the alarm woke me up.' Meredith pressed herself against me. I could feel her small body shivering through her Peppa Pig pyjamas. 'I thought it was Daddy getting up for work but it wouldn't stop. And then I started coughing and coughing.'

'I don't know why I didn't notice earlier,' Bridget said, clasping her hands together and squeezing them like she was doing a Covid-era hand-sanitising routine. 'I must have been miles away. And I was responsible for Patrick and Niamh.'

My eyes met Patch's over Bridget's head and the flash of panic in his face made me realise how desperately he'd been trying not to confront the knowledge that things with his mother weren't right.

'Mummy.' Toby pulled at my hand, and tugged again when I didn't respond straight away. 'Mummy?'

'What is it, darling?'

'If the house burnt down, would the firemen rescue Blue Bear?'

Stupidly, the thought of my son's beloved teddy being lost to the flames brought me closer to tears than I'd been all evening. 'Sweetheart, the house didn't burn down. If there'd been an actual fire – which there wasn't – the fire fighters would have come and put it out long before that could happen.'

'But what about Blue Bear?'

'He'd have been found soggy but unharmed upstairs in your bed,' I said firmly.

I had no idea whether this was true – or whether telling my children reassuring half-truths was the right thing to do in the circumstances or the worst parenting cop-out ever. Rationally, of course, I knew that in the event of a fire Blue Bear and Meredith's beloved orange camel would have been consigned to the flames without anyone thinking twice about it, along with my wedding dress and all our other treasured possessions.

'Would you like to stay over, Mum?' I heard Patch saying gently. 'You're more than welcome, if you'd prefer not to go home on your own. You've had a shock.'

'I should wash up that lasagne dish,' Bridget fretted. 'It'll need a good long soak with a scoop of biological washing powder and then a scrub. That's the thing with Pyrex, burnt bits get caught in all the nooks and crannies.'

'Come on, Meredith and Toby,' I encouraged. 'Let's get the two of you to bed. It's late now. Everything's going to be all right, and I'll stay with you until you both fall asleep, okay?'

Leaving Patch to comfort his mother, I took the children's hands and led them upstairs. There was still a whiff of smoke in the air, but it wasn't as bad as the kitchen. I opened the window in their room and tucked them up, planting kisses on their foreheads and reassuring them that everything would be all right now, Mummy and Daddy were here.

My mind kept returning to the possessions we might have lost, but hadn't. Every time it did, I tried to force it away – to tell myself that those things, however important they felt, were just stuff that could either be replaced, or would remain in our lives in the form of memories.

Then I realised – they weren't insignificant. They represented not just the past, but our future together as a family. One day, Meredith (or Toby, obviously – there was no way I wanted to be that kind of parent) would ask to try on my wedding dress, and I'd watch them parade around in it and tell them they looked beautiful. Toby's teddy would be there for him as long as he needed it, and when eventually he didn't, I'd know it meant that Blue Bear had played his part in my son becoming secure and independent. The Christmas decorations would be brought down from the loft year after year – the cheap, moulting tinsel Patch and I had bought the first year we lived together; the set of three glittering glass spheres the Girlfriends' Club had given us for a wedding present; the cotton wool snowmen the children had made at a craft session, which were already dusty and greying – and as the children grew older they'd come to recognise their favourite ones, confident that they'd be there to hang on the tree every time.

It wasn't just stuff – it was the physical fabric of what made us a family.

And it could all have been lost – not by a fire that had never actually happened, but by me. By me deciding that the foundations on which Patch's and my marriage was built were too insubstantial to withstand further construction – that because the way things had started had been flawed, the future automatically would be, too.

'Jesus, Naomi,' I muttered. 'What a bloody fool.'

Toby was sleeping now, his thumb resting near his mouth in case he needed it during the night. Meredith was dropping off, her eyelashes fluttering involuntarily over her cheeks, their smoothness marred by drifts of dried tears.

As silently as I could, I stood up and tiptoed across the floor, giving them one last look before turning the light off and pulling the door closed behind me. The lights were still on downstairs, but I couldn't hear voices – Patch must have organised a taxi to take Bridget home.

I found him in the kitchen, slumped over the table, a glass of whisky in front of him.

When he heard my footsteps, he raised his head. 'Kids down?'

I nodded. 'Is there any left in that bottle?'

'Plenty. You want ice?'

'Yes, please.'

'Quite the night, hey?'

'It was awful.' I sat down opposite him and sipped my drink. I never normally drank whisky and this reminded me why – it was vile. The peaty taste that was meant to make it special just made it taste medicinal and burnt to me. But then, I supposed, lots of things were going to taste burnt for a while.

'I mean, it wasn't awful really,' Patch said. 'It was just a false alarm – literally.'

'You did well, though. Quite the Boy Scout, with your wooden spoon.'

He laughed. 'Be prepared, right? Except I wasn't – I had to get it out of the drawer. Maybe I should carry it with me all the time.'

'Like your pocket knife.'

'A pocket spoon. Good shout.'

We smiled at each other – a tentative agreement that the almost-row we'd had earlier could be forgotten, set aside, deemed unimportant in the light of what had happened afterwards.

I couldn't change the past, anyway. I could only apologise to Zara and explain to Rowan, Kate and Abbie that I genuinely hadn't known about the overlap between our relationships with Patch. Explain that had I known, I'd have acted differently. Hope they understood that a matter of weeks when things were complicated wasn't enough to undermine a marriage that had lasted years.

Then I thought of something else.

'Patch?'

'What?' He swirled the whisky in his glass, the ice cube clinking against its sides.

'That camera. The one Zara had. What's on it?'

'Photos,' he said, his face expressionless. 'What do you think?'

'Yes, but photos of... what? Of the time when you and she were still... and I was already...?'

He looked up at me, his immobile features suddenly slackening with what I guessed must be relief. 'That's right.'

'So that's why Zara gave it to me.' Anger and remorse flared inside me. 'To prove that she was right and I was wrong.'

'Except she didn't have to prove anything. I've told you now.'

With a scrape, he pushed back his chair and left the room. I heard his feet on the stairs – *For God's sake, don't wake the kids*, I thought – and then the snap of our bedroom light switch and the rumble of a drawer opening and closing.

When he returned, I thought at first he was empty-handed, and then I saw the tiny sliver of grey plastic in his hand, a gold label shining on its side. He held it out to me.

'The memory card?' I asked, although it was obvious that was what it was.

He nodded. 'We don't need it now. It's all out in the open.'

I turned it over in my fingers, looking at it. I remembered what I'd said to Zara all those years before, in Paris: *All you have left is trust.*

I handed it back to him and he took it delicately, then flexed his two thumbs and forefingers around it and snapped it in half. He snapped each piece in half again, then dropped them all in the bin.

Then he stepped over to me, placed those same strong fingers tenderly on the sides of my face, and kissed me.

'There,' he said. 'That's done. I think I'll head up to bed.'

'I'll join you when I've finished my drink.'

I waited until I heard our bedroom door close, then walked softly over to the bin and opened it. The four fragments of plastic, each less than half an inch across, lay on top of a discarded teabag. Of course, they weren't just plastic. In there somewhere would be a microchip, possibly made of silicon, tiny transistors and resistors and other things I didn't know the names of, metals like copper or perhaps even gold. And also, maybe, the data itself, undamaged and recoverable.

Except I wasn't going to try and recover it. Patch had told me the truth and I was choosing to trust that.

I closed the bin and fetched my phone from the hallway where I'd abandoned my bag earlier. The Girlfriends' Club WhatsApp had been quiet that day, as it had been for the past couple of weeks. The question of the second, secret group that might or might not exist niggled at my mind, but I posted anyway.

NAOMI:

> Evening all. How's everyone's day been? Just wanted to let you know Patch and I had a good chat tonight.

ABBIE:

> Evening. Just got into bed, I'm knackered. What about?

NAOMI:

> The whole Zara thing. Turns out there was an overlap between her and me. He admitted it.

KATE:

> Oh no. Shit, Nome, that's a lot to take in.

ROWAN:

> Babe, I'm so sorry. What are you going to do?

ABBIE:

Jesus. No wonder Zara was angry. You must be
raging too. Why did he do that?

NAOMI:

I don't know. I feel really bad for Zara,
obviously. But I can't chuck it all away over
something that happened years and years ago,
can I?

I watched my screen. Two blue ticks appeared next to my
message. Abbie started typing, then stopped. Then Rowan
typed something, but didn't post it. My screen stayed blank.

It stayed blank for a long time. I imagined all of them over
on another group, talking about me. It felt horrible. All the
emotions of the evening rushed in on me – anger; fear; the
looming presence of grief that had never descended; the sure
knowledge that, now, Bridget could surely never be left alone
with my children again.

My friends didn't know what had happened, but they knew
I needed their support, and they were choosing to withhold it,
and the pain of that was almost worse than all the other things.
Now that they knew Zara had been right about what I'd done,
they were choosing to take her side over mine, and I couldn't say
I blamed them.

Especially now Zara had been diagnosed with cancer.

As soon as the thought entered my mind, I hated myself for
it. I tried to erase it, to unthink it, but of course I couldn't.

Instead I tapped the top of the screen, scrolled down to the
bottom and tapped the red words that said, 'Exit Group'.

TWENTY-SIX

SUMMER 2011

Two weeks after that first night with Patch, I took Rowan and Clara out for ice cream in a park near Rowan's flat. Clara had strawberry, Rowan coffee pecan, and I had pistachio. Although, inevitably, Clara spilled hers down her front and Rowan and I had to share ours to console her.

'God knows if she'll sleep tonight,' Rowan said. 'They weren't shy with the espresso in that.'

As if she'd already felt the caffeine hit, Clara went dashing off over the grass, her legs chubby and strong under her blue cotton dress.

'Ro? Is it okay if I tell you something?'

'You're seeing Patch, aren't you?'

I twisted my sticky fingers in my paper napkin. 'Yeah. I mean, kind of.'

'I hope it's not "kind of",' Rowan said sternly.

'What? Why?'

'Because it's been blatantly obvious from day dot that you were head-over-heels smitten with him, and if there's any "kind of" about it, you'll get hurt for sure.'

'It's been over between him and Zara for weeks.' I felt compelled to get this vital detail in early.

'I figured. I mean, you wouldn't have let it happen if it wasn't, right?'

'Of course not.' I realised I was biting the skin around my thumbnail, and tucked my hand down in my lap. 'I feel bad enough as it is.'

Rowan sighed. 'I'm not surprised. It's not going to be easy.'

'But it's okay, isn't it?' I pleaded. 'He wasn't cheating on her with me.'

'I'm sure he wasn't. Zara's going to be cut up about it, but relationships end. Shit happens. Have you told her about it?'

I shook my head. 'Patch has. He said she's okay about it – well, okay-ish.'

'Don't you think you should speak to her?'

I put my feet up on the bench and hugged my knees, watching Clara run across the grass then plop down on her bottom and start pulling up daisies with her chubby little hands. If only my life could be as simple as hers was, I thought, with love guaranteed and heartbreak solved by a spoonful of gelato.

'Nome?' Rowan asked. 'Don't you think—'

'I should speak to Zara? Yeah, I know I should. But I'm...'

'Scared?'

I nodded.

'Look, I'm not saying you've done anything wrong.' Rowan turned to look at me, pushing up her sunglasses. There was only kindness and concern on her face. 'But at the same time, you need to own what's happened. There might be consequences. Zara probably won't take this well and putting off speaking to her isn't going to make it any easier.'

'But she—' I began, and then I stopped myself. The suspicions I had about Zara's own behaviour towards Patch – more than suspicions, now, more like a cast-iron certainty – would change everything, if I were to disclose them to Rowan and the others.

But I couldn't do that. I'd made a promise to her, and I didn't break promises to my friends. And besides, if the truth got out to the wider group, it would be only a matter of time before Patch found out. He'd be hurt – more than hurt – and I didn't want to be the cause of that. Also, what if he were to probe me and discover how long I'd known about Zara's infidelity without having told him? I didn't want that, either.

Zara's secret would have to remain a secret. There was simply no alternative.

'But she what?' Rowan persisted.

'She's in Paris,' I said feebly.

'She's coming to London on the second Wednesday of next month,' Rowan said firmly. 'She told Kate and Kate told Abbie and Abbie told me. Put it off until then, if you want. Speak to her when we're all there. What's she going to do, bite you?'

I giggled nervously. 'I guess not.'

'Exactly. Big girl pants on, and just do it. It'll be okay.'

She hugged me and kissed my cheek, her lips smelling of coffee, and a few seconds later Clara ran over and jumped on the bench with us and we all had a cuddle in the warm sunshine.

Despite Rowan's assurances, I felt more and more anxious as the next Girlfriends' Club meeting approached. Patch was offshore again, so we could only communicate through text and brief phone calls and I didn't want to burden him with my worries about Zara. Every time my phone rang or vibrated, I felt a leap of excitement and hope that it would be him, then immediately a lurch of fear that it would be her.

Rowan was right, I told myself. The sooner I'd spoken to her and cleared the air, the better. I might not get her blessing for Patch's and my relationship, but at least we'd all be able to move forward. Our friends would be there, on hand to support me

and comfort Zara. In time, I thought in my rare moments of
optimism about the whole thing, we'd all be able to look back on
this and laugh.

Still, as that Wednesday approached, I found myself as
nervous as if I was going to a job interview – or had a perfor-
mance appraisal at which all my shortcomings would be laid
bare and judged. I longed to seek reassurance from Patch or
Rowan, or even pre-empt the evening's confrontation by
messaging Zara. But I couldn't think what I would say to any of
them. All I could do was wait, resolve to turn up and take whatever punishment Zara was going to dish out to me.

By seven thirty, I was at the appointed meeting place – a
busy Central London wine bar with glass tables, tubular
chrome chairs and face-brick walls hung with abstract artworks
in lurid shades of purple, green and orange. It was a venue we'd
never visited before and, fighting my way through crowds of
noisy City office workers to reach the bar, I hoped we never
would again.

I eventually managed to secure a bottle of rosé, five glasses
and a tiny bowl of olives that I parsimoniously calculated cost
about 50p each, and made my way back to our table. There I
sat, my glass dripping with condensation and my palms damp
with sweat, and waited.

Rowan was first to arrive. She hurried in, pausing at the
entrance and glancing around with worry in her eyes. All the
way from across the room, I could read her thoughts: *I'm late.
Am I too late?* I half-stood and waved to her and she hurried
over, relieved.

'Oh, thank God. Bloody Paul was late picking Clara up; I
was worried I'd abandoned you.'

'It's okay.' I managed a nervous smile. 'The others are even
later.'

'Now, you need to stop worrying, okay?' Rowan splashed
wine into her glass. 'It's just the Girlfriends' Club, right? Zara's

your friend. Even if she takes this badly, it'll be okay. You'll get through it.'

'I hope so.' I realised my hands were shaking, and took a big gulp of wine.

And then I saw them: Kate, Abbie and Zara, arriving together. Abbie was wearing faded skinny jeans and trainers. Kate was in one of the tailored shift dresses she wore when she needed to impress someone at work. Zara was wearing a silk scarf-print mini dress that showed off her slim, tanned arms and legs, outsize black sunglasses obscuring most of her face.

As soon as I saw the three of them, pushing shoulder-to-shoulder through the glass door, laughing, the sun bright on their hair, I thought, *They've been talking about me.*

Rowan must have seen the alarm on my face. 'It's okay, Nome. We've got this.'

As I watched, they exchanged a few more words, laughing again. Then Zara headed to the bar and Abbie and Kate came over to join us. We all exchanged hugs, just as we always did, but something felt different – wrong.

Before anyone could launch into the usual chat about how everyone's day had been, how glorious it was to see sunshine after weeks of rain, the excitement of the forthcoming London 2012 Olympics and all the rest of it, I felt the need to set out my stall.

'This is kind of awkward,' I began, fortifying myself with another large gulp of wine. 'Seeing Zara. I feel like I have to apologise to her.'

I looked at the three faces around the table, watching me silently. Rowan's was supportive – *Go on, Naomi. I'm here.* But Abbie and Kate looked more solemn, almost stern.

I felt as if I was a defendant in the witness box, my barrister preparing to let me speak my truth, the prosecution lining up to catch me out in any inconsistencies, and the victim waiting in the background for justice to be served.

'Is she okay?' I asked tentatively. 'I haven't spoken to her since... you know.'

'Since you nicked her boyfriend off her,' Kate said. Her voice was lighthearted, but there was an edge to her words I couldn't hide from.

Abbie gave her a look that said, Steady on.

'Is that what she thinks?' This was getting off to an even worse start than I'd feared. 'Is it really? Because that's not what happened.'

Over at the bar, I could see Zara leaning over, chatting to the barman, his smile flashing out at something she'd said.

'She's hurting, Naomi,' Abbie explained. 'Of course she's upset. She feels kind of betrayed by what happened.'

'I suppose she does,' I said miserably. 'I never meant for it to turn out this way, but it has.'

Zara turned back towards us, a silver ice bucket in her hands, and started to make her way towards the table. To anyone else in the room, she must have looked like just another attractive woman, maybe more than usually well dressed for a Wednesday evening. To me, she looked like an avenging angel.

She slipped into the free chair, setting the ice bucket down on the table, and looked at me. Her green eyes were like chips of glass.

I took a deep breath. 'Hi, Zara.'

'Hi, Naomi.' Her tone was mocking.

'It's good to see you,' I began. 'It's good because I wanted to say all this to you in person, and try and explain. About Patch and me. The thing is, as long as you were with him, nothing would've ever happened. I promise. I would never have let it and nor would he, because it would've been wrong.'

Zara nodded. 'And so you had to make sure he and I weren't together any more, so you could make your grubby little move.'

'I didn't!' I felt my face flame. 'I liked him. I'm not going to deny it – it would be stupid to deny it. He and I wouldn't be together now if there hadn't been something – the potential of something between us. But I'd never, ever have acted on it unless you'd split up.'

'You must be able to see how it looks, though, Nome,' Kate said. 'I love you – we all love you. But, you know. Girl code.'

'What does girl code say, though?' Rowan interjected. 'That Patch isn't allowed to get together with anyone Zara knows? Or that he and Naomi could date, but only if they waited however many months or years, like a Victorian mourning period? Help me out here, because I don't understand.'

'People deserve to be happy.' Abbie herself looked abjectly miserable. 'But when it's at the expense of someone else's happiness it makes it all... It makes it difficult.'

'Come on,' I said. 'Let's say I decided I wanted to steal Patch from Zara. Let's do a whatchamacallit – a thought experiment. Let's say he had no say in the matter at all, and it was all down to me. Let's say everything was perfect between them. How would I have done it? Because I know for a fact I couldn't have, even if I'd wanted to.'

'You did, though.' Zara looked at me steadily. 'You did the one thing you knew would work. Because he wouldn't have ended it with me any other way. You told him I'd been cheating on him. You lied to get him for yourself.'

I was blindsided – not just by the falsehood of Zara's accusation, but by the truth that lay so close to its surface. And as her words began to sink in, the injustice of them smarted even more. I could have done what she was accusing me of, months or even years before. Even when my feelings for Patch had been barely more than friendship, I could have told him what I knew, not out of self-interest, but to protect his feelings.

But I hadn't, because of the promise I'd made to her.

'Did you, Naomi?' Kate asked. 'Seriously? Because that would be—'

Again, I looked at the faces around the table: Zara's alight with anger, Kate doubtful, Abbie looking like she might be about to cry, Rowan flushed with rage on my behalf. Suddenly, I didn't want to defend myself any longer. I didn't want to do anything that would widen the fault lines I could sense already opening up in our friendship. I didn't want Rowan, Kate and Abbie to be forced to take sides. I didn't want me or Zara to be forced out. I wanted things to stay the way they were between us, and I was willing to do whatever it took to achieve that.

'Stop,' I said. 'Please. Can't we just stop? I'm sorry what happened hurt you, Zara. I really am. And I'm sorry it's put the rest of you in an impossible position. I never said anything to Patch about you, Zara, and I never would. But that's not important. What matters is us – this friendship. I don't want to fuck it up, not for anything. Not for a man. Not even for Patch.'

'What are you saying?' Rowan asked, her eyes wide.

'I'll end it with him,' I said. 'If it's going to cause a rift between the five of us and that's what it'd take to fix it, then that's what I'll do.'

'Don't be mad, Nome.' Abbie looked like she had just awoken from a dream. 'That's just – it's not necessary. Relationships end. You can't throw away your happiness because—'

'I agree with Abbie,' Rowan said. 'Honestly, Zara, I know it's tough for you. We'll all be here for you. But you can't blame Naomi for what happened. She's said she would never have deliberately set out to hurt you and I believe her.'

'I believe you too, Nome,' Kate said. 'I'm sorry I didn't for a while. It was unfair of me.'

Zara's eyes darted round the table, not still like glass any more but like dragonflies in flight, skimming over the surface of water. For a moment, I felt as if I was able to step inside her head, think what she was thinking.

They've chosen Naomi. They've chosen her over me, same as Patch did.

It wasn't true, but I could see why she felt that way. Perhaps I'd have felt like that too, in her position.

'Really, Zara.' I half-stood, reaching my hands out to her. 'I'm sorry. I'm so very—'

'No, you're not.' Her chair scraped back at she got to her feet, the table tilting and the glasses slipping as she leaned over to me, her lips twisted with anger. I could smell cigarette smoke on her breath and perfume on her hair. 'You're not one bit sorry. I know women like you – you act like a timid little mouse but you're a snake. You've got what you wanted now. Wait and see if it makes you happy – I know where my money is.'

'Zara, come on,' Kate interjected. 'I know you're upset, but try and calm—'

'Calm down? You're seriously expecting me to calm down after what she's done? And all of you falling in line because sweet little Naomi deserves to get what she wants? I'm not going to calm the fuck down and I'm not going to be part of this pathetic little clique for one more minute.'

Zara's hand swept over the table and for a second I wondered whether she was going to send all our glasses crashing to the floor, like a magician's trick gone horribly wrong. But she didn't.

She picked up her bag and drained the last of the wine in her glass, perched her sunglasses on top of her head and looked at us.

'Girlfriends' Club,' she spat. 'My God. You women wouldn't know friendship if it bit you in the arse. And it will – just wait and see.'

She wheeled round on her high heels and stalked away, straight through the crowded room to the exit door and out into the street.

There was a moment of dead silence after she left. Then Kate burst into shocked, almost hysterical laughter; Rowan started to cry; Abbie embraced her and found her a tissue.

Everyone asked if I was all right, and I said I just hoped Zara was all right. We talked of little else that evening – what we could have done differently, whether Zara would change her mind and whether the friendship could ever recover if she did, whether we should contact her and if so who, and when.

I don't think I contributed much to the conversation, though. I was torn between guilt, relief and an overwhelming shadow of fear: what if Zara wasn't done with me yet?

TWENTY-SEVEN

I woke early the next morning, feeling the warmth of Patch's body in bed next to me, then hearing the trill of his alarm and the rustle of the sheets as he stretched over to snooze it. Still half asleep, I lay still, conscious that something was different – something had happened.

My first realisation was of what hadn't happened. My house hadn't burned down. And my children hadn't woken up in the night.

The idea that the two things might somehow be connected made me sit bolt upright in bed, fear waking me more effectively than any alert on a mobile phone could have done. The events of the previous night came rushing back to me – my talk with Patch, Bridget's panicked call, the dash home, the discovery that everything was all right. But what if it wasn't? What if some sort of toxic fumes had been released into the air, and poisoned the twins in their sleep?

I pushed my feet into my slippers, snatched my dressing down off its hook on the back of the door, and stumbled to the children's room, opening the door slowly and fearfully.

They were both in bed, where I'd left them the night

before. As I watched, Meredith turned over, flinging one arm above her head outside the covers. Toby muttered something, reached for Blue Bear, found him, and burrowed deeper under the duvet.

Bewildered, I returned to our room and found Patch sitting on the edge of the bed, yawning, his phone in his hand.

'What's wrong?' he asked.

'Nothing. I mean – nothing's wrong. It's just weird. The kids slept through.'

'What? Are you sure?'

'They're both still sparko. This literally never happens.'

'You don't sound very pleased about it.'

'I am. Obviously. But – seriously, how do we even wake them up?'

'God. You're right. I have no idea.'

We looked at each other, then started to laugh. Of all the things I'd learned how to do as a parent – change nappies, breastfeed without flashing my tits to all and sundry, pick my battles, all the rest of it – this was a skill I'd never had to acquire. Of course, there might have been the occasional night when one or the other of them hadn't interrupted my sleep, but they'd always come into our room before I was fully awake, or called for us, or otherwise jerked me out of bed, grumbling and exhausted.

'Do you think this is it now?' Patch asked. 'Do you think they've cracked it and they'll do it for, like, ever?'

'I very much doubt it. Well, maybe when they're teenagers we'll have to drag them out of bed, kicking and screaming.'

'Them or us?'

'Dunno. Probably both.'

Together, we returned to the children's room. I'd left the door ajar and we stepped in, silently watching them for a second, lost in delighted surprise. Then Patch went over and pulled the curtains open. Morning light filled the room; I could see a rectangle of blue sky filling the window frame, bright with the promise of a warm spring day.

Patch and I stood together for a moment, looking down at our sleeping children. It was an amazing thing we'd done, I thought – the most amazing thing ever, creating these two perfect, small people out of our bodies and our love.

The idea should have filled me with joy, but it didn't – it made me feel inexplicably sad. If I'd known, on whichever of the countless occasions when we'd slept together that had resulted in a sperm and an egg – or rather, in the random case of my body, two eggs – that our relationship hadn't been what I'd trusted it was, would I have done things differently?

If I'd known when we were first together, delighted with the newness of our love, that I hadn't been the only woman in his life, would I have stuck around?

I wanted to believe that I wouldn't – that I'd never have allowed any of it to happen. But I'd been so besotted, so head over heels with him, so enthralled with the knowledge that he was finally mine, that I hadn't allowed any doubts to cloud my happiness.

But you did know, I reminded myself. *You knew, all along, when you were busy falling for him, that he was taken.*

But he told me he'd ended it.

Not until after you'd kissed him. He hadn't ended it then, but you went ahead and did it anyway.

I shook my head, as if I could physically dislodge the thoughts that were whirling through my mind. The children had woken while I was musing – Meredith instantly alert as she always was, Toby drowsy and yawning. On auto-pilot, I got them up and dressed, my distraction preventing me from entering the dreaded morning fishwife mode.

I made coffee for Patch and myself, stuck some bread in the toaster, then hurried upstairs and dressed, dragging a brush through my hair and wondering how on earth the likes of

Imogen managed to emerge from their houses groomed and stylish each morning. Did she have a nanny? A house husband? A time machine? Whichever it was, I needed some of it.

I'd made my choice – I was going to have to make the best of it. I'd made my bed (actually, I hadn't – the duvet was still scrunched up at its foot, Patch's pillow on the floor where he always threw it during the night) and I was going to have to lie in it.

'What time are you home tonight?' I asked Patch, noticing with a flicker of pleasure that he didn't have his gym bag over his shoulder as usual.

'Early. Seven thirty, eight? Maybe we could...?'

'I'll cook something nice,' I promised. 'Early night?'

'For sure.' He leaned in and kissed me, not the usual quick peck but a lingering contact between his lips and mine that felt like a promise.

Or perhaps not a promise – perhaps it was something else. A request, or even a plea for something. Something I wasn't sure I was able to give.

But I had to try. I owed that to Patch, and to myself. So, after dropping the children off, I flew into action. First, I went round to Bridget's and found her in good spirits, laughing about her mishap the previous night and apparently able to recall every detail of the incident clearly.

'You'll have to show me that wooden spoon trick of Patrick's,' she said. 'Next time, I'll know what to do and I won't have to interrupt your night out.'

Just a few hours before, I'd been certain that I'd never be able to ask her to babysit again, but now I second-guessed myself – what if it had just been a blip, a mistake anyone could have made? Depriving her and the children of the pleasure they took in one another's company on the basis of that seemed like an over-reaction. But still, it had happened. It had been real. And I was worried about her.

'Bridget,' I asked, 'when was the last time you saw your doctor? Just for – you know, a once over?'

'Are you suggesting I'm losing my marbles?' She put her teacup down firmly. 'Because I'm not. I'm perfectly fine.'

I felt a pang of sadness for her, and fear for what lay ahead. I loved her; she'd always been welcoming to me and her adoration of her grandchildren was one of the best things in their lives. And I hated doing this – ahead, I could see my role in managing her health and wellbeing increasing while Patch stood back and let me get on with it.

If I was going to take on that responsibility, I might as well start now.

'I'm not saying anything of the kind,' I told her firmly. 'I'm not a doctor – I have no idea. But I – and Patch and the children, and Niamh and her kids – want you around and well for as long as possible, right?'

She nodded slowly.

'There's probably nothing wrong at all,' I went on. 'But why not make an appointment, just for a check-up? Where's the harm in that?'

She made a vague, helpless gesture with her hands. 'I'm frightened they'll find something wrong, of course.'

'Oh, Bridget.' I got up and squatted down next to her, taking her hands in mine. 'Of course you are. But if there's anything wrong – and there might not even be – putting it off isn't going to help, is it?'

She looked down at me, and for a second I saw the fear in her eyes. 'I'm only seventy-five, you know.'

'Exactly! You'll be around to see Toby and Meredith graduate from university for sure. So why not stop worrying and just do it?'

'All right,' she promised. 'I will.'

Shortly afterwards, I hurried home and set about cleaning the house from top to bottom. I walked to the high street and bought lamp chops at the fancy organic butcher rather than raiding the supermarket as usual. I begged the woman in the beauty salon for a last-minute appointment and had the hair ripped off my legs and bikini line with hot wax.

I kept myself so busy that I barely had time to think of the Girlfriends' Club WhatsApp, or wonder what might be being said on there without me – about me.

Overnight, the feeling of outraged injustice had died down and been replaced with hollow sadness. For well over a decade, my friends had been my sounding board, my home base, my lifeline. And now I'd chosen to walk away.

Or perhaps I'd chosen to jump before I was pushed. When I'd needed them most, they hadn't been there. They'd heard the other side of the story – Zara's side, no doubt told to them when I wasn't there, and then confirmed by me – and their little jury of three was still out on who to support.

Well, I'd made my choice. Without my friends, I'd have to make my own way, and that meant I needed my husband more than ever. I was going to stick by him – stand by my man, as a tabloid newspaper would have put it, if Patch was a philandering footballer and I was his long-suffering, hair-extensioned wife – and my family, even if it meant sacrificing my relationship with my friends.

Already, with my initial anger having cooled, I could feel the void. Looking at the package of lamb chops, blood seeping through their paper wrapping, I remembered the incredible potato dish Kate had once made, loaded with cream and garlic, and thought how, just a few days before, I'd have messaged to ask her for the recipe. I thought how I could have shared the news of the twins' sleeping through the night with Rowan, and how she'd join me in punching the air triumphantly but be there to console me if – as would almost certainly happen – it all went tits up again in a night or two. I imagined commiserating with Abbie over the excruciating pain of my Brazilian wax, and how she'd be able to recommend exactly the right combination of ice packs, aloe vera and paracetamol to soothe it.

But there was no point dwelling on that now. While the children splashed in the bath, I had a lightning shower. Then I dried them off, got them into bed and read them a story, trying to conceal my urgency. (*Hurry up and go to sleep. Don't mess me around tonight. And once you're asleep, it would be fricking amazing if you could maybe stay that way for, like, eight hours? Maybe?*)

And then, dressed in my nicest underwear and a jersey wrap dress that Patch had always liked and which by some miracle still fitted me, I went downstairs, set the kitchen table, lit candles and opened a bottle of wine.

On the morning of Andy's funeral, I'd asked myself when I'd last had sex with my husband and remembered that it had been Christmas Eve. And now, Christmas Eve was still the last time.

And the time before that? On Patch's birthday, obviously. In June.

It was normal, I'd told myself, after pregnancy, a painful, infected C-section wound, endless breastfeeding and broken nights. We'd get back on track, I'd thought.

But now the children were just months away from starting school and our track was nowhere in sight.

With relief, I heard Patch's key in the lock. I filled my wine glass, poured one for him, and met him in the kitchen doorway with a kiss.

'You look lovely.' He sounded surprised, which made his words less flattering than they should have been.

'Wait till you see what's for dinner,' I joked back. 'It'll be ten minutes. Want to grab a shower?'

Patch took in the candles, the smell of meat sizzling under the grill, the open bottle of wine.

'Sure.' He grinned and kissed me again. 'Be right back.'

After we'd eaten, I opened another bottle of merlot – excessive, probably, but in that moment I felt I needed all the Dutch courage there was going.

'Shall we sit on the sofa?' I suggested.

Patch slotted the last plate into the dishwasher. 'Sure. Unless you want to go upstairs?'

'Don't want to risk waking the kids.'

'Gotcha. Fail to prepare, prepare to fail.'

I laughed. Knowing he felt the same way I did about this – that it was some kind of make-or-break moment, a challenge to be risen to – gave me hope. We were a team – we were in this together.

He took my hand and led me out of the kitchen, flicking the light switch off as we went. The lamp next to the sofa glowed softly. The television was off. A Spotify playlist of nineties chill-out classics was playing.

'So,' he said, 'do you remember how we do this? Because it's been a while.'

'I think first you take off your shoes,' I joked, trying to hide how ridiculously nervous I felt.

'On it. Jeans as well?'

'As far as I can recall, yes. I mean, you could leave them on, but that would be...'

'Tricky?' He raised an eyebrow and I giggled, reassured that he was finding this just as awkward as I was.

'Yeah, I think I read that somewhere.'

We laughed. Feeling as apprehensive as someone about to go into a job interview, I watched as Patch unlaced his shoes and stepped out of his jeans. The muscles of his thighs were hard and defined. When he raised his arms to take off his shirt I saw his skin stretch taut over his abs and chest. Untying the belt of my dress, I felt painfully conscious of the extra few pounds I'd been meaning to lose for years, the stretch marks on my belly and thighs, the way my breasts would sag when I removed my bra.

It doesn't matter, I told myself. *You gave birth to his children. He loves you.*

But still, I wished I'd turned the light off.

Dropping my dress to the floor, I stepped towards him, feeling his strong arms around me, the warmth where our bodies met. I closed my eyes and waited for his kiss, and when it came I kissed him back, feeling the familiarity of his lips and tongue, waiting for the equally familiar surge of desire to fill me.

But it didn't come. And after a few moments, I realised it wasn't going to – and neither was I. I'd loved him more than I'd ever loved anyone. He was the father of my children. He was the most handsome man I'd ever kissed.

So why couldn't I make myself feel desire for him?

I didn't ask him to stop. I tried my best to enjoy it, without actually faking it. I told myself it would be all right; we loved each other, we were just out of practice. I told myself that trust could be rebuilt and intimacy return.

All the same, when it was over, I was conscious of a surge of bitter sadness.

Is this what I've signed up for? Is this how it's always going to be now?

TWENTY-EIGHT

For the next couple of weeks, I felt as if I was existing rather than living – enduring rather than enjoying my life. I woke every morning (or during the night, because the twins' smashing-it-out-the-park night's sleep was only occasionally repeated) feeling fairly normal, and then after a few seconds reality would kick in and a black cloud of gloom descend. I went through my daily routine on autopilot: getting dressed, getting the children dressed, making breakfast, taking them to nursery, dropping in on Bridget, doing housework, collecting the children, going to one or other of many activities, going home, giving them dinner, getting them to bed, preparing dinner for Patch and me.

It felt relentless. It felt soul-destroying. Even the weather wasn't helping – the promise of spring that had brought me so much cheer had lapsed into a wet, chilly, blustery May that tore the new leaves off the trees and had apparently frozen fledglings in their nests.

'Only a few months until they start school,' the other mums said at the nursery door. 'Hasn't it flown by?'

But even that landmark in my children's lives felt like it would be little more than a comma in my own. So they'd start school – then what? My own life would stay unchanged, endless days the same, only I'd be wrestling Toby and Meredith into uniforms each morning and dropping them off at a different building.

Sometimes, like a child peering through its fingers at a scary movie, I allowed myself to look further into the future. The children would grow older. Their primary school uniforms would be replaced with different ones. There'd be activities to ferry them to after dinner as well as before. And then, eventually, they'd leave home altogether, to university or homes of their own.

And then what? I'd be fifty-two, unemployed and probably unemployable, stuck in an empty house in a marriage I felt I'd achieved under false pretences. Bridget would be older, frailer, needing more care. Perhaps I'd have learned to play bridge, or joined the Women's Institute or a swingers' club, just to have something to do.

Not that anyone would want to play bridge with me, given that my brain would have atrophied from disuse. Or have sex with me, given that my vagina would have atrophied from menopause. Hopefully at least my scones would be decent, only I'd probably have given myself type two diabetes because I'd have no one to share them with.

And there was the crux of it. I was missing my friends. I wanted to have people I could complain to about the tedium of my life, who'd sympathise and then make suggestions about how I could make it less tedious. I wanted to shriek with laughter at the unthinkable cringeworthy images of swingers' parties. I wanted, when the time came, to compare notes on hot flushes and progesterone pessaries.

Maybe I'd make new friends. I'd already been for a coffee with Imogen and had a few glasses of wine with some of the other nursery mums after a playdate. One had suggested I join her yoga class.

But it wasn't the same. Those women – pleasant as they were – weren't my tribe. They weren't the Girlfriends' Club. They weren't the friends I'd believed were the only friends I'd ever want or need.

Patch seemed to sense my gloom.

One evening over dinner, when I was pouring the last of a bottle of wine into my glass, he asked, 'Is everything okay, Nome?'

'Fine,' I said, not looking him in the eyes. 'Just tired. Been a long day.'

'Wasn't yesterday the second Wednesday of the month? You didn't go out.'

'You were at the gym, and I don't feel comfortable leaving the kids with your mum. Not since the thing with the smoke alarm.'

'I'd have come home early.'

'It's been in the diary forever. You didn't offer.'

It was true – but also not true. I'd added the monthly Girl-friends' Club to my calendar years before and set it to repeat in perpetuity. Almost always, I'd gone, sorting out childcare one way or another. Occasionally, I hadn't been able to make it and then I'd grumbled to Patch about how miserable I was to miss it. But this time, I hadn't mentioned it. Sometime, I supposed, I'd delete the recurring event from my schedule, but I couldn't bring myself to do that just yet.

'How are they all, anyway?' Patch asked.

'Okay, I guess. Busy.'

And 'busy' was a guess, too. Every day, I'd looked at my WhatsApp home screen hoping that I might have been added back to the group, but I hadn't. Rowan had sent me a message asking if I was okay, and I'd replied coolly, saying I was all right, and how was she?

ROWAN:

Good

I miss you, Nome.

I'd left that olive branch there, read and unreplied to. I missed her, too – I missed them all so much it was like a part of me had been torn out, leaving a wound that wouldn't heal. But I stopped myself from reaching out to Rowan and asking her to meet up, or to intercede with the others, or to – something. Something that would make things go back to how they were.

One gloomy Tuesday afternoon, in the time when the children had been at nursery long enough for me to start missing them but pick-up time wasn't close enough for me to wish I could leave them there a bit longer, I was hunched at the kitchen table with my computer. The house was silent apart from the muted hum of the laptop fan. The day wasn't cold enough to have the heating switched on, but for some reason it appeared to have gone into overdrive. Perhaps it wasn't used to being worked so hard – a bit like my brain.

I wouldn't have been surprised if my own CPU had been about to burst into flames.

But I was getting nowhere.

I stood up from the kitchen table, stretching my tight shoulders, and poured another glass of water from the tap. I'd been sitting there, hunched over in a posture that was unfamiliar to me after so many years of not working at a desk, since getting back from dropping the children at nursery, and now it was almost time to pick them up again.

I'd sat down with the intention of catching up on LinkedIn, putting out some feelers to recruitment agents to let them know I might be back on the job market in the autumn. But my mind kept veering to Zara. The fragments of information she'd shared with me about her past. The different stories she appeared to have told my friends. The version of her past that Patch had kept secret for so long.

And, overshadowing it all, the revelation from Rowan that Zara was ill – Zara could be dying.

I couldn't believe it – I didn't want to believe it. But the picture Rowan had shown me on Zara's social media had all the hallmarks of authenticity. Before, when I'd felt vague doubts about the truth of something Zara had said about her background, or her family, or her whereabouts, I'd been able to brush it off – *It doesn't matter. She's our friend, and that's all that matters.* Besides, all the versions of her history I'd been exposed to before had been second-hand – something she'd said to Kate, or Patch, or Rowan, that didn't quite match with what I recalled her saying to me.

But this was about Zara today, not some shadowy past Zara.

The more I thought about it, the more puzzled I became. And then something had awoken in my brain – a part of my own past that felt so foreign to me now it was like a different version of me. Way back when I was at university, before the Girlfriends' Club, before Patch and the children, I'd imagined myself qualifying as a lawyer, prosecuting people who'd done wrong or defending those who'd been falsely accused.

I'd imagined my working life becoming a remorseless quest for justice and truth.

In the end, of course, it hadn't happened. My final degree was good, but not good enough for law school. So I'd decided to find work as a legal secretary, learn the ropes, gain contacts and experience, and seek to qualify later on. But life had got in the way – the need to pay the rent, the fact that I found the job I was doing interesting and absorbing enough not to hunger for more. Then I met Patch and our relationship took on such importance that I was happy to put my career on the back burner – and once we had the children, I'd had no choice but to put it on hold entirely.

Now, though, I could feel that old Naomi resurfacing – the girl who'd studied all night long, only realising when my alarm clock went off that I hadn't been to bed. The girl who'd loved to read and research and remember details.

I could put those rusty skills to work now, I thought, and discover the truth about Zara.

Except I couldn't.

A Google search for her name brought up a handful of unsurprising results – Zara Lovejoy reporting on the Fendi show at Milan Fashion Week, Fall 2015. Zara Lovejoy on the return of the over-the-knee boot. Could Natalie Bryant be the next Tyra Banks, asks Zara Lovejoy.

All of it was consistent with what Zara had told us about being a freelance fashion editor and stylist. But it all seemed – incomplete, somehow. There was no Zara Lovejoy profile on LinkedIn – well, there was, but she was a structural engineer based in Michigan. Entering zaralovejoy.com into my browser tab took me to a page offering to let me register the domain myself. Searches for freelance fashion writers in Paris yielded a number of names, but not Zara's.

So I turned back to social media, where I knew she had a presence. I was reluctant to look at her Facebook feed, because that would have meant following her again, and I didn't want her to see a notification warning her that I had. Fortunately, I discovered when I logged out of my profile and searched for hers, it was public, so I was able to view it anonymously.

Until recently, her feed had been full of fabulous clothes, trips to Milan, New York and Shanghai, Zara exuding effortless glamour. Then a few months back – shortly before Andy's funeral, I realised – all that had stopped. There was a post from early January with no picture accompanying it; it was just a few words on the screen.

So I went for a smear test last week. It's true what they say – French gynaes are the best! Dr Hubert can look at my bits any

time he likes, haha! And he'll be seeing a lot of them over the next
while, because I got the results back and they're not good.

There were a couple of dozen replies. Mostly along the
lines of, *Oh no, hun, are you okay?* but others saying things like,
Try not to worry. This happened to me and I freaked out! But I
had a procedure to zap the cells and now I'm fine. Bet you will
be too.

A few of the responses were in French, which I could only
read at the most basic level, but as far as I could tell they were
all saying much the same thing.

Then, three weeks later, there was another post.

So I had the surgery. Out of theatre now (general anaesthetic is
fucking bliss – they suggested going it under local but I said NO
NO NO). Feeling a bit woozy but okay. Hopefully they won't
need to keep me in overnight and me and what's left of my cervix
can go home. They kind of garrotted the dodgy bit off rather than
lasering it, so they can analyse the cells. Hope whoever's job that
is has fun with it – it'll be the most action my vag has seen in a
while.

This time, there were many, many more replies – over a
hundred of them. It seemed that somehow, since her initial post,
Zara had gained new friends. Again, the responses were loving,
supportive, exchanging the writers' own experiences.

A week later, she'd posted an update. This time, it was
accompanied by a photograph – Zara standing by an open
window with a soft-focus view of tree-tops and blue sky behind
her. She was wearing a dressing gown, but not the shabby
towelling variety that was the only sort I owned – a glamorous
garment in what looked like silk, with a print of trees and birds.
Her face was bare of make-up but she still looked impossibly

beautiful, her skin pale and luminous, violet shadows under her eyes the only sign that she might be unwell.

And the results are back. It's not looking good. Dr Hubert says there appears to be some malignancy there, which is medic-speak for cancer. The big C. It's the same word in French so I don't even have a foreign term to make it sound a bit more... I don't know. A bit more exotic? A bit less scary? Either way, it's not exotic and it is scary as hell. Apparently, we're looking at surgery in the first instance and then drugs – chemo and radiotherapy; just typing those words makes me feel like puking, and I've not even started the treatment yet. Guys, I'm scared. What if I can never have a baby? What if – and yes, I'm thinking about this a lot – all my hair falls out? I know none of you wonderful people have the answers, but I could do with a handhold. Or possibly a kick up the jacksy to tell me to get on with it and stop cata-strophising.

This time, there were even more responses – they numbered in the hundreds.

And after that was the post Rowan had shown me, of Zara in her surgical gown in hospital.

I read through the sequence of posts again. They didn't make sense to me. Perhaps, if Zara was ill, she might still have come to London for Andy's funeral – she might have thought it was the right thing to do. She would probably have been feeling fine at that stage – she'd certainly looked the picture of health.

But after that? As far as I knew, Zara had been in the Airbnb apartment in London the whole time, not in Paris having tests. I'd met up with her to collect Patch's camera. She'd been to the Girlfriends' Club meet-up when I'd been ill.

It didn't add up.

Almost without thinking, I picked up my phone and scrolled rapidly through to Rowan's name. I was about to hit the call button when I stopped, scrolled down one more place to find her work number, and dialled that. She might not be at her desk but if she was, at least she'd be sure to answer.

She was, and she did. 'Walkerson's Elite, Rowan speaking.'

'Hi, it's me.' I spoke as quickly as I could. 'Please don't hang up. Have you got two minutes?'

'Yeah. But probably only two.' Her tone was guarded. 'I've got to leave for a viewing in five.'

'Okay, I'll be quick. Will you hear me out?'

She didn't say anything. I imagined her nodding reluctantly, the phone trapped between her ear and her curtain of dark hair. I was going to have to get this right – be convincing, give no hint of my suspicions, persuade her I wanted to do what was right.

At least, I told myself, if I was wrong I'd still be doing the right thing. No one would ever need to know my true thoughts – except me, and I'd have to live with that knowledge.

'It's about Zara. The cancer thing. Listen, Ro. I feel terrible about all this. I know I've been a bad friend to her, and I want to try and make things right.'

'How?' Rowan asked.

'I want to go to Paris. See her, if she needs support. Apologise to her in person.'

'Seriously? You're going to go and see her? What about Patch?'

Patch. Shit. In my haste to speak to Rowan, I hadn't even thought of that.

'I'll tell him I could do with a break – a weekend away from home and the kids.'

'By going to Paris on your own? Really?' she asked incredulously.

'Not on my own. I want you to come with me.'

TWENTY-NINE

JULY 2012

Through a crack between the heavy cream curtains, I could see Kate, Rowan and Abbie, all crowded together around the tall, gold-framed cheval mirror. Next to them was a little splayed-leg table holding a bottle of champagne and four glasses; on the other side, its twin held a vast arrangement of fleshy white lilies.

Abbie was wearing jeans and a jumper. She had her back to me, so I could see the hole in one of the elbows – I remembered her telling us that she and Matt had recently been fighting the equivalent of the Cold War against a plague of clothes moths, and it looked like the Iron Curtain wasn't going to be lifted any time soon.

But speaking of curtains... I peered again through the gap. Abbie turned around, her face shifting from the delighted smile I'd seen in the mirror to a worried frown. I yanked the gap closed and turned back to the smaller mirror in the cubicle.

Kate and Rowan had both looked gorgeous. The strappy lilac satin dresses suited them perfectly with their dark hair, even though their skin tones were quite different.

I, on the other hand...

'Nome?' Abbie called. 'Are you okay in there? Is the zip stuck or something?'

'I'm all right,' I managed to say, turning away from the mirror.

But it was no good. I knew what I'd seen, and I'd see it again when I came out.

And there wasn't a thing I could do about it. This was Abbie's wedding, her and Matt's big day, and as one of her bridesmaids, I had to wear what she'd chosen, like it or not.

No one will care, I told myself firmly. *It's not about you. Suck it up, buttercup.*

Taking a deep breath, I parted the curtains and stepped out.

There was a moment of silence. I forced myself to smile.

And then all at once, we started to laugh. Abbie came over and hugged me. Kate and Rowan pressed their hands over their faces like kids watching a particularly scary bit of *Doctor Who*, occasionally peering between their fingers and then laughing some more.

The sales assistant hurried over, tape measure looped around her neck, to see what all the commotion was about.

'Delightful!' she cooed. 'I always think that a soft, cool pastel suits everybod— oh.'

'Oh my God,' Abbie said, when eventually she could breathe. 'I'm so sorry, Nome.'

'You look like you died a couple of weeks ago and someone just dug you up,' gasped Rowan.

'I know we shouldn't laugh.' Kate grabbed a tissue from the box on the table, presumably intended to mop up the joyful tears of overcome mothers-of-brides, and wiped her eyes. 'But Naomi – you just – you poor thing.'

'It's okay,' I said. 'It doesn't matter, honestly. I'll wear it. It's fine.'

'You'll do nothing of the kind.' Abbie had stopped laughing

now; she looked absolutely mortified. 'Seriously, Nome, I just didn't think. I've never seen you in lilac before. I didn't know...'

'That she'd look like something on the mortician's slab in *CSI*?' suggested Kate.

'I mean, I should have known there was a reason you never wear it,' Abbie went on, 'but it didn't occur to me. Mum said, "How about lilac for the bridesmaids? It'll look so fresh," and I agreed without thinking.'

'Fresh like something on ice at the fishmonger,' giggled Rowan.

'You can't change the whole colour scheme just for me,' I said.

'Can't I?' Abbie argued. 'Just watch me. What are a few flowers and table napkins compared to my best friend feeling like shit on my wedding day and looking like a corpse in the photos? Of course I'll change it.'

'Ah, it's the photos you were worried about,' teased Rowan. '"Who's that woman who came back from the dead for your wedding, Matthew?" everyone would ask for ever more.'

'Stop it,' Abbie scolded. 'Get these off and we'll try something different.'

The sales assistant looked at us, her head on one side. 'How about a nice fuchsia? That would warm your skin tone up beautifully, and it always suits dark-haired girls, too.'

'Fuchsia sounds great,' agreed Abbie. 'Let's give it a go and if it works I'll get Mum on the case with the florist. Come on, all change, please.'

Half an hour later, we were all sitting around a table in a nearby pub, already a bottle of wine down, a waiter placing steaming plates of sausages and mash in front of us.

'Crisis averted,' Kate said, topping up our glasses. 'Strong work there, Abs. I do risk management for an actual job, and you handled that like a pro.'

'It's not that big a deal.' Abbie forked up a mound of mashed potato and peas. 'Not nearly so much as having one of you not being comfortable on my big day would have been. I mean, that's partly why...'

'Why what?' I asked.

Abbie took a breath. 'Why when I kind of asked Zara if she could be a bridesmaid too and she said she was too busy, I didn't push it.'

I swallowed, the piece of sausage I'd been eating suddenly feeling like a golf ball in my throat. 'You asked her? I never knew.'

'I'm sorry, Nome.' Abbie smiled. 'I know I should've checked with you first. I knew you wouldn't be comfortable with it, after what happened. But it felt like the right thing to do. I'd have felt awful not asking, and I was ninety-nine per cent sure she'd say no, so I took the risk.'

'You see?' Kate said. 'Handled it like a pro.'

'What would you have done if she'd said yes?' asked Rowan.

'I honestly don't know. But she's in New York now, apparently, so there's no way she could have come out for the hen night and dress fittings and everything. I was pretty confident.'

'I...' I took a breath and admitted, 'I don't know if I could have gone ahead with being a bridesmaid if she was too. I'm sorry, Abs. I'm glad she couldn't. It would have been just... too awkward.'

'Because of Patch?' Rowan asked.

'Of course. But also – the way she was the last time we saw her, it was like she hated me. Hated all of us. Even if we'd all apologised and hugged it out and stuff like that, I still feel like – like we can't be friends in the way we were before. Not ever again.'

It was true. Zara's dramatic departure from the group had left me grappling with conflicting emotions: fear that she'd somehow return to seek revenge for what I'd done; regret that things had turned out as they had; but mostly, overwhelmingly, relief. I'd quietly unfollowed her on Facebook and although I felt guilty about doing that, it was nothing to the general background noise of the guilt I felt about Patch and me being together.

I'd have said it cast a shadow over our relationship and in a way it did – but it was the shadow of a distant, passing cloud on a sunny day, because I was happier than I'd ever been. Although Patch's work still took him up to distant Aberdeen for weeks at a time, we texted constantly, saw each other as often as we could, and our reunions were blissful and passionate. Already, we were talking about having a future together, and what that might look like. Lying in bed together, we'd teasingly discussed the names of our future children, where we might live and – with Abbie and Matt's wedding approaching – had joked about him one day putting a ring on my finger and making an honest woman of me.

'Has anyone actually been in touch with her, apart from you, Abs?' Kate asked.

'Andy still speaks to her sometimes,' Abbie said. 'That's how I found out she'd moved to New York. She's put so much distance between us – not just physically, you know what I mean. When we used to be so close. And we haven't done enough to stop her.'

'Zara's a complicated person,' Rowan said carefully.

'It's like she was always part of the group, but also kind of separate,' agreed Kate.

I felt as if we were swimmers taking our first steps into dark, cold water, not knowing how deep it would be, where the current would take us, or whether the others would follow. As a group, we didn't gossip about one another. I could only recall discussing one of my friends when she wasn't present on a handful of occasions, and then it had been positively – when we'd agreed on a gift for Kate's birthday, organised flowers for

Abbie's engagement, or talked about ways we might murder Paul after he and Rowan split up.

'It must come from having grown up in care,' I said. 'Isn't attachment disorder a thing, or something like that?'

Abbie looked at me like I was speaking a foreign language. 'Zara didn't grow up in care. Her dad was something massive in the oil industry and she spent her childhood in some kind of palace in Saudi Arabia with millions of servants. Boarding school, yes, but not care.'

My face must have looked just as blank with surprise as Abbie's had. I remembered how I'd felt when Zara had confided in me about her past – shocked, of course, but also sorry for her, admiring of how far she'd come, proud that she'd chosen me to confide in.

And it hadn't been true. Or if it was, she'd told Abbie something completely different, which wasn't.

'I kind of assumed wealthy parents, too,' said Rowan, 'although she never explicitly said. I mean, you have to have money to live the way she does. It's not like fashion pays well, unless you're Kate Moss or someone.'

I remembered the seedy hotel in Bloomsbury where I'd dropped Zara off that drunken night. It certainly hadn't seemed like a place where someone who had money would choose to stay. At the time, my thoughts had been so occupied with questioning the presence of the man I was sure I'd seen there to reflect on what it meant about Zara herself.

'But it did pay her well,' Kate argued. 'Wasn't she, like, a child star and made a fortune doing that, but then when she was a teenager she was hospitalised with anorexia and had to stop because she nearly died? Or – hold on – was it only me she told that to?'

'I think it was only you,' Rowan said, after a moment's silence. 'It's like she – I don't know – tailor-made versions of herself to tell each one of us, because she knew we'd never talk about her behind her back.'

'And we never have,' I burst out. 'Not until today. Kate, did she make you promise you'd never tell us – tell anyone – about the anorexia stuff?'

Kate nodded. 'She bloody well did. She swore me to secrecy. I'd have felt bad keeping secrets from the rest of you normally but I went along with it because – you know – you want your friends to trust you. It's kind of important.'

'And we trusted her.' Abbie raked a hand through her hair, like she was trying to reorganise the contents of her brain. 'We never questioned any of it.'

'I can't believe I never asked her about her work in more detail.' Rowan was looking past me, out of the window, as if it would allow her to see into the past, remember the detail of conversations she'd long forgotten. 'If I had, I'd have realised things didn't quite add up. I just took everything at face value.'

'Why would someone do that?' Abbie asked. 'Just why? Did she feel she wasn't good enough for us, or something?'

'Did she not trust us enough to tell us the truth about herself?' Rowan fretted. 'Whatever the truth is?'

'I don't know,' I said. 'I don't think we'll ever find out the truth.'

We all looked at one another around the table, baffled. The Zara I thought I knew had come from a background of under-privilege and poverty, making her own way in the world, scraping by to pursue the career she loved. The Zara Patch knew had attempted suicide. The Zara Abbie knew had been an entirely different person, cushioned by wealth and luxury.

How many Zaras were there?

'Okay.' Kate picked up the wine bottle and refilled all our glasses. 'If any of you bitches has also been living a double life, why don't you spill right now? Amnesty time.'

There was a moment of silence, and then we all burst out laughing.

'That's it,' Abbie said. 'No secrets between us, right? Not any more.'

'Not ever,' Rowan promised.

'No secrets,' Kate echoed.

'I'll drink to that,' I said.

We all raised our glasses and tapped them together in the centre of the table, as if we were signing a pact in blood, not just toasting with red wine.

Feeling the closeness and love of my friends wrapping around me like a blanket, I felt a new confidence: we could move forward now, a group of four, without Zara. I could be secure in my relationship with Patch, because surely now there could be no question of my having betrayed Zara – not after how she had betrayed us all.

And there was no need for me to break my promise to her and tell them the secret she'd shared with me about her infidelity – even though I was sure that, unlike her other false confidences, this one had been true.

THIRTY

In the end, it was almost a week before Rowan and I were able to get away. I had to square my last-minute trip with Patch – no easy task, because it meant him spending an entire weekend looking after the children – and Rowan had to arrange the Friday and Monday off work.

But eventually, on a Friday evening, she and I stepped off the Eurostar at Gare du Nord. Of course, I couldn't help being reminded of our previous trip to visit Zara, but this was different in so many ways. There was no Kate, Abbie or Matt. There'd be no Patch meeting us there. There was no giddy, festive atmosphere or cans of gin and tonic on the train. I had no excited butterflies in my stomach, only a hollow apprehensiveness at the knowledge that I was going to see Zara, fear at how she might react to seeing me, and a complete blank when it came to what I was going to say to her.

It didn't help that Rowan's attempts to contact Zara on social media, email and phone had all been unsuccessful, and thinking of the possibility that I might never get the chance to make things right made my confidence in my plan evaporate and be replaced with cold dread.

At least the frosty atmosphere there'd been between Rowan and me seemed to have thawed now that we were united in a common goal.

'Chin up, Nome,' Rowan said. 'We've got this. Let's find our hotel, check in, get something to eat and make a plan.'

Her brisk efficiency reassured me, and we did as she suggested. The hotel Rowan had booked was tucked away on a cobblestone street in the Marais and was basic but pleasant, with a twin room – we weren't here to live it up, as Rowan had pointed out. But once we'd dropped off our bags and headed out into the street, I felt the magic of the city captivating me as it had the first time. It was early summer now. The trees lining the boulevards were in full leaf, shading the pavements as if we were walking beneath giant green parasols. The evening was warm and there was a gentle breeze disarranging the chic bobs of the women who crowded the pavement with their well-cut, neutral-coloured clothes, their high heels and their expensive handbags. We walked past magnificent stone mansions where it was impossible not to imagine living as a seventeenth-century aristocrat, through an elegant garden square with a vast fountain at its centre and down to the river, sparkling in the setting sun.

Everyone seemed to be smiling; it felt like a city where you could fall in love. I remembered the last time we had come here, and the desperate yearning I'd felt for Patch, the agony of love I'd believed would never be reciprocated. I imagined coming here with him again, leaving the children with my parents, strolling hand-in-hand with him through the streets, eating croissants at a pavement café, returning home in the evening tipsy from rosé and having sex with the curtains blowing into the room from our balcony, like a second honeymoon.

Actually, I realised, coming here with Rowan was something not unlike a honeymoon, and almost more important. It felt like a chance to heal the fractures in our friendship, to begin to make things right between us and somehow recover from the damage that had been done by Zara's return, and my actions in the past.

When we'd met at St Pancras station, our conversation had been – not cold, but kind of formal, limited to our travel arrangements and the plans we'd made for our children to be looked after while we were away. But now, glancing sideways at Rowan, I could see a lightness in her step, a smile on her face when the breeze blew back her hair.

'It's got you, hasn't it?' Rowan asked, and I realised she was looking sideways at me too.

'What has?'

'Paris, dimwit.'

I laughed. 'Yup, you've got me bang to rights. And don't pretend it's not got to you, too.'

'Course it has. Paris and – being here with you, Nome. It's nice.'

I grinned, my heart lifting. 'Yeah, it's all right, isn't it?'

'So, food. This place looks decent, if you're happy with cassoulet or something? When there's just a short menu like this it generally means they do it perfectly.'

I looked through the window at the paper-covered table-cloths where studenty-looking couples sat drinking red wine, their faces illuminated by candlelight. I was starving, I realised.

'Works for me.'

'So,' Rowan said, once we were seated and smearing salty butter thickly on to slices of baguette. 'We need a plan.'

'Did you try calling the hospital?' I'd vaguely suggested this when we spoke the previous day.

Rowan shook her head. 'I tried googling, but I could tell straight away I was on a hiding to nothing. There are loads of different ones and I can't tell from Zara's Facebook posts which one she's in. Same with Dr Hubert – there seem to be about three gynaecologists called that in Paris and even if I got the right one, there's no way he'd tell me anything. They're even hotter on data protection here than in the UK.'

'So plan B – we go to her apartment. She must have been discharged by now. Unless...'

We looked at each other in silence over the flickering candle flame. We didn't need to say the words – *Unless something went wrong with the surgery. Unless it was even more serious than she thought. Unless something went wrong and she...*

'We'll cross that bridge if we come to it,' Rowan said firmly. 'I'm sure she's fine. I bet this Hubert guy's whipped out more uteruses than you've had hot dinners.'

'And speaking of which...'

A waiter had appeared with our food, chunky white china plates piled high with glorious smelling beans and sausage, a green salad glistening with oil and another basket of bread. He filled our wine glasses from the carafe on the table and smiled at Rowan the way men always smiled at Rowan.

We ate and drank in silence for a while, then I said, 'Do we even know where she lives?'

'She used to have a flat in Canal Saint-Martin – hipster as hell, like you'd expect. I remember her saying she shared with another girl – a model. But I don't know if she's still there, or even what her name was.'

'I remember her mentioning it. Danielle? Something like that.'

'Yeah, we could start by having a look on Facebook and working our way through all the Danielles in Paris.'

'Or maybe not.' I sighed. 'So hitting Danielle up on social media and telling her we've come to visit Zara looks like a non-starter. It was ages ago, anyway. Zara's moved all over the place since then.'

'I mean, we could just go there,' Rowan suggested. 'She might have left a forwarding address.'

'You mean, like, now?'

Rowan glanced at her watch. 'It's gone nine thirty. I reckon we should sleep on it and try Danielle in the morning.'

Relief washed over me. One night wasn't much of a reprieve, but it was a reprieve all the same. We paid for our meal and walked back to the hotel through the buzzing Friday-night streets. Back in our room, I FaceTimed Patch, heard to my relief that the children were safe in bed, then fell into bed myself and – to my surprise – slept dreamlessly all night.

The next day was glorious – sunny and fresh, the air sparkling and the scent of coffee and croissants drifting out from the pavement cafés. Rowan and I picked one of them for breakfast, and she perused her phone while we ate.

'I reckon I'll be able to find the place,' she said. 'One good thing about being an estate agent is it gives you a killer memory for where houses are. And if Gabrielle – that's her name, not Danielle at all, I remembered at like five a.m. – if she's not there, we can leave our numbers with the concierge or someone and ask her to ring us.'

'And if Gabrielle doesn't live there any more, we can come up with a plan B,' I said, thinking, Or give up the whole idea and go home.

But the prospect of there being a concierge – an anonymous taker of messages rather than an old friend of Zara's to whom we'd have explain everything – emboldened me. We finished our coffee and I followed Rowan to the Metro station, on to one line and then on to another, and then out again into a pretty neighbourhood with tidy terraced houses lining the banks of a slow-flowing canal.

I hurried to match Rowan's long stride as she strode confidently past a little parade of shops, away from the meandering water of the canal, and into a maze of narrow cobbled streets. Occasionally she'd stop, frowning, consulting her phone then apparently her own memory before backtracking and turning off again.

At last, she stopped. 'I'm pretty sure this is the place. Rue de l'Église, number fifteen. I can't for the life of me remember the apartment number, though.'

We stood there in the sunshine for a moment, looking up at a series of tiny wrought-iron balconies, many with geraniums spilling from window boxes or pots of herbs spreading their leaves in the morning sun. The impetus that had carried me so far abruptly faded away.

What were we doing here? The idea that I'd somehow be vindicated by catching Zara out in a lie seemed absurd now that the prospect of it happening was real. And, of course, if I was wrong and it turned out Zara's illness was not a fabrication – well, I'd feel every bit as terrible as I deserved to.

On the wall outside the building was a panel of bells next to a metal fretwork security gate. We stood for a moment, looking at them.

'I don't think this is—' I began.

'Shall we—' Rowan said at the same time.

'Look, I really don't think this is a good idea, Ro.' I grabbed her arm and pulled her back from the entrance.

'What? Why not? We can't have come all this way for nothing.'

'She's not here,' I gabbled desperately. 'Even if this Dan—Gabrielle still lives here, what are the chances of her knowing where Zara is? We shouldn't have come.'

Rowan looked at me, her face softening. 'Hey, Nome. I get it. It's scary. I'm scared too. But what's the worst that can happen?'

There were so many possible worsts, I couldn't find the words to tell her which I was dreading the most. Dragging in a lungful of the fresh morning air, I looked up at the facade of the building, as if the clashing red and magenta flowers or the faint scent of basil would give me courage. And then I froze.

'Ro. Shit. Look up there.'

Rowan looked. 'What? The cat? Cute.'

Between the metal railings of the balcony above us, a pair of green eyes was looking curiously down at us. The cat's fur was dark brown and glossy, mottled with spots like a miniature leopard's. The sun glinted off its whiskers. Its long tail was tucked around its haunches.

'That's not just some random cat. That's Zara's cat.'

'Are you sure?'

I realised Rowan was just as nervous as I was. 'Positive.'

'She must be here, then.'

'We'll have to ring and see if someone will let us in.'

But before we could, there was a click and the security gate swung open. A woman stepped out, very tall and rail-thin, wearing faded jeans with a white shirt half-tucked into them. Holding on to her hands were two little girls, one a bit older than Meredith and the other a bit younger, immaculately dressed in little velvet frocks, the older one's navy blue and the younger one's yellow.

The woman said something to her children, smiling down at them. Then her eyes settled on us and she stopped. '*Puis-je vous aider?*'

Rowan spoke to her in French, a short stream of words of which I could only recognise 'Gabrielle', 'Zara' and 'Londres'.

The woman's face broke into a tentative smile, which vanished almost as soon as it had appeared and was replaced by puzzlement. She replied, at more length than Rowan had, but I understood almost nothing apart from a gesture up to the balcony from which the cat was still watching us, and an annoyed click of her tongue.

Rowan looked mystified and spoke again – 'Zara', 'Facebook', '*hôpital*'.

The woman shook her head and launched into another stream of French, too rapid for me to make out any words. Rowan answered briefly, and a couple more short exchanges followed, the woman looking more and more confused and Rowan more embarrassed.

At last, Rowan fished in her bag for a notebook and pen, wrote her name and mine and our phone numbers on one of the pages, ripped it out and handed it to the woman.

'*Alors*,' she said. '*Au revoir, Gabrielle. Désolée de vous déranger.*'

'*De rien*,' said Gabrielle. Taking her daughters' hands again, she walked away, giving us one last puzzled, slightly annoyed glance over her shoulder.

'Come on,' Rowan said. 'Let's get out of here.'

'What's happened? What did she say? Is Zara...?'

'Zara's fine. Come on.'

Rowan almost ran back along the street the way we'd come, in the opposite direction to which Gabrielle had been headed. She didn't stop until we reached the canal. She sat down on a wrought-iron bench and I flopped down next to her, dabbing beads of sweat from my forehead.

'That,' Rowan said, 'was the most bizarre conversation I've ever had in my life.'

'Tell me. I don't understand.'

'Zara's not there.' Rowan turned to face me, looking utterly perplexed. 'She was staying with Gabrielle for a bit, but she's not any more. She left her cat behind and Gabrielle's not best pleased about it.'

'So where is she now?' I pressed. I was almost sure I knew which way this was going to go, but not quite sure enough.

'Gabrielle doesn't know. Sounds like she did Zara a favour and she feels taken advantage of. She had no idea about all the Facebook stuff – her husband's something in politics so she doesn't do social media.'

'So she never saw Zara's posts about having cancer? But she had her to stay anyway?'

Rowan nodded. 'She said Zara was in hospital for a minor

procedure a couple of weeks back and she couldn't go to a hotel because of the cat.'

'A minor procedure?' Relief flooded me. 'So not cancer?'

'Not cancer at all. Nome, I don't get it. I genuinely have no fucking idea what's going on here. But I think you do, and I feel like I'm being taken for a mug here.'

I took a deep breath and reached for Rowan's hand. 'I'm sorry, Ro. I kind of brought you out here under false pretences. I thought – I doubted that what Zara was saying about having cancer was true. I know that sounds terrible but… after everything we know about her… I just had this feeling it might all be made up.'

'But everything – the photos in the hospital—'

'I know. That's why I doubted myself. And genuinely, hand on heart, if I'd been wrong, I'd have apologised to her and I'd have meant every word of it.'

'But you weren't wrong.' Rowan's eyes were bright with tears. 'I was wrong. We were wrong. We believed Zara. And I behaved horribly to you, Nome.'

I shook my head. 'It doesn't matter. That one thing – the thing about Patch and me – that was true. I didn't know it at the time but it was. And when I said I wanted to apologise to her for that, I meant it – and I still do.'

Rowan covered her face with her hands. 'It's all a right mess. The Girlfriends' Club – things haven't been the same since she came back and I don't think they ever will be again.'

'Come on, Ro. Don't cry.' I edged along the bench and put my arms around her. Hugging my friend again was the best feeling ever, even though her shoulders were shaking with sobs. 'We'll make it right again. I'm not sure how, but we'll find a way.'

'Are you sure?' She looked up at me. Her face reminded me of Meredith's when she'd cried after an injection and I'd pointed out to her that it didn't actually hurt any more.

'I'm absolutely sure.' Then I asked, 'Ro? This minor procedure?'

'What about it?'

'What actually was it?'

'It was removing some haemorrhoids.'

'What? That woman – Gabrielle – told you that?'

'She's French. They don't get embarrassed by bum stuff.' She started to giggle, and after a moment I joined her. I wasn't sure why it was funny, but her laughter was infectious, and soon we were rocking backwards and forwards on the bench like schoolgirls, helpless with mirth, literally crying. When one of us stopped for a moment, we'd catch each other's eyes and start all over again.

I felt limp with relief, like I'd been hollowed out and there was nothing inside me to support the weight of my body any more. All the guilt I'd been feeling had been washed away, all the fear that Zara might die and we'd have to live, together, with the loss of her the way we were living with Andy's had evaporated.

The knowledge of what had happened between Zara and Patch was still there, of course, but it felt like a small thing – an insignificant thing, compared to the hugeness of the blame I'd been willing to place on myself and the possibility of losing my closest friends in the world.

I looked at Rowan. The sun was shining on her face and there were tears sparkling on her cheeks.

In a small voice, she said, 'I'm just so relieved. I feel like the world's biggest mug for believing her – again – but I don't actually care.'

'I'm relieved too.' I squeezed her hand. Then I looked at her again. 'There's something else, isn't there. That you're relieved about?'

Rowan nodded slowly. 'You see, if this wasn't true, then the other things she said to me aren't true, either.'

I thought of what Zara had said to me – the seeds of doubt she'd sown in my mind. How her telling me that she'd felt on the sidelines of the group had reminded me of feeling that way, too, making me wonder afresh whether my friends weren't really my friends at all, and how that knowledge had been eating away at me.

'What did she say to you?' I asked.

Rowan blinked back tears. 'She said – oh God, I don't know why I even let myself believe it for a second, but I did. She said... she said you'd told her you thought me moving in with Alex would be – you know. Inappropriate. Because of Clara. She said that when she was Clara's age, her mum had a boyfriend who... you know. Abused her. And that she'd told you about it and you'd said you wondered why I wasn't concerned about the same thing happening to Clara.'

'Hold on. Are you saying she said I thought there was something – that Alex—'

'I mean, not in so many words. I know it's not true, of course I do. I know Alex isn't like that. I mean – ugh! If I had even the tiniest hint of that I'd be calling the police, never mind going out with him and introducing him to my daughter. But the idea that you thought something wasn't right hurt. It hurt a lot.'

'Of course it did. Jesus. I can't imagine how that must have felt. But you know it's not true, right?'

'I do now. I always did, really. But she made me doubt myself. Not a lot, but – you know. Enough.'

'And you're not doubting yourself any more?'

She shook her head.

'Thank God for that,' I said.

'I'm so sorry, Naomi. I feel terrible. I should have known you'd never have thought that, never mind said it. To Zara, of all people.'

'I believed stuff she told me, too, you know. In spite of myself.'

'What stuff?'

I shook my head. Now, sitting in the sunshine with my best friend, it seemed ridiculous. But by saying it, I knew I could reduce its power forever.

'She made me feel like I was the odd one out, of us. Actually, she told me she'd felt that way, and it reminded me that I used to, as well. But I always thought she was the one who fitted in and I wasn't. God, it sounds so pathetic when I say in out loud.'

Rowan laughed, but it was a hollow sound, different from the laughter we'd shared earlier.

'Wow,' she said. 'She really knows how to push our buttons.'

'And I bet that's not all.' I stood up, feeling lighter somehow, full of determination. 'She'll have said things to Kate, too. And to Abbie.'

'My God,' Rowan breathed. 'Yes. You're right.'

'And I'm going to find out what. And I'm going to make things all right between us again.'

THIRTY-ONE

There wasn't much point staying in Paris after that – our mission was accomplished, after all. But, somewhat guiltily, Rowan and I stayed anyway. We might as well, we agreed – the tickets were paid for, my children were safe with Patch and Clara was spending the weekend with a friend. We were free; we might as well enjoy ourselves.

And so we did. We went to a patisserie with an array of cakes in the window that looked like jewels, and took as long deciding which to have as we did eating them. We walked along the river in the sunshine and climbed what felt like a million steps up to Montmartre to see the city spread out below us like a printed silk scarf. I bought a beautifully cut slate-grey blazer that would form the basis of my future work wardrobe.

Being there with my friend was a reminder of how things used to be and a promise of how they'd be again – if only I could find a way to make it so. All the way home on the train, I carefully considered my strategy. I wasn't going to descend on Kate at work the way I had on Rowan – I knew that wouldn't work. I needed to be careful and tactful. I knew how to do that – or at least I used to, back when it was my job to manage people's demands and needs and moods just as much as it was to manage my boss's diary.

So, on Monday afternoon, I sent Kate an email asking if I could meet up with her. It was the first time I'd been in contact with her since I'd left the Girlfriends' Club group; I imagined her seeing my name in her email inbox and reacting with – what? Happiness? Anger? Disdain? I couldn't be sure, which was why I'd approached her saying that I needed advice, without specifying about what. I knew that whatever doubts she was feeling about our friendship, Kate would be willing to help me if she believed I needed her.

And I did need her. What she didn't know was that she needed me, too.

She replied after an hour or so, with her typical efficiency.

Sure – want to come round to my place this evening? Or I could come to yours if you can't leave the children?

Fortunately, Patch had reluctantly taken the day off work and hadn't yet left for the gym, so I was able to apologetically inform him that his plans were changing, and he'd have to stay in to give the twins their dinner.

'But you've been away all weekend,' he objected.

'But I give them dinner every single day of my life,' I countered. Then I decided I'd catch more flies with honey than with vinegar, and added, 'Please? It's important.'

'Fine,' he grumbled, and I grabbed my bag and fled before he could change his mind.

When I arrived at Kate's apartment just south of the River Thames, the door to her balcony was open and a bottle of wine in an ice bucket, two glasses and a dish of cheese straws which I could smell were freshly out of the oven awaited us on the table outside.

I felt briefly encouraged by this welcome, before remembering that even if Kate's worst enemy had called on her unexpectedly, she'd have insisted they have a cup of Earl Grey and a scone.

'How was Paris?' she asked.

'It was good. Interesting. I'll tell you all about it soon. But first, there's something I really wanted to ask you.'

Kate gestured to one of the chairs, poured the wine and sat down. 'Go ahead.'

'It's about Bridget.'

'Bridget? Your mother-in-law?'

I nodded. 'I've been worried about her. She's getting absent-minded – well, more absent-minded. She keeps calling Toby and Meredith Patrick and Niamh, and the other day she almost burnt our house down when she was babysitting.'

I poured out the story and Kate listened, her head on one side as she nibbled a cheese straw.

'I thought you might have some advice,' I finished, 'because of all the stuff you do with your lonely older people who meet for coffee and company at St Mildred's church.'

'St Mungo's,' she corrected. 'And I don't actually do anything. Mona organises it all. I just turn up and drop off cake for them when I've been up all night baking because I haven't been able to sleep.'

I knew this, of course – but I also knew that Kate loved nothing better than a problem she might be able to help solve.

'But I suppose I pick up a bit,' she went on. 'Just through chatting to Mona. When elderly people are isolated, it can sometimes accelerate symptoms of dementia – if it is dementia. And often it isn't. Other things can present in the same way – urinary tract infections, deafness, plain old loneliness.'

'I see,' I said.

'So it sounds like a trip to her GP is the first step,' she said. 'And why not bring her along to St Mungo's? I know it's a bit of a journey for you but they're a friendly lot. Mona's got a real gift for getting people to open up about their problems. They meet every Wednesday and Saturday at ten.'

'I will,' I said. 'Thank you.'

Kate smiled and sat back in her chair. Beyond her, I could see the setting sun glinting off the river, Tower Bridge silhouetted in front of it. The cries of gulls rang out over the water and I could hear a group of young men laughing as they walked along the path below.

I can do this, I told myself. *I can get everything back to how it used to be – before Zara came back.*

'Now, tell me about Paris.' The tentative ease there'd been between us seemed to have faded now; Kate was looking down at her hands instead of at me, twisting her fingers together in her lap. 'Did you see Zara?'

I said, 'No, we didn't. We tried, but we didn't. We did see her old flatmate, though – Gabrielle. And we saw her cat.'

Kate's face turned white, as if there was no blood left in her at all. 'Oh no. Does that mean she—'

'No! Not that,' I hastened to reassure her. 'She's fine. There's nothing wrong with her. Well, nothing except...'

Quickly, I filled her in on the story, watching as her expression went from bemused to incredulous to amused.

'My God,' she breathed, when I'd finished. 'That's – I mean, I'd say it was incredible. But it's not, really, is it?'

'Not really.'

'And it's a massive relief, obviously.' I could see the analytical part of her brain working – *If that wasn't true, what else isn't true?*

I seized the moment. 'So that made me realise there's something I need to ask you.'

The smile faded from Kate's face. She looked closed again, guarded. 'Go on.'

'When you met up with her, back in February, what happened? What did she tell you?'

Kate sighed. 'She told me she felt partly responsible for what happened with Andy.'

'Wait, what? She did?'

'She told me about a time Andy visited her in Paris. It was a couple of years back, she said, during his sober period. They went out together, and they – you know. Partied.'

I sighed. 'You know what Andy was like. You could have dropped him down on the surface of the moon and he'd find a dealer. Go on.'

'And she said she felt guilty about having been there when he relapsed. She said that was why she'd come to the funeral. To get – you know. Closure.'

'But even if that did happen, it doesn't mean Andy's death was Zara's fault.'

'I know. That's what I told her.' Kate pushed her hair back from her face. It looked like it took a huge effort to move her hand at all. 'I wanted to make her feel better. I told her that I'd always blamed myself for it, for years and years. All the times I was there with Andy when he relapsed and I did nothing.'

'But you did. You did everything you could. Everything anyone could.'

Kate held up a hand to stop me. Her fingers were silhouetted against the sunset now, obscuring the distant bridge. 'It didn't feel that way. I told Zara that. And she was sympathetic – she said she got it. And then she said...'

'What?'

'She said that all of you thought I was responsible. Because I'd been there all along. I'd been closest to Andy. He and I were – you know. More than friends, all that time, and I hid it from you. She said she understood how that felt, because she felt responsible for what happened too, and blamed herself.'

'But we never blamed you. Never.'

I could see it now. Zara's manipulation – so subtle, but so effective. The same as what she'd done to me – telling me that she'd always felt like the odd one out in the group, reminding me – as she must have guessed – that I had felt that way. And that, along with all the guilt I'd felt when I first fell for Patch, causing me to doubt my friends and turn away from them.

'I wanted to move on from it,' Kate went on. 'But I couldn't. Not quite. Because I wouldn't have blamed you for blaming me. It made things between us – not the same.'

'I get it,' I said. 'I really do. But can't you see – that was what she wanted. To drive us apart. And she succeeded.'

Kate nodded. 'I suppose she did.'

I asked her the question I hadn't asked Rowan. 'Why did you believe her? Why did any of us believe her? After what happened before?'

'That's what I thought,' she said. 'I asked myself – why are you buying this? You know she lies about stuff. But everything she told us before – that was about her. Details about her life and her past that didn't really matter. This felt different. It felt like it could so easily be real.'

I thought of what she'd told Rowan – introducing doubt and mistrust and fear. Souring things with lies that were based on the things we most feared could be true. Same as she'd done to me.

'Kate?' I said. 'Did she speak to Abbie as well? What did she tell her?'

'I don't know. But we should ask her.'

'We have to. We have to find out. All of us together.'

THIRTY-TWO
OCTOBER 2012

When you ask Abbie about her and Matt's wedding, she says that the best bit – the bit she remembers most clearly – is Matt's speech. Which is funny, because he never actually made a speech.

I remember that bit too, of course – Matt standing up, tall and awkward in his suit, surrounded by his friends and family, all willing him to do his best, make them proud, not fuck it up. And Abbie next to him, gazing adoringly up at him, seeing the exact moment when the words he'd composed so carefully and practised so thoroughly simply refused to come, leaving him standing there mouthing mutely like a goldfish. That's when Abbie stepped in, stood up, poised and graceful in her white dress, made the speech for him and brought the house down.

For a good few months after that, anyone who went round to their house had to watch the wedding video. If you protested because you'd seen it before (perhaps multiple times), she'd say, 'Okay then, just the best bit,' and make you watch that, while Matt laughed, shook his head ruefully and said he had no idea what had come over him.

That's not the bit I remember best, though – not at all.

I remember when we were all standing together at the entrance to the chapel – or rather, the hotel function room where the ceremony was to be held. Abbie was trembling with nerves, white as her dress under her glowing make-up, surrounded by her three bridesmaids: Kate, Rowan and me.

Abbie's mum fluttered around us, taking a final look at her daughter before she would become a married lady. Her father stood to one side, waiting to walk in with his daughter on his arm, proud but shy, as if he wasn't used to being surrounded by all these women. Abbie pulled herself upright, shaking out her skirt, and said, 'Come on, let's do this.'

Just in time, Rowan clocked the tissues someone had tucked under Abbie's arms to soak up her nervous perspiration, and whipped them out. Abbie's mum took them, used one to wipe away a tear from her cheek then tucked them in her handbag and sailed through to take her seat, her rose-coloured hat almost too big to fit through the door.

'Are we doing this or are we going to hang around out here forever and have me die single?' Abbie demanded, her nerves apparently forgotten.

'Come on then, let's go,' Kate said.

And then Zara arrived. In defiance of all convention, she was wearing white – a full-length satin dress so long it dragged on the floor like a train. Her hair was longer than I remembered ever seeing it, and seemed to fly out behind her like the banner of an invading army.

'Don't mind me,' she said. 'Late as always, haha.'

She swept into the room as if her entrance was the most the important thing that would happen that day. At the end of the aisle, I saw Matt turn, his face alight with excitement and then falling into bewildered surprise – *Wait, what? They've changed who I have to marry?*

Just in time, we hustled Abbie out of the way so that he

wouldn't see her, even though he was going to in a few seconds anyway.

'My God,' Kate whispered. 'What is she like?'

'Unreal,' murmured Rowan.

I might have said something too, but I have no idea what it was. I felt numb with shock, all the excitement of the day vanishing like the bubbles in a bottle of champagne that had been shaken so vigorously there was no fizz left.

Somehow, we got Abbie into the room and up to the table where Matt, his brother and the celebrant were waiting. Then we took our seats and the ceremony began.

I can't recall a word of it. Throughout, I was conscious of Zara behind me, feeling her eyes burning the back of my carefully pinned-up hair like lasers, so I could almost smell the popcorn fumes of it. Patch was there too, somewhere behind me. I imagined her sitting next to him, her hand in his where mine should have been.

I wouldn't have put it past her.

'It's okay,' Rowan whispered to me, in the few moments when the register was being signed and a ripple of happy chatter filled the room. 'You've got this. Just ignore her.'

And so I did. As best I could, throughout the champagne reception and photographs and into the dinner. We bridesmaids were seated at the top table with Abbie, Matt and their families. I could see Patch, a couple of tables away, sitting next to a woman in a yellow hat who I didn't know, Andy on his other side. He'd been briefed by Matt, clearly, because I saw him topping up Andy's glass with water whenever it was empty, before filling it with wine again when the water was drunk.

Zara had found herself a seat, somehow, over in the corner of the room with a group who I guessed were university friends of Abbie's. Out of the corner of my eye, I could see her chatting, drinking, laughing, the plate of food in front of her untouched. Although she was in my peripheral vision, her presence filled my mind as if she was inches away from me, laughing in my face.

The speeches happened. The cake was cut. Abbie and Matt had their first dance, their bodies pressed together and their smiles radiant.

Then other couples began to fill the dance floor in the appointed pattern: Abbie's mum and Matt's dad, Kate with Matt's brother Ryan, me in the arms of a colleague of Matt's whose name I can't recall. He'd spilled something down the front of his shirt, and I worried that it would rub off on my dress.

Zara was dancing with Patch. Of course she was. I couldn't know whether she'd asked him or he'd asked her, but there they were, the best-looking couple in the room – her hair the same colour as his black jacket, but shinier, her skin almost as pale as the white shirt pressed against her cheek, only pearly and perfect – her body twining against his like jasmine climbing a wall.

But she was also drunk. I could see how she needed to cling to Patch's shoulders to stay balanced in her high heels, and when I caught a glimpse of her eyes I noticed that their brilliant green irises were red-rimmed.

Leave him alone, my mind screamed. *Stay away – he's mine. Don't break what I've waited so long to have.*

My relationship with Patch had never felt as fragile as it did in that moment, or my love for him as intense.

When the music changed and the couples pulled away from each other, laughing, clapping and regrouping for the next dance, Zara stayed where she was, her arms around Patch's neck, her face turned up to his. I smiled at the man I'd been dancing with – or tried to – and muttered something to excuse myself.

Pushing my way through the crowd, I moved to the other side of the room, trying to get closer to Patch – to rescue him, or rescue myself. When I got close enough for him to see me, he caught my eyes and smiled, a rueful, weary, eye-rolling smile, then held up his hand, the fingers outstretched to make a number two.

I'll be with you in two minutes.

That wasn't good enough. I needed to reach him now, prise Zara off him if I had to, claim what was my own.

But before I could approach them, I felt a gentle hand on my shoulder.

'Don't stress, babe,' Rowan said. 'Abbie's going to throw her bouquet now. Chin up, smile. You're beautiful and he loves you.'

'But she—'

'It's going to be okay. We don't want a scene, do we? It's Abbie's day.'

That was the reminder I needed. I reached over and squeezed Rowan's hand and let her lead me away to the table where the cake was resting, three tiers of white icing as smooth as Zara's dress, twined with green leaves and silver bells.

'Gather rounds, folks!' Ryan called over the music, which immediately dropped in volume. 'Ladies at the front. Let's see who's going to be the lucky one.'

Someone helped Abbie up on to a chair. She teetered as if she was about to fall, laughing, and then grasped Matt's shoulder to steady herself, her bouquet held high in her other hand.

'I was always shit at PE,' she warned, 'this might not go very far, so come close.'

Zara hadn't needed telling. She was already there, pushing to the front of the polite little circle of young women who were gathered round, no one wanting to seem too eager, too desperate.

Abbie reached behind her, the bunch of white roses and

trailing ivy gripped in her fist. As she brought her arm forward again, I saw that her eyes were squeezed tight shut.

She hadn't lied – she couldn't throw for toffee, bless her. But it wouldn't have mattered if she'd pitched the flowers like an international cricketer, because Zara was right there. It was impossible to tell whether the bouquet had even left Abbie's hand before she snatched it in mid-air and held it triumphantly aloft.

There was a little ripple of surprised applause and laughter. Someone towards the back of the group said, 'Hey, that wasn't fair,' and someone else said, 'Sssh.'

'I got it!' Zara's voice carried clear as a bell over the background voices. 'He's mine!'

'What's she on about?' grumbled the woman who'd complained about fairness.

'Not that it makes any fucking difference,' Zara said. 'No one will ever marry me. Ever.'

She gripped the bouquet in her two hands, lifted it high over her head and pulled. At first nothing happened – the florists had done their job well. But Zara was strong – I could see the definition of the muscles in her arms and back as she pulled, and quickly whatever was holding the stems together gave way in a cascade of petals.

Her initial fury apparently spent, Zara's arms fell to her sides, the two halves of the ruined bouquet dropping to the floor.

'Fuck you,' she said. It wasn't clear first who she meant, then a second later she added, 'Fuck you all. Especially you.'

She turned to me with a look so full of venom that I physically recoiled, my hands flying up to protect my face.

And then I put them down again, clenched into fists by my side. I took a tentative step towards her and then another.

'Why are you doing this?' I asked, keeping my voice as calm

as I could. 'Why are you trying to ruin Abbie and Matt's day? I don't understand.'

'Ruin their day?' Her voice rose, clear in the suddenly silent room. 'Who cares about their bloody day when my whole life is ruined, thanks to you?'

'I never wanted to hurt you,' I said softly, my eyes stinging with tears. I tried again to approach her, but I couldn't – it was as if the force field of her rage was blocking me. 'Please, Zara. Don't do this. We can make it all right again. We can be friends.'

Zara stared at me for a second, then gave a shriek of high, hysterical laughter that turned almost immediately to tears. Her hands over her face, she pushed through the watching guests, now all standing immobile with shock.

'Oh no,' Abbie whispered, 'make it stop.'

Someone helped her down off the chair. Someone else – perhaps the girl who'd complained about not catching the flowers in the first place – picked them up off the floor.

'I'd better go to Zara,' Kate whispered to me.

She hurried away, but seconds later I heard Zara's voice, high-pitched with distress, saying, 'Don't touch me! Don't come near me.'

Trembling, I turned to Abbie. 'I'm so sorry. Your special day. It's all my fault.'

I saw her stand a little straighter, squaring her shoulders and determinedly smiling – a physical manifestation of the phrase 'pull yourself together'. It was as if, in that moment, she faced a choice – to have her day ruined, or not. And she'd chosen the second.

'Don't be daft, Nome. It wouldn't be a wedding without a bit of drama, would it? Come on, Matt, let's cut that cake.'

I tried to recover my own composure – I really did. But I could feel myself shaking, shock and embarrassment threatening to overwhelm me. Biting my lip, I forced myself to stand and watch while Abbie and Matt, their hands clasped together, sank a knife into the perfect white surface of their wedding cake. Then someone came and took it away to the kitchen to cut it up properly and serve it.

There was something about that moment – the last of the key points that marked the day, the cake someone had laboured over for so long being whisked away and transformed from a centrepiece back into just food, Abbie and Matt standing there together, united in their refusal to allow their happiness to be spoiled – that broke me.

A choking lump in my throat, tears beginning to course down my cheeks, I turned away and fled to the toilet. I couldn't see Patch anywhere, but that didn't seem important – I just wanted to be alone with my shame and my sadness.

Because all of this was my fault. If I hadn't done what I'd done – fallen in love with a man who was taken, pursued the relationship in spite of a friendship that mattered to me, broken the sanctity of the unwritten but inviolable Girl Code – none of this would have happened. Zara would have been here today as Patch's date. Abbie would have had four brides-maids instead of three. I would have been the single girl who'd hustled to catch the bouquet, and maybe there'd have been someone else out there for me, someone who I could have a relationship with without breaking another woman's heart.

I pushed open the door of the ladies' loos, ignoring the trio of women already in there, gossiping while they freshened up their lipstick, locked myself in a cubicle and sobbed.

I don't know how long I spent there before I heard a tap on the door and Rowan's voice saying, 'Naomi? Babe? Let me in.'

A wad of soggy tissue clutched in my hand, I unlatched the door. Her face full of concern, Rowan put her arm round my shoulder and led me out.

'You poor thing,' she soothed. 'Honestly, what a drama. You couldn't make it up. Come on, let's fix your face. There are still a few people dancing and there'll be bacon rolls in a bit. We'll get you a glass of fizz.'

'I don't think I can. Where is she?'

'Zara? She went outside. She's sitting in the garden smoking.' She hesitated, then admitted, 'Patch is with her. He was the only person who could calm her down. We couldn't leave her alone – she was hysterical.'

'I don't want to see her.'

'You won't have to. Don't worry. There's no way she's going to swan back in there and start troughing bacon like nothing happened.'

'Still. I can't.'

'Okay. It doesn't matter. Do you want to come up to my room with me? I've got the most amazing make-up remover – it's SkinCeuticals and it's like magic.'

I noticed my reflection in the mirror about the basins and saw why she'd mentioned it.

'Okay,' I said. 'Thanks. I don't want anyone to see me.'

'Mate.' Rowan pressed her hands on my shoulders and looked down at me, her face stern. 'When you rugby-tackle your way to a bunch of flowers then rip them apart like you're one of those muscle-men who tear up telephone directories, then start effing and blinding at all and sundry, then you'll have something to be ashamed of. I'll be sure and remind you if I catch you doing it by mistake.'

I felt a watery smile reach my face, and giggled.

'And until then, you can hold your head up high,' she went on. 'Understand?'

'Okay,' I said. 'Next time I feel the urge to do that, I'll clear it with you first.'

'That's my girl. Come on now, bedtime.'

I let her lead me out, guide me discreetly round the edge of the room, out to the lobby and into the lift. She took me to her room, cleaned my face and lent me a pair of her pyjamas. Then we made tea and sat on her bed, sipping and chatting about things that had nothing to do with Abbie's wedding, or Patch, or Zara.

And I must have fallen asleep at some point, because I woke up there the next morning, Rowan asleep in the twin bed next to mine, my mind feeling oddly clear, like it had been scrubbed with Rowan's magic make-up remover.

I'd tried my best – everyone had seen it. Everyone would understand that I'd done nothing wrong. Everyone had seen the real Zara.

THIRTY-THREE

It was dark by the time I left Kate's flat. The warm sun – a promise of spring that had filled me with hope that I could take back control of everything that had unravelled since Zara had walked back into our lives – had long set, and the chill of evening seemed to sap my confidence.

Despite the cold and the wind that whipped along the river, tangling my hair and cutting through my thin denim jacket, I walked across Tower Bridge over the river instead of heading to the nearest Tube station. I barely registered where I was going; my feet moved on autopilot, my thoughts scattered. I felt as if I was close to a resolution, the solutions to the problems that had almost shattered my marriage and placed my closest friendships in jeopardy almost within my grasp.

Rowan and I could tell the others about Zara's final lie, reveal her for the person she was, definitively not to be trusted. The fog of mistrust could be cleared. I could tell Patch what she'd done and maybe one day we'd laugh about it. I could rebuild my marriage, put my selfish personal ambitions on the back burner for now, embrace the life that until Andy's death and Zara's reappearance had felt safe if not satisfying.

I could make it all work.

The prospect sustained me all the way home, through kissing my children's sleeping faces, holding my breath so as not to wake them, through telling Patch that I wasn't hungry and microwaving a ready meal for him as if he wasn't capable of doing it himself, through cleaning my teeth and putting on my pyjamas and getting into bed.

But as soon as I switched off the light, it was as if a light inside my head came on.

I couldn't turn back the clock. I needed to face up to the insecurities that had made me doubt my friends and made all of us believe Zara's lies. I needed to face up to my own role in the break-up of her and Patch's relationship. I needed to start afresh.

I needed to see Zara.

I spent the night sleeping fitfully, itching to contact her, to arrange to meet up, to say my piece. But five thirty in the morning – when I officially gave up on sleep – was too early to contact anyone, even Zara. Perhaps especially Zara, who had always been a night owl.

I lay in the darkness, my eyes open and my mind whirring, until Patch's alarm went off and I heard Toby call me from his bed.

Then, of course, the carnage of the morning began, and it was almost ten before I was able to sit down with my phone, drinking coffee on the sofa in the slanting morning sun, and compose my message.

Zara replied almost immediately, and we arranged to meet in town, not for lunch or drinks, but in Trafalgar Square, like we were spies organising a dead drop or something.

Unusually – although perhaps inevitably – I was early. I'd decided not to bother dressing up or putting on make-up – she knew what I looked like, after all, and stunning her with my highlighted, contoured beauty wouldn't change the fact that she'd always been more beautiful than I could dream of being.

Sitting in the sunshine on the steps of the National Gallery, my jacket draped over my shoulders, looking up at Nelson's Column soaring into the sky, down at the eagerly pecking pigeons and around at the crowds of tourists, I felt oddly at peace. Whatever happened today would probably not change anything, but might at least clear my conscience.

Zara arrived exactly on time. Like me, she wasn't wearing make-up – the first time I'd ever seen her without it. Her skin was alabaster flawless, but her eyes looked smaller, her jawline rounder. In her gym leggings and jumper, she looked very young and somehow defenceless.

She sat down next to me and wrapped her arms around her knees.

'Hey, Naomi.'

'Hey. Thanks for coming.'

'It's okay. I had nothing on. I'm going back to Paris this afternoon – I only came back to check out of my Airbnb.'

'Then I'm glad I caught you. This won't take long. I – basically, I just wanted to say sorry.'

I angled my body sideways so I could see her face. We were close enough that, over the scent of roasting nuts from a street vendor's cart and a cloud of sweet, fruity vapour from a passer-by's e-cigarette, I could smell her familiar perfume.

'You're sorry?' Her eyes widened in surprise.

'I... Yeah.' I looked down, my fingers twiddling the strap of my handbag, then forced myself to meet her gaze again. 'I did a shit thing, back then with Patch. You trusted me and I betrayed your trust. I was in love and I thought that made it okay, but it didn't.'

Zara laughed. The sun emerged from behind a cloud, illuminating her face and the brilliant green of her eyes. She squinted against it, the sides of her nose wrinkling, and pushed her sunglasses down from her head.

'I didn't think you'd go through with it, you know,' she said.

'What do you mean?'

'With Patch. Come on. I wasn't stupid – I could see how you wanted it to go. And he fancied you too. What a man, honestly. Lovely to look at but as subtle as a brick.'

'Is that why you told me you'd been unfaithful to him?' I asked. It felt strange articulating the secret I'd kept to myself all these years.

'I had to, didn't I? You'd never have got on with it and shagged him if I hadn't. There was a risk you'd tell him, of course, but I didn't think you would.'

My sleep-deprived brain reeled. I felt like I was in one of those funfair halls of mirrors, all the reflections of myself and the people I thought I knew suddenly distorted and unfamiliar.

'Hang on.' I looked up at her again, but saw only my own face, reflected in the black lenses of her shades. 'You meant for me and Patch to get together? I don't understand.'

'It's simple.' She turned to me, her blank gaze direct. 'You wanted something that was mine. I didn't want it much myself, but that wasn't the point. And I wanted something you had. So I figured we'd do a trade.'

'Zara, I don't get it. What are you talking about?'

'You had them – Kate, Rowan and Abbie. You were right there in the inner circle and I wasn't.'

'But you weren't even here. You were in Paris.'

'Doesn't matter. I could have been camping out in their front room and it would have made no difference. You were their friend and I was just someone who was around because she was dating their mate.'

'But we all were. The Girlfriends' Club – the clue's in the name. That's how it started. And anyway, you said—'

But she interrupted me before I could continue. 'Sure. For about five seconds – which was approximately how long it took for Kate to dump Ryan and stop being a girlfriend, if you remember. You and Whatshisname didn't last much longer. Then Rowan and Paul split up. And Andy was never anyone's girlfriend.'

I stared at her, my face no doubt as blank as her black-covered eyes. 'I don't understand. I thought this was about Patch, but you're talking about our friends.'

She sighed, like she was explaining something very simple to someone very hard of thinking. 'It was about him, like I said. I thought if he cheated on me with you, they'd want you out of the group and me in, because they'd feel sorry for me.'

'But that's mad.'

'Possibly. It made sense to me at the time.' She shrugged. 'Anyway, it didn't work, did it?'

In a small voice, I said, 'That's because no one knew. They thought you'd already split up. I even thought that.'

'Did you, now?'

'I... Okay, we'd flirted. We even kissed. But that was literally all. That's why I wanted to see you today – to say I was sorry for that. By the time – you know, before anything more than that happened – you weren't together any more. At least that's what I thought. I only found out recently that that wasn't true.'

The sky had clouded over once more and the breeze was picking up. On the hard, cold stone of the step, I could feel my buttocks going numb. I shifted, pulling my jacket closer around my shoulders. Zara pushed her shades up again.

'How did you find out?' she asked.

'He told me. But only because I asked.'

'He's quite the player, isn't he, your husband?'

'He says he made a mistake. He says he didn't want to hurt you.'

'Funny, that. That's what he told me, the morning after Abbie's wedding.'

'That he didn't want to hurt you?' Even as I asked the question, I knew what the answer would be.

Zara laughed, a small, humourless sound. 'That he didn't want to hurt you.'

My mouth suddenly felt dry and my stomach tight, so it was hard for me to get air into my lungs. I remembered that next morning – waking up in Rowan's room, hungover and confused. Borrowing some clothes from her because I couldn't do what would look like the walk of shame along the hotel corridor in my bridesmaid's dress. Hurrying back to my own room and finding Patch there in the shower, and wondering in confusion why housekeeping had already been in and made the bed, and him explaining that he'd woken early and already been down for breakfast.

And me not wanting to disbelieve him, not wanting to think for even a single second that there was any reason to doubt him, even though the last I'd heard the previous night he'd been outside with Zara, calming her down while she smoked in the garden.

Adrenaline coursed through me, making my skin prickle. 'What are you saying?'

'Do I really need to spell it out? We slept together that night. He never could resist me. I was pissed, but that's not really why I did it. I can show you the texts he sent me, if you like. He did feel terrible about it, to be fair. Although not terrible enough not to come and see me in Paris a few weeks later.'

'I don't believe you.' I could barely get the words out.

My mind was scrambling like a spider when you catch it in a glass to put it outside, struggling to recall those few weeks, when Patch had been up in Aberdeen with work, which had been normal then. But then there'd been a weekend when he was supposed to be home, but hadn't because there was some problem that had kept him there.

It had all seemed plausible at the time – it hadn't even crossed my mind that there was anything to worry about. Just a blip, an inconvenience. Just missing him. Not this.

'If you don't believe me, you should take a look on that camera,' she said. 'I can't believe you haven't already. There are photos of us together on there. Time stamped and everything. But it didn't last; he said he wouldn't do it any more, because he wanted to be with you. And it was pretty clear by then that what I'd thought would happen with you and the other girls wasn't going to happen, so...'

She shrugged, as if dismissing a minor inconvenience – her favourite shade of lipstick being discontinued, say, or not being able to get a table at a restaurant she wanted to try.

'So you gave up?'

'I was busy. I had other things going on in my life. It just wasn't that important.'

'And then Andy died.'

'And then Andy died,' she agreed. 'You know, I did care about him. He and I were quite similar in lots of ways. Both fucked up.'

I wanted to scream, *Andy was nothing like you! Andy was kind, deep down. He cared about his friends.*

But I could see where she was coming from. Whatever it was in her that was fragile – so damaged it was almost broken – must have found an echo in Andy, wrestling with different demons.

'So you decided to come back for the funeral and try and wreak havoc with our friendship all over again?'

'It wasn't a decision, really. It just sort of happened.'

She made it sound so casual, as if what she'd almost succeeded in doing wasn't in the least important.

'And pretending you had cancer? Did that sort of happen, too?'

'Oh.' Now, surprisingly, Zara blushed. I couldn't see much

of her skin between the high neck of her jumper and the stark black rims of her shades, but the ivory pallor was briefly suffused with mottled pink. 'You weren't supposed to find out about that. Never mind come dashing out to Paris to check up on me. Honestly, that was above and beyond.'

'What the hell did you think would happen, though? You can't just lie about shit like that.'

'Well, no one wants to admit they've got a nasty case of thrombosed piles, do they? I had to tell Gabi, because I needed a place to stay, but I didn't want it all over my social media, obviously. So I came up with something that sounded a bit more – *émouvant*. And you know what it's like when you start telling a story. Sometimes you get carried away.'

I was silenced – shocked by the lightheartedness with which Zara dismissed her lies. And then I realised it was just more of the same – more of the elaborate stories she'd told us all, different ones for different people, tailored according to what would have the greatest appeal to each of us.

My appalled disbelief must have shown on my face, because Zara said, 'Come on, Naomi. It wasn't that big of a deal. No one got hurt.'

'It is a big deal, though. Can't you see that? Lying to people who care about you is a massive deal.'

'And you've never done that? Really? Not even the teeniest snow-white lie?'

I felt my own face colour now. Of course I had. Telling Patch I was too tired for sex when the truth was I just didn't want it. Telling the children I'd forgotten to bring their Easter chocolate home from Bridget's when actually I'd left it there deliberately so they could have a bit every time they visited and hopefully rot their teeth gradually instead of all at once.

Telling myself I could make my marriage work, even though I was pretty certain that I couldn't.

'It's different,' I protested.

'Maybe.' She shrugged again. 'I just don't see it that way.'

'Zara.' I stood up. 'I guess there are a lot of things you and I don't see the same way. I hope maybe one day you'll realise that some things we do aren't okay, and we've got to deal with the consequences.'

'God, don't lecture me, Naomi! It's not like you're perfect.'

'Oh, no,' I said. 'I'm as far from perfect as it gets. I've done plenty of things I'm not proud of. But I've got to own them, and try to make amends. That's why I wanted to apologise to you, and I meant it. I'm sorry, Zara.'

I took one last look at her, hunched and small on the stairs like a doll, or a figure made by a child out of pipe cleaners. I didn't say goodbye – I just walked slowly away. She'd done her best to hurt me, and she'd succeeded. She couldn't hurt me any more – not if I didn't let her.

THIRTY-FOUR

'What, no picnic this time?' Patch joked.

It was Saturday afternoon and we were on Hampstead Heath, sitting on a bench overlooking the London skyline, the world literally at our feet. I knew he was remembering, as I was, the time we'd come here years ago, on one of our first dates as an official couple. We'd sat on a rug in the May sunshine and eaten smoked salmon sandwiches and drunk champagne, and he'd told me he loved me for the first time.

It had been one of the happiest days of my life. It was still right up there with the day Toby and Meredith were born, the day I graduated from uni, and the day I got cast as Desdemona in the school play.

The memory of that happiness was almost physical, as real a thing as the wisps of cloud in the sapphire sky and the shrieking parakeets wheeling overhead, and as impossible to capture. I wondered if Patch felt it too.

But I didn't ask him. I just said, 'I've got a couple of packs of those dehydrated carrot puff things the kids like in my bag. They might be a bit squashed.'

'Thanks, but I think I'll pass.'

We'd dropped the twins off at Imogen's daughter's birthday party, with a clear two hours before we needed to collect them (no doubt hyper and exhausted after too much cake), so I'd suggested a walk.

Not that I wanted to walk, particularly – but I did need to talk. The blindsiding shock of my meeting with Zara had gradually left me, replaced first with fury and now with a kind of leaden dread.

I knew what I needed to do, but that didn't make doing it any easier. Looking at Patch's face, the familiar lines of his half-smile, the threads of grey in his hair, the deep brown eyes the children had inherited, I felt overwhelming sadness.

When we'd come here all those years ago, I'd been filled with desire for him, leaping joyfully into our future together like a swimmer on a hot day. Now, I was living that future. We had our life together, our home, our children – all the things I couldn't have dreamed of back then.

And I was about to throw it all away – dismantle it, somehow, untangle the very fabric of what we'd created.

Are you sure? I asked myself. *You don't have to do this.*

I didn't, of course. I could just put the past behind me, look to the future, move on. But it didn't feel like it would be moving on at all. It felt like it would be taking a step back, far into the past, making myself revert to the person I'd been then, denying who I was now – older, sadder, perhaps stronger.

Only I didn't feel strong. I felt more weak and fragile and alone than I'd ever felt in my life.

Unexpectedly, the image of Andy's face came into my mind – not as he'd been when I first met him, the party boy whose yearning for fun and freedom had trapped him in the darkest of places, but the man he'd become before his relapse, strong and serene.

You've got this, Naomi, I imagined him saying. *One day at a time, as they never stop fucking telling us in the programme.*

Andy was gone. He'd died because he'd let his past reclaim him. I wasn't going to allow that to happen to me.

'You look glum as hell, babe,' Patch said. 'What's up?'

'I was just thinking about Andy.'

'Andy? Poor sod. I still miss him, you know. We had crazy times.'

'I know. It's like he packed loads of lives into just one, like a cat or something.'

Patch laughed. 'You say the daftest things sometimes, Nome.'

I laughed with him, but my laughter soon died down. Remembering Andy had made me even more conscious of what I'd brought my husband here to do – choosing this place, with its memories of the past and its promise of the future lying before us, hazy and glimmering in the sunshine.

'It's made me think, though. Really, you only get one life. When you make mistakes, like Andy did, you don't get to unmake them. You can only live with them, or change what you do next.'

'That's all very profound, Nome. Not sure I'm up for such deep thinking on a Saturday afternoon. How about we head back and have a pint before we collect the kids?'

I remembered Zara's words – subtle as a brick. It was true – for all his amiability, I realised, I'd never really been able to talk to Patch about the things that mattered most.

Now, I was going to have to.

'We can have a drink later, maybe,' I said, thinking that what I was going to need most in the world before this day was out was an enormous gin, tonic optional. 'First, there's something I need to talk to you about, and I don't want to do it in a pub with loads of people listening.'

'Look, is this about you going back to work? I want to support you, Nome. Maybe in a couple of years...'

'It is, and it isn't. That's part of it. But, Patch...'

I stopped. *Now's your last chance, Naomi. You can not say it – not now, or even not ever. You can keep what you've got in the present and make the most of it.*

'What is it, babe?' He reached over and took my hand. 'If something's bothering you, you can tell me, you know.'

His kindness was like a knife in my heart. *What if I never find someone this nice again?*

I forced air into my lungs past the lump in my throat. 'I want to split up.'

'You want what? Hold on, run that past me again.'

'I want to end our marriage. I've been thinking and thinking about it. I don't like what my life's become and I can't see another way to change it.'

'This is about Zara, isn't it? A couple of sympathy shags, years and years ago, and you're jacking in our marriage and breaking up the kids' home over it? Have you lost your mind?'

Already, I could feel my calm deserting me. 'It wasn't just a couple, years and years ago. It was a couple more, months after that. After Abbie's wedding.'

'Who the fuck told you that?' His face was blank with shock, as if I'd slapped him.

'Zara did.'

'Zara's a bullshitter.'

'Yes, she is. But I think she was telling the truth about that.'

'Right. So you'd rather believe that crazy woman over your own husband? She always had it in for you, you know. She never wanted us to be together even though she was fucking other men while she was seeing me.'

His words shocked me – the casual admission of the secret I thought I'd kept to myself all these years. 'You knew about that?'

'I found out a few days before you and I went to that gig in Camden.' He sighed, as if remembering pain that was so distant it had become nothing more than a theoretical concept. 'She sent me a text meant for some other guy. Maybe she did it on purpose; I don't know. She's crazy, Nome. She's a loose cannon. And you're seriously saying you're going to let her get her way over some casual, drunken thing that meant nothing?'

His sudden belligerence alarmed me, then amused me. What did he think I was going to say? *Oh, now you put it that way, of course I'll change my mind?*

It had been a pattern in our relationship, I realised: Patch holding out for whatever he wanted, me going along with it for the sake of a quiet life, conscious that I was so lucky to have him, I was punching, I mustn't do anything that could drive him away, back to Zara.

Well, that ship had sailed. He'd been lured back to her without me having to do anything wrong at all.

'I don't really care what Zara wants. Honestly, this isn't about Zara at all – it's just that she sees things for what they are. I love the children and I love your mum and I love you – I really, really do, and I always will – but I can't keep putting myself last. I've lost myself somewhere along the way, and I need to—'

'To "find yourself"? What is this, *Eat, Pray* fucking *Love*?'

I forced a steadying breath into my lungs. 'Take the piss if you want. I don't mind. Here's the thing, though, Patch. You want your life arranged to suit you. Your work, your hobbies, even your sleep. Even sleeping with Zara. It's not so much that it hurts me, although it does. It's that you went ahead and did it because it was what you wanted to do, and you didn't care that it would hurt me and hurt her.'

He turned to me, his mouth twisting with anger that I knew was a mask hiding pain. 'Oh, so it's not about you finding your-self, after all. It's about me being public enemy number one.'

'You are the person you are. I knew from the get-go – I can't blame you for it. But it's because of who you are that I can't get to be who I want to be.'

'Lots of women would kill for your life, Naomi. Look at it –

great house, lovely kids, not having to go to work, husband who loves you. You don't know you're born.'

'I know. I know I'm lucky and plenty of people would want what I've got. But that doesn't mean it's all I want. It's not, and I'm allowed to make that choice.'

'And anyway, what about the kids? How the hell do you think would work? Because I'm not going to let you have them full time and never see them. They're my children.'

'And you're their father, and they love you. I wouldn't dream of not letting you see them. The more time you can spend with them, the better.'

He flinched, as if realising he had fallen into a trap. 'Fine. Then move out if you want to. I'll keep the children with me and you can rent some poky flat somewhere and live on benefits. See how you like that.'

I sighed. 'Patch, we'll have to work all of that stuff out. It isn't going to be easy, I know. But we both want what's best for the children.'

'What's best for the children is having their mother and father living together under one roof with them.'

'Not when their mother doesn't want to be there.'

He stood, the muscles in his legs propelling him powerfully upwards. For a second, I wondered what I'd do if he hit me, but I forgot the thought immediately. Patch had never raised a hand to me and I knew he never would. But his anger was still frightening.

'I'm not going to stay here and listen to this. You need to get your head straight – get over whatever this craziness is and come to your senses. And then apologise to me.'

I watched as he turned and strode away down the hill, feeling the breath release from my body in a long, weary sigh. It had gone both as well as I'd hoped and as badly as I'd feared. But it was done – I'd taken the first step on the path that led to my future.

And the first step, Andy had always said, was the hardest one.

I waited a few minutes, imagining Patch leaving the park, finding a pub, ordering a pint of Guinness and sitting alone, drinking, calming down, waiting for me to text and say I was sorry, it had all been a mistake.

The grass felt springy under my feet, as if I'd shed a heavy load, as I walked down the hill to fetch my children from their party.

THIRTY-FIVE

My mood of buoyant optimism lasted the rest of the weekend, in spite of Patch giving me the silent treatment, maintaining a face like thunder and only addressing me via the children.

'Meredith, where did Mummy put Daddy's gym bag?'

'I don't know what a man has to do to get anything to eat in this house, do you, Toby?'

Resolutely, I ignored his sulking. I'd expected it; it was inevitable. He was hurting and this was how he was expressing it.

Still, when I woke alone in our bed on Monday morning, I realised that the sunshine had vanished and with it my positivity. I dragged myself up and embarked on the morning routine, discovering that, unsurprisingly, Patch had already left to go to the gym before work and the children were at their most cantankerous.

By the time I opened the front door to begin the walk to nursery, I'd already endured a screaming fit from Meredith because she didn't want to wear her raincoat, Toby throwing his breakfast toast on the floor Marmite side down, and the discovery that the back of the sofa was soaked with rain because Patch had left the living room window open.

'Come on, you two,' I urged as cheerfully as I could. 'Hurry up or we'll be late.'

'I need a wee, Mummy,' Meredith whined.

'Well go upstairs and have one then. Come on.'

'Mummy, I'm hungry,' complained Toby.

'Serves you right for twatting your breakfast on the floor,' I said under my breath, then, 'I'll put an extra cereal bar in your bag. Let's make a move.'

But by the time we made it to the nursery gates, my exasperation had been replaced with a deep sadness. These were my children – only slightly larger versions of the tiny babies I'd carried inside me and loved so much I wanted to lick them from the moment I first saw their furious, scrunched-up faces.

I was tearing their world apart. Everything they knew – the corner of the kitchen where Meredith sometimes curled up in the sunshine like a cat, nodding off on the floor and needing to be carried upstairs to finish her nap; the young apple tree in the garden Toby still studiously watered with a can even after it had rained; their bedroom, their climbing frame, their parents – all of it would be left behind.

And it was all my fault: my urge to unmake past mistakes, my desire to get a job and a life outside of motherhood, my refusal to forgive and forget my husband's transgression.

You could just suck it up and stay, Naomi, I thought.

But the prospect of that was intolerable. I couldn't imagine ever sleeping with Patch again, knowing what I knew now. I could already feel the resentment I harboured over his selfishness, his assumption that anything to do with the house and the children was my problem, his prioritisation of his own ambitions over mine, emerging from the place where I'd kept it submerged for so long.

If I stay, I'll end up hating him, I realised.

'Are you okay, Naomi?' I'd barely noticed Bronwen taking the children's hands from mine and their bags from my arm. 'You look miles away.'

'Sorry.' I forced a smile on to my face. 'Monday morning, you know. Just getting through it on autopilot.'

'Aren't we all?' She laughed. 'You have a good day, now.'

I bent down to kiss the children, feeling the first hot tears on my cheeks mixing with the cool rain. Somehow, I managed not to cry properly until they were out of sight, but as I walked away the street in front of me went all blurry and I couldn't catch my breath for sobs.

Then I heard hurrying footsteps on the pavement behind me and felt a warm hand on my arm.

'Hey, Naomi.' It was Princess Lulu, once again in her sleek work attire instead of her sleek sportswear.

'Morning, Imogen,' I managed. 'Sorry. Having a bit of a bad day.'

'I can see that. Come on, let's go for a coffee.'

Part of me wanted to tell her to leave me alone, brush off her concern, head home and lick my wounds in peace. But suddenly, the company of another adult, another woman, felt like a promise of much-needed comfort.

'But won't you be late for work?' I asked.

'I'm the boss. I can be as late as I like. Let's do this.'

Firmly grasping my elbow, she led me down the road and pushed open the door of a coffee shop – a chichi new place I'd been meaning to visit but never found the time, all artisan espresso and avocado on sourdough toast.

'Hello, Imogen.' The bearded young man behind the counter beamed at her like she was his long-lost sister. 'Your usual? Extra hot oat milk latte?'

'Yes, please, Duncan.'

'And for you, madam?' His face was solicitous – carefully kind, but not so kind as to make me start crying again.

'Just a black coffee, please,' I said.

'I'll bring it right over.'

Before I could protest, Imogen had tapped her phone on the payment device and led me to a table by the window.

'Now,' she said, 'what's up? You don't have to tell me if you don't want to – I'm just some random, after all – but if you want to talk, I'll listen.'

'Thanks,' I muttered. 'You're very kind. It's nothing, really.'

But also everything.

'The twins are all right?' she asked gently.

'They're fine. At least, they are now. But my marriage has gone tits up and I don't know how long they're going to be fine for. And I haven't got a job or any money or anywhere to live and it all just seems like...' I trailed off, a tear splatting on to the dark, opaque surface of my coffee.

'A lot? That's because it is.' Her blue eyes rested on me as she sipped her latte. 'Look, feel free to tell me to butt out. But I've been there. I know what it's like.'

'You have? But I thought...' My image of the wealthy banker husband, the perfect home, the life without financial or marital woes, materialised in my mind and just as quickly vanished.

'I was happily married? I thought so too, until I wasn't. That was when I'd just found out I was pregnant with Jesse. It was grim – the worst thing that's ever happened to me. But I got through it, and you will, too.'

'How, though? I haven't had a job since before I had the twins. And Patch works stupid hours and has hobbies and stuff – would he have the kids on weekends and then I'd never see them? And how will I afford to even live? I just can't see how it's ever going to work.'

'Now, listen to me,' she said firmly. 'It's not easy, I know. But you won't get anywhere by being defeatist about it. Your husband's not an unreasonable person, is he?'

'No,' I admitted reluctantly, 'he's not. The reason we're

splitting up is – well, it's complicated. But it's not because he's violent or anything like that.'

'That's a good start.' The way she said it made me wonder if, perhaps, her own ex-husband had been something like that. 'So, really, it's just practicalities you need to focus on, isn't it? Where you can afford to live, how you split childcare – all that stuff.'

'I guess so. But all that – it feels kind of overwhelming right now.'

'Of course it does. So we break it down. Can you spare ten minutes?'

I nodded, automatically taking my phone out of my bag. Then Imogen started talking and I listened and made notes. She talked about pensions and equity and divorce law and all the things I'd been too terrified to think about on my own, and sent me links to documents I could read later on.

Listening to her, I was reminded of Rowan, who'd separated from Paul shortly after their daughter was born, and managed to make it work. Rowan, too, would be able to help me navigate all this.

'I think that's probably enough for you to be getting on with for now,' she said at last. 'I'll send you the details of the solicitor I used – she's sharp and she's kind. She'll help you.'

'But first, I need to help myself.' I felt my spine straighten against the back of my chair. 'I need to find a job.'

'What is it you do?'

I laughed. 'For the past four years, change nappies, clean up sick and do the nursery run. Before that, I was a legal secretary.'

'Not my area, unfortunately. But I run a recruitment company and I'd be happy to help you polish your CV up a bit. It's a candidates' market out there; you'll find something.'

'I really hope you're right.' I drained my coffee, encouraged by her confidence.

'Let me give you my card,' she suggested, handing over a

glossy scarlet rectangle. 'And get in touch, okay? Otherwise I'll chase you next time I see you at nursery.'

'I will, promise. And thanks for the coffee and – you know. Everything.'

After that, I hurried to the supermarket and picked up some shopping for Bridget. She seemed more cheerful today and less confused, so I took the opportunity to ask her how her appointment with her GP had gone.

'You can't be too careful at my age, Naomi,' she said. 'So they've referred me for some tests at the hospital next week.'

'You can't be too careful at any age.' I hugged her. 'I'll come and keep you company there, shall I?'

She accepted my offer gratefully and I left shortly afterwards. I didn't tell her about Patch and me – it wasn't my thing to tell. It was news for Patch to break to her alone or for him and I to reveal together. But I knew that whatever happened, she'd always be a presence in my life, my children's grandmother, a woman I'd grown to love.

Back at home, instead of tackling the household chores, I opened my laptop and spent the day sitting at the kitchen table, getting up and making endless cups of tea whenever I began to feel overwhelmed by the task ahead of me.

All the work I'd already done on my CV and my LinkedIn network was going to stand me in good stead – there, at least, I was prepared. Summer was almost here and it wasn't the ideal time to be job-hunting, but I was confident that by the time the children started school in September, I'd be employed, even if it wasn't in my ideal job.

In a fit of optimism, I even googled law conversion courses: now might not be the perfect time to resurrect that old dream, but it wasn't the right time to let it go, either.

And, when Patch got in from work, the children asleep and the dinner things cleared away, I suggested he join me at the table, and got my laptop out again.

'We need to talk,' I said.

I knew that the conversation would take all my resolve and courage, and that it would be only the first of many. But I was prepared. I had my ducks in a row.

And even more importantly, I had three responses to the message I'd sent earlier to Kate, Abbie and Rowan in a new WhatsApp group using exactly the same words.

NAOMI:

We need to talk.

THIRTY-SIX

I looked at the three faces sitting with me around the table at the Prince Rupert. Actually, thanks to a mirror on the wall next to me, I could see my own face, too, and it bore the same expression as the others' – unsmiling, wary, a bit sad. If I looked the other way, I could see a slice of green space, lit by the lowering sun – the football pitch where our men had played all those years ago.

It was almost two decades since we'd first drunk in that pub, and the first time we'd returned to it for ages – the Prince Rupert, as I remembered now we were actually there, had never been the most salubrious of places, which was why (once we'd dropped any remaining pretence of actually watching our menfolk play football on Wednesday evenings) we'd made the decision to decamp to other, nicer venues.

But now, here we were again, at my instigation – in fact, my insistence.

I couldn't help thinking of that first night – how we'd abandoned the rainy, freezing football pitch in search of warmth and alcohol, none of us with high expectations of how the evening would unfold. And how, in the end, we had found so much more. How, from more or less the first drink, the first shared laugh, the first tentatively offered confidence, we'd been friends.

I thought of all the monthly get-togethers, bright beads on the intertwined chains of our lives. Everything we'd been through: the births of Clara, Meredith and Toby; Abbie's wedding and mine; new jobs and new homes and new cats; and, of course, our shared grief over losing Andy. The stream of our daily chats with requests for support with everything from a domestic squabble to a broken Hoover, trivial speculation about whether metallic jeans would still be around next season or were a waste of fifty quid and made your legs look like leftover sausages wrapped in foil.

I imagined it all falling silent: no more 'Good morning's, no more 'Night all, love you', just a blank screen.

Tumbleweed.

Kate had her phone on the table in front of her, and occasionally glanced down at it impatiently, as if she had better things to do and places she'd rather be. Abbie's mouth turned down at the corners like a sad emoji, her shoulders slumped as mournfully as they'd been at Andy's funeral. Rowan looked close to tears. And I – my reflection in the foxed surface of the mirror told me – looked like I was sitting face to face with an interview panel, rather than my closest friends in the world.

We've had a good innings, I told myself. *Nothing lasts forever. At least you've tried.*

But I didn't want to be philosophical about it. I didn't want to accept that people change, friends move on, life comes at you fast. I wanted to fight with everything I had for the survival of us as a unit, for what I knew the Girlfriends' Club had meant to us all.

'Shall I get a round in?' Abbie asked, smiling hesitantly. 'What did we drink that first time, mulled wine?'

'They won't be serving it now,' Kate pointed out. 'It was November then and it's summer now.'

'Mulled wine's pretty gross anyway,' Rowan said. 'And it's even grosser when it's cooling so you have to drink it really quick.'

'And then you end up puking up your mini stollen bites all over Father Christmas's boots,' I agreed.

They all looked at me, their faces still. *Shit*, I thought, *that one didn't land. Tough crowd.*

Even the way we were sitting felt alien. Usually, we'd be leaning forward across the table, our elbows propped on its surface, our faces so close I'd notice if one of my friends was wearing new perfume or had had her eyebrows reshaped. Today, we were upright in our chairs, our hands in our laps, like board members negotiating a hostile takeover.

Always the peacemaker, Abbie tried again. 'They've got Pimm's. It might be drinkable.'

'So long as we get them to make it with soda water instead of lemonade,' Kate agreed reluctantly.

'And slosh in some extra gin,' suggested Rowan. 'I think we all need it.'

'I'm on it.' Relieved that the ice was, if not broken, at least perhaps beginning to crack, I hurried to the bar. I strained to hear their voices behind me but there was nothing – no hum of chatter, no bursts of laughter, no snap of a camera as someone took a group selfie. A few minutes later, I returned with a tray holding a jug, four glasses and two packets of pork scratchings.

'I see they still haven't raised their bar snack game here,' Kate observed, carefully pouring the amber liquid into our glasses, slices of cucumber and strawberry splashing after it.

'I guess it's better than a Scotch egg with extra salmonella.' Rowan ripped open the bags of snacks and pushed them to the centre of the table, but no one ate.

'Well, cheers, I guess.' Abbie reached out across the table

and we all followed suit, the rims of our glasses clinking together in a ritual as old as our friendship. I wondered if I'd ever hear that sound again without longing for these women.

'Cheers,' Rowan, Kate and I echoed.

I cleared my throat, feeling that job-interview feeling twist my stomach. 'Thanks for coming, guys. I know it's a pain. But I think we've all got things to say to each other.'

Kate's face was still and wary again. 'Right. Why don't you go first?'

No, you go first. Or Ro, or Abs. Don't make me do it. But I had to – this had been my idea after all. In a sense, I'd started it.

I said, 'So, first off. Patch and I are splitting up.'

My friends' – or former friends' – faces segued from expressionless to sad.

Rowan reached out and touched my hand, just a brush of a fingertip like she was scared I'd burn her – or contaminate her. 'I'm sorry.'

'So am I,' said Kate.

'Are you okay?' Abbie asked.

'Yes,' I said slowly. 'Well, no. Not really. But I will be eventually.'

'What happened?' Rowan asked. 'I mean, you said you'd decided that the other stuff – the stuff with Zara – didn't matter.'

'I had. And it felt like the right decision at the time, even though I know you guys didn't agree with it.'

'It wasn't about that,' began Rowan. 'It was—'

I held up my hand. 'Let me finish. I know how things started with Patch and me wasn't right. I know it wasn't fair to Zara. I can see that now – I guess I could see it all along. I was selfish and so was he. If there'd been a way to make that not have happened, believe me, I'd have done it. But there wasn't. And with the kids and everything – why uproot their lives because of a shit thing their mum and dad did years ago?'

Slowly, I saw Rowan nod, then Kate and Abbie follow suit.

'But then there was another thing.' I paused, the pain still too fresh for me to get the words out easily. 'You all remember what happened at Abbie's wedding?'

'When Matt forgot the words to his speech?' Abbie asked, smiling. I saw her smile mirrored on Kate and Rowan's faces, and felt it on my own.

'Who could forget that?' I said. 'It was the best bit, right? But no. After that. When Zara turned up and nicked your bouquet.'

'She really lost it, didn't she?' Rowan shook her head. 'What came over her?'

'She felt like I'd taken what was hers by right,' I explained. 'So she was going to take – something. I don't know what she actually meant with the bouquet. Maybe she didn't know herself. But after that, when Patch went outside to talk to her and we went up to your room, Ro—'

'Oh my God,' Rowan whispered. 'Don't tell me she and Patch...?'

I nodded miserably. 'That night and a few times after. She says she's got texts from him to prove it, and photos, but I didn't need to see them, because he says it's true.'

'Oh, Naomi.' Abbie reached over and squeezed my hand. 'That's awful.'

'Yeah, it's not great. But it's also not everything. I know cheating's meant to be the ultimate deal-breaker, the thing you can't get past. But it isn't always. I think I could have moved past it. But it made me realise things about Patch and about me – about where things had got to in my life.'

'Go on,' Rowan said.

'I realised I'd lost me.' I shrugged. I didn't know how to find the words, but I hoped that the knowledge and understanding my friends had formed of me over the years would be enough for them to interpret what I meant. 'I'd let my life become all about being Patch's wife and the kids' mum and there was nothing left for me any more. I guess I gave myself permission to be more selfish. More like Zara. So I decided I had to leave.'

'You don't want to be like Zara.' Kate's face was pale with shock.

'Not in every way – of course not. But one thing she does is fight for what she wants. She wanted to – to take revenge on me, I guess, for what happened all those years ago. And she did.'

'What are you talking about, exactly?' Rowan picked up her glass, touched it to her lips and then put it down again. She looked like Toby with his puzzle toy, putting a shape in the wrong hole at first, then trying another and another, knowing eventually he would get it right.

I took a deep breath. Telling them about Patch was the easy part – I'd already figured it out in my own head; I knew what to believe and what not to. But this was different.

'She told me she'd always felt on the sidelines of the group. Which she was, of course, because of not being here all the time. But it was like she was holding up a mirror to me and making me feel that way too. She made me doubt our friendship.'

I saw understanding gradually dawn on their faces.

'And then when I decided to try and make a go of things with Patch, even after I knew how things were when he and I first got together, I felt like you were all judging me. I felt like if you could, you'd take her side over mine.'

I stopped, looking around at them. Kate's hands were wrapped tightly around her glass, her knuckles white. Rowan was biting her lip. Abbie was fiddling with her hair, winding a strand round and round her finger then letting it go and starting again.

'It sounds so petty, doesn't it?' I went on. 'It's like we learned how to do friendship when we were teenage girls and never really figured out a different way.'

My words fell into silence. I could hear a beep from the card reader at the bar, the whoosh and clunk of the toilet door opening and closing, the hum of traffic on the road outside. But my friends made no sound – I couldn't even hear them breathing.

Then Kate said, 'I know what you mean, actually. Because I felt the same way.'

'About something Zara said to you?' Abbie asked softly.

Kate nodded.

'What was it?' I asked, although I already knew.

Kate cleared her throat, hesitated, then the words came out in a rush. 'She told me that she felt responsible for Andy's addiction, and his death. Because of how they used to party together when he visited her in Paris. And I do, too – I always have, no matter how much everyone tells me it's not my fault. And she made me think that you guys felt the same, and blamed me for it.'

'But you know we don't!' Rowan's voice was high, almost pleading.

'Why wouldn't you?' Kate asked. 'Come on. If I hadn't had that relationship with him and kept it a secret for so long, and let him stay with me when he was using, and all that stuff. If I hadn't done that, he might still be alive. I thought that, deep down, and there was no reason to believe you guys wouldn't think it too.'

'Oh my God,' Rowan said. 'That's so cruel. And so not true.'

'I told you it wasn't true,' Abbie said, her voice thin and small. 'But I don't think you believed me.'

Kate said slowly, 'I did and I didn't. I didn't really believe you'd say something like that about me to Zara, of all people. But you see, I've always blamed myself for it. And Zara must have guessed that. She knew the seed was there so she poured a load of shit on it and then it grew.'

'You mustn't blame yourself,' Abbie protested. 'You know

it's not your fault. You were the best friend Andy could have possibly had.'

There were tears in Kate's eyes. Abbie pulled a pack of tissues from her bag and passed one to Kate, then blew her own nose. I could see – as if it was a physical thing – the wall between them beginning to come down.

'Rowan,' I said. 'She told you something about me, too, didn't she?'

I felt as if I was cross-examining a witness in court – the role I'd dreamed of. It wasn't nearly so much fun as I'd thought it would be.

'I...' Rowan began, a dark flush creeping up her cheeks. 'Yes, she did. It's too horrible, I can't say it.'

I looked at her and waited, and after a few seconds she went on. 'Years ago, Zara told me she was abused when she was a teenager, by a boyfriend of her mother's.'

I could almost hear the thought rippling around the table – *Zara told us all lots of things*. But no one spoke.

'I know what you're thinking,' Rowan went on. 'But the way she talked about it – it was so vivid, so awful. It's stayed with me. So when I told her about Alex and me getting together, the best thing that's happened to me in ages, and she asked me to remind her how old Clara is, it all came back to me.'

She stopped, and we sat there for a moment, waiting, until Kate said, 'Go on, Ro. We're listening.'

'Of course, I didn't think Alex would be capable of anything remotely like that. But it made me feel guilty about what I could have exposed Clara to, you know, if Alex wasn't a good person. And then Zara said that you – Naomi – you'd said you wondered about Alex being... you know. Safe. Around Clara. And whether he was actually only with me because of her. And suddenly it wasn't about me trusting Alex any more, it was about me trusting you.'

'And that's why you were being so cold towards me,' I said. 'I don't blame you, but God, it hurt.'

'Of course it did.' Abbie's voice was so soft I could barely hear her. 'I know just how much.'

We all turned to look at her, slowly, like if we were too hasty she would take fright and run away. I reached a hand out across the table towards her, but I didn't touch her; I just waited for her to speak.

Abbie – the kindest and gentlest of us all. She'd been through so much, so recently, and it had almost broken her.

'Zara told me she can't have children,' Abbie said, her words coming out on a long sigh of breath. 'She said she was in Poland at the beginning of the pandemic, and lockdown happened and she had to stay there. She found out she was pregnant while she was there and of course abortion isn't legal, so she had to find someone who'd help her.'

Kate and Rowan's faces bore the same look of blank disbelief I knew mine did. Here it was – another of Zara's stories, carefully calculated to have the maximum impact on its audience. I felt a surge of anger – we should have known not to believe her, but we had. We all had, because she knew exactly how to draw us in.

'She haemorrhaged and nearly died,' Abbie continued, 'and when they got her to hospital they had to take her uterus out, she said. She was crying when she told me. So of course I told her about Matt and me, and how we went through infertility treatment but it didn't work. And then she said it was a relief for her, in a way, because she'd have been a terrible mother.'

'I'll drink to that,' Rowan said darkly, and I felt another, almost imperceptible lightening of the mood around the table – as if, once we were able to laugh about this, we'd be able to laugh at absolutely anything that ever happened to us in the future.

Abbie went on, 'I told her Matt and I have made peace with

it now. And it's true, we have. It's been a relief in a way. But she told me that Kate had said – that you'd said, Kate – that you were relieved too, because you thought if I had a baby we wouldn't be able to be friends in the same way if we weren't the only ones in the group without children any more.'

'I never said that,' Kate burst out furiously. 'I promise I never did. But I...'

'You thought it,' Abbie whispered.

Reluctantly, Kate nodded. 'I'm sorry. Long ago, I did think that. But once I knew what you and Matt were going through, it didn't matter any more. I just wanted you to be happy.'

'It's okay.' Abbie managed a smile. 'The only thing that would have made it not okay is if we weren't friends any more.'

'Don't you see,' Rowan asked, 'what she tried to do? She tried to split Naomi and Patch up, all those years ago. And then when that didn't work, she came for us, as friends, to try and destroy what we have together.'

'And it's working,' Kate said sadly.

I nodded slowly before saying, 'The question is, are we going to let it?'

I'd barely noticed that, outside, clouds had formed and it had been raining – one of those summer showers that catches you unawares, making you pack up your picnic and run for the car or dash into Boots and buy an emergency umbrella. But now the rain had stopped and the clouds had parted. A shaft of bright sunlight spilled through the window, reflecting off the varnished table so it was almost too bright to look at.

'No way,' Abbie said fiercely.

'No,' Kate echoed.

'Hell to the no,' Rowan almost shouted.

A few minutes before, I hadn't been able to hear my friends' breath breaking through the oppressive silence. But now I could – an audible sigh, a shared release of tension from us all. I felt relief so heady and intense it was like being drunk.

'You know what,' Rowan said, 'I think we need another jug of that Pimm's.'

'I'll get it.' I jumped to my feet and hurried over to the bar. The surly, tattooed landlady stopped wiping its surface and looked at me curiously, and I realised I'd practically skipped across the pub, like I'd just been proposed to or something.

'Same again, please.' I beamed at her. 'Pimm's with soda water, not lemonade, and plenty of extra gin. And two packets of pork scratchings.'

My mood must have been infectious, because she actually cracked a smile when she pushed the jug across to me.

'Thank you so much.' I tapped my phone on the card reader and heard its familiar beep.

And then a new notification caught my eye and all my elation melted away.

THIRTY-SEVEN

Slowly, I returned to the group with the jug and snacks. My friends were in the familiar posture: leaning in, elbows on the table, laughing. The setting sun streamed in through the window, reflecting off Rowan's glossy hair, making the diamond on Abbie's finger sparkle with rainbows, turning Kate's eyes an impossibly bright blue.

'Guys,' I said, 'I think you need to see this.'

I held out my phone so they could all see what I'd seen: a new WhatsApp message, a strip of paler grey against the black screen, a white 'play' arrow at one end, a green dot alongside it, and the thumbnail image of Zara's face at the other end.

'She sent you a voice note?' Kate asked incredulously.

'Looks like it.'

'I mean, what are we meant to do, play it right here in the pub?' Rowan said disbelievingly.

'We're not doing that,' said Abbie. 'Hard no. Only twats put their phones on speaker in public.'

We all laughed, the tension easing a bit again, and I sat down. I didn't really have much choice – my legs felt wobbly with adrenaline, like they didn't want to support my body.

'Maybe,' Kate suggested slowly, reaching into her handbag, 'she's sent it to all of us.'

As if they'd been choreographed, three phones appeared in my friends' hands. Three thumbs swiped the screens to life. Three faces waited an impatient second for the camera to recognise them.

'I've got it,' Rowan said.

'Me too,' said Abbie.

'Yup,' said Kate.

'We don't have to put it on speaker, then,' I said. 'We can all listen to it together.'

'Or we could just delete it.' Rowan picked a slice of cucumber out of her drink and ate it. 'And block her number.'

'We could all burn our phones,' suggested Abbie.

'And then move to Uruguay and start a new life,' Kate joked, but she wasn't smiling.

'I think we have to listen to it,' I argued. 'Remember Andy's voice notes, Kate?'

She nodded sadly. 'I've still got one saved on my phone. I listen to it sometimes, when I'm really missing him.'

'He always said they were for people who think the sender's time is more important than the recipient's,' remembered Abbie. 'The rudest form of communication ever.'

'But he sent them anyway,' went on Rowan, 'long streams of consciousness going on for five or ten minutes.'

'Longer, if he got distracted and forgot he had the Record button pressed,' I said.

'This is only a couple of minutes.' Kate filled up our glasses. 'I reckon we should go for it. What's she going to say that she hasn't already?'

'She can't hurt us any more,' said Rowan. 'Surely not? After today, I reckon we're officially Zara-proof.'

'Okay,' Abbie agreed. 'Someone's going to have to hold my hand, though.'

'We'll all hold each other's hands.' I placed mine in the centre of the table. 'Come on. Hand sandwich.'

After a moment, I felt the warmth of Rowan's palm on my fingers, then additional pressure as Abbie's hand joined it, then Kate's.

'Ready when you are,' I said.

'Let's do this.' Kate lifted her phone to her ear. 'One, two, three...'

I pressed Play. There was a moment of crackly silence, and then I heard Zara's voice, as clear and present as if she was right there at the table with us, the fifth member of the Girlfriends' Club.

Hello. It's me. But you know that. It's the second Wednesday in June, and I bet you're at the Prince Rupert, aren't you? For old times' sake. I thought about joining you in person, and I almost turned up. but then I decided this way was better. I wanted you all to hear me out, just this one last time. And besides, that place is an absolute shithole.

Anyway, here I am. Or here I'm not. You know what I mean.

I wanted to say goodbye.

Don't panic, I'm not going to top myself. I'd never have the guts to do that and besides, it's really difficult isn't it? So don't worry, whenever you listen to this, I won't be dead.

Just in Wigan, which is pretty much the same.

It's where I'm from, and my parents still live there. I know what you're thinking – not the grim care home with predatory staff and not the luxury mansion in – where was it, Dubai? Just a normal terraced house in a not very nice part of a pretty grotty town. I was desperate to escape it, and now if I'm honest I'm desperate to go back.

It's all gone pretty much tits up. I couldn't carry on living the way I was, running away and pretending and telling people things to make them think I was more special than I am. I'm tired. I'm over it.

I'm seeing a shrink, who thinks I've got narcissistic personality disorder or an avoidant-dismissive insecure attachment style or something. He's going to have a good old rummage into my brain and see if he can figure it out. Maybe he will and maybe he won't, but God loves a trier, right?

So you don't have to worry about me turning up at your monthly drinks.

The other thing I wanted to say was sorry.

I don't know why I did the things I did. Hopefully my shrink will figure it out some day, and if he does, maybe I'll get the chance to explain. I wanted to be your friend, but then when I was I couldn't stop myself messing it up. I wanted to be liked, but I did so much to make you all hate me. I won't blame you if you do.

But maybe, one day, if I'm ever fixed, you'll give me the chance to apologise in person. I'd like that.

You're the most amazing women ever and I was proud to be your friend, even if I had a funny way of showing it.

Uh… bye then. Take care.

There were a couple more seconds of dead air and then nothing – just the faint rustle of friction where my phone was pressed against my ear.

I lifted it away and put it down on the table. Kate's followed it and then Rowan's and then Abbie's, and then, slowly, we unstacked our hands.

Without the warmth of Rowan's resting on it, mine felt cold.

'So that's that, then,' Kate said.

'It kind of makes sense,' Abbie mused. 'I mean, no one would behave like that without some sort of... thing. Disorder.'

'I'm glad she's getting help.' Rowan's voice was throaty, as if she might be about to cry.

'I'm glad she's okay,' I said. 'Safe, I mean. I was really worried when she said—'

'Goodbye,' finished Kate. 'After Andy, I couldn't have borne that.'

We looked at each other, our faces grave, and together we all nodded. After the loss of Andy, another loss would have been too much to endure.

But then, what choice would we have had? No more than we'd be able to choose to bring Andy back.

'We couldn't help Andy,' I said. 'We tried so hard. But Zara...'

'If she ever contacts us again...' Abbie began.

'We'll be here, won't we?' Kate finished for her.

'I mean, we won't get sucked into her drama ever again.' Rowan spoke quickly. 'That won't happen again. No way. But if she needs us...'

'If she needed us, we wouldn't abandon her,' I said.

Briefly, we piled our hands in the centre of the table again, this time in a different order: Kate's first, then Abbie's, then Rowan's, then mine. And then we moved them away again, like their work was done for now.

'Wigan, though,' Kate said. 'Who'd have ever thought it?'

And we all burst out laughing, just as the last of the sunlight disappeared and the lights of the pub came on.

THIRTY-EIGHT

FIVE MONTHS LATER

The first time I'd heard the knock on the door, it had sounded so strange I'd jumped out of my skin, before walking slowly and tentatively into the hallway and opening the door just a crack, peering out as if I was expecting an intruder before relaxing and allowing myself to step back in welcome.

Now, it was entirely familiar – the rhythm as distinctive as a signature. Tap-tap, tappity-tap-tap-tap. The sound brought a smile to my face and the children dashed down the stairs, their feet beating out a different rhythm.

'Have you got your school bag, Toby? Meredith, go back and brush your hair. Quickly, or you'll make us all late.'

'But you're not going to work today, Mummy. You've got the day off,' my daughter said.

'Can't we have the day off, too?' wheedled Toby.

'No, you may not. Bag – now. Daddy's here.'

I hurried to the door and opened it. Patch smiled at me, the special smile I'd noticed him giving me when we saw each other briefly like this. It was warm but distant, friendly but somehow sad. A smile, but also a shield.

'Groundhog day?' he asked.

'You've got it.'

I smiled back, appreciative that, at last, he did get it. Having the kids four nights one week and three the next had made him familiar with the morning carnage, the afternoon panic-dash from work to school, the evening spent trying to get two knackered twins fed, bathed, read to and asleep before they got so overtired there was zero chance of any of those things happening.

'Can you show me again how to do that braid thing in Meredith's hair? I tried copying a YouTube video but she kept wriggling and it was a mess.'

'Maybe when you drop them off on Saturday? There isn't really time now. You'll be all cack-handed and it'll take ages.'

'Daddy, Mummy's going to sail toy boats and we aren't allowed,' Toby pushed past me, thrusting his hand into his father's.

'We'll go and play boats on the pond at the weekend, okay?' Patch promised. 'And your fingers are all sticky. Did you have jam for breakfast?'

'Mummy made me a poached egg,' Meredith said. 'They're my new favourite.'

Patch looked at me, that smile on his face again. 'Damn. You're going to have to show me—'

'How to poach an egg? It's trial and error, I'm afraid. At least you'll get your protein macros in eating all the ones she won't touch because they're too hard or too snotty.'

'YouTube to the rescue again, then.' He rolled his eyes conspiratorially.

'You'll get there. Just like I did with the origami boats.'

'Should've asked me. I make a mean boat.'

'And you'll take your mum to St Mungo's church on Saturday?'

'Sure thing.' He grinned. 'I might even stay for the canasta. There's cake, you know. Right, you two – let's get going.'

Automatically, I pulled the sagging bobble out of Meredith's hair, smoothed it back from her face and retied it more securely. 'Sure you don't want to come? You could drop the kids and meet me after?'

He shook his head. 'Got a meeting. Anyway, this is your thing. I hope it goes well.'

'Me too. Especially since I've got a meeting too, at half eleven. So we're going to have to make it quick.'

'Gotcha.'

With one child holding each of his hands, he paused. Like the smile, I'd grown used to this – the moment of hesitation on the doorstep of my flat, as if he wanted to stay but also didn't. My own hesitation was familiar, too – the moment when I longed to beg him to take care of the children, bring them back to me safe, not allow them to forget about me while they were in his care.

I never did, though. I didn't need to; he was their father.

I was saved by the cat darting between my legs, making a bid for freedom through the open door as the often did.

'Come on, you, inside.' I scooped her up, pressing my face against the silken seal-coloured softness of her head. 'Have a good day. See you on Saturday evening. Love you.'

'Love you, Mummy,' the children chorused. 'Love you, Bisou.'

The door closed and I turned back into the flat, the silence roaring in my ears as it always did in the few moments after Patch collected the kids and I was left alone, until I got used to it again only to be shocked by how noisy it was when they returned. It was at times like this that I was extra grateful for the company of Bisou, who I'd almost stopped thinking of as Zara's.

Gabrielle had called Rowan first, because it had been her number that was uppermost on the scrap of paper Rowan had given her. And it was just as well, because I'd never have been able to understand the story, told in French, of how Zara hadn't returned to collect her, one of Gabrielle's children had developed an allergy, and Gabrielle couldn't bring herself to abandon her at an animal shelter.

'I can't take her, either,' Rowan had fretted. 'You know what Balthazar's like. He'd eat her for breakfast.'

So I'd made the trip to Paris on the Eurostar, this time alone, and returned with a companion. To my surprise, Bisou had fitted into my life as if she'd always been there, greeting me at the door when I got home from work, curling up on my lap while I worked on my law conversion course assignments at the kitchen table in the evenings, sleeping on the kids' pillows at night.

She was just one of the many things in my life that had changed. At first bewildered by the idea that Mummy and Daddy wouldn't be living together any more, Toby and Meredith had settled relatively quickly into their new routine, and Patch and I had – well, we were adjusting, too.

Just the previous week, on my way to work, I'd gone past the school gates and seen Patch dropping off the children. I'd stopped, keeping well away, not wanting to interfere or potentially upset the twins at the start of their day – even though a big part of me had wanted to dash over, squeeze them tightly in my arms and tell them that Mummy would always love them.

There they were, so grown-up in their uniforms but so small, too, one of them holding on to each of Patch's hands. He was walking slowly, his head lowered, apparently deep in conversation with them. What were they saying? I longed to know, but also I was enjoying being a spectator – a spy almost – in this little slice of my ex-husband's life with the children we'd always share.

I watched as he squatted down on the pavement and kissed them both, the teaching assistant looking on in approval. With a pang that was part remorse and part relief, I remembered that for the next two days, if one of them felt ill and needed to be taken home and put to bed, it would be Patch they called, not me.

Then I noticed another familiar figure hurrying along, a charcoal wool coat swinging from her shoulders, a leather laptop bag in one hand, her daughter clutching the other. Princess Lulu – Imogen.

She, too, stopped at the gate and relinquished her child with a kiss. But she didn't turn and hurry away – instead, she fell into step next to Patch, the two of them walking together in the direction of the Tube station, chatting easily like they were old friends. Then I saw Imogen laugh at something Patch had said, the morning sunlight catching her glowing skin and shiny hair, and I thought, *Hold on a minute*.

When they were safely out of sight, I resumed my own journey to work, my mind whirling. Were they seeing each other? And did I mind if they did?

To my surprise, I realised I didn't. Patch was a good man, a good father. I hadn't been able to get past his infidelity with Zara – and I could see now that it was also my own behaviour I'd been unable to move beyond, to truly put behind me – but I bore him no ill will. Our children were an unbreakable link between us, one that had been forged with love. Whatever I did, and however I responded to what Patch did in his own life, had to be in their best interests.

Somehow, between us, we needed to make this work amicably, and if that meant giving him my blessing for a new relationship, I'd do that willingly.

And as for me – well. At Kate's fortieth birthday party a month or so back, she'd introduced me to her friend Claude. Handsome Claude, who I'd met up with for coffee and a walk, the most tentative first date ever, and discovered made me laugh and feel instantly at ease. Who'd surprised me by messaging the next day to say how much he'd enjoyed it, and ask me out again. Who I was meeting for drinks and dinner on Friday night.

But now wasn't the time to think about Claude, or even about Patch. This morning was about another man.

I pulled on my coat, tucked my laptop into my bag and then carefully placed the little paper boat on top of it. It would probably get a bit squashed on the journey, but I'd done enough practice runs that I knew I'd be able to reshape it easily once I reached my destination. Then I locked the flat behind me and hurried out into the street.

It was a glorious, golden November day, the sun low in the blue sky, slanting through the last crimson and amber leaves that clung to the plane trees. The wind that had scattered leaves over the pavement last night had dropped now and the air was still and clean-smelling. Around me, the faces of people hurrying towards the Tube station as I was looked far more cheerful than they would have on any other autumn Tuesday.

'Happy birthday, Andy,' I whispered, stepping down the stairs into the station.

There'd been no way for us to arrange to scatter our friend's ashes. They'd have been delivered to his mother by the undertaker, to do with as she thought best. Perhaps she'd deposited them in the water of a Scottish loch, or into the Mediterranean on one of her cruises. Perhaps she'd buried them under a rose bush in her garden. Perhaps they were still sitting in an urn on her mantelpiece, a grim reminder of the son she must once have loved.

We'd never know. And so we'd decided to hold our own ceremony, not on the anniversary of Andy's death but on that of his birth.

'We could do a balloon release,' Kate had suggested.

'We could not,' Rowan countered. 'Clara would never let me hear the end of it – they're so environmentally unfriendly.'

'Andy would have loved it, though,' Abbie argued.

'Andy might not have cared about choking some poor otter to death, but I do,' said Rowan.

'Doves, maybe?' I'd suggested.

'Hell to the no,' Kate said. 'Horribly cruel, and besides they'd shit everywhere.'

'We could plant a tree.'

'Where, though? None of us has a decent-sized garden.'

'We could do a memorial plaque on a park bench.'

'God, imagine what Andy would have said about that? "Like I'm some ninety-year-old dear called Phyllis?"'

'We could blow bubbles?'

'We're not four.'

And so, eventually, we'd settled on launching paper boats into the Thames off Westminster Bridge. Clara had been tasked with researching biodegradable paper and I'd got Patch to find an idiot-proof boat-folding tutorial for us to follow. Abbie had researched the tides and informed us that on the morning of Andy's birthday, the river would be high and there'd be a good chance of our vessels being carried all the way out to sea.

The previous night, I'd neglected my law studies to write a letter to Andy and eventually copied my fourth attempt carefully on to the knobbly surface of the paper.

And now the time had come to say our final goodbye.

I emerged from the station into the bright morning and threaded my way through crowds of commuters and tourists on to the bridge. The water was the brightest blue, reflecting the sunlight so brilliantly it hurt to look at it. The paving stones still gleamed with last night's rain. The air was full of the scent of candied nuts coming from a street vendor's cart, whose smell I'd recognise anywhere but which I'd never tasted.

Rowan, Abbie and Kate were already waiting on the bridge, in the middle as we'd agreed, facing east. Abbie had a rainbow-hued golf umbrella furled by her side. Kate was wearing the purple coat she'd bought for Andy's funeral. Rowan was holding a bright pink insulated coffee mug.

'There you are, Nome.'

'Sorry I'm late.'

I walked into the circle of their arms and our four bodies pressed together for a moment, warm against the autumn chill.

'I tell you what, this thing was a right fucker to make.' Kate took her boat out of her pocket and carefully eased its corners back into shape. I could see that both sides were covered with her tidy royal-blue handwriting.

'Clara did mine in the end,' Rowan said. 'I told her if she didn't help we'd go for balloons, and sod the otters.'

'I couldn't decide what to write,' fretted Abbie. 'I tried and tried, but in the end I left it blank. I hope that's okay.'

'Andy wouldn't have minded,' I assured her. 'He knows how you feel.'

'That's good, because I'm not even sure I know how I feel.'

'I'll never stop being sad.' Kate sighed. 'But you get used to it, don't you?'

'It's kind of like background noise, now,' agreed Rowan.

'And we're all here,' I told them firmly. 'That's the main thing. If we weren't – or if one of us wasn't – that would have been the worst.'

'The very worst,' agreed Abbie, wiping her nose on her sleeve. 'I'd rather Andy was still here but since he isn't – well, at least we are.'

'Come on then, let's do this,' urged Rowan.

We turned and leaned over the water: Kate, then Rowan, then Abbie, then me. Linking arms, we reached out over the balustrade, our fragile crafts in our hands.

'I love you guys,' I said.

'Love you,' the others echoed. 'Love you, Andy. Happy birthday.'

'Three, two, one,' Kate counted, and together we released the little paper crafts. Gusts of wind caught them, whirling them upside down and then back upright as they neared the water. Somehow, all four landed and floated, the current bearing them rapidly away.

We watched until we couldn't see them any longer, and then turned back.

On the other side of the bridge, I saw her. Or at least, I thought I did. Watching us from behind oversized black sunglasses, a cream trench coat fluttering around her legs in the breeze, her hair shining in the sun as if it had been polished.

Zara.

I lifted my hand and waved, but then a stream of red double-decker buses passed between us, hiding her from view.

And when they'd gone, so had she.

A LETTER FROM THE AUTHOR

Huge thanks for reading *The Fall-Out* and joining Naomi and her friends on their journey. If you'd like to be kept up to date on future Sophie Ranald releases, please take a moment to sign up to my author newsletter.

www.stormpublishing.co/sophie-ranald

Twenty years ago, newly married and still quite newly arrived in London, I made a decision that would change my life: I started a book club. At the time, it felt like a way to widen my circle of friends; provide some regular, fun social interaction; maybe even support me through a marriage that I was already realising had been a mistake. Oh, and read some books.

What I didn't expect – and, to be honest, would never have dared to hope – was that two decades later, that book club would have become by best friends in the world. Through weddings, births, divorces, illness, heartbreak and all the tumult and minutiae of life, we've supported one another. We've hugged, cried and laughed until we've almost puked. We've talked about everything. We've had the best fun.

But there's one thing we occasionally mention that casts a shadow over us: *What if there was to be an epic fall-out?* It hasn't happened yet, but the value I place on our friendship makes me conscious of its fragility, and the huge void that would be left in my life were our friendship to somehow fracture.

The three books in The Girlfriends' Club series that

precede *The Fall-Out* (they are *P.S. I Hate You*; *Santa, Please Bring Me a Boyfriend*; and *Not in a Million Years*) were written as a celebration of female friendship as much as they were romances. *The Fall-Out* is an exploration of how things might go wrong – and in a way, I suppose, an insurance policy against that ever happening to my friends and me.

If reading this novel inspires you to take a moment to appreciate your own friends, share a bottle of wine with them, and perhaps even have a chat about books, then my work here will truly be done!

I hope you enjoyed reading *The Fall-Out*. If you have a second to leave a review, please do so – I read every single review of my books and hugely appreciate your thoughts. If you'd like to stay in touch, you can follow me on Instagram, through my Amazon author page or via my website.

Thank you again for reading *The Fall-Out*, and my very best wishes.

Sophie

www.sophieranald.com

facebook.com/SophieRanald

instagram.com/sophieranald

ACKNOWLEDGEMENTS

Before I started writing novels as a career, I imagined that being an author would involve wafting around in a sort of haze of creative bliss, occasionally having long lunches at glamorous restaurants and collecting large royalty payments.

The reality, unfortunately, is rather different. Writing is hard, and the process that begins with an idea and ends with the book you're holding right now is nothing short of a slog at times. Fortunately, though, I have the support of amazing people who have helped me every step of the way along what has been a particularly arduous journey.

Thanks as always go to the wonderful Alice Saunders and her colleagues at The Soho Agency. My brilliant editor, Claire Bord, has worked incredibly hard through multiple drafts to get this novel into shape, with the support of an incredible team at Storm: founder Oliver Rhodes, Editorial Operations Director Alexandra Holmes, Publicity Manager Anna McKerrow, Head of Digital Marketing Elke Desanghere, Digital Operations Director Chris Lucraft and Editorial Assistant Naomi Knox. Thanks also to copy editor Liz Hurst, proofreader Becca Allen, cover designer Rose Cooper and audio narrator Eilidh Beaton.

I'm also fortunate to have a wonderful crew at home – my partner, Hopi, and cats, Purrs and Hither – offering a sounding-board, cuddles when I need them and strategic walking-over-my-keyboard when I don't.

Finally, there are no words to express my gratitude to the

beautiful women of STBC for twenty years of friendship. Amanda, Becky, Carla, Catherine, Eleanor, Hazel, Helen, Jen, Jess, Katie, Lisa, Lou, Lucy, Lynda, Nikki, Rache, Sarah and Sian – I love you all.

Made in United States
North Haven, CT
22 July 2024

55262777R00200